"I am not what you seek. I am only a forester. A farmer."

She gave him a small bow of her head. "For now," she said. "But know this, when you need us. When you have accepted what must be, then call and we will come."

"You will wait a long time," he said.

"Time, Cahan Du-Nahere, is a currency we are rich in. You will call."

"I do not even know your name."

"I was named for my god, when Our Lady of Violent Blooms passed from the memory of the people, so did my name."

"Then I cannot call you."

"What would you name me, Cowl-Rai?"

"Nahac," he said, and it came unbidden. Unwanted, as if her question were more than that. As if it compelled him to speak a name from the past, the name of one long dead and much missed.

"A good name, Cahan Du-Nahere, one from your past?" He nodded. "Fitting, for we both know that is what will bring death to your feet."

Praise for RJ Barker

"A vividly realized high-seas epic that pulls you deep into its world and keeps you tangled there until the very last word."

—Evan Winter, author of *The Rage of Dragons*,
on *The Bone Ships*

"*The Bone Ships* is excellent. Aside from the standout writing, it's one of the most interesting and original fantasy worlds I've seen in years."

—Adrian Tchaikovsky, Arthur C. Clarke
Award–winning author of *Children of Time*

"I absolutely loved it. A whole lot of swashbuckling awesomeness by RJ Barker. He has crafted a fascinating world and a twisty plot, both rooted in characters I came to care about. A definite winner for me."

—John Gwynne, author of
The Shadow of the Gods, on *The Bone Ships*

"An epic tale of duty and obligation and honor, and what bravery really means. I can't recommend it enough."

—Peter McLean, author of
Priest of Bones, on *The Bone Ships*

"Simultaneously gritty and full of a sense of wonder, *The Bone Ships* is the perfect adventure for anyone who's ever had dreams of the sea—or of dragons....An excellent book for any reader in search of a fantastical journey."

—*BookPage*

"A unique and memorable world—harsh and brutal and full of sharply realized, powerful female characters. Barker has managed to craft a story inspired by *Moby Dick*, *Game of Thrones*, and pirate lore, and readers will be drawn in and fascinated."

—*Booklist* (starred review) on *The Bone Ships*

"Often poignant and always intriguing, *Age of Assassins* reveals its mysteries with the style of a magic show and the artful grace of a gifted storyteller."

—Nicholas Eames, author of *Kings of the Wyld*

"Outstanding. Beautifully written, perfectly paced, and assured. Kept me reading well into the early hours of the morning. A wonderful first book—a wonderful book, period—that should be at the very top of your to-read list."

—James Islington, author of *The Shadow of What Was Lost*, on *Age of Assassins*

By RJ Barker

THE WOUNDED KINGDOM

Age of Assassins
Blood of Assassins
King of Assassins

THE TIDE CHILD TRILOGY

The Bone Ships
Call of the Bone Ships
The Bone Ship's Wake

THE FORSAKEN TRILOGY

Gods of the Wyrdwood

GODS
OF
THE
WYRD
WOOD

The Forsaken Trilogy:
Book One

RJ BARKER

orbit

orbitbooks.net

Orbit
Hachette Book Group
1290 Avenue of the Americas
New York, NY 10104
orbitbooks.net

First Edition: June 2023
Simultaneously published in Great Britain by Orbit

Orbit is an imprint of Hachette Book Group.
The Orbit name and logo are trademarks of Little, Brown Book Group Limited.

The publisher is not responsible for websites (or their content) that are not owned by the publisher.

The Hachette Speakers Bureau provides a wide range of authors for speaking events. To find out more, go to hachettespeakersbureau.com or email HachetteSpeakers@hbgusa.com.

Orbit books may be purchased in bulk for business, educational, or promotional use. For information, please contact your local bookseller or the Hachette Book Group Special Markets Department at special.markets@hbgusa.com.

Library of Congress Control Number: 2022952443

ISBNs: 9780316401586 (trade paperback), 9780316401784 (ebook)

Printed in the United States of America

LSC-C

Printing 3, 2024

For Ed Wilson, an agent and a friend

Harm none, and remain unharmed.

Beginning

The boy liked Ventday best. He had always liked Ventday because on Ventday the processionals happened and there was no work when the processionals passed the farm. The tools and staffs were put away and the mothers made them wear their best clothes and the fathers made sure they were clean. Then they all stood on the grass, cold whistling around them, trying not to shiver as they waited for the monks to make their way through Woodedge from Harn towards Harn-Larger.

The monks always came in the first part of the day, but they never stopped at the farm.

Monks had no time for clanless tenant farmers scratching a life from the frozen land. But it was exciting for the boy. Though all followed Chyi, the god of the Cowl-Rai, there were a thousand gods who paid Chyi service, and you never knew which god the monks would worship, or even what they would look like. Sometimes they looked kind and sometimes they looked rich and sometimes they looked fierce and sometimes they looked frightening and sometimes they were all of those things. He had seen the monks of war gods, with warriors who whirled and danced with blades, monks of the night who went naked and painted their bodies midnight blue. Some wore their hair long and some had no hair at all and the only way to know what they would look like was to be there when they came out of the forest path. To the boy that seemed like the most exciting part.

Who would they be?

"Can you hear the bells, Cahan?" said his sister. She was older, not by much, but enough to be in charge when they were in the fields. "They are coming."

"I hear them, Nahac," he said. "And I will be first to see them."

"Quiet," said firstfather and he did so because firstfather had a temper.

"Lorn," said secondmother softly, "let the children be excited. Life is hard enough."

"Harder if the monks think us disrespectful," said firstfather, and secondmother said nothing, which meant she thought firstfather was right. So Cahan looked down as he had been taught to do. But he only tipped his head a little, not enough to show true obeisance. Otherwise he would not see them, and he so wanted to see them.

When the monks came, they were a disappointment. There were no musicians, no pristine robes, no dancers or warriors. Only a parade of tired people, their long hair filthy with mud, their clothes spattered with dirt from travel. The only one who was grand at all was a man who wore a mask carved into a fierce face with long teeth. Their Skua-Rai, the speaker of their god. He had a long white beard and they carried him in a chair which was wrapped with floatvine to lighten the load and swayed from side to side in time to their chiming bells. A Star of Iftal was held above him on a long pole, but the wood was old and the eight arms around the central circle wobbled as the procession moved. But still, they were monks, which meant they were important so the boy bowed his head and tried to hide his disappointment with them.

Then they stopped.

The monks never stopped. Not at their farm.

"These people were not at the gathering for Zorir-Who-Walks-in-Fire in the village," said the man on the chair. His voice was very soft.

"They have no make-up, no clanpaint, they are clanless," said a monk who was bald and fierce-looking, as if his words explained everything, and of course they did. Even the boy knew that to be clanless was to be less than every other. Worth less even than the crownheads on the farm, and crownheads were the most stupid animals alive. Without garaur to herd them they would be dead in a day.

"So," said the old man, "no one stops here?"

"As I said, Skua-Rai, they are clanless."

"Of no family. Of no loyalty, living on the edge of the forest," said the old man. Then he turned back to them. "I think we will stop here."

The boy found he was shaking and he did not know if it was with fear or excitement. He watched, while trying not to be seen to be watching, and the chair was anchored, a step set up and the old man stood. He was helped down by the bald monk.

"It is forbidden, Skua-Rai," he said softly to the old man.

"Well, Laha, many things are forbidden until they are not, eh?"

"But the teachings . . ." began the man.

"As Skua-Rai, Laha, I do not think you need to tell me of Zorir's teachings, eh?"

"No," said the man, and he went to his knees. "Forgive me, Skua-Rai."

"Always," he said and walked forward, standing in front of where they knelt in the mud. "I bring Iftal's blessings to you, farmers," he said. "I am Saradis of Zorir-Who-Walks-in-Fire and I bring greeting to you in my god's name also. May the fire warm but never burn you. May your sacrifice ease great Iftal's pain through his servant Chyi."

No one spoke. No one knew what to say, as the clanless were never blessed. The boy glanced at firstfather and did not understand the look on his face. He looked scared, like when they saw swarden in Harnwood and had to run for their lives.

"Thank you," the boy's sister spoke. Cahan tensed all his muscles as he heard firstfather breathe in, a sudden and dangerous noise. The sort of noise he made just before his hand came out and delivered a stinging blow.

"You're a brave one," said the Skua-Rai and took a tentative step towards his sister, moving carefully on the wet, slimy, half-frozen ground. The boy's heart began to beat so hard he thought it would escape as the man came to stand before Nahac. The air smelled sharper, the boy suddenly aware of the dirt on his clothes and body. He could smell the grass, bruised beneath the man's feet. She is in trouble, he thought, my sister is in trouble and these people are important and they will cut her lips off for talking out of turn. "Look up, look at me," said the monk. "You can all look at me." He did. The old man was nearer and the boy was not at all sure he was a man now. His voice was softer, more like secondmother's. His shape under the robes not as wide at the shoulder as firstfather's, and more curved at the waist.

"Please forgive the girl," said firstfather, words falling from his scarred mouth in a rush. "She does not know her place yet, neither of them do. Punish me for what she has done, not her." The Skua-Rai blinked behind the mask. Stared at his scarred face, and where his bottom lip was missing.

"It appears you have already been punished," said the Skua-Rai, adding softly, "but I am not here to punish." They looked to Nahac, the girl stared back like a challenge and Cahan waited for the order, for monks to grab his sister and knives to come out for the punishment of clanless who spoke out of turn.

"Tell me, Firstfather," their tone was soft, curious, "do you ever travel to Wyrdwood?"

"It is forbid—" She cut him off with a look.

"Do not worry about what is or is not forbidden. Tell me only the truth and none will suffer." Firstfather bowed his head. The way he did before the Leoric of Harn when they requested to trade.

"Sometimes it is hard to make ends meet, with rent and what we are paid for our crops and crownheads and—"

"That is all I needed to know."

The Skua-Rai turned from him and back to the two children, cocked their head and the polished wood of the helm caught the weak light of the afternoon. The boy saw the beard was attached to the mask and was sure now the Skua-Rai was a woman. They reached out a hand towards Nahac, paused halfway, shook her head. "It is not in you," she said. Then turned, walked over to Cahan and studied him. She knelt, letting out a groan as her joints complained, her light blue robe becoming soaked by the wet grass. The world paused. She stared at him for a very long time. He could hear the breathing of his family around him. The low growl of the garaur tethered near the house. The lowing of crownheads down near Woodedge.

The Skua-Rai held out her hand.

"I am Saradis, Skua-Rai, the head of my order and the speaker for my god. Take my hand, boy," she said. He swallowed. Did as she said. Her hand felt like crownhead skin after softening in the pits and hanging on the racks. Warm and dry.

Do not be afraid.

"I am not," he said, the words coming unbidden to his mouth, more bravado than truth. He knelt straighter. The woman smiled. He looked across at Nahac, at firstfather and secondmother and thirdmother and secondfather behind them. At thirdfather who watched from within the hut. They stared back at him, as if they barely knew or understood him.

"Few would have heard the words I said, boy," said the

woman, and she nodded at his first and seconds and thirds, "they did not." She looked towards the forest. "You have been in there. To the depths."

"No," he said, because they were not meant to go deep into the forest, and what the family did there was forbidden.

"Do not worry," said Saradis. "I want you to be brave while I try another thing."

He felt something then. The monk kept hold of his hand and the boy felt something strange, so strange he had no words for it. It was as if the flesh under his skin rippled. It made him want to laugh and it made him want to be sick at the same time. His immediate feeling was one of revulsion, of wrongness and then it was gone. But, though it had only been there for a moment, and though it had felt terrible, he found he wanted it back.

He stared at the eyes behind the mask. They stared back at him. He felt the warmth leave his skin as she took her hand away and, like the strange feeling, when it was gone he wanted it back. She reached up with both hands and, with a click, removed the polished wooden mask and the false beard from her helmet so that he could see the face beneath. She was not as old as he thought, though her hair was white like someone over thirty harvests. But her face was young beneath the caked make-up and red lines. A long gap in the make-up revealed intricate clanpaint running around her eye and down her cheekbone. "This," she held up the mask and smiled at him, "is a very strange thing. It scares some people. It makes some people do as I say without even thinking to question me." She reached out, touched his cheek. "It gives me power," she said, "how would you like to come away with me, to learn about power, forest child? To a place where it is always warm. I will teach you to read the symbols you are forbidden." She smiled. "And I will teach you so much more."

"On my own?" he said. The woman looked around, her gaze resting on Nahac.

"This is your sister?" He nodded. "You are close?" He nodded again. "Then she may come also."

"No!" that was secondmother, crying out. Her hand came up to her mouth. Fear on her face. "I mean only that we barely pay our rent on this farm as it is. Without the children to help us work it we will be thrown off. We will die."

The woman looked at secondmother, then she took off a necklace, beads of shiny, multi-hued bladewood.

"You are aware of the price of speaking to one such as me out of turn?" said the Skua-Rai. Secondmother nodded. A tear ran down her face.

"I birthed him," she said. "I birthed him", and she fell forward, weeping into the dirt.

The Skua-Rai stared at secondmother as she wept. Firstmother and secondfather stood, terrified, unable to move or help.

"Laha," the monk said to the man behind her. He sported different, less intricate, clanpaint and fewer lines of red drawn across his face. "Take these beads back to the village. Speak to the Leoric and use them to buy this farm for our temple." She turned back to secondmother. "Run this farm for me in the name of Zorir," she said, "keep whatever coin you can make and know your children will have a better life with us than any you could ever provide."

"Why?" said firstfather. "Why do this? We are clanless." She stood, but her attention remained on the boy as if firstfather's words were barely of any interest to her.

"Do you know what a Cowl-Rai is, boy?" He nodded. "Tell me," she said.

"They rule for Chyi. And do magic. Big magic," he said. "Like Rai but even more powerful."

"You are very clever, boy," she smiled. "The Cowl-Rai can wave a hand and whole armies vanish. They can change the fortune of our world with a thought. Like Rai they are gifted power by a god, and use that power in their name." He could not take his eyes from her. But she looked away from him now, to his firstfather and secondmother. To his firstmother and secondfather. "Do you know the prophecy of the true Cowl-Rai?" said the woman.

Firstfather nodded.

"They will rise, and overthrow the Old Cowl-Rai. Then tip the world so it is warm in the north once more."

"A simple version of it," she said. "But there is more. The true Cowl-Rai will serve the true god, they will restore the link between the gods and the lands broken in the war with the foul Osere. The gods will no longer need to work through the people so we will be free." She looked around the gathered family. "There will be no more Rai or Leorics or even Skua-Rai." To the boy, it felt as if she grew taller as she spoke. "It will not matter that your ancestors did not fight the Osere. There will be no shame, all will be free and we will walk the Star Path to paradise."

Firstfather stared at her.

"I have never heard the village monks say this."

"Because they would have to admit Chyi is not the true god," she said. "Zorir is the true god, and their voice tells me your son is to be the true Cowl-Rai." His firstfather only stared. Then he looked to Cahan but the boy could not think or move or say a word. The world was closing in on him, strange and huge and terrifying.

"Pack your things, boy," said firstfather. "And remember us."

Then all was action and business, all fuss and running though he barely saw it. The boy stood in a numb, in a cold daze as his few things were packed and he was told to walk behind the seat of the Skua-Rai. At first he did not move, only watched as she placed the mask back on and sat in her chair. He was frightened, not excited. This was all he had known, his only warmth found with those who loved him. He did not want to go.

He felt a warm hand in his and looked round to see Nahac smiling at him.

"Come, Cahan," his sister said. "We will always have one another." She pulled on his hand and he began to walk, thinking only about placing one foot in front of the other.

As they approached Woodedge on the other side of the clearing the Skua-Rai turned to him. "Take a good look at your farm, boy, for this will be the last time you will ever see it."

Like many things she said, this would turn out to be untrue.

1

The forester watched himself die. Not many can say that.
He did not die well.

The farm in Woodedge was the one rock in his life, the
thing he had come to believe would always be there. Life
had taken him from it, then returned him to it many years
later – though all those he had once loved were corpses by
then. The farm was mostly a ruin when he returned. He
had built it back up. Earned himself scars and cuts, broken
a couple of fingers but in an honest way. They were wounds
and pains worth having, earned doing something worthwhile and true. He liked it here in the farthest reaches of
Northern Crua, far from the city of Harnspire where the
Rai rule without thought for those who served them, where
the people lived among refuse, blaming it on the war and
not those who caused it.

His farm was not large, three triangular fields of good
black earth kissed with frost and free of bluevein that
ruined crops and poisoned those foolish enough to eat them.
It was surrounded by the wall of trees that marked
Woodedge, the start of the great slow forest. If he looked
to the south past the forest he knew the plains of Crua

stretched out brown, cold and featureless to the horizon. To the west, hidden by a great finger of trees that reached out as if to cradle his farm, was the village of Harn, where he did not go unless pressed and was never welcome.

When he was young he remembered how, on Ventday, his family would gather to watch the colourful processions of the Skua-Rai and their servants, each one serving a different god. There had been no processions since he had reclaimed the farm. The new Cowl-Rai had risen and brought with them a new god, Tarl-an-Gig. Tarl-an-Gig was a jealous god who saw only threat in the hundreds of old gods that had once littered the land with lonely monasteries or slept in secret, wooded groves. Now only a fool advertised they held onto the older ways. Even he had painted the balancing man of Tarl-an-Gig on the building, though there was another, more private and personal shrine hidden away in Woodedge. More to a memory of someone he had cared about than to any belief in gods. In his experience they had little power but that given to them by the people.

The villagers of Harn were wont to say trouble came from the trees, but he would have disagreed; the forest would not harm you if you did not harm the forest.

He did not believe the same could be said of the village.

Trouble came to him as the light of the first eight rose. A brightness reaching through Woodedge, broken up into spears by the black boughs of leafless trees. A family; a man, his wife, his daughter and young son who was only just walking. They were not a big family, no secondmothers or fathers, and no trion who stood between. Trion marriages were a rare thing to see nowadays, as were the multi-part families Cahan was once part of. The war of the Cowl-Rai took many lives, and the new Cowl-Rai had trion taken to the spire cities. None knew why and the forester did not care. The business of the powerful was of no interest to him; the further he was from it the better.

He was not big, this man who brought trouble along

with his family, to the farm on the forest edge. He stood before the forester in many ways his opposite. Small and ill-fed, skin pockmarked beneath the make-up and clan-paint. He clasped thin arms about himself as he shivered in ragged and holed clothes. To him the forester must have seemed a giant, well fed during childhood, worked hard in his youth. His muscles built up in training to bear arms and fight battles, and for many years he had fought against the land of his farm which gave up its treasures even more grudgingly than warriors gave up their lives. The forester was bearded, his clothes of good-quality crownhead wool. He could have been handsome, maybe he was, but he did not think about it as he was clanless, and none but another clanless would look at him. Even those who sold their companionship would balk at selling it to him.

Few clanless remained in Crua. Another legacy of Tarl-an-Gig and those that followed the new god.

The man before Cahan wore a powder of off-white make-up, black lines painted around his mouth. They had spears, the weapon the people of Crua were most familiar with. The woman stood back with the children, and she hefted her weapon, ready to throw, while her husband approached. He held a spear of gleaming bladewood in his hand like a threat.

Cahan carried no weapon, only the long staff he used to herd his crownheads. As the man approached he slowed in response to the growling of the garaur at the forester's feet.

"Segur," said Cahan, "go into the house." Then he pointed and let out a sharp whistle and the long, thin, furred crea-ture turned and fled inside, where it continued to growl from the darkness.

"This is your farm?" said the man. The clanpaint marked him of a lineage Cahan did not recognise. The scars that ran in tracks beneath the paint meant he had most likely been a warrior once. He probably thought himself strong. But the warriors who served the Rai of Crua were used to fighting grouped together, shields locked and spears out. One-on-one fighting took a different kind of skill and Cahan doubted he had it. Such things, like cowls and good food, belonged to the Rai, the special.

"It is my farm, yes," said Cahan. If you had asked the people of Harn to describe the forester they would have said "gruff", "rude" or "monosyllabic" and it was not unfair. Though the forester would have told you he did not waste words on those with no wish to hear them, and that was not unfair either.

"A big farm for one clanless man," said the soldier. "I have a family and you have nothing, you are nothing."

"What makes you think I do not have a family?" The man licked his lips. He was frightened. No doubt he had heard stories from the people of Harn of the forester who lived on a Woodedge farm and was not afraid to travel even as far as Wyrdwood. But, like those villagers, he thought himself better than the forester. Cahan had met many like this man.

"The Leoric of Harn says you are clanless and she gifts me this land with a deed." He held up a sheet of parchment that Cahan doubted he could read. "You do not pay taxes to Harn, you do not support Tarl-an-Gig or the war against the red so your farm is forfeit. It is countersigned by Tussnig, monk of Harn, and as such is the will of the Cowl-Rai." He looked uncomfortable; the wind lifted the coloured flags on the farm and made the porcelain chains chime against the darker stone of the building's walls. "They have provided you with some recompense," said the man, and he held out his hand showing an amount of coin that was more insult than farm price.

"That is not enough to buy this farm and I care nothing for gods," said Cahan. The man looked shocked at such casual blasphemy. "Tell me, are you friends with the Leoric?"

"I am honoured by her . . ."

"I thought not." The forester took a step around the man, casually putting him between Cahan and the woman's spear. The man stood poised somewhere between violence and fear. The forester knew it would not be hard to end this. The woman had not noticed her line of attack was blocked by her husband. Even if she had, Cahan doubted she could have moved quickly enough to help with her children hanging onto her legs in fear. A single knuckle strike to the man's throat would end him. Use the body as a shield to get to the woman before she threw her spear.

But there were children, and the forester was no Rai to kill children without thought. They would carry back the news of their parents' death to Harn, no doubt to the great pleasure of Leoric Furin as she could offer these new orphans up to be trained as soldiers instead of the village's children.

If he did those things, killed this man and this woman, then tomorrow Cahan knew he would face a mob from the village. They only tolerated him as it was; to kill someone above his station would be too much. Then the Leoric would have what she wanted anyway, his farm. Maybe that was her hope.

The man watched the forester, his body full of twitches. Uncertainty on his face.

"So, will you take the money?" he said. "Give up your farm?"

"It is that or kill you, right?" said Cahan, and the truth was he pitied this frightened man. Caught up in a grim game Cahan had been playing with the Leoric of Harn ever since he had made the farm viable.

"Yes, that or we kill you," he replied, a little confidence returning. "I have fought in the blue armies of the Cowl-Rai, to bring back the warmth. I have faced the southern Rai. I do not fear clanless such as you." Such unearned confidence could end a man swiftly in Crua.

But not today.

"Keep the money, you will need it," said the forester and

he let out a long breath, making a plume in the air. "Farming is a skill that must be learned, like anything else, and it is hard here when it is cold. You will struggle before you prosper." Cahan let out a whistle and Segur, the garaur, came from the house. Its coat blue-white and its body long, sinuous and vicious as it sped across the hard ground and spiralled up his leg and chest to sit around his neck. Bright eyes considered the forester, sharp teeth gleamed in its half-open mouth as it panted. Cahan scratched beneath the garaur's chin to calm it. "The far field," he told the man, pointing towards the field between the rear of the house and Woodedge. "The ground there is infested with root-worm, so grow something like cholk. If you grow root vegetables they will die before they are born and that attracts bluevein to the fields. The other two fields, well, grow what you like. They have been well dug over with manure. There are nine crownheads, they stay mostly at the edges of the forest. They will give you milk, shed their skin for fur once a year, and allow you to shear them once a year also."

"What will you do?" said the man, and if Cahan had not been giving up his livelihood such sudden interest would have been comical.

"That does not concern you," he told him, and began to walk away.

"Wait," he shouted and Cahan stopped. Took a deep breath and turned. "The garaur around your neck, it is mine. I will need it to herd the crownheads." The forester smiled; at least he could take one small victory away from this place. Well, until this new tenant ran into the reality of farming and left, as others had before. The man took a step back when he saw the expression on Cahan's face, perhaps aware he had pushed his luck a little further than was good for him. Wary of the forester's size, of his confidence even though he was walking away from his home.

"Garaur bond with their owners. Call Segur by all means.

If you can make it come it is yours, but if you knew anything about farming you would know it is wasted breath." With that he turned and walked away. The man did not call out for Segur, only watched. Cahan found himself tensing his shoulders, half expecting a thrown spear.

They were not bad people, not really, the forester thought. They were not ruthless enough for this land either. Crua was not the sort of place where you leave an enemy at your back. Maybe the man and his family did not know that, or maybe they were shocked by how easy it had been to steal the farm.

"And stay away," shouted the man after him, "or I'll send you to the Osere down below!"

Nothing easy turns out well was a favoured saying of the monks who trained Cahan in his youth. In that there was a truth these people would eventually discover.

He made camp in the forest. In Harnwood, where it was dangerous, and definitely not in Wyrdwood among the cloudtrees that touched the sky, where strange things lived, but also not so shallow in Woodedge that the new owner of the farm would notice him.

Further in than most would go, but not far enough to be foolish. Good words to live by. There he sat to watch. He thought a sixth of a season would be enough, maybe less, before the family realised it was not an easy thing to scratch a living from ground that had been cold for generations. No one had stayed yet. War had taken so many lives that little expertise was left in the land and Cahan, barely halfway through his third decade, was considered an old man. The farmers would not last, and in the end the fact that Cahan could reliably bring spare crops to market, and knew how to traverse the forest safely, would be more important than the small amount of sacrifice he refused to give.

Though it was a lesson the Leoric struggled to learn. But the people of Harn had never liked outsiders, and they liked clanless outsiders even less. He pitied them, in a way. The war had been hard on them. The village was smaller than it had ever been and was still expected to pay its way to Harnspire. Lately, more hardship had been visited on Harn as the outlaws of the forest, the Forestals, were preying upon their trade caravans. As it became poorer the village had become increasingly suspicious. Cahan had become their outsider, an easy target for a frightened people.

No doubt the monks of Tarl-an-Gig believed the struggle was good for Harn; they were ever hungry for those who would give of themselves and feed their armies or their Rai.

Cahan had no time for Tarl-an-Gig. Crua used to be a land of many gods, its people had an unerring ability to pick the worst of them.

It was cold in the forest. The season of Least, when the plants gave up their meagre prizes to the hungry, had passed and Harsh's bite was beginning to pinch the skin and turn the ground to stone. Soon the circle winds would slow and the ice air would come. In the south they called the season of Least, Bud, and the season the north called Harsh they called Plenty. It had not always been so, but for generations the southerners had enjoyed prosperity while the north withered. And the southern people wondered why war came from the north.

Each day throughout Harsh, Cahan woke beneath skeletal trees, feeling as if the silver rime that crunched and snapped beneath his feet had worked its way into his bones. He ate better than he had on the farm, and did less. Segur delighted in catching burrowers and histi and bringing them to him; brought him more than he could eat, so he set up a smoker. Sitting by the large dome of earth and wood as it gently leaked smoke. Letting its warmth seep into him while he watched the family on the farm struggle and go hungry and shout at each other in frustration. They were colder than he was despite the shelter of the earth-house. Their fire had run out of wood and they were too frightened to go into the forest to collect more. Cahan watched them break down a small shrine he had made to a forgotten god named Ranya for firewood. They did not recognise it as a shrine – few would – or get much wood from the ruin of the shrine tent, covered with small flags. Of all the gods, Ranya was the only one he had time for, and the one least able to help him – if gods even cared about the people.

He had learned of Ranya from the gardener at the monastery of Zorir, a man named Nasim who was the only gentleness in the whole place. He did not think Nasim would begrudge the family the wood of the shrine. Cahan tried not to begrudge them the wood either, though he found it hard as grudging was one of his greatest strengths.

He did his best to ignore the people on his farm and live his own life in Woodedge. It was true that much in the forest would kill you, but largely it left you alone if you left it alone. Especially in Woodedge, where, if you ran into anything more dangerous than a gasmaw grazing on the vines in the treetops, you were truly unlucky. "Take only what you need, and do not be greedy, and none of the wood shall take a price from you." They were vaguely remembered words and he did not know where from, though they carried a warmth with them, and he liked to imagine it was the ghosts of the family he had left when he was young.

The death of the forester – the death of Cahan Du-Nahere – happened towards the end of Harsh, when the circle winds were beginning to pick up once more and the ice in the earth was starting to slip away. Frosts had kissed the morning grass and the spines of the trees, making the edges of the forest a delicate filigree of ice. He heard the drone of flight as a marant approached. The sky it cut through was clear and blue enough to please even a hard god like Tarl-an-Gig. Far in the distance he could see a tiny dot in the sky, one of the skycarts that rode the circle winds, bringing food to trade for skins and wood.

The marant was not big for its kind: long body, furred in blues and greens. The wide, flat head with its hundreds of eyes looking down, and there would be hundreds more looking up. Body and wings the shape of a diamond, the wings slowly beating as it filled the air with the strange hiss of a flying beast. From its belly hung the brightly coloured blue pennants of Tarl-an-Gig and the Cowl-Rai in rising. In among the blue were the green flags of Harnspire, the Spire City that was the capital of Harn county, and on its back was a riding cage, though he could not see those within.

It had been long years since Cahan had seen a marant. When he had been young and angry and striking out at the world they had been a common sight, ferrying troops and goods to battles. But marants were slow and easy targets so most of the adults died early in the war. It was good to see one; it made him smile as they were friendly beasts and he had always liked animals. For a moment it felt as if the world was returning to how it had been before the rising of the Cowl-Rai, and the great changes of Tarl-an-Gig had come to pass.

Those changes had been hard for everyone.

He was less pleased to see the beast when it did not pass over. Instead it turned and began to slow before floating gently down to land on eight stubby, thick tentacles before his farm.

From the cage on its back came a small branch of troops, eight, and their branch commander. The soldiers wore cheap bark armour, the wood gnarled and rough. Their officer's armour was better, but not by much. After them came one of the Rai who wore darkwood armour, polished to a high sheen and beautiful to look at. They all wore short cloaks of blue. Four of the troops carried a large domed box, as big as a man, on long poles and their branch commander was pointing, showing them where to put it. That struck Cahan as strange, worrying. He had seen the new Cowl-Rai's army use such things before. It was a duller, to stop cowl users performing their feats. But the man who had taken his farm was no cowl user, Cahan was sure of that. If the creature which let the Rai manipulate the elements had lived under the man's skin Cahan was sure he would have known it, just as he knew it lived within the Rai who led the troops, even if their armour had not been painted with glowing mushroom juice sigils, proclaiming power and lineage.

The Rai was larger than the soldiers, better fed, better treated, better lived. Cowlbound, like all Rai, and with that came cruelty.

"Why hobble their Rai's power, Segur?" asked Cahan as he scratched the garaur's head. It looked at him but gave no answer. It probably thought people foolish and useful only for their clever hands. Who could blame it?

The woman, not the man, left Cahan's house and walked out to meet the troops. She stayed meek, head down because she knew what was expected of her. The Rai said something. The woman shook her head and pointed towards Woodedge. A brief exchange between them and then the Rai motioned to the branch commander, who sent their troops towards the house. The farmer shouted and she was casually back-handed for it, falling to the floor before the Rai, clutching her cheek. He heard more shouting from within the house but could not make it out. Cahan crept nearer, using all the stealth of a man raised in the forests of Crua, staying low among the dead vegetation of Harsh, right up to the edge of the treeline where young trees fought with scrub brush for light. From here he could hear what was being said at the farm. The beauty of living in such a quiet place was that sound carried, and the arrival had quietened the usually boisterous creatures of Woodedge.

The man who had taken the farm was dragged from the house. "Leave me be!" his voice hoarse with panic. "I have done nothing! The Leoric gave me this place! Leave me alone!" As he was dragged out the troops followed, spreading out around him, spears at the ready. No obscured sightlines here.

"Please, please," the woman on her knees, entreating the Rai. She grabbed hold of their leg, hands wrapping around polished greaves. "We have done nothing wrong, my husband fought on the right side, he was of the blue, we have done nothing wrong."

"Do not touch the Rai!" shouted the branch commander, and he drew his sword, but the Rai lifted a hand, stopping him.

"Quiet, woman," said the Rai, and then they spoke again, more softly, dangerously. "I did not give you leave to touch me." The woman let go, went down on her face, sobbing and apologising as the Rai walked over to her husband.

"I come here on the authority of the Skua-Rai of Crua and the High Leoric of Harnspire, carrying the black marks of Tarl-an-Gig, who grinds the darkness of the old ways beneath their hand, to pronounce sentence on you." The Rai grabbed his hair, pushed his head back. "Clan marks that you are not entitled to. Punishable by death."

At that, Cahan went cold. He had wanted to believe this Rai and their soldiers were here for the man. A nonsense, a lie, but he had ever been good at lying to himself.

"I am of the clans," shouted the man. "My firstmother and firstfather and secondfather were all of the clans! And all that came before them!" The Rai paused in their pronouncement, looking down at the man.

"The first action of the condemned is always to deny," they said. "Your sentence is death, you can no longer hide." They raised their sword. It was old, carved of the finest heartwood from the giant cloudtrees that pierced the sky. Sharp as ice.

"It is not my farm!" shouted the man. The sword stayed up.

"Really?"

"Please," weeping, tears running down his face, "please, Rai. I was given this farm by the Leoric of Harn and the priest there."

"And where is the previous owner?"

"Gone, into the forest."

A brief pause, the Rai shrugged.

"Convenient," they said, "too convenient." The man began to beg again but for naught, the sword fell. He died.

Silence. Only the chime of flags and the hiss of the marant. Then his woman screamed, she remained prostrate and was too frightened to look up, but her grief was too great to be contained.

"Rai," said the branch commander, paying no attention to the screams or the corpse spilling blood into the soil, "there are children in the house. What shall we do?"

"This well is poisoned," said the Rai. "No good will come of it." The woman screamed again, scrambled to her feet and turned to run for her house. Never got the chance. The Rai cut her down with a double-handed stroke, more violence than was needed. From his place Cahan saw the Rai lift their visor and smile as they bent and cleaned their bloody blade on the woman's clothes. Two of the Rai's soldiers moved into the house and Cahan almost stood, almost ran forward to try and stop them as he knew what they intended. But he was one man with nothing but a staff. What would one more death serve?

They were quick in their task at least. No one suffered. Once the farm was silent they tore down his colourful flags and strung the building with small blue and green flags, so all would know this was done on the authority of the Cowl-Rai.

Cahan watched them load the duller and board the marant, heard one of the troops say to another, "That was a lot easier than I thought," and the creature lifted off, turning a great circle overhead. The forester stayed where he was, utterly still, knowing how hard it was to see one man amid the brush if he did not move. Once the shadow of the marant had passed over he watched it glide away into the blue sky towards Harn-Larger and Harnspire beyond. Then he looked back at his house, now strewn with dark flags, as if spattered by old, dry blood.

He heard a voice, one meant only for him, one audible only to him.

You need me.

He did not reply.

2

He did not go back to the farm that day, or the next. Only a fool would go back to be found among corpses.

Instead Cahan waited until the villagers of Harn had found the bodies, which took them not a fourday or even an eightday, but two eightdays. Then the villagers waited another fourday before doing anything, fearful the troops of the High Leoric in faraway Harnspire would return. Eventually they cleared the bodies, took down the warning flags. Cahan worried they might take everything of value from the farm, but they did not. He watched their monk, Tussnig, an undesirable sort in a filthy grey smock and a hat made of twigs woven to resemble the eight-branched Star of Iftal, if you squinted. He pronounced the area cursed and haunted by the dark spirits of the Osere, for which Cahan was thankful as it meant nothing would be removed. He worried that Tussnig would set the earth-house alight but he did not, probably because the monk was lazy and earth-houses are hard to get burning. Cahan gave it another week before he called Segur and they moved back in.

He was pleased to find the previous owners had done little damage, mostly because they had done very little.

It took him a week to clean the house, remove the blood-stains and get it back to how he liked it. Segur spent most of that time sniffing and growling at unfamiliar scents. He thought of rebuilding the small shrine to Ranya but decided against it. He had another that was better hidden, and the Rai might always come back.

On the last day of cleaning he found a small wooden model of a crownhead; it must have belonged to one of the children. Cahan sat and looked at it for a long time, turning it over in his big, rough hands.

Was it his fault? If he had interfered he would have died.

We would not.

He ignored the voice. That was the ghost of another life, another person. Someone dead who should stay dead. Someone who had brought nothing but pain where he walked.

He took the crownhead toy to the woods and buried it in the small, hidden grove of his own making that he had dedicated to Ranya, the lady of the lost. No doubt the family had worshipped fiercer gods, Tarl-an-Gig, or maybe Chyi, though he doubted they would have admitted it in the north. They were not gods Cahan could find any truth in, or believed there was any truth in. He had been raised for Zorir, a fire god who he had been told was the only true god.

Another lie.

Travelling through Crua, selling his anger, he had heard monks of Chyi and Tarl-an-Gig preach. What they said, it was not that different from what the monks of Zorir had told him. Names changed, stories differed slightly, but the end was the same. Bow down and give of yourself, or be denied the Star Path and paradise when you die. He knelt before the shrine to Ranya, a rough pyramid of found wood strewn with colourful flags, and placed the toy within it. This was the best he could do for the child.

Cahan hoped it woke in gentler lands than these. It was

not the first life laid down in the grove, but it was probably one more deserving of mercy.

That done, he headed back to the farm to do what must be done to restore order. The fields would need digging over. The family had planted root crops which were, as he warned, rotting in the ground and good for little else but providing compost for next year's planting. He worried he might find traces of bluevein in them, but his land looked clear. The water pool had run dry. He hoped they had simply let the wetvines run from Woodedge heal, but if they had destroyed them then it was a long job to fix, not only growing them thick enough to keep the pool filled but digging channels to keep them safe from the crownheads, who would gladly chew through them for a drink rather than walk a little further to a pool. They were stupid, obstinate animals, but they were his livelihood. The people of Harn called him Forester because he did not fear the woods, but the truth of it was he was a farmer. The crownheads were what brought in enough money for him to survive the months of Harsh without having to leave the farm he had been born on and live off the forest.

And though he knew the forest and its ways, it was not always a welcoming place.

He whistled for Segur and set out with his staff to find his lost creatures.

While he searched, he had to force into the back of his mind the voice of the thing that lived beneath his skin.

Those soldiers came for you, Cahan Du-Nahere.

Had they? No names had been asked. It could simply be that word of someone clanless owning property had reached the ears of those who ruled Harn-Larger, or Harnspire. They would be aggrieved by such a thing. Cahan would not put it past Harn's monk, Tussnig, to tell tales on anyone who he thought threatened him or Tarl-an-Gig. Cahan spat. The Rai were cruel and they kept power not only with their cowls but by dividing the people, and most were too foolish to see it.

Cahan had heard it said, among those that knew, that the more a cowl was fed the crueller the user became. But the truth was the people of Crua were cruel to begin with, and maybe they deserved the Rai and all they brought.

He took a deep breath and fought down the writhing of the thing beneath his skin. The man who had taken his farm was dead. Even if they had been looking for him the Rai would consider their job done. He would be safe to continue his life here.

One of many lies he told himself.

He knew the family had killed one of his crownheads for food, which annoyed him though there was little he could do about it. Cahan considered the animals far too valuable to eat, especially when the forest and fields were full of histi, delicate raniri and burrowers that could be caught with traps. Even more annoyingly, they had lacked the skill to smoke or salt the meat to preserve it. They had eaten the choice cuts and the rest was wasted. He wondered where those people had been raised, no doubt in the crumbling tops of a spire city among the poor where the skills of the forest were never needed. They had not killed more than one crownhead, probably because crownheads could be hard to catch once warned you might hurt them. He had a suspicion as to which they had taken, which made him a little sad. Even crownheads, stubborn and often foolish as they were, had personalities, and Cahan had his favourites.

Nasim, a good man who had tended gardens for people who considered themselves wise, had told the forester that only a fool borrows trouble. In the whole of the fire god's monastery Nasim's garden was the only place he found any real wisdom. So Cahan tried not to be a fool and not to mourn the loss of his favourite, and most valuable, animal without being certain it was gone.

He found two crownhead corpses, one just within Woodedge. It had become caught in a trapvine and as it had not been freed had simply continued to struggle, driving the thorns deeper into its flesh. It was not a kind way to die but it had happened long enough ago that the corpse was mostly bone now. Cahan gathered the bones up into a bag; they could be ground into bonemeal for the crops and the horns had many uses. The next dead crownhead was nearer the farm clearing, not bone yet but dead long enough that there was no good meat to recover and many-coloured mushrooms were fruiting from it. Cahan made a mental note of the place so he could return later.

The rest of the flock had fled into the forest and Cahan would never have found them without Segur; the garaur was invaluable when it came to crownheads. It could always find them and enjoyed imposing its will upon them. When it had gathered them together and driven them back towards the farm Cahan realised, with a sigh, that he was correct about which animal had been slaughtered. The family had killed his only male. It had always been more friendly than the females and the easiest to catch for those unskilled in looking after the beasts. He cursed the man and his wife to the Osere for being so short-sighted. He would have to go into Harn. If the male was not replaced there would be no young come Least. A visit to Harn meant a day of shearing the remaining crownheads so he had wool to sell.

Though if someone in Harn had told the Rai about him going into the village could end up bringing the soldiers back. Not that it mattered, or that was what he told himself, without a male crownhead he was done anyway.

He sheared the crownheads. It took him long into the dying light of the second eight of the day and brought only an increasing sense of disappointment. The fleeces were of poor quality: the beasts had spent too long in the forest using twigs and branches to scratch at their wool, filling it with burrs, thorns and tags. If it had been shedding season at least he would have had the skins to sell.

When he had the fleeces, he bound them tightly with floatvine into a pack that bobbed above the ground at head height. It was too late to go into Harn, so he tethered the package and went to sleep.

In the morning he tied the bundle onto his belt and set off through Woodedge towards Harn. It was not a long walk; the light barely moved across the sky, but the pack kept catching on the branches of trees and the smell of the wool attracted the tiny biting flyers that usually followed the crownheads about. Segur happily snapped at them, but it made the journey a frustrating one and he was in a poor mood by the time he saw the village through the trees.

There were many who would say he was never in a good mood.

A ring of wooden walls, built from trees cut and split and twice the height of a person, surrounded Harn. In front of the walls was a further ring of stakes, facing outward. They looked fierce but were placed too far apart to be of any real use as a defence, and up close the wood was mostly rotten. At the far western edge of the clearing was a gasmaw farm, the creatures contained by huge nets of woven vine. Gasmaws were forest creatures, but the whole of Crua relied on them. They came in many colours and sizes: some were huge, others so small they could barely be seen but the form was nearly always the same. A gasbag made up most of the body, long and triangular shaped with two vents the animal could open and close to control its height. The front was a head with a powerful beak for cutting through vegetation. Two large main eyes on either side, and four eyes facing down and four facing up. Around the beak grew tentacles, four that they used for grasping and movement when they were not jetting through the air, two longer tentacles with flatter ends that could be used to manipulate things and two stinging tentacles they used for defence or to catch prey. Gasmaws generally fed off vegetation but would take meat if they could, and their relatives, the spearmaws, ate nothing but meat.

Farmed gasmaws had the stingers cut from them when they hatched, and these domestic gasmaws never grew quite as big as their wild cousins, though they were also never going to sting you either, which Cahan thought a worthy trade-off. The stings were painful at best, lethal at worst.

At the northern edge, outside the wall, was the tanners' house, a circular earth-house much like Cahan's farm, surrounded by tanning pits and supplied by multiple wetvines that ran into a small lake to feed the pits. Tanners were always on the northern side of a settlement as the circle winds blow the stink away, except in the south of Crua, where everything was the other way around.

Harn had two gates, like every other village. The Forestgate faced north towards the forest and the tannery, and the Tiltgate faced south towards Tilt, the centre of Crua where the new Cowl-Rai ruled and from where they continued the war with the old Cowl-Rai. If they won they would tip the world once more and the north would be warm and the south cold.

As Cahan left Woodedge, Segur whined. He stopped. "They are only people, Segur," he said, leaning on his staff. "They will not hurt you while I am there." The garaur hissed at him and Cahan laughed at it. "Very well, go and hunt in the forest, and join me when I leave." It whined once more and then vanished into the undergrowth.

Though Harn was a small settlement, little more than a hundred and fifty people in it and the surrounding farms, it was too many for Segur, and more than Cahan was comfortable around.

A pair of guards stood at the Tiltgate. They wore armour made of wool soaked in sap and dried until it became hard. It was old armour, the chest plates fraying and cracked, the helmets long ago softened by moisture into little more than uncomfortable hats. Each held a spear of hardwood in their hand and a wooden shield on their arm. They had the white face paint and black swirls common to the clans of Harn, subtly different on each of them. The one on the right was missing a hand; the wars of the Cowl-Rai had left few of fighting age untouched.

"Forester," said the one-handed guard, "I thought you gone." Cahan recognised the voice, even though he had done his best to avoid the place knowing the gate guards were unavoidable. As was paying the sacrifice they asked of any visitor.

"My farm was taken, Gussen," Cahan said, "but those who took it must have been criminals, as the soldiers of the Rai came for them." He stared at the guard, wondering if she would give something away. "But I have taken my farm back, though it is in a poor state." She stared at him.

"You'll be wanting in then?" said the other guard, Sark.

"Guard duty, Sark?" said Cahan. "I thought you were a hunter?"

"We must all do our bit for the village," he said, and the gate guards crossed their spears to bar him entry. "Outsiders who do not contribute are not welcome in Harn." Cahan had, long ago, decided that if the people of Harn were going to consider him an outsider then he would be one. He felt no guilt for not paying the village tribute or refusing to do guard duty or help build walls and houses or the hundreds of other tasks they found to do.

"You know me," said Cahan, "I come here to sell my wool, and your village will make good profit from it." Sark looked away.

"We're being extra careful now, Forester," said Gussen. "The Forestals have been preying on our merchants when they set out for Harn-Larger. They've got much braver. You aren't one of us, Clanless, you could be here to scout out the village for them." She stared at the long staff in Cahan's hand. "Long staff that you have, just for a walk."

"It is useful to have a stout staff if you venture into the forest."

"Reminds me of them forestbows the outlaws use." She stared at him. "Bows are against the law."

"Then it is a good job, Gussen, that this," he lifted the finely carved wooden shaft, "is a staff and not a bow." The guard stared at it but said nothing. Cahan waited, but when the silence continued he sighed and went into his purse, taking out a shiny wooden coin.

"Will this help you trust me?"

"Might help," said Gussen. "But Sark," she nodded at the other guard, "he's a suspicious one." Cahan took out another coin and passed it over.

"There," he said, and they uncrossed their spears.

"Iftal's blessings on you, Forester," said Gussen, "it's a pleasure to have you back in Harn." Cahan did not answer, only pulled his floating bundle of wool on into the village.

Deep in the Forest

He walks the fire.
You are the fire.
You watch him walk.
Used until you are broken.
Run and hide.
You are running.
Where have they all gone?
Do not forget.
But you are not running fast enough.
You are the fire.
        Everything is burning.
                He is burning.

And you are the fire.

3

The huts and houses of Harn were well cared for but shabby. Life was hard this far north. All trade in Harn was brought through Woodedge on floating rafts from Harn-Larger and as there was little money in Harn few chose to make the journey. With the Forestals being seen in Woodedge then even fewer were coming now, still, the market was busier than Cahan liked.

As he entered he saw a young woman sat in the cold mud by an earth-house, her felt clothes not thick enough for the northern weather and her hair fashioned into huge spikes with white mud and wooden rings. The same mud had been used to draw whirls and lines on her face. She was very thin.

"Spare a coin for a monk of a forgotten god?" she said, holding out a thin hand streaked with dirt. He had little time for others' gods, forgotten or not, but did not like to see someone go hungry and knew how Harn treated outsiders.

"Avoid the bread," he told her and threw her a splinter, "and do not let Tussnig see you. He does not like competition, forgotten god or not."

"I know that," she said, and sprang to her feet, suddenly looking far less feeble. "The monk of Tarl-an-Gig who-walks-without-humour has sharp boots and a blunt wit, but a real readiness to kick." She grinned and vanished between the side of the house and the wall, leaving Cahan wondering whether he had been conned out of his coin. Not that it mattered. The coin and the woman were gone.

Something that always struck him about towns was the smell. He was used to open spaces and the rich, green smells of the forest. Harn smelled of towns, of latrine pits dug too near the walls and a myriad other unpleasant smells trapped between the houses, along with the smoke from wood fires. Then there were the people. He had always found the press and smell of people crowded together overpowering. In his youth, in the monastery of Zorir, he had washed every day. Wetvines were run in to make pools and even fountains. But the monastery had been in Mantus, where it was warmer and life was easier. There was even rainfall from the great geysers of Tilt. Here in the north they got only occasional snows that lay on the ground for an age during Harsh and left slowly and resentfully in Least.

People did not wash as much in the far north.

That was not to say they did not look after themselves, for they did. The people of Harn were a colourful lot. Their closeness to the forest provided plenty of plants with which to dye their clothes and, though they exported the majority of the skins and wool from the crownheads, there was still enough left over to be pressed into thick felt for warm clothes. They painted their faces, as was the tradition, in white with black lines and clan patterns. Despite all this, they always looked tired. To survive here was to struggle.

If he had known the market was on he would have waited until it was quieter, but he had not known and now had not only the people of the village to contend with, but also the people from the outlying farms. Those milling around the few stalls were a rainbow of colour: brown and yellow jerkins of thick felt with pressed-in stripes and whirls of bright colour. They wore conical hats in bright blues or reds or purples dyed from berries and mushrooms. For their trousers and kilts they tended towards more sombre dark blues and blacks. Between the adults ran children in simple one-piece gowns, screeching and laughing. In them was the only merriment to be found in Harn.

He passed stalls: butchers, weavers, felt pressers, a pot seller and a woodcarver. Stalls set up by those who hunted or gathered in the relative safety of Woodedge. On the other side of the village he could see Tussnig, the monk of Tarl-an-Gig, who stood before the shrine of his god; a figure made of sticks. Like all representations of Tarl-an-Gig it was standing on one leg, the other leg held out, foot on the knee, creating a triangle, arms clasped in front of the head. It was not a great representation, but then the monk was no great artist. Behind the statue of the god was the eight-branched Star of Iftal. Before it was the village taffistone where sacrifices were made. In Tilt the taffistones were as big as a person and they glowed with a strange light. Harn's stone was badly chipped and barely reached the monk's hip. Once it had been marked for Chyi, but that had been erased with a chisel, like the names of many gods before. Now it was marked for Tarl-an-Gig in flaking paint. Usually the sacrifice was a simple laying on of hands and promise of service or strength to the god. Today the stone was streaked with blood and the head of a crownhead, staring up blindly, lay before it. It was an expensive sacrifice.

Tussnig dressed exactly the same way he always did, with an eye headdress and a long felt robe of undyed wool. He had painted his face a bright blue for his god. The monk watched the people of the market as they milled about, buying and selling goods. Cahan tried to keep out of the monk's line of sight but was not quick enough.

"Forester!" shouted Tussnig. Like most weak men he

liked nothing more than an easy target. "Forester!" he shouted again and the bustle of the market was stilled. Faces, shaded by wide-brimmed hats, stared at Cahan in the weak light of the cold day. "We do not welcome the clanless here! And do you bring a sacrifice? Do you bring a gift for Tarl-an-Gig as is befitting? Will you give of yourself to your betters?" He let that hang in the air, which, despite the smell of Harn, felt crystal clear and sparkling, the better to let every eye in the village see Cahan.

"A gift for you, more like, monk," he said. He heard more than one indrawn breath at his rudeness. "I follow no gods, no one rules over me."

"Did you hear?" shouted Tussnig. In his hand he held a wooden forked wand and he pointed it at the forester. "Did you hear that, good people of Harn? He follows none! Tarl-an-Gig comes, casts out the false gods, shows their power through the victories of our Cowl-Rai! And this man scorns them! Does he wish Chyi back? Does he worship old forest gods, go on bended knee to the forest nobles? I say he does!" The monk was working himself up into a fury, jumping up and down on the spot and whirling his wand around. "Tarl-an-Gig will gift his power to the Cowl-Rai and tilt us back to warmth! This man would bring back old darkness! He will bring the boughry from the forest to prey upon us! Swarden will mass at our borders! Rootlings stand under our walls!" The monk was punctuating his words with his wand, thrusting it towards Cahan. "You will pay the price, Forester. Iftal of the burning star, the broken god before whom all others bow will judge you! The Cowl-Rai will bring his judgement. Tarl-an-Gig will drag you in chains before Iftal, you will be cast down to the Osere!" Cahan began to back away, too many eyes were on him that could be easily turned to violence. "Look at him! Ignorant and indolent. A clanless man who thinks himself above us, when he is lower even than the Osere under us! I say let you burn! Let the Rai burn you slowly to feed their cowls. Let them flay your skin from you for the glory of Tarl-an-Gig! They will thank us if we do it for them!" The man was frothing at the mouth and Cahan could feel danger growing as his words gained ground with the crowd. "Take up your—" A clod of dung hit him in the face, cutting short his rant. The shouting and dancing and frothing stopped. "Who did that?" he shouted.

"Call yourself a monk," came the reply, and Cahan saw the young woman with the spiked hair he had given a coin to. "I have had better monks fall out of my arse!" She turned and flipped up her gown to bare her rump at him. The tension fled, the market erupted into laughter and Tussnig, seeing himself thwarted, screamed at the woman.

"Osere take you!" He ran from his shrine after her, and she vanished between the houses pursued by the irate monk and the laughter of the people. Cahan turned away. If he saw the young monk again he would give her another coin.

Even with Tussnig gone Cahan was still a figure of suspicion among those of Harn; they moved out of his way as he walked, not to ease his passage but because he was clanless and they considered it unlucky to be near him. Still, it made passing through the crowd with his floating bundle of fleeces easier and he had to put up with the smell of them a little less.

Gart, the wool merchant of Harn was older even than Cahan, white-haired and bearded, and he had always paid a fair price for goods, despite Cahan being clanless. He suspected he gave others a fairer price, but such was life.

"Iftal's blessing on you, Forester," he said, eyeing up the floating bundle, "six fleeces is it? Less than your usual."

"Lost three of my flock," said Cahan, and pushed the bundle over. Gart cut the fleeces loose, letting the floatvine go and it spiralled up into the cold air. A good sign, if he were not in a buying mood he would have tethered the weed to his stall to reuse it. Others often let the floatvine go to inconvenience him, but Gart was not a petty man.

He watched as the wool merchant began to lay the fleeces out, one on top of another, with hands gnarled by his great age.

"You should have given the monk a gift, Forester," he said, as he smoothed a fleece down with the ease of long practice, "it would have shut him up."

"I doubt it."

"Aye," he looked up, "you are probably right. He is weak, the Rai send us the scraps from their table and call it a feast." Cahan said nothing. Gart could pass judgement on their monk if he wished, but it was not safe for him to do so. "Not of your usual quality," said Gart.

"I had some trouble. I need to make enough for a new male."

"Not with these," said Gart. Cahan had expected as much.

"These, and the promise of all my skins and fleeces in Least." It was a fair offer.

"Would if I could, Forester," he said, "you are good for your word. But you know the Leoric's rules on you. No favours." Cahan nodded, he had also expected to hear that but it was worth a try.

"I'll take coin for them then," he said. Gart reached into his pouch and took out an amount of coin that, even knowing the fleeces were not great and that he was clanless and therefore ripe to be exploited, Cahan found disappointing.

"I will make sure a male is set aside for you in Least," Gart said, "a good one." Then he looked away, like a man caught stealing and Cahan wondered if the monk Tussnig had returned.

Instead he found Furin, the Leoric of Harn, standing behind him, a guard on either side, and her second, Dyon, a tall, thin man, behind her. Despite they were often at odds Cahan had always thought her a handsome woman, the Leoric, of a similar age to him, her dark hair beginning to silver, creases at the corners of her dark eyes. She thought him nothing but a problem. Furin wore the same felted clothes as everyone else but in the deep blue beloved of Tarl-an-Gig. Her face was caked in white make-up and she wore elaborate swirls across her forehead. Dyon wore the same paint but his stripes were much thinner; as if to make up for it he wore the paint of his lineage larger than most.

"I would speak with you, Forester," she said.

"My business here is done," he replied, "and my farm is in need of attention." He made to leave but one of her guards, as ill-kempt and crack armoured as the gate guards, stepped in front of him.

"I heard your request of a loan from Gart," she said. "Come speak with me and maybe I can help, despite that your fleeces are of poor quality."

"That they are poor quality has more to do with you than me, Leoric."

"Speak with respect to her," said Dyon. The Leoric held up her hand to silence him, then gave Cahan a small nod, accepting what he said as truth.

"I have warm drink in my longhouse. Come share it with me," she said. "I will not take up much of your time."

The Leoric's longhouse was the largest building in Harn, larger even than Cahan's farm. He leant his staff by the door as he entered. A fire burned in a pit within and saplamps threw out a dim glow. A small boy played before the fire with dolls made of dry grass.

"Issofur," said the Leoric, "I would speak with this man, play in the back." The boy stood and ran to the rear, vanishing behind the screens of woven reeds. The gloom hid much of the building, but there was the sense of a large space beyond the stools around the small fire. It was warmer in the longhouse than without, but Cahan's breath clouded in the air. Not even the Leoric of Harn was rich enough to warm her rooms well. She ladled out a warm drink from the smaller of two clay pots suspended over the fire and passed the cup across. Then she poured a drink for herself.

Cahan waited until she drank before he did, such things having been drilled into him as a very young child; clanless wait.

The Leoric did not notice.

The drink, a broth of bones and herbs, was good.

Furin, the Leoric of Harn, did not talk straightaway. For all she disapproved of Cahan and made his life difficult, he thought she was an honourable woman, in her own way. She cared about the village. Not that it made him trust her any more, or want to stay with her, handsome woman or not. When she still did not speak, he did.

"Do you intend to help me buy a male crownhead in recompense for sending those poor fools up to take my farm?"

"No," she said, and stared at him over her cup. "You are clanless," she said, "you found a building that was derelict and made a place for yourself. I respect that. But you live within the lands of Harn, and should either be part of us or leave. Times are hard in Harn, we all need to contribute."

"Times are hard for all of us, Leoric," he said, sipping from his cup. "Even harder for those with no idea how to work the land if you give them a farm."

"He said he was a farmer, and that he would make sacrifice." She took another sip of broth. "Can you wonder I gave him permission to take your farm?"

"Well, he was not a farmer, and that has cost both of us. Me in coin, and you in the amount of goods you have to trade." She said nothing to that as she had nothing to say, instead changing the subject.

"The monk, Forester, does not want clanless running a farm." She sat straighter on her stool. "He thinks it an affront to Tarl-an-Gig and the ways of the new Cowl-Rai." She looked away. "That you can travel through the forest means little now. The old gods are gone, along with the old ways." She looked back. "It would be easier for you if you had some friends here."

"And you offer your hand in friendship?" She shook her head. "What then?"

"You have heard that the Forestals have been coming out of Wyrdwood and preying on our trade?" Cahan nodded, and knew what was coming. "We send our fleeces to Harn-Larger in three days. If you go along to protect Gart I will pay the remaining cost of your new crownhead as recompense."

"You cost me that crownhead." He was surprised by the sudden vehemence in his voice, the anger, the way the thing beneath his skin moved in response to it. He took a deep breath, every hair on his body standing on end as if a freezing breeze had crept beneath his clothes and passed across his skin. He thought he had better control over himself. To the Leoric's credit, she did not shrink from him or his anger.

"Well, as we have said, times are hard. Not only will it get you the animal, Forester, but it will get you some much-needed goodwill that the monk will find it hard to go against. I sent a farmer, he would send a mob with fire."

"Did he send the soldiers?" he asked. She shook her head once more. "Did you?" At that she laughed.

"Osere under us, Forester," she smiled to herself, "we have barely enough to live on here as it is. The last thing I want is the eyes of the High Leoric and her Rai turning on Harn and taking what little is left." She leaned forward. "You come across as a man who has travelled; you know what the Rai are like." He did not answer. His past lay in a shadow he wanted none to cast light upon.

"I am no soldier, to protect caravans of trade," he said, wondering if she could see the lie in him. If somehow she sensed his past or if it hung around him in a cloud, a poisonous one.

"Maybe not, Forester, but you are big, bigger than most here, and that may be enough in itself to scare away the Forestals." She looked him up and down, and graced him with a smile, a small one. "They want easy pickings. This may end up being little more than a walk to Harn-Larger and back for you, and a well-paid one." A sensible man would have said yes there and then. Would have agreed with her and seen the logic and, in some ways, the kindness of her offer.

But Cahan had found that to be proud and headstrong was the best armour against the pain of the world, and it was a hard armour to take off. He stood.

"I think you send me for someone to blame if it goes wrong."

"No, I do . . ." Cahan walked away, took up his staff from where it leaned against the wall. "You have your own guards, Leoric. Use them," he said and left, stomping out of the village. No one bothered to try and stop him as his anger was apparent in each stride and maybe, even if he did not know it himself, it was not only the Leoric, Harn, or even the monk he was angry with.

Deep in the Forest

There is a firepath set out and you wonder why. There has been no mention of a firewalk. No readying a celebration as is usual. The firepath, it is longer, far, far longer than is normal. You wonder why everyone is gathered. You wonder why there is no meat cooking and no cakes or bread being baked. No tables up. No fancy flags of Broken Iftal blessing the fire god Zorir. No sense of celebration.

Saradis is there and you try not to tremble. Try not to show fear because you know she hates weakness. They all hate weakness. They beat weakness out of you.

"The firewalk!" shouts Saradis, "is the test of the faithful! Those who have betrayed Zorir will be consumed!"

These words scare you.

4

Kirven Ban-Ruhn sat back on her throne, uncomfortable, no matter how many cushions she added. Its woodwork was carved in the northern style that she did not care for, no adornment apart from geometric shapes. Brutal and cold, like the people here.

She was the first High Leoric of Harnspire in generations that was not Rai and, of course, the Rai hated her for it.

She hated them back.

She hated them *more*.

Not that long ago, Kirven had been glad to make it through a day alive. Now those who had once oppressed her danced to her tune. They might mutter and hiss behind her back. They might spread rumours and plot, but they would not move against her because she had been chosen by the Skua-Rai of Tiltspire, voice of Tarl-an-Gig and the one who bathed in the light of the Cowl-Rai.

She sat in splendour on the bottom level of the central and largest of the city crown's spires. The great banners of the blue, mixed with the green of Harnspire falling from the snaking ribs of the vaulted ceiling. Huge wooden figures of Tarl-an-Gig, the balancing man, lined the walls. Between each one hung the star of Iftal. Lining the great hall were her guards – *hers* – in burnished wooden armour. Fires burned in each of the forty fireplaces, keeping away the chill of the north. A thousand servants ran to do her bidding. Here she sat and received the report of her soldiers and her Rai.

"We cast out old ways," she said under her breath, "we burn out the old gods, so that the one may thrive."

The last of her trunk commanders had reported on the search for more trion and left. Now only a small group of Rai were left, splendid in their expensive armour. Resentful in every look and movement.

They wanted her to be scared but they did not know her. Madrine, her firstwife and a Rai of Chyi, had once left Kirven and her child alone in Wyrdwood. One of the many lessons Kirven had been forced to endure. Less violent than the others maybe, but more terrifying. Wyrdwood was no place for a woman with a babe. But Kirven had survived Wyrdwood. She had survived Madrine where a firsthusband, secondhusband, thirdwife and two trion had not.

She was strong.

It took a lot to scare Kirven now and she ruled simply; cross her and die. It would not be a drawn-out and tortuous death the way the Rai preferred. Die swiftly, die quietly and be replaced by someone who was not as foolish.

No fools survived the first months of her reign.

Kirven had spent the day receiving reports to the throne of Harnspire; it was taking so long that the light above had moved through three of the great windows at the far end of the hall. It was her duty to hear how the hunt for followers of the old gods of Wyrdwood went. Despite her physical discomfort the destruction of every shrine felt like a small victory. So she sat upright and wished they would hurry. The soldiers were done, now was the turn of her more specialised hunters.

Falnist, her trion major-domo, stepped forward, holding

a staff topped with the star of Iftal, their clothes were stiff and angular, bleached to the purest white.

"Rai Harden Van-Gurat and Rai Galderin Mat-Brumar, approach and speak." The two Rai came forward, confidence in their walk, arrogance in it, but Kirven did not waver or show her distaste.

"Tell me of your successes, Rai," she said. Falnist took the papers held out by Rai Van-Gurat, gave her a small bow and presented Kirven with three hand-sketched portraits. She unrolled them and looked at the pictures. A thin woman with hair that looked like it had been hacked off with a knife. A sour-looking man with hollow cheeks. Another man who looked beaten, small and squashed, his hair patchy.

Van-Gurat watched her with pale eyes. The other Rai, Mat-Brumar, stayed where he was. He was the more powerful of the two; it showed in his ornate and beautifully painted armour. No doubt he did not want to enter the influence of the duller beneath her throne that cut him off from his cowl. The Rai found the experience unpleasant. Van-Gurat was about to speak when Kirven raised a hand to silence her.

"All should leave, now, except my Rai." She watched and waited as her soldiers and servants turned and left the long room. It took a long time. Falnist remained by her throne and she turned to them.

"And you." Their eyes widened in annoyance, then they bowed and followed the rest.

She did not need to send them away, but enjoyed annoying Falnist and making Van-Gurat wait within the duller's field. The Rai stared at her, their dislike of her plain as Falnist walked past them.

Kirven tried not to smile as she watched the trion walk away down the hall and out of a door.

"High Leoric," said Van-Gurat as the last guards left. The discomfort of the dulling field plain on the woman's face. "The woman in the portrait is named Tamis Du-Carack, brought into being as false Cowl-Rai by the monks of Hast-Who-Walks-For-Death. Their Harnwood Shrine is destroyed. She is captured and in your dungeon. As is the first man, Urdan Mac-Varsa, who was raised as false Cowl-Rai for Gadir Made-of-Blood. His monastery is burned along with those monks who would not bow to Tarl-an-Gig."

"What of the other?" asked Kirven. Her voice echoed through the long room.

"We have not yet found the false Cowl-Rai Virag Par-Behian, brought into being for Loun the Wet Blade, High Leoric. The monastery in Stor was empty, no sign it has been occupied for many years." She looked up. Her skin sickly looking, more like paste than flesh. "We will find him. We have interrogators and searchers looking."

Kirven wondered if they hated this. Crua had always been riven by war. Cowl-Rai would rise, the world would tilt and either north or south would become prosperous until the process was repeated. Tarl-an-Gig would stop that, they were eradicating every cult, monastery and forest shrine they could find.

There would be no new Cowl-Rai rising. Ever. But the strife of war was when the Rai rose, when they could swap allegiances and become strong by betraying those they had once called friend.

All that would be gone, the Cowl-Rai brooked no threat. Kirven smiled. Maybe the Rai would be next to fall.

"Well," said Kirven, "what are you standing there for, Rai Van-Gurat? The Cowl-Rai has demanded you capture these pretenders, burn the monasteries and shrines of their gods. You have not yet completed your work." The Rai stood, gave a short bow of her head and then turned and marched from the throne room. Galderin Mat-Brumar stared at Kirven for a moment. He gave her a nod and an unpleasant smile before following his companion, though he would not leave Harnspire with her, Kirven needed him for something else.

A third Rai waited, watching. Her wooden armour scarred and scratched. Her face not quite as harsh as the others.

"What of you, Sorha Mac-Hean?" This one did not bow. It was not in her to bend the knee unless forced. She took off her helmet, letting red hair fall free. Uncommonly beautiful, you are, thought Kirven as the Rai approached. But it was a cold beauty, more like a statue than one of the people. Sorha twitched as she walked into the influence of the duller and the connection between her and her cowl was severed. A brief pause, then she ascended the three steps that led up to the throne and held out a rolled-up portrait. She held it just out of reach. Making Kirven lean forward to take it. The picture was a man, bearded, long hair. Deep-set eyes marked as brown. Tired looking.

"Cahan Du-Nahere," said Sorha, backing away with a sneer. "False Cowl-Rai brought into being for Zorir-Who-Walks-in-Fire. The monastery long ago destroyed, when the Cowl-Rai first rose. Found at a farm in the far north."

"And he is in my dungeon?"

Sorha shook her head. "He is dead, and his family with him."

Kirven did not speak, not at first.

"The Cowl-Rai bids you bring them back to me."

Sorha shrugged. "It saves a lot of time and effort if I kill them, rather than waiting for you to do it."

"That is not your decision to make," said Kirven softly, staring at the picture and wondering what this man had been like. Few prospective Cowl-Rai had family and put down roots.

"Do you think this duller could save you, if I decided to kill you?" asked Sorha conversationally, staring up at the ceiling. Kirven rarely looked up, the ceilings of the spires were strange, like the corridors of the upper reaches. They made her head ache if she looked at them for too long.

"No, the duller would not save me," said Kirven. It was true. The Rai were trained to fight from the moment they could walk, well before they took on their cowl. She met Sorha's stare. "But I know you would only survive my passing by moments."

Sorha's eyes narrowed, then she looked around. Saw the holes in the walls, knew something that endangered her must wait behind them. Smiled to herself, nodded and took a step back.

"To own a bow is punishable by death," she said.

Kirven ignored her, looked at the picture.

"You made sure it was him?"

"I killed the man who was where you sent me." That shrug again. "He had shaved the beard, cut the hair. Those pictures are mostly useless anyway." She was staring at Kirven, intent on her. "They are made from rumours and the ravings monks of old gods spit out under torture." Kirven did not dispute that. Still, she could not let Sorha be so openly insolent whether she spoke the truth or not. Kirven Ban-Ruhn ruled here, not the Rai. Not any of them.

"I think, Rai Mac-Hean, we may need to find you a new assignment." Sorha only continued to stare. "You can leave now."

The Rai walked away, so sure of herself. Of them all she thought that one was the most likely to make trouble. She was ruthless and impetuous, a bad combination.

Kirven would deal with Rai Sorha Mac-Hean another time. She had other business to attend to now. The dead man she could forget, the prisoners she would deal with later. She scratched at her head. In her previous life she had worn her long, dark hair loose, but the position of High Leoric demanded a set of elaborate braids that made her head itch.

So much here needed her attention, such was power.

And in Crua, power always came at a cost.

5

The forester's mind was clouded with anger as he
approached his farm. He had stomped through the ferns
of Woodedge with more force than necessary, Segur hanging
back because, although he would never hurt the garaur,
sometimes he would shout and the creature did not like it.
He was soaked and in a worse mood than when he had set
out, convinced that every branch had chosen to drip icy
water on him and it was not his own temper causing them
to shake as he pushed past.

A figure was sitting on the stone wall around his farm,
utterly motionless. He could make out a shield and a spear
in the dying of the light. Had the Leoric run out her patience
and sent some warrior ahead in the hope of dealing with
him? No. There was no one in Harn with the skill to over-
take him in Woodedge without his notice.

Were they Rai? Come to correct the error they made in
killing the family and not him? The figure was not dressed
like Rai. And Rai did not wait, not alone. They came with
soldiers.

He thought of vanishing back into the forest, or sneaking
around the back and approaching in secret but he was

overcome with annoyance. What was the point? If they were innocent, someone lost who had stopped in hope of help he would only scare them, and if they wanted something darker they would only come back. He stood. Best to face this head on.

The figure turned at the sound of his approach but made no attempt to stand. Up close he saw they wore a long cloak in dull grey that swathed their body, almost entirely covering them. But beneath the folds of the cloak he could see the shape of greaves, a chest piece and the wrist guards of a warrior. They watched him walking towards them and their cloak fell open, showing the wood of their armour, laminated with fanciful designs. In their lap lay a crested helmet laid over the haft of a long spear. Their shield they put on the wall. The only skin they showed was their face and on seeing it Cahan felt shock. The woman's skin was as grey as her cloak and he wondered if he had made a mistake in approaching. There were few warriors he could not best, but the woman waiting on his wall may well be one of them.

She did not stand, nor go for her weapon as he approached, which he took to be a good sign. As good as it could be when a legend sat on your wall. Cahan pushed fear away, even as the cowl beneath his skin squirmed.

You need me.

"You own this farm?" she said. Her voice soft, like a breeze through trees. Segur let out a low growl and spiralled up around the forester's body to sit around his neck where it felt safe enough to chatter and growl at the intruder.

"Who asks?" He scratched the garaur's head to calm it.

"I am unnamed." Closer he could see her grey skin was as soft and lifelike as his own, though entirely the wrong colour for the living.

"You are of the reborn," he said. "What brings the reborn to my house? Where have you come from?" The moment he finished asking where she was from she stopped listening to him, started talking.

"I fell on the fields of Yarrat in service to the Foul-Rai. When I woke again I served Cahrasi Who Enslaves, and when the Foul Rai was vanquished and my soul was weighed, I was found unworthy of the Star Path and cursed. Rather than join the Osere below I chose to walk the land." When she finished talking he saw panic pass across her face, like someone who had gone to sleep in their bed and woken in a strange place.

"Apologies, Reborn," said Cahan. "I have only heard talk of your kind long ago, I forgot about the curse of your kind, and did not mean to ask of your genesis."

"Well, my past is out for all to see now," she said, her voice once more flat and emotionless. "It is best that way." She glanced at the ground. "And that you triggered the curse tells me we are in the right place. You are Cahan Du-Nahere." It was not a question.

"I know no one of that name."

"I am not hunting you, Cowl-Rai."

"Do not call me that," he said, too quickly and he knew it. "I am not that. Have never been that and I do not know this Cahan Du-Nahere you speak of. The man who owned this farm was killed by the Rai, maybe it was him you seek." He had heard it said the reborn could hear a lie from a thousand leagues away. If so, his words must have deafened her.

"Would the farmer have set off the curse?" she said. "I do not think so." She stared at him. "They will come back for you, denying what you are will not help."

"Who will come back?"

"Those who killed the family that took your farm."

"You saw that?" She shook her head and the glass trinkets in her braided hair chimed.

"The dead whisper to me. The boy that lived here," she said, her eyes no longer looking at him, "he is glad to have his crownhead back, he thanks you."

He took in a breath and walked past her to the wood-block by the door and picked up his chopping axe, a rough and ready thing of old wood. He could not help thinking that, despite all he wished for, he had so often ended up with an axe in his hand.

"Why are you here and not fighting in the south for the new Cowl-Rai?" He placed a log, let the axe fall. Split the wood. Placed another log. "That is what reborn do, they fight."

"The new Cowl-Rai," she spat upon the floor, "I care that for the Cowl-Rai, both the one that is and the one that will be and all that have been before them." Though he concentrated on the wood he could feel her stare as if it were the light above burning his skin. "Cowl-Rai made me this, reborn, who feels nothing, tastes nothing. I know neither heat nor cold and only feel when I kill. Only death lets me remember what it was to be alive."

"Plenty of death to be found with those Cowl-Rai you scorn."

"I would kill either given the chance."

"And yet," he let the axe fall again, "you say you are not here to kill this Cahan Du-Nahere you seek. And you call him Cowl-Rai, who you say you hate."

"You are different," she stared straight at him.

"I am a farmer and forester, that is all." She did not move. Her stillness was wrong, something out of nature. It was almost as if she faded out of the world unless she was moving, making herself part of it.

"The dead follow us in a grand procession, Cahan Du-Nahere, and they never cease to speak, to beg, to hate. In our life, before we were reborn, we served the Lady of Violent Blooms and few warriors were our equal. Few still are. We offer our services to you, as guard, as assassin, as whatever you need us to be. You are Cahan Du-Nahere. Unwilling Cowl-Rai. The Fire of Crua." The axe fell again. This time he let it embed itself in the softer wood of the chopping block and turned to the reborn.

"If I truly was this man you think I am, I would have little need of a guard, would I?" She nodded.

"You think that, but you underestimate what they set against you. Cowl-Rai rise, they brook no pretenders or rivals. Monasteries and forest shrines burn. Crops become poisonous. Land creaks and breaks. The darkness brought by Cowl-Rai varies in its intensity, but I have known nothing like this."

"I am no Cowl-Rai."

"I sense death, Cahan Du-Nahere," she said, "and it is coming to you. Deny who you are all you wish, it is still coming. Death cannot be stopped."

"I say again, I am not what you think I am, a mistake has been made is all." He looked at her, the skin of his hands red and tingling from swinging the axe. "I am no bringer of death." She shrugged and slid off the wall, placing her helmet on. She pulled down the visor and he stared into a blank face of polished wood. Beautiful, probably hundreds of years old.

"No man or woman brings death, Cahan Du-Nahere, death is a contrary companion, it comes unwelcome and uninvited." Her spear had fallen when she stood, and she used her foot to flip it up into her hand. "Many of my fellows are dead, yet we still live," she said. "When death is all we wish for."

"We?" Cahan said. He picked up the axe again and looked about him. Only then seeing a second figure in the treeline to the west, dressed identically to the woman before him, the carved face on her visor serene. The reborn saw him find her compatriot and nodded. "Anyone can die, reborn," he said, nodding at his wood block, "put your head on there and I will cut it off. Then I will throw your remains in a fire and char them to ash if release is really what you want." The visor stayed fixed on him. When she spoke her words were a little muffled. She had told him she did not feel, but he was sure he heard a sadness there. Behind it something more, a terrible longing.

"Do you think we have not tried such things?" She pointed at the other reborn with her spear. "She and I, we have tried every way you can imagine to die. And each time we awake, sometimes in a day. Sometimes in a season. Sometimes in a year. Our bodies are remade just as they were when we died."

"What do you think I can do?" he said softly. She had conveyed such horror to him in her voice that he had forgotten to lie about who, and what, he had once been.

"Cowl-Rai raised us, Cahan Du-Nahere. So we hope, that if we make ourselves useful enough, if we can create a debt so great that even a Cowl-Rai cannot deny it, then you will find a way to put us down." For a moment he had no words. He cleared his throat, laid the axe on the block. A shiver ran through him. The air felt colder than usual.

"I am not what you seek. I am only a forester. A farmer."

She gave him a small bow of her head. "For now," she said. "But know this, when you need us. When you have accepted what must be, then call and we will come."

"You will wait a long time," he said.

"Time, Cahan Du-Nahere, is a currency we are rich in. You will call."

"I do not even know your name."

"I was named for my god, when Our Lady of Violent Blooms passed from the memory of the people, so did my name."

"Then I cannot call you."

"What would you name me, Cowl-Rai?"

"Nahac," he said, and it came unbidden. Unwanted, as if her question were more than that. As if it compelled him to speak a name from the past, the name of one long dead and much missed.

"A good name, Cahan Du-Nahere, one from your past?" He nodded. "Fitting, for we both know that is what will bring death to your feet." She turned and walked away without looking back, the figure from the edge of the forest coming to join her. He watched until they had vanished into Woodedge then went back into the house and sat at the table. Lit a saplamp and stared into the flame.

How could he be so foolish to think he could continue here.

If these reborn knew who he was then others must also. The soldiers had not been sent by Harn. His past was coming and he would have to leave or face it. He would miss this place, it was the nearest he had known to a home since being abandoned by the monks of Zorir-Who-Walks-in-Fire.

He packed a bag, the bare minimum needed to survive, and called Segur. With the garaur curled around his neck he walked to his grove in the wood. There he moved the shrine, being careful not to break it, and used his hands to burrow in the ground below it like a histi, digging up the coin he had buried in case he needed it. "Well," he said to Segur, "the day has finally come." He hid the money in a purse he wore against his skin then stood, looking around. Thinking about other secrets buried beneath the earth. Then he let out a long breath and turned away, heading towards Harn. The Leoric would finally have his farm and though he did not want to admit it, leaving this place was hard. It was the only place he had any happy memories attached to. He had lived there until he was six. What he remembered of that time was hazy, but he was sure his parents had been good. That they cared for him. He thought they laughed a lot. They had taken him even as far as Wyrdwood and taught him skills he still used.

But he did not laugh much after he was taken away, for Zorir was a stern judge and looked poorly upon frivolity. Everything was serious, hard. His childhood subsumed by what he was to be. Maybe only children are ever happy, he thought, maybe people are cursed to become more serious and sad the older they get. Maybe it was a blessing in disguise that Nahac died when she did.

In the morning he made his way back to Harn, striding up to the Tiltgate only to be stopped by the guards.

"You are not welcome here any more, Forester," said Gussen, barring his way with a spear, "by order of Leoric Furin."

"Tell her I will do what she wants," he said. "I will guard her traders and help the village." Surprise washed across Gussen's face.

"Very well," she said. "Wait here."

6

It was a custom in the spiretowns of Crua, like Harnspire and its sister towns further south, that the richer you were the lower in the spire you lived. It was true, thought Kirven, that to be higher up gave you a better view, and removed you from the day-to-day stink of the city but there were disadvantages. Mostly that the spires were old and given to tumbling, and the lower down the spire you were the more likely you were to survive if the thing came crashing down.

Harnspire was arrayed in a crown formation like all spire cities. Eight black trunks reaching for the sky, their walls thick with rills and frills like the bark on trees. They rose to needle-sharp points around a central, thicker spire. Or that had been Harnspire, once. Now there were five spires around the centre, their walls gaudy with climbing plants and small trees that had taken hold, roots working their way into the material of the buildings, doing their slow and destructive work.

The fallen spires of Harnspire lay as skeletons, surrounded by the longhouses of the people who lived and worked there. The carcasses of the buildings were occupied of course, they made a useful covered space for markets and barracks and a place to live for those who were well off enough to claim them, but not well off enough to claim the actual spires, which were the sole property of the Rai and the old families who bore them.

It was also true, thought Kirven Ban-Ruhn as she walked up the winding staircase of the central spire, her legs aching and her heart thumping, that the further up the spire you went, the more disturbing the place became. She did not understand the minds of the people who had built the spires; what lost wisdom they had possessed must have addled their minds. In some ways the oddness of them became normal with time and you ceased to notice it, the way a doorway did not seem quite designed for ease of use, or how the corridors felt wrong in their proportions, too wide for how tall they were. Even the walls were strange, built of the same black material as the spire that begged you to touch it, made you think it glistened with moisture, but when you placed a hand against it the wall felt dry and hard as baked rock. And there was always light, from some unseen source. She had heard people say the spires were grown not built, and she had no trouble believing it. There was, colour apart, something of the tree about them, not hard to imagine the contours and swellings that many took as decoration of the walls as great veins to lift sap from the land far below.

She did not like it.

It was easy to die up here too; the corridors played tricks on the eye, and you could turn a corner to find it open to the air. A moment's inattention and you would be falling. They blocked the openings, of course, but even after generations of living in these places they had not found them all and to Kirven there was something malicious about these places. As if they desired to lead you astray.

Still, it was quiet in the high reaches of the central spire, at least when there was no skyraft tethered to it. Kirven walked with purpose, following a path marked with small, blue-painted figures of Tarl-an-Gig that marked the way. Her heart hammered in her chest as she approached a familiar door high in the central spire. Outside it sat the trion Falnist, one of the third gender of Crua, placed between man and woman by Iftal as a conduit to understanding. That was how the monks of her youth described them. Funny how when she was nervous these things came back to her. Falnist stood, no longer wearing the white robes that, strictly speaking, were only for monks. Tall and thin, head shaved bald. Face painted white and the marks of their family in blue. Falnist also wore the blue line of a trion over one eye and it gave them the impression of having drawn on one eyebrow, comical really, if you did not know how ruthless they could be. She could not imagine Falnist being the calming influence between anyone but she took them as a lesson. Do not judge people by what they are meant to be. Judge them by what they are.

"High Leoric," said Falnist, giving her an almost imperceptible bow.

"How are they today?" she said.

"The same as they ever are, High Leoric." Was there a sneer at her title there? Maybe. She chose to ignore it. "May I suggest, High Leoric, that it has been well over a year now. Maybe it is time for harder measures?" She paused, hand on the doorknob.

"That is my child you speak of, Falnist."

"A child with a higher purpose, as you well know, High Leoric," said the trion. "The Skua-Rai, who gifts us both our place in this world, will not wait forever. The Cowl-Rai wants results." They paused, that quizzical painted-on eyebrow shifting a little. "I took the liberty of starting to make arrangements and—"

She cut them dead with a look. Letting go of the door and stepping right up to the trion.

"I rule here, Falnist, not you. Harn is mine and you do

not make 'arrangements'," she hissed the word at them, "without consulting me first. Especially when it is to do with my child." Falnist did not move away. They smelled of some citrusy forest fragrance. It made her feel ill.

"You should not forget, Kirven Ban-Ruhn," the trion said, their voice light, falsely friendly, "that I also answer directly to the Skua-Rai of Tilt, who speaks for Tarl-an-Gig and the Cowl-Rai. Results are expected."

"And they put me above you," she said, "so who is the living embodiment of the god in this place?" Falnist met her gaze. "Be careful, Trion," she said, "these corridors are a maze, they care nothing for power and anyone can have a fall." Falnist smiled and bowed their head.

"How true, High Leoric", and though Kirven knew this was as much a threat as her own words she let it pass. She generally tried to avoid conflict with Falnist. They were one of the few she could not simply have killed, they would be missed. Worse, she knew the trion was right in many ways. Time was running short and she had been rehearsing what she would say today, sure that at last she had found the right words.

She opened the door and walked in.

A small room with few comforts.

It smelled of animals. An open-topped cage in one corner contained two histi. Kirven felt her stomach turn as she saw they were still alive. On the far wall a window gave her a view out over Harn county past the greenery of the northernmost spire. It was beautiful, the season of Harsh showing itself in mists that drifted over the lands, casting gauze over the grasslands and obscuring the dark and forbidding lines of the forest far to the north. The sight of the forest worsened her mood. She would burn it all down if it were up to her. She had to settle for destroying its gods for now.

A few old tapestries hung on the bulging walls of the room, showing the breaking of Iftal in a fiery star over the great tree in the lost city of Anjiin. The moment when the gods sacrificed their link to the world to cut off the Osere. Iftal had freed the people from servitude, but now the paradise of the Star Path could only be found through death where the guidance of the gods, or the god now, waited. Iftal had saved the people but made the land hard, because the gods could no longer service it. They could only give power to their chosen, the Cowl-Rai and the Rai, and wait for the day when Iftal was reborn and then the Star Path would open to the living once more.

The tapestries were old, threadbare and rather than Tarl-an-Gig rising over Iftal they showed hundreds of nameless gods breaking from the trees and the forest, taking on countless forms. Things of the past on the walls, but the future was also in the room.

Her future, what put her above the Rai and above Falnist, lay on the bed with their back to her. Pretending she did not exist. That she was not there.

"Venn," she said.

No answer.

"Venn."

No answer.

"Venn, I am not going away. We must speak."

Still no answer. She shut the door behind her and took a step forward. Standing between the bed and the cage with the histi in it. The animals were brown, covered in thick fur and with large green eyes. They looked up at her, curious.

"This cannot continue, Venn."

"Then let me go." They were speaking. That at least was better than her last few visits.

"I cannot, you are too important. You know that."

"Then we have nothing to talk about. Not as long as I remain a prisoner." The figure on the bed pulled the blankets more tightly about them and for a moment Kirven felt only despair. Then she took a deep breath and sat on the bed. The histi continued to stare at her from their cage.

"Do you remember, Venn," she said softly, placing one hand on the trion's back, wanting to die a little when she felt them flinch, "the festivals?" No answer. "How you used to watch the Rai juggling fire, or making snow and laugh and wish you could do it?" They moved, only a little but she felt them move. She wanted them to speak. She had watched four seasons pass in this room and been met with silence, then argument, then silence again from its occupant. A stubborn and complete refusal to believe that she did what she did for both of them. An inability to understand that in Crua sacrifices had to be made. "Can you try to understand that I saw possibility for you, and took it?" The body beneath her hand moved. Pushing itself round and up until they were sat looking at her. Sickly looking, too thin. Skin sallow from time locked away from the light. Cheekbones too sharp in their face. "They are only histi, Venn," she said. "You gladly eat them, I ask you to use what is within and . . ."

"Did you know?" they said. The words as dead in their mouth as they became in the air. "Did you know when you gathered us together, when I made friends for the first time. Met people like me. Did you know what would happen?" She stared at them. A thick blue line painted over their deep-set brown eyes, dry with lack of sleep, or maybe weeping, or both. "You never answer."

"This was a long time ago, Venn," she said. "We must take the world as it is now, move on." She reached out for them and they moved back on the bed, out of her reach. "This is bigger than you. Than me." As she said the words she felt her frustrations rising, losing the calm she had worked so hard to bring into the room with her.

"Did you know?" they said again.

"I know nothing in Crua is safe, Venn." She tried to move closer. "I knew this was the best chance for you, for us."

"You knew I might die." She felt a coolness settle on her, the same coolness that had settled when she had made the decision. When she had been given the option of taking power.

"I thought the risk was worth it." Her child stared at her, their breathing ragged, their expression one of utter confusion.

"Shall I tell you what it was like?"

"Venn, I know it was unpleasant, you do not . . ."

"Unpleasant?" the word a shriek and then they were near her, right in her face. Their teeth bared, words hissing out. "Let me tell you of it, you keep asking me to speak to you. Well, I shall speak to you, Firstmother," they said. "I shall tell you all about it." She felt fear, odd, as she knew Venn would not hurt her, this whole thing was because the child would not hurt anyone, would not even kill a histi. But still, she felt fear. Pain was not always physical. "Those two histi," Venn pointed, "I call them Hargis and Lensier. Do you know why? I will tell you why." The trion was shouting. Breathing hard. They stopped, calmed themselves. "The first day they brought us together, thirty trion, they fed us well and I met people, made friends who were not sneering Rai. Found people I liked. We thought it a fine thing to be among people who understood us. The monks of Tarl-an-Gig, they warned us the first part of our test was not pleasant, explained the blooming rooms were dark and smelled bad and might appear frightening. But we found comfort in each other. So many trion, we joked it must be like the old days when we were everywhere, not simply traded between powerful families."

"Venn, I would never seek to . . ."

"Listen!" the trion shouted it at her. Then said it again, more quietly. "Please listen. I want you to understand." Kirven nodded slowly. "They took us to the blooming rooms. The first thing that hits you is the smell. You were a soldier, Firstmother, you know the smell of rotting corpses. How overpowering it is. Well, that is the blooming rooms, every dead Rai from a battle brought back and piled in the back. A stack of rot. Some of the trion with me were barely old enough to walk, they did not understand what was happening. They wept. Many were sick though you could not smell the vomit over the stench of death." They were speaking quietly now, gaze far away and back in that place, that time. "Some of the thirty tried to escape but they shut the doors behind us. Trapped us in complete darkness. We knew they would of course, they had told us the process needs darkness. It did not stop the screaming or lessen our fear." She knew what happened but to hear it from the mouth of her child made it something more real, more terrible. "Then we saw the glow. The corpses, piled high at the back were glowing. And in the glow, we saw the mushrooms, saw them push their way out of the dead. I remember a voice, I do not know who said it, but I remember the words. 'It is starting'. And some, the bravest, the most eager or maybe the most gullible. They rushed forward. As they approached the mushrooms bloomed, they opened, wide and flat and tall and with that strange glow. It got brighter, they let loose clouds of spores. They were so colourful, beautiful even." Venn's eyes were wet with tears, voice thick with misery. "Those closest, Firstmother, they were first to die. It was not quick, or painless. They did not scream. I think they could not. It was as if their bodies rebelled, their muscles working against them. I remember the awful sound of bones breaking. The rest of us, we hammered on the doors, begging to be freed but no one freed us. In the end, it was only me, a very young trion called Hargis and another about my age called Lensier. I watched them die the same way I watched all the rest. In agony as their own bodies betrayed them."

"But you did not die, Venn," she said softly. "You did not die."

"Did you know?" they were shouting it now. "Did you

know it kills most trion? I was one out of thirty! Did you know that when you sent me?" For a moment she could not speak. Then she found herself, slowly and calmly repeating her words.

"But you did not die, Venn. You are Ban-Ruhn, we are strong."

"I have had enough of death, Mother," they said, shrinking away from her. "You sent me in there, not knowing if I would walk out. You sacrificed them, and were ready to sacrifice me."

"You are special, Venn," she said, sure they must hear her desperation. "You must forget the past, the Cowl-Rai needs you. Me and you we can . . ."

Her child was screaming in her face.

"You do not care about me! You used me for your own power!"

She stared at them, so many confused feelings and thoughts flowing through her. A single, shining moment where she must decide what she could be, who she would be. A desire rose up within her, knowing she had done the unforgiveable, piling it on acts already unforgiveable. She should apologise. She should apologise for everything, beg for Venn's forgiveness. She had put her child through something intolerable and they were right, she had done it for herself. She could take them away. Take their hand and run from this place. She could do it now.

It would mean losing everything.

All her pain. All her child's pain. It would all be for nothing. She would become nothing, another village woman scratching a living from the dirt. Venn would be nothing, or worse, driven to madness by what lived within them if they did not learn to control it.

She slapped them.

She had never hit her child before. Never. Always prided herself on it. She stood. Looking down on her child who stared, unbelievingly, at her. Holding their throbbing cheek.

In a moment within a moment, she had made a realisation and a decision.

"We are Ban-Ruhn, Venn," she hissed it through clenched teeth. "We are stronger than Rai as we worked for what we have rather than simply being given it. You have a cowl within you. The first trion in generations with one. It gives you power like none in our family have ever had. It frees us both from fear of the Rai. It makes you beloved of the Cowl-Rai themselves, you are to be the conduit of Tarl-an-Gig and you will change this world." She wanted her words to stir them, for them to understand, but they only stared at her. Guilt and pain whirled around her, mixing, until they became something acidic and poisonous and angry. She grabbed one of the histi from the cage by its neck. It screamed and squealed and struggled in her hands. "If you cannot be strong, Venn, then this world will chew you up and," with a twist of her hands she broke the neck of the animal, silencing it, "then it will swallow you." The trion said nothing, but a single tear tracked down their face. She threw the little corpse at them, hitting them in the chest. "Use your power, Venn. Kill the other one, wake your cowl. And if you do not then we will start investigating other ways to do it. You are Ban-Ruhn!" She spat the name at them.

Venn stared at her, then they reached out and took the dead histi in their hands. Blood dripped from where a bone had broken the flesh and her child, her beautiful child, her hope in the world, wet their thumb in the blood. Tears ran down the white make-up of their face, tracking blue from the long strip that ran over their eyes. Venn lifted their hand. Blood on their fingers. They looked at the blood for a count. Looked at her. Then began to rub the side of their head, a frantic, hard, furious motion, using their bloodied fingers to smear the clanpaint into a black and red and blue mess.

"I am not Ban-Ruhn, I have no family," they said.

She could not speak. Not without saying something final. Too much. So she turned, opened the door and walked out. She did not look at Falnist, still sitting by the door, though she knew they must have heard every word said in the room.

"The arrangements you were making," her words came breathlessly. She smoothed her clothing, such finery was easily creased and she could not look anything but unruffled.

"What about them, High Leoric?"

"Complete them," she said, her words cold, calm and collected as she knew she must be. "I am done coddling my child, Falnist, they must learn the truth of our world and take their place in it. No matter what the cost."

"Of course, High Leoric," said Falnist. "No matter what the cost." She did not look at them, she could not bear to see the expression of triumph she knew they would be wearing.

7

They made him wait outside the gates. He sat on a rock and tracked the movement of the light across the sky, watching the shadows of the trees reach out for the walls of Harn as the light passed through the early eight. Above him the clouds, long and smooth, like smears of fungal bloom that pointed north across the sky. The circle winds would push them on until they came upon Wyrdwood, and the wall of cloudtrees which would shatter them into lifegiving water. That to fall into the forest to trickle back into the land through a thousand streams and creeks. Little of that water reached as far as Harn, as it was sucked up before it left Harnwood and water had to be stolen from the vines and trees.

If he squinted he imagined he could make out the line of mist where cloud met tree, the way the black trunks and vast branches stuck out below, giving the impression that the massive trees had a canopy of foggy air. Few people of Harn, or Crua, ever made the journey into Wyrdwood. The dangers far outweighed the benefits and unless there was a truly worthwhile reason, like treefall, it was unlikely most would ever see the cloudtrees or walk among them.

He had, though; sometimes it was as if the great forest called to him in a voice he could not deny and, despite the dangers of Harnwood and Wyrdwood, he was drawn to those quiet, dark and lonely places among the vast trees.

He met no others there, except the occasional Forestal, those who entirely rejected, or chose to reject, society. Generally they kept to themselves. If they raided it was from desperation or to strike at the Rai. They had little interest in one man toiling through their forest, or small villages like Harn, as they were places they could trade should they need to. The Forestals had access to valuable woods which made the risk of dealing with them worthwhile.

He wondered why they were attacking Harn's traders now, it barely seemed worth their while to come all this way for a few fleeces.

"Forester!" He turned to see Dyon standing between the guards of the gate, tall, thin and austere as ever. He had painted his bald head with fungal juices, the mystic swirls of Tarl-an-Gig glowing faintly upon his pate. "The Leoric will hear your entreaty now."

Cahan bit back a bitter reply. It was just like Dyon to make the fact that he was doing Harn a favour sound like he was the one coming begging to them. Like most in Harn he had never travelled further than Harn-Larger and was suspicious of anything outside of his small world. He watched Cahan approach and scratched at the painted symbols that ran down the side of his face proclaiming his lineage. It looked like the inks irritated his skin and though it was small of Cahan it made him smile – that this badge of belonging should trouble its owner so.

"Lead on, Dyon," he said. The man nodded and walked away without checking Cahan followed.

Furin the Leoric waited in her cold longhouse, sitting before the glowing embers of her fire sipping on her broth.

"I am glad you saw sense, Forester," she tried a smile

but it did not quite reach her eyes. "I will have the crown-head sent to your farm." He nearly said more than he meant, that she could keep the farm as he no longer wanted it or needed it. The reborn's visit had made up his mind and he had no intention of coming back from Harn-Larger. It seemed foolish to tell these people. Harn may not have brought the soldiers down on him, but it did not mean they would not give him up. The less they knew of his plans the better, though it saddened him that his remaining crownheads would be left to look after themselves. Most likely they would die.

"I would rather have the coin," he said.

"You do not trust us to choose you a decent animal?"

"No," he said, while thinking it was good of her to provide him with an excuse. Furin looked at him, some expression he could not decipher on her face, shook her head and stood with a grunt. The Leoric rubbed her back and then vanished into the rear of the longhouse, behind the screen. Returning from the gloom with a bag of coin. It was not a large amount, but enough. With what he had already dug up from his grove it was probably more than most people in Harn would ever see in their lives. He stowed the money in his pack among the clothes.

"I am sorry you were made to wait outside, Forester, that was not my instruction," said Furin. "I told Dyon to have you wait while the caravan was made ready, but he should have brought you in to do so."

"I did not see the caravan."

"It is by the Forestgate, when I knew you were here, well," she smiled again but the smile was as cool as her house, "I did not want to give you time to change your mind. When you return, maybe we can become closer than we have been, eh?" With that she led him out of her house and through the quiet village to the Forestgate where the caravan was readying itself.

It was larger than he expected. There was a raft, and

rather than being suspended by floatweed as was usual, it was held above the ground by a net containing over a hundred young gasmaws, each about the size of someone's head. They darted back and forth, fighting the edges of the net with writhing tentacles, looking for a way out. Sengui, the gasmaw farmer, was carefully checking her knots to make sure none could find an escape. On the other side stood Gart, checking over the sides of the raft to make sure they were solid. With him was the butcher, Ont, a huge man, far bigger than Cahan and a man the forester had never cared for.

". . . and I tell you," he was booming, "I have more dried meat I wish to send."

"Meat and skins," said Sengui softly, "are heavy. The net will not take more of the maws to balance the weight out."

"Then get another net," said Ont.

"The rest are too young, no one will buy them. If you want to add more goods then you must deal with Gart," the wool merchant smiled and shook his head at Ont.

"If you match Diyra's price that she paid me to remove my wool and put on more skins, I will take your coin." The big man huffed but said nothing. Cahan turned away from the arguing traders, looking for the Leoric.

"You said you needed me for my size," he said, "but Ont is far bigger than I am."

"Two men of great size is better than one, right?" She shrugged, "or that is what my first- and secondhusbands said to me."

"Do not try and deflect this with jokes." The beginning of a real smile fell away at the seriousness of the forester's tone. "Tell me why you really want me to go with your traders or I will walk away."

He stared at her.

She stared back.

Cahan wondered how much she actually knew of him. Or if he simply did not hide his past as well as he thought and the echoes of the warrior he had been followed him wherever he walked. Footprints left behind in red from the blood he had spilled. "If you do not reply true, Leoric, I will walk away. Why do you really need me?"

She took a deep breath.

"Very well, I know we cannot hope to match their coward's weapons with what little strength we have here."

"You think one more man can stop a group of Forestals with bows?" The fire inside him burning brighter. "Clearly, you have never seen a good archer in action." He should not have been surprised that she was unfamiliar with bows; they were banned throughout Crua and reviled by the people. "Why not bring in the Rai? They will protect your village and punish the Forestals for attacking, especially if they bring bows. They have little patience with weapons that kill from such a distance." She let out her breath, took his arm and moved him away from the traders – who continued with their own argument, oblivious of his.

"I know nothing of you, Forester," she said, "not even your real name. But I know you are not like these people," she said, inclining her head to indicate the traders behind her. "You have seen the world, you know it and not simply from marching in an army to fight, seeing nothing but camps and battlegrounds." Her eyes searched his face, looking for some sign that she was right. "I am the leader of these people, and they know nothing of the Rai but stories of great heroes. To them Rai are warriors seen at a distance on the battlefield. But we know the truth of them, yes? Our leaders are cruel, and they would treat my people badly if I called them." He could not deny that. "You are a forester, you know the forest and its ways." She looked over at the squabbling traders. "They will argue, and they think themselves better than the Forestals. They will try to fight if they find them. At best they will lose everything, at worst they become corpses feeding the trees and the fungi." She looked back to him. "I had hoped you might be able to speak with the Forestals, agree some sort of deal to let my people pass."

"Do you know why they are attacking you?" he asked. She looked away, back at the caravan. "You should send a message, offer the Forestals a portion of your goods, and a place here to trade if they want it, as long as they leave you alone." She stared at him.

"You think I have not tried?" Furin sighed, lowered her voice. "Harn is dying, Forester, we need to be able to trade with Harn-Larger. It is our link to the skyrafts and from there to the rest of Crua. The bluevein blights our fields and without trade the forest will reclaim Harn and these people will lose everything." Behind them the caravan finally sorted out its differences and the traders put on the rope harnesses and began to move it through the village. He watched it pass, the net of gasmaws bobbing above the heavily laden raft. They passed without looking at him. At the Tiltgate the two guards waited with the monk Tussnig who held a screaming histi by its ears.

"You should join them for the blessing," said Furin.

"I do not think I would be welcome, neither do I want the blessing of a god such as Tarl-an-Gig." The moment he finished speaking something wet hit him in the face. He turned, ready to be angry at some villager cursing him for his lack of piety, or the simple truth that he was clanless. Instead he found the monk he had given coin to, squatting before an earth-house. Her hands filthy with mud and an impish smile on her face. The spikes of her hair rose tall above her.

"I have blessed you, Forester," she said, lifting a handful of mud, "with good earth, as befits a traveller through the forest." She brought her hand down and sniffed it. "Well, good earth as much as you can find it in this place. It's full of filth." At the gate the histi squealed as Tussnig cut its throat and spattered blood over the raft and travellers. "But it's still cleaner than that old fraud," she said, glancing towards the Tiltgate.

"Udinny," said the Leoric, "sometimes I think you wish to be banished from here as you have been banished from so many other places." The monk made a mocking look of contrition at the Leoric, sticking out her bottom lip. "If you wish to clown then go and do it for Issofur, he at least delights in it. The Leoric sounded serious but he did not believe her, there was an edge of amusement there. "Issofur's affection for you is the only reason I protect you from Tussnig. So do not ignore him and fall out of favour with my child." Udinny hopped up into the air from a crouching position and gave the Leoric a bow.

"As you wish, great leader." She trotted off towards the Leoric's longhouse.

"And do not teach him any of your bad habits!" she shouted after her, then turned back to the forester. "I am sorry about that one," she said, took a piece of cloth from a pocket and, reaching up, wiped mud from his face. Such a simple and thoughtless action on her part, and it shocked him. The expression on his face strange enough to cause her to pause. "Sorry," she said, and was there something playful there, in her voice? No, there could not be. He was clanless. "Sometimes the part of me that is a mother cannot be put aside and I act without thinking." The hand holding the cloth fell to her side. "I had an older boy once, but he died in the war along with my firstwife and our firsthusband." She held out the soft cloth and he took it from her, cleaning the mud from his face.

"Thank you," he wiped at the mud, "few are so kind to the clanless."

"Anyone can draw a few signs on their face," she was staring quite intently at him and it made him uncomfortable. He gave the cloth back, felt the familiar frown returning to his face. Furin's smile faltered and she turned away, towards the gate. "It looks like the blessing is over," she straightened up, and once more she was leader of the village, not simply a woman talking to him, "you should lead them to Woodedge."

"Aye," he said, "I should", and he walked away but his mind was not on the forest or the caravan. It was on the touch of a cloth upon his face, and the realisation that no one had touched him in anything but anger since the day an old gardener in a monastery far away had died a terrible, terrible death.

Deep in the Forest

You are running but you are not running fast enough.
The Trainer of Body has a whip
Whip!
You are fighting but you are not fighting hard enough.
The Trainer of Arms has a whip
Whip!
You are understanding but you are not understanding
   deeply enough.
The Trainer of War has a whip
Whip!
You are connecting but you are not connecting strongly
   enough.
The Trainer of Spirit has a whip
Whip!
You are running but you are not running fast enough.
The Trainer of Body has a whip
Whip!
You are running but you are not running fast enough.
You are running.
Running.

8

It was a busy day for Kirven and she could not let the effect Venn's disobedience had on her show. Her greatest wish was to rant, to find someone who had let her down or betrayed her and take out her anger on them, but time did not allow for it.

Not yet.

It was her duty to attend the sacrifice to Tarl-an-Gig in the great clearing before the central spire. Then she could see to these false Cowl-Rai that had been brought in. She let herself smile a little. At least there was an outlet for her rage there, in the cages below Harnspire.

How could Venn not see that she had no option?

Not see the truth?

They were strong, the only survivor of thirty trion taken to the blooming rooms. No, that was not true, of far more than thirty if you counted those before. And it was still happening. All over Crua trion were being put to the bloom but Venn had no need to know of that. Of them all only Venn had been chosen: they were chosen out of hundreds. She paused in her hurried walk to the square. Maybe if she told Venn that hundreds had died, *hundreds*, and only they survived. Only they had a cowl growing beneath their skin. Becoming part of them. Waiting for that first death so it could come to life. Born from death, and woken by it.

Maybe then they would understand.

Did she shudder. Balk at the cycle of horror she had willingly thrown her child into? If so it was only for a moment before she set off on her way. Her regret changing and reforming, diluting itself into self-pity.

She should not have sent word to the Cowl-Rai of Venn. She had been too hasty, too excited by the opportunity. At least war still raged in the south, there was that. Venn would not be needed until the war was done and the lands had settled under the hand of their new ruler, and their new god. But when Tarl-an-Gig ruled everywhere she must have the trion ready or they would both pay the price. She stopped at the great doors of the spire.

Took a breath.

Walked out.

The cold air bit her skin. The smell of the city, effluent and woodsmoke, stung her nostrils.

Before the central spire lay the great square. It was not actually a square, the angles and lengths of its sides were not quite right, a little unpleasant. The place was full. She could not see it, not yet, but she did not need to as she could hear the crowd that filled it, a thousand feet upon the huge mosaic of Iftal's star.

Before her, backs to the spire, stood the ranks of Harnspire's rulers, the Rai in their beautiful darkwood armour. Each stood before a small taffistone, their hand on it. Beyond the Rai stood Harnspire's great stone, as tall as three people standing on each other's shoulders. It obscured her view of the square. She heard the droning voice of one of the monks, Jaudin, who acted as Skua of Harnspire, as they ended the rite.

"Give of yourself to Tarl-an-Gig!" he shouted. In reply the crowd shouted back.

"We give, to Tarl-an-Gig!" Though they did not. This was not a true sacrifice of giving, where the people lined up to touch the great taffistone, each leaving a portion of their life for the cowls within the waiting Rai. Paying the price asked by the gods so the land did not dissolve beneath their feet.

When she had first taken over Harnspire the sacrifices had been every other day. She knew how such sacrifices took the strength from you and how war had tired the north. Harnspire's production, of crops and animals and weapons, had been steadily dropping. The soldiers they recruited were becoming noticeably weaker and Kirven had been tasked with reversing this, turning the county round. Now true sacrifices only happened once each month of the eight of Least, and once every two months during the eight of Harsh. The Rai did not like it, but the Cowl-Rai had chosen her so they could not complain. The bluevein blighted crops and tremors cracked the land, both had taxed the people sorely. Something had to give somewhere and the sacrifice of giving was a thing she could control. To appease the Rai she had increased executions to daily, which pleased both the people and the most powerful of the Cowl-Rai who benefited from them.

Today there would be two executions. One of a thief, and one of a woman who had been murdering the guests at her inn. The Rai who would be carrying out the executions, Galderin Mat-Brumar and Vanhu An-Derrit, were both strong and old. She trusted them, not because they would not plot against her, or kill her should they think she truly threatened them, but because she understood them, could manage them. As Rai became older the cowl burned away their softness, made them very pure. Simple in their own way. They lived for power and cruelty; give them what they wanted and they would protect you.

"Tarl-an-Gig blesses the people of Harn!" shouted Jaudin. A great flower of fire exploded from the top of the taffistone. A roar of approval exploded from the crowd.

Kirven smiled. She was not in the mood for humour but sometimes it was hard not to be amused. From where she stood she could see the Rai behind the stone who made the plume of fire that tricked the crowd. How simple it is to lead, she thought. It is all show.

When the fire was finished she ascended the stone apron before the taffistone. Saw Jaudin's look of disappointment when he realised she would oversee the execution and bask in the appreciation of the crowd. She gave him a small nod, then commanded the condemned to be brought forward. Her guards made them stand either side of the taffistone, attached the ropes, and the crowd jeered and hooted at them. Then the Rai came. Rai Galderin to stand behind the thief, Rai Vanhu behind the murderer. The crowd quietened. Sensing the nearness of death. So many faces below her, expectant, waiting for her command.

She had been surprised at how easy it was to win the love of the crowds. When the Rai, Madrine, had her join her family she had watched her carefully. She had learned. Give them gods, free them from a few of their responsibilities, keep them entertained and give them someone to hate. Then they were yours.

Not all, of course, and she was ruthless against those who stood against her; another lesson Madrine had taught her.

"We are gathered here for justice," shouted Kirven, felt a great wave of approval from the crowd. Justice was always a good start: tell them it was just and they felt right about what happened. "Two proud Rai will feed their cowls," her voice echoed around the square, "and the souls of these criminals will be sent to the Osere below!" A roar from the crowd almost made her forget the anger she felt with Venn – her pain. The crowd's approval and desire washed away any doubt she may have in her actions.

This was her place.

This was where she should be.

In charge.

"I will not make you wait for your justice, for I do not think justice should wait!" Another roar. She turned to the condemned. "First, the thief." She looked down on the man, he had been beaten, bound, gagged and stripped. The people loved them to be naked. She did not really understand it but she gave them what they wished. He looked frightened and she could not blame him. Of all the ways to die, executed by Rai might be one of the worst. Behind the thief stood Galderin. The man was not tall, but he was broad and handsome if you could ignore how dead his eyes were. He wore the white make-up that was popular throughout Crua, small blue stars above his eyes and the black sigils of his lineage ran down the side of his face. She gave him a nod. Galderin raised his arms and fire leapt between his hands. The crowd hooted their approval. The condemned man tried to move but could not; he was firmly tethered to the stone below him. The Rai let the fire stutter and burn out. Looked at his hands as if disappointed.

Someone in the crowd shouted, "Feed your cowl!" The chant was taken up and Galderin let it swell, waiting for the right moment. The thief whimpered, Kirven doubted anyone heard, or cared. Galderin placed his hands on the shoulders of the condemned, a brief moment of nothing. Then smoke rising, the thief's eyes widening and Galderin let out a sigh. The thief crumpled to the floor.

She liked that about Galderin, he was efficient, did only what was needed. For that reason she had given him the thief. Most of the people in the crowd were only one or two steps from thievery. It did not do for them to see suffering and think it could be them that ended up before the stone.

Murderers, however, were a different story.

That was why she had chosen Vanhu for the murderer.

All the Rai loved cruelty, but Vanhu gloried in it. He was more squat than Galderin, less handsome, his white make-up carelessly applied, clanpaint smudged. She left the smouldering body of the thief, and walked over to the woman. Stood for long enough to feel the crowd getting restless before she turned to them.

"How many!" she shouted to them, "lost sons, daughters and trion, to this woman and her greed?" Screams and jeers from the crowd. "A thief, we can all understand a thief, though it does not mean they should not be punished." She gave a theatrical look at the body behind her before turning back to the woman. She did not look scared, maybe she had come to terms with her death. Well, Kirven doubted she knew what was coming. "But murderers," shouted Kirven, "should suffer before the Osere get them!" A great roar from the crowd and she bathed in it. Then gave a nod to Vanhu.

He did no theatrics, he juggled no fire. Only placed his hands on the woman's naked shoulders, smiling all the while. The woman closed her eyes, as if ready, finding peace in the moment of her death.

Kirven watched.

Kirven waited.

The woman's eyes opened. She tried to scream but the gag in her mouth prevented it. She fought the ropes that tethered her. Smoke rose from her fingertips. Rai Vanhu's face remained impassive as he began the burning. Kirven had seen this before, the ember, the slow burn. It started at the fingers and toes, moving inward towards the body. She knew it was an impressive show of control, a way of showing off to the other Rai as well as entertaining the crowd. The very skilled could start it and walk away, leaving their victim burning for days. The woman would be slow in dying, but not too slow as the crowd were not patient. Kirven had no wish to stay and watch, and had more that needed to be done. She nodded to the Rai, turned and bowed to the crowd. Then straightened, raised her fist and shouted, "Justice!" and left, wishing for a moment she could have burned the woman alive herself. It may have made her feel better.

Less angry.

But she could not. Though she was not without recourse to ways of causing pain and punishment. With that thought in her mind she returned to the central spire and headed down, into the darkness of the underspire.

Kirven walked quickly through tight corridors, lit by the same unseen light as the rest of the tower, until she came to a room only she could enter. Two soldiers guarded the door, loyal only to her, who would listen only to her. These guards were sent by the Cowl-Rai and their Skua-Rai from faraway Tilt. The two on the door, faces hidden behind visors, eyes a gleam behind slits in polished wood, moved out of the way as she approached.

They did not speak to her, they never did.

She opened the door and went into the room. Inside were cages for prisoners, a door leading out to another part of the underspire and two more guards holding long spears.

Seven cages in all, though only the two on either side of the door were occupied. Behind the cages stood duller pods. The cage immediately before her held nothing but a small taffistone, a twin to the ones the Rai stood before in the square above her.

No, not a twin, that was not true. This one was different, strange in some way she could not quite fathom. Sometimes she thought it glowed with a light that was not a light. If she stared at it for too long it made her head ache and her stomach threaten to rebel. Even its arrival had been strange, coming from Tilt under cover of darkness. Brought on a crownhead raft, rather than the skyraft which delivered most of their goods. With it had come the ten soldiers who guarded the stone and the cells. The first thing they had

done when it was fitted and the cages built was kill the
rafter who had brought them.

Kirven had not understood, not then.

Understanding came later. When the lists of old monasteries arrived, along with the men and women who came
and went under cover of darkness, dropping off names
overheard in lonely villages, rumours of abandoned places.

To the left and the right of the cell with the stone sat
the two false Cowl-Rai. The man and the woman.

"Give me your spear," she said to the guard nearest her.
He passed it over without complaint or question. It was
long, longer than the usual fighting spears. Long enough
to reach the back of the cage with its elegantly curved and
finely carved blade. She approached the woman first,
looked her up and down. Nothing special to look at, they
generally were nothing special to look at. "Do you know
who I am?" The woman shook her head. "I am Kirven
Ban-Ruhn, the High Leoric of Harn." The woman went to
her knees, began to apologise, to beg. Kirven did not want
to hear it. "Quiet!" a harsh bark. "Do you know why you
are here?" The woman shook her head and Kirven watched
for some sign she was lying before continuing in a quieter
and more measured voice. "You are here, because we have
been told you were raised under the lie you could be
Cowl-Rai by monks of a false god." The woman's face was
a picture. Whether it was through genuine surprise or
because she had been discovered Kirven did not know. But
she would find out. Kirven carried on speaking because
she knew that if she let them talk then they would not
stop, blabbering out their dull lives and excuses in hope
of pity. "All you need to do to save yourself, to prove these
rumours false," said Kirven, "is to swear allegiance to the
Cowl-Rai on that taffistone over there." She pointed at the
stone in the other cell.

"That is all?" said the woman. Kirven nodded.

"Will you do it?"

"Yes," said the woman. No hesitation or fear. "I fought for the blue, see, the Cowl-Rai already 'as my allegiance'."

"Good," Kirven pulled on the lever that opened the door between the cages. "Place your hand on the stone, and say 'I swear allegiance to the Cowl-Rai of Tarl-an-Gig'." The woman blinked, got up from her knees and walked into the cage. She looked down at the stone. Then back at Kirven. "Your hand." The woman nodded to the High Leoric and placed her hand on the stone.

"I swear allegiance to the Cowl-Rai of Tarl-an-Gig," she said. The air stilled, though whether that was real or Kirven's sense of expectation she did not know. The woman did not seem to notice. "Is that it?" she said after a moment.

"Yes," The High Leoric smiled at her. "Kindly return to your cell." The woman did as asked and Kirven pulled the lever closing her in then walked over to the other cage. The man stood.

"You want me to do the same?" She nodded, looking him over. There was a confidence about this one the woman lacked. "Then open the cage," he said, almost an order, "I will swear." She pulled the lever. "Same words?" he said.

"Yes," replied Kirven, he gave her a nod and a smile and walked from his cage to stand before the stone. "Put your hand on it." Again, the nod as he put out his hand, his eyes on hers, never wavering.

"I swear allegiance to the Cowl-Rai—" He stopped.

The confidence fled.

Eyes widened.

He made a noise, an utterance of pain so pure and complete that it made Kirven wince. His head bent back, exposing his neck and he began to choke as the muscles of his neck worked against his desire to breathe. His body began to vibrate and more not-words, sounds of agony, escaped from his constricting airways. For a count she was sure the stone glowed more brightly, a pale blue. Then he collapsed, crumpling to the floor. She could already feel the effect of the stone. She wanted him away from her, and knew that when he opened his eyes they would be white, strange and upsetting to look into. She turned to the soldiers.

"Have him taken to join the Hetton." One of the soldiers nodded. "I had hoped he'd go the other way. They need dullers in the south." The soldier said nothing, had no comment. They never did.

"What happened to him?" said the woman. She was staring, had moved as far away from the man as she could get in her small cage. Kirven walked over, spear in hand.

"He really was a false Cowl-Rai, but you are not."

"Did not know false Cowl-Rai was a thing," said the woman.

"Most don't, but it is a dangerous secret to have," said Kirven. And she put all the anger that had been simmering within her since she saw her child into thrusting the spear through the bars. A thing she knew had to be done. Had been hoping she would get to do, thinking it might clear some inner turmoil she was unable to calm. The woman looked surprised when the spear cut into her.

It did not make Kirven feel any better.

She wanted to feel better.

9

To Cahan, Crua was a land of paths running through forest and over plain. The creatures that walked rather than floated or flew created byways through which they followed their food, webs of travel and communication, of sight and scent. The people of Crua found and used these paths, and those that led in useful directions widened and hardened under the light above. Those that did not were quickly reclaimed by the land. In the plains and fields of Crua these paths often existed for many generations.

In the forests, if not maintained they were quickly erased.

The forests existed in layers: the soil, and all that lived and slowly decomposed within it. The layer of low plants, the wildflowers, herbs and grasses. Trapvines that caught the feet of unwary walkers, or the throats of smaller creatures then tightened about them until their thorns pierced something vital and life flowed, warm and wet into the ground. Flowers that dazzled and closed about the tiny flyers attracted by their treacherous beauty. Above that the shrubs, the bushy plants that grew berries that burst with sweet juices in the mouth, some bringing joy, but the wrong ones, just as bright and enticing, bringing a slow and lingering death. All clad with thorns to protect their fruits, long and sharp and often dripping with poison or armed with vicious barbs. Hiding the berries were ferns, with great fan-shaped leaves, some as small as a finger, others taller than a person, shading ground busy with a thousand tiny creatures. Plants grew that shot clouds of seeds into the air, plants dropped seeds that burrowed into flesh and doomed the creatures they attached to into becoming the medium of their growth.

Then the understorey, the young trees struggling for room, thrusting up in their hurry to reach the light and crowd out their rivals. Some saplings thin and bendy, some growing stout and strong, each another placed bet in an eons' long gamble on the best way to achieve life.

Above them, the canopy, the mature trees.

Life everywhere.

In Woodedge the trees were not so great, the undergrowth not so thick. Near Harn the trees were cut regularly, managed by the villagers for fuel to burn and carve, but beyond Woodedge, in Harnwood and Wyrdwood, the trees grew to heights it was difficult for most to imagine.

But the forest did not stop with the canopy.

Above the canopy where few would ever see, was the emergent layer, the domain of the Rai of the forest, the great old trees which had grown above their competition and looked down upon all.

Knitting all of this together were the vines, thick and thin, some carrying water, some with bladders that allowed them to float, some with thorns and some with poison and each and every one, like any other plant in the forest, had a place and a use. Where there were not vines there was moss, hanging in great carpets, coating trunks and rocks. And within this huge organism of many parts, a final hidden layer, a secret web that united every plant and animal within the forest. A web of unseen cilia that pushed through the earth and the plants and even the creatures that lived there. The only proof of it the explosions of fungal blooms that were its fruit. They appeared in dark corners or on damp mornings to be harvested if they were familiar, and ignored and feared if they were not. Others grew hard and strong, and outlasted even the trees.

The caravan fought its way along a path marked with waysticks, their flags torn and mossy. Going was slow, constantly stopping to trim twigs from trees which had grown over the path and could rip the gasmaw net. Ont complained continuously, until Sengui pointed out that if they lost the gasmaws they would have to gather floatvine to keep the heavy raft off the ground, and that would take far longer than trimming a few trees.

The air was thick with whistles and howls and cracks and the drumming of forest creatures. The scent of the forest, healthy and green, filled his nostrils. Cahan was uncomfortable with these people he travelled with, wary about treating the wood in anything but the most respectful fashion. Take from it if you must, but not too much or it might take back. Though he felt no great threat from Woodedge, the great forest was weak here.

"We should camp soon," he said, "before the light is fully gone."

"I would rather be out of the forest," said Ont. He spoke in the way of people who believed themselves important, with scant regard for how little he knew and how loud he was. "I have heard there are orits about." His words made the other traders, Gart and Sengui, nervous.

"Orits are rare in Woodedge," said Cahan, striding ahead of them. "And if you keep away from them and have nothing they want to eat then they have no interest in you." He stopped and turned, addressing his words to Ont. "And, before anyone starts talking of them, swarden are found even deeper in the forest, and never in Woodedge." Ont gave him a look that suggested he thought him half-Osere. "The worst we can expect is wild gasmaws, drawn by those in the net. If Sengui has some long spears in that raft we can puncture their gasbags if they bother us." He walked on, not looking back to see if they were comforted by what he said.

"Another Osere-brought tree in the way," said Sengui from behind him. "I don't remember it being this overgrown before."

"That's because the Forestals weren't preying on us before," said Gart. "Ont here is scared of forest beasts when it's forest people we should worry about."

"I have seen an orit," said Ont, "terrible it was, bigger than four people stood on each other's shoulders and it roared and screamed and . . ."

"Whatever you saw," said Cahan, "that was not an orit."

"Listen to him, the forester thinks he knows more about—"

"There is probably a reason we call him Forester, Ont," said Sengui, and that shut up the butcher. The light, filtering through the trees that dappled and spotted them as they walked was fading to a browner twilight, the way the leaves of the trees would fade when Harsh began to bite.

"There should be a campsite soon," said Cahan, "but from the way the path has been we will need to clear it before we can rest."

"And I cannot imagine the maw cages there will be in a decent state," said Sengui. She turned to one of the guards, a man called Furden, the other guard was his firsthusband, Duhan. "You two, go ahead and find the clearing, make it as ready as you can."

"But we are to protect . . ."

"You think you can stop Forestals who are armed with bows?" she said. "The Leoric sent the Forester for that, so he stays with us. You go ahead."

"But what if we . . ." began Duhan.

"The Forestals want our goods, not our lives," said Gart.

"You will be fine and if they are out there now then I suspect they will be more likely to come for us than you." The two guards waited a second then nodded.

"Very well, but if anything happens, you can tell the Leoric." The two traders watched the guards walk away.

"Nothing will happen tonight," said Cahan.

"You seem very sure," said Ont. Cahan suspected he would have liked them be attacked, if only to prove him wrong.

"Listen to the wood, butcher," he said. "Listen to the creatures. If people were out there they would not be so loud. You can hear Woodedge settling, the change from night to day creatures. And the night creatures are the most shy. Nothing is out there."

"I have heard the Forestals are ghosts," said Ont. "They move through the wood without being seen or heard and can even vanish into the air."

"Such rumours do nothing but help them," said Cahan. He was tired and his mind ached from being around people. As he finished speaking, Gart picked up a fallen branch blocking their path and threw it into the wood to be lost among the mass of creepers, bushes and moss-covered vines. They walked on. Despite what he had said, Cahan was wary. He had the feeling there was something out there, something watching them. He did not say so as he did not want the traders any more worried than they already were.

He smelled smoke as they approached the camp, then saw it. Thick and white, hanging in the spaces between the branches, curling around trunks and seeping through the leaves and bushes. The two guards had cleared much of the overgrowth of vines and plants from the old camp and used them to build a fire. Now they were fixing holes in the cage meant to keep gasmaws in. Sengui took one look at their work and shook her head.

"We are only here for the night, it will take us longer

than that to make that thing escape proof," she nodded at the cage. "I will feed them once we have eaten, they will have to survive in the net. Help me tie it down." When that was done they settled in to eat and then sleep, though Cahan spent the night listening to the forest, straining to hear sounds that should not be there.

In the morning Cahan made sure the fire was fully out, splitting a wetvine so it ran into the place where they had set the fire and whispering an apology to the forest, asking it not to be angry and telling it how this place would be fertile now. Shoots always grew greener from ashes.

He stood, sniffing the air, listening. There was something subtly different about the forest this morning. Cahan was tempted to put it down to the fire. The forest and its creatures hated fire, and deep in the forest lighting one could be lethal. But here, in Woodedge, not so much, not enough to account for the difference in sounds.

But if there were people out there, that would account for it.

He put a hand to the forest floor, digging his fingers into the dirt. There were ways available to him, to reach out and feel what was about him. What moved within the forest that was not part of it.

You need me.

He pulled his hand from the dirt as if he had touched a hot coal.

"We should go," he said. He thought he saw something, a flash of grey in the undergrowth. A branch moving the wrong way from the wind. The reborn? Following him? Was that why he felt watched?

They walked all morning, through the slowly quietening wood, stopping occasionally to clear the path and make way for the net of gasmaws. Wild gasmaws were noisy, they whistled and buzzed and whooped but the farmed ones, those cut and broken ones made safe for people to use as they saw fit, did none of those things. They let out only a low mournful hum and it put Cahan on edge, the same way the slowly changing sounds of the forest did.

The Forestals were out there, he was becoming sure of it.

Only a matter of time before they sprang their trap.

10

The skyraft had been docked at Harnspire for three days of almost non-stop celebration, always the way when the skyrafts came in bringing trade and news from the farthest edges of Crua. She wondered where the people got their energy from. After the first night she had been forced to put soldiers on the streets, not because she feared revolution or riots, but because the fires were getting out of hand and most of Harnspire outside the spire ring was wood. There had already been one fire that had burned down half the city while she ruled, and keeping her hands on power during that crisis had reminded her how precarious her grasp was. If not for Rai Galderin she would have lost her seat.

She had first met him when he brought her news of treachery. A group of Rai had used the smokescreen of the fire to feed their cowls on a few unlucky citizens. Then they had stormed the spire, full of their own power. Only to walk into a trap set by Galderin.

Kirven was not a fool. She half suspected that Galderin had goaded those rebellious Rai into action, if not personally then through some intermediate who no doubt went on to feed Galderin's cowl. Then used their rebellion to advance himself. The Rai loved nothing more than finding ways to destroy their rivals and cement their own power. Knowing who hated who was often her best weapon.

She could hear the markets of Harn; they had begun to move out of the central ring as the skyraft was getting ready to leave and trading there was done.

The skyraft family were the Harrender. All brightly dressed in tight fitting yellow and blue wool, bound tightly with straps as any loose material was likely to get caught in the many pulleys and winders that were used, not only to steer and sail the raft, but to power its lifts and doors. Two lifts were currently in operation, a large cargo lift that went into the belly of the raft; it was filled with crownheads, and a smaller one with a cage around it went through a hole in the centre of the raft to the main deck, for passengers and crew.

On the lower hull of the skyraft they were getting ready to load on new gasmaws to keep the thing in the air. The huge nets that held the creatures against the bottom of the northern side of the raft had been loosened, freeing the gasmaws to fly around inside it. Without their buoyancy a quarter of the raft was listing noticeably.

Rafters hung from long ropes by the loose net, shouting to each other and laughing as they weeded out sick gasmaws that had lost their buoyancy and were sinking towards the bottom. They used long piercing saws, jabbing the used-up gasmaws and slashing their gasbags, the serrations on the saw ripping large holes. Then the broken maws fell into the bottom of the net. There the children of the skyraft families gathered up the dying gasmaws and threw them into a huge bag to be hoisted up into the body of the raft where they would be used as feed for healthy maws. It seemed very wasteful to Kirven to kill so many, though she knew the truth of it that was there was no other way. Once sick gasmaws always died, and they could not be eaten as their flesh was poisonous.

But gasmaws were easy to breed, they laid eggs in the thousands and grew quickly. The economy of many smaller villages depended on the constant churn of gasmaws to the skyrafts, skippers and rafters. To the villagers the creatures were valuable. To the people who used them they were disposable. Their lives short and their destiny to be ground up to feed the next generation of maws tethered beneath the rafts.

There was metaphor there, she supposed, for the whole of Crua and the way it worked. Be a gasmaw, or be a rafter.

She would never let herself become a gasmaw.

The raft family were packing away what they had bought or bartered into large boxes. They were a merry lot, singing as they worked. Somewhere an instrument was being played, something made of wheezing bellows and no doubt the sound was pleasant to those with an ear for it. Kirven had never enjoyed music. Madrine had been a keen musician.

The High Leoric was dressed for travelling. She would have preferred armour but it was not fitting for her to wear armour, it would be seen as an insult to the Rai chosen as her guard. She could not risk that. Instead she wore the clothes of wealth, the softest wool, folded many times over as much for warmth as it was to show she could afford it. The trousers so wide they were more like skirts, the top so big it made moving her arms uncomfortable. She wore only a light powdering of white on her skin, as was becoming fashionable, and it left her feeling naked. The paint of her lineage did not show as well, though she had no need to proclaim who she was. All knew Kirven Ban-Ruhn.

"High Leoric!" she turned. Rai Vanhu approaching and with him came Kyik, a Rai Kirven barely knew, one of the new recruits from the southern families. By Kyik was Sorha, she carried her helmet in one hand, better for Kirven to see how annoyed she was with this duty. She thought herself better than this and Kirven knew it. She had hoped that some time doing guard duty under Vanhu would teach the woman her place. Sorha saw the High Leoric looking at her, sneered and turned away. Between Vanhu and Kyik walked Venn in full armour, expensive, well-fitted. She felt very proud, seeing them as what they would become. Rai. Powerful. Played right, her child would be the left hand of the Cowl-Rai. The conduit for power. It would give them both a strength and security she had never dreamed of in the days she sat and waited in fear for Madrine to return.

She smiled at them. Venn looked away and her blood slowed in her veins.

"Vanhu," she hissed, "come to me." The Rai nodded and turned to Kyik.

"Take them to the lift, I will join you." Unlike Kirven, Vanhu wore his white clay thick on his face. His lineage painted in red today rather than black and she wondered if this was a subtle nod to Chyi, who he had once served. She almost wished she could have seen Vanhu's face when he discovered Rai Galderin was also on the raft. They were not friends. "You wanted me, High Leoric?" he said. She nodded. He licked his lips. The double meaning of his words implicit in his eyes.

It had been a long time since she had taken a lover and was conscious of the space left in her life, but Vanhu was not the person to fill it. He was cruel, and she had no wish for Rai as lovers. Besides, they would be on a skyraft for the next few days, and there were no secrets on a skyraft.

"Is this really necessary, Vanhu," she said, looking over as Venn stood before the lift, their back to Kyik and Sorha. "Could whatever it is you and Falnist plan not be done in the spire?" He smiled at her. It was not a pleasant smile.

"The child is comfortable there, High Leoric." She had no doubt he thought her at fault here. Thought she had coddled them. "They know they are safe in the spire," the man's voice was a growl, as though his throat had hardened and made words difficult to form. "We must break that idea, put them somewhere they no longer feel safe."

"And you think that is Harn-Larger?" She stared over at Venn as they watched a cage full of histi being taken to the goods lift. "They are not afraid of mud."

Again, Vanhu's smile, a hollow thing, more an old habit than an expression of emotion.

"Not Harn-Larger," he glanced over at Venn. "I said I wanted to stop them feeling safe, I will take them to Harnwood."

"You would take my child into the forest?" She spoke too quickly, too harshly. Vanhu blinked, sensed some break in her armour he might be able to use one day.

"You are afraid of the forest, High Leoric?"

"The forest is . . ."

"Dangerous," said Vanhu, "as you well know. But you need not worry. Three Rai accompany your child, and we will not go in too far. Only enough to unsettle them."

"And then?" she said.

"Then," said Vanhu, "I will use what they believe against them. I will turn weakness into strength, High Leoric, and we both will advance ourselves through it."

11

The Forestals found them in the afternoon.

Cahan had known it was coming since they entered the second eight of the day; there had been a quietening around them that had nothing to do with nature. The noose was closing.

His hand tightened on his staff.

You need me.

But he did not need the cowl to find them. He did not need to draw upon a power he had forsaken long ago and neither did he intend to. The faintly mocking voice in the back of his mind could stay there. Cahan walked closer to the traders. They had brought spears of hardened wood. Not great workmanship, but good enough for defence and to trade. A whole pile of them on the raft they pulled. He hoped they would not need them. Traders with spears stood little chance against Forestals with bows.

"Is something wrong?" said Gart.

"Maybe," said Cahan. "Be on your guard." Ont stopped and as the raft neared him he reached for a spear.

"No," said Cahan softly, watching the gentle movement of the wood around them, taking deep breaths of the fresh forest air. "Keep walking and act as if nothing has changed."

"If we are to be robbed I want my weapon, I will stop this . . ."

"The Leoric said they had bows," said Cahan, "you will not have time to draw back your spear arm before they drop you if that is true."

"Cowards," he spat, "with cowards' weapons."

"They kill you no less for it." Cahan walked away, leaving the traders pulling the raft while he listened to the forest telling tales of people hidden within its soft green folds in a language few understood.

The Forestals sprung the trap as the light was fading and the thoughts of the traders were turning towards making camp. It was not a dramatic trap, there was no hail of arrows, no screams, no demands to give up or die. Only a figure waiting on the path before them. Their woollen clothes dyed green and brown better to hide within the vegetation, thin branches and fern leaves woven through them, their face hidden beneath a hood. In one hand a bow nearly as tall as they were.

"Good evening, traders of Harn," said the figure before them. "May the Forest Nobles look away from you."

The raft stopped. The traders stiffened. The guards began to lift their spears but Cahan stepped between them, gently pushing the spears down.

"And Iftal's blessings to you, stranger," he said. Stepped a little closer and stopped, leaning on his staff. "Do you come from Harn-Larger?"

"I am simply from around," they said.

"And do you have a name?" The figure laughed. Cahan stepped a little nearer.

"Never wise to give your name out to strangers you meet in the forest," they said. Now he was closer Cahan was sure the speaker was a woman. "Close enough, friend," she told him and took an arrow from the quiver on her hip. She did not nock it, only held is loosely in her free hand. "You have probably not seen one of these before." She lifted the bowstaff. He said nothing: give no information to your enemy that they do not already have. Something they taught him in the monastery of Zorir. "This is a forestbow. It can put an arrow through you, and through the big man behind you and carry right on along the path as if you had never existed." Cahan turned. Ont stood behind him, between the guards. Gart and Sengui stood on the other side of the raft, frozen. Behind them a flash of grey, a figure vanishing into the wood. "It would go through another behind him, if there was one," added the Forestal.

"Impressive," said Cahan. She gave him a nod, tipping her head to the side. Then she nocked the arrow, drawing the bow a little but not fully tensioning it.

"Of course, bloodshed and violence are ever unpleasant," she said, "and who knows what corpses may attract, even in Woodedge." A smile under the hood. "So it would be better for all if you simply gave over your goods to me and then you can return whence you came."

"We are five," shouted Ont, "and you are only one." Again, that tip of her head.

"It does seem a little unfair," she said, and then let out a high-low whistle. From the bushes around them more Forestals appeared, bows at the ready. Cahan counted eight. Saw the shock pass across Ont's face, and wondered if he thought they had sprung magically from the bushes. "Now," said the woman, and he could hear the smile in her voice, "things are a little fairer. I suggest you take off those harnesses you pull the raft with and hand it over." Cahan wanted to curse Ont for interfering. The woman had been talking and now she had moved on to simply robbing them.

"Wait," said Cahan, taking a step forward. Stopping when she drew her bow and aimed it at him. He raised his hands. Holding his staff loosely so that it did not appear to be a weapon. "How good are you with that bow?"

A moment of silence, apart from the chirp of creatures in the trees, the tiny ones you barely saw and the larger ones that you only saw as fleeting movements in the corner of your eye.

"I am better than most," she said.

"Do you care for a wager?"

A cry, a howl, a whirr of wings.

"I have shot enough targets to find such wagers tedious, stranger. I shoot only living targets now."

"Do you think you could hit me?" he said.

A whirr of wings. A chirp. A howl. A laugh. The last from the woman before him and she pushed her hood back. Beneath it her curling hair was a deep brown, almost black.

"With my eyes shut."

"I wager you could not," he told her. "In fact, I would wager my life on it and all of our goods." Ont began to protest but one of the others stopped him. "If you kill me, we will not stop you taking them. If you do not, then we will pay sacrifice of ten per cent of our goods to you, and you will allow us safe passage to Harn-Larger and then back to Harn." She was staring intently at him, probably trying to work out if he was afflicted by some disease of the mind.

"And those with you, they will agree to that? To your death?"

Cahan nodded. "You heard the big man there, 'the five of us'," he said, "when there are plainly six." He glanced back at the traders and the guards. "They do not count me as one of them, I have no clan mark on my face. I am employed to get these goods to Harn-Larger. If I fail I am dead anyway."

"You should join us," she said, a twist upon her lips that Cahan thought might pass for a real smile. "We put no value on birth, only on who you are." He heard an intake of breath behind him and for a second he was tempted to take the freedom of the forest. But that was to put himself into the Forestal's trust, and he did not trust them any more than he trusted the people of Harn.

"I have never been much of a joiner," he said, "and, besides, I have given my word." She blinked, then nodded and without preamble, talk or pause, drew and loosed her bow.

It was an excellent shot.

A well-practised archer was a thing of beauty to him. The people of Crua told tales of archers as wicked outlaws and cowards who used a weapon of the weak and honourless. But Cahan knew that was not true. A bow took years of constant repetition and practice to master, not only to aim well but to build the upper body strength to draw it properly.

This woman had put in the years.

She drew the bow back until the string was taut. The blink of an eye as she paused. The wooden ends of the arching bow quivering as she checked her aim, even at such a close distance. She was no fool about to miss because of overconfidence. Then she let the arrow fly. So quick it could not be seen.

An arrow like that was only ever felt.

The impact harder than any punch, the wood streaking through flesh, ripping it apart, sending shock waves through the target that caused damage far out of proportion to the thin and fire-hardened shaft.

Over in a moment.

It was over in a moment.

The arrow flew. Cahan brought his staff across. The sound of wood on wood. The dull thud of an arrow hitting a tree. He did not look to see where the shaft had gone. It was enough that he had deflected it. She looked at him. Her eyes widened in surprise. Then slit in malice and she pulled another arrow, began to nock it.

"Ania!" A voice shouted from the undergrowth and the archer stopped mid-draw. "You took the bet. We stand by our word."

"I would have hit him," said Ania. She let the tension out of her bow as the speaker came to join her. His cloak a mixture of greens and greys. "He cheated."

"The bet was his death, and he is alive. Unstring your bow, sister." The new Forestal pushed back their hood, revealing a lean-faced man with long, dark hair. "We will take a measure of dried meat," he said, "and two crownhead fleeces, one is in lieu of gasmaws," he pointed at the net. "We have no use for them."

"But that is not fair on me," said Gart.

"Sort that out among yourselves," he said as the Forestals came to take their due, "it is not our concern." He studied Cahan. Staring at his staff then grinning. "That was a good trick, I have never seen the like." He looked friendly, then all levity fled from his face. "But it will not work again. You have safe passage to Harn-Larger and back this one time." He came closer. Cahan could feel the warmth of his breath as the man whispered into his ear. "You give the Leoric a message from me. Say that Tall Sera says she knows what we want. That she will give it to us if she does not want her village strangled."

Cahan wondered what it was he wanted, and if he should tell the Forestal that he had no intention of returning to Harn to deliver the message, but he did not think it would go down well and was not willing to push his luck further. Once the Forestals were gone and the raft restowed to balance properly they set off once more.

"Fine guard you are," said Ont as he pulled the raft past while Cahan scoured the woods, looking once more for hints of grey figures dogging his steps.

"We have our lives, Ont," said Sengui, "and most of our goods."

"And the Forestals still live," said Ont, "to trouble us the next time. A real guard would have ended the threat." Cahan said nothing as the butcher must have known that what he said was foolish even as the words left his mouth.

There were very few alive in Crua who could have taken on all those Forestals and won.

Cahan kept to himself that, of those very few people in Crua, he was one.

Deep in the Forest

You see the Skua-Rai, high priest Saradis in all her regalia, the bearded mask, the shining, glowing cloak. She sits upon a throne which, up close, has hundreds of flaming, screaming faces carved into it. No matter how cold it is outside the throne room is always too hot. The many fires of Zorir burn constantly and the Skua-Rai barely covers her flesh in a way that you have been raised to believe is wrong outside of the family. So much they tell you to do seems wrong. But the Skua-Rai is chosen of Zorir, so how can anything she does be wrong? You are as confused by her and this place as ever. She shimmers, her voice overlaid by a hissing, scratching voice.

You think it is the voice of your cowl.

But how can it be?

That time has not yet come.

12

He left the traders in Woodedge within sight of Harn-Larger. Its walls were similar to those of Harn, but much taller. The buildings within made of wood rather than being mostly mud and woven sticks. The Larger was a maze of narrow streets, houses built and rebuilt to no plan after the fires that regularly destroyed lives and livelihoods. It was also the gateway to the plains of Harn, the sweeping grasslands, studded by copses and cut through with ravines. The plains were good for grazing and little else.

Still a full morning's walk away, a black wart on the muddy green landscape. He watched a message skipper heading towards the town, a balloon of either floatvine or gasmaw above them to balance out the massive pack, twice the size of the person who held it. They moved in huge leaps towards Harn-Larger. Lines of people were making their way towards the town, and from the south a huge skyraft was coming in towards the mooring spike. He realised why Sengui had been making the trip, why there had been time pressure on them. The price for gasmaws shot up whenever the rafts came in as they needed to replace the sick or dying ones, and in large numbers.

"You'll not come in with us?" said Gart. Cahan shook his head.

"I've done my job now." He stared at the skyraft as it floated serenely towards the town, its huge and gaily painted balloons billowing as the rafters started to release hot air. "I will make my way back to Harn to claim the rest of my coin." He intended no such thing of course, but if they thought he was going back towards the village and he never arrived most would presume some forest creature had got him, or maybe the Forestals had taken their revenge. Few would mourn his loss.

"The Leoric paid you to escort us there and back," said Ont.

Cahan shrugged. "She paid me to protect you from the Forestals," he said. "And they will not bother you on the way back, they gave their word."

"What use is the word of outlaws?" said the butcher.

"Do you wish to spend more time in my company?"

"No," said Ont. He was very poor at covering his thoughts. Cahan could see in his eyes that he was scheming something. Probably realising he could tell the Leoric that Cahan had abandoned them. That it was Ont who protected the party on the way back.

"Come, Ont," said Sengui. "The Larger will be busy, it always is when the raft tethers. I want to be in the trading hall, not stuck out in the square."

He watched them go, gradually reducing in size as they crossed the plain to join the long lines of people and carts heading towards the town. Then he returned to the forest. Tomorrow, when the raft was tethered the town would be busy and he could slip in and buy supplies for his journey. Few would look twice at him in a town, though neither would they welcome him much as he was clanless. He would get what he needed and get out of the place, head to somewhere he was unknown. He would become nomadic, travelling from town to town, picking up work where he could. Maybe he would sign on to the raft crew for the journey east towards Mantus where the raft would pick up the winds going south. He did not want to go as far as Seerstem; war still raged there and the new Cowl-Rai fielded their armies in the name of Tarl-an-Gig. He could earn well as a soldier, but found it impossible to hide what he knew, what he had been taught in his youth, and it either brought him into conflict with those who led the troops or brought him to their attention as someone who should be promoted.

Attention was the last thing he wanted.

No. That was not true.

Death was the last thing he wanted. He had seen too much of it. Been the cause of too much of it. Power and death, to him, were inextricably intertwined. With the attention of the Rai came death, always. It was inevitable and he was done with it. No more a soldier. He was a forester, a farmer. There was always work for a farmer.

Tilt should be safe for him. The people there were comfortable and the climate good. He would avoid Tiltspire, far too many Rai there, and as long as he had shelter when the geysers erupted then life would be better and more comfortable than it had been on his farm. And even if he could not find shelter when the geysers erupted? Well, he had been wet before and it would not kill him.

He felt something warm against his leg and looked down to see Segur. Now the villagers were gone the garaur had returned.

"We are going south, Segur, in a day or so," he said softly. It wound itself up and around him to sit around his neck. "Do not get too comfortable there, Segur." The garaur chattered in his ear and he scratched it between its ears, a thing he knew it loved.

He slept fitfully, woken in the night by one of the earthquakes that were becoming more and more common.

In the morning he left Segur in the wood and headed, cold-necked, to Harn-Larger, slipping and sliding over freezing mud trodden by many before him as they made their way to the town to sell whatever goods they brought in the shadow of the skyraft.

Out of the shelter of the woods where the circle winds were cold and cutting, he wrapped his felt coat tighter, leaned into his staff. He met few people on his way to Harn-Larger. Most were already in the town, and the few heading in now showed no interest in him. He stopped to watch another message skipper, clad in green and bounding down the path in huge leaps, the balloon of floatvine creaking as they jumped. They moved far more quickly than Cahan could ever hope to.

The skipper's progress drew his eye to the town. He could see what looked to be a balloon partway there, and wondered what it was. As he walked the balloon grew larger and he could see a small raft below it. When he reached the raft it was coming toward him, pulled along a rope that stretched across a deep crevasse. It was not massively wide, but too wide to jump, unless you were a skipper.

"Three splinters to cross," said the rafter as she brought her craft in to grate against the edge of the crack in the land. Earth fell into the hole, some spilling onto the raft. He heard stones clatter against the wood of the craft but nothing from those that fell into the hole.

"How long has this been here?" he said, nodding at the hole.

"Not long enough for 'em to bridge it," she said. She was very old, with a creased face beneath a conical yellow hat. "I'll move on when they do. Always some new hole opening in the shakes."

"Three splinters is a lot to cross such a small gap," he said. He leaned over, looking into the split in the land. Deep down in the darkness a trick of the eye made it look like lights were twinkling.

"You can go around," she said, her voice creaking like

the wood of the raft, "but it's a day's walk in either direction. No guarantee we won't shake again, open it further as you walk."

"Do you ever wonder what's down there?" he asked as he dug coins out of his pocket. She shook her head.

"Some fellows came along with ropes in the early eight of yesterday, says they were going to look."

"What did they find," he said as he stepped onto her raft and felt it dip under his weight. She shrugged.

"Don't know, fools never came back up. Osere got 'em, I reckon." She pushed off with a heave on the rope and they drifted across the gap. He looked into the twinkling depths, wondering whether the creatures who had once enslaved the people and fought against gods really lived in the depths. Though he did not wonder for long. The journey across was swift.

Cahan half expected the guards to stop him as he passed through the gates of Harn-Larger. But the fact that he was clanless hardly mattered to them; he was just another face among many. Above the gates hung the curfew bell, a ragged figure shown begging on its porcelain sides. The bell was rung to empty the streets of vagrants as the second eight ended, but he did not intend to become a vagrant. He had money and would rent a room, even though it would cost him dear with the skyraft being in. Still, he would stay only one night, buy some travelling supplies and then move on.

From above came the shouts and calls of the rafters. The raft was bigger than the town, and shaded most of it. Three huge masts slung underneath, one pointing straight down, the others at angles and all were connected by a web of rope through which the crew moved as if it was their natural habitat. Against the hull were nets of gasmaws, hundreds and hundreds tethered in position by the web of rope. The top of the raft was given over entirely to cargo, cabins for travellers and the woodburners for the balloons. Above that the huge balloons which would be inflated for flight, though now they were stowed away. Ropes had been lowered and goods were being slid down them, the weight countered by tethered maws. On the far side he could see passengers walking across a gangplank to the tether tower. Unlike the town, which was strewn with lines of flags in blue for Tarl-an-Gig and green for Harn, the raft had no flags of allegiance, though it was painted in many bright colours.

These rafts were independent of Crua, seen as small principalities of their own under the rule of families who had plied the circle winds for generations. He had travelled on the skyrafts in the past, and found the command families to be a strange and insular lot, though they kept their word, always.

He stopped in the town square, one of Harn-Larger's Rai was fire-juggling. Easy enough to do for those with a cowl, and impressive to the common passer-by. There was art in what they did, wheels of fire and bright flashes of colour spinning hypnotically. They ended the display with an explosion, which would usually have elicited an awed shout from the people but the skyraft was drawing the eyes of most. A round of desultory applause greeted the end of the fire show, most of that encouraged by a woman he took to be the Rai's servant.

The skyraft's arrival was timed for what would have been the festival of Rahini, the Stern Judge. Now it was simply another festival of Tarl-an-Gig. In the central square filthy monks, scarred with burns, robes dirty with charcoal, danced and sang around pyres with figures of the judged tied to posts atop them. Thankfully figures of rags, not flesh. Cahan had little stomach for executions, especially burnings. Even these false burnings set a bitter taste in his mouth.

He turned from the main square, pushed past a recruiter, singing out the glory of war and telling the town that the strongest would get rich mopping up the remnants of the red in the south. He tried to catch Cahan's eye, his size always attracted recruiters, shouting of the Cowl-Rai who had fulfilled the prophecy and heralded the coming of warmth and plenty to the north. Twenty years since the Cowl-Rai had risen and ten since they had taken the great spires of Tilt, and still war raged. Cahan had seen little plenty and felt no warmth. By the recruiter was an information broker, paying for news of those who did not follow the new ways.

He wanted nothing to do with them.

Cahan had long ago found it true that in the worst of places the least questions were asked, so he sought out those places and found one near the wall of Harn-Larger. A rickety building with a drinking den downstairs and what were laughably called "rooms" – beds divided by thin wicker walls – on the second floor. The place was rowdy, filled with filthy men and women and the smell of them hit him harder than the raucous noise. They had little interest in him and he in them which suited his purposes. In the back of the room was a door and from behind the door came more noise. His feet took him in that direction as if there were a path there he must follow.

Curiosity had ever been his undoing.

In the back room, a place larger than the whole of the Leoric of Harn's house. He heard the yattering of garaur but did not see them. There was much laughter, much drunken joy, and the smell of blood which he did not like, not in a place like this. It was the smell of the hunt and it had no place in a town where people hid behind walls.

Too late he realised he had stumbled into blood sport, a fighting den. He tried to retreat but the weight of the crowd denied him, pushing him towards a large wicker cage.

In the cage, shivering and frightened, sat a rootling. The sight of it stopped him dead. Froze him to the spot.

Cahan knew the great slow and layered forests of Crua as living things in more ways than greenery and great trunks. The forests had ideas and desires which manifested in ways that were strange and frightening to those of the towns. Strange and frightening to him too, quite often, but of their place, and he knew and respected them for it. Sometimes the trees would take a creature, one of their own, and change them, make them look more like the people and so rootlings were born. Whether this was to try to communicate with the people of Crua or to fight them off Cahan was never sure. Rootlings could be fierce when backed into a corner, but were generally shy. The most he usually saw of them was a sparsely furred arm or leg vanishing into the thicket.

It was not right it being here, it was not its place.

The one in the cage had been a garaur once. At first glance it looked like one of the people, not the size of a fully grown person, but bigger than a child. If you looked more closely then you realised it was not like the people at all, the eyes, intelligent, wide and oh-so-scared, were too large, the teeth in the mouth too sharp, the nose too small and ears too big and pointed. The body, covered with fine hair that was too long and too thick.

The rootling was plainly terrified. It had curled itself into a ball in the centre of the cage, as far away from the jeering crowd as it could get. Scattered around the floor of the cage were dead garaur. Cahan counted eight and mourned every one of them for they were good and noble animals. He had seen this before, setting rootlings against the creatures they had once been and betting on it. Once it would have been unthinkable, too many of the gods came from the forest, and their creatures were revered. Those who did not revere them at least feared the vengeance of the boughry, the Forest Nobles, the greatest of the forest spirits. But Tarl-an-Gig had no time for the forest, its gods, or any other gods. Such cruelty as this was becoming more common, and one of many reasons he stayed away from towns.

"Four at once, next!" came the voice of the cagemaster. He stood on a box to see over the crowd, "How long do you think it will survive, eh? How long? Will it survive at all?"

To survive is often to walk away from cruelty. But is that to live?

This gardener had told him that.

Saradis, the Skua-Rai of Zorir, always said cruelty was inevitable, and that was the way of life. But the old gardener said cruelty was a choice, and if you wished to live easily then you must be ready to let the cruelty of the world pass you over, but to do that was also to take the cruelty into yourself. To accept it was to become part of it. Cahan had learned all about cruelty from the fists of the tutors of Zorir who found him wanting, and he liked it little.

Real strength, the gardener had said, meant to stand against cruelty. Cahan did not want the attention such a stand was likely to bring.

To survive is often to walk away from cruelty. But is that to live?

"Osere take you, Nasim," he said. Somewhere, deep within, Cahan knew it was not the gardener he should curse, but himself. He had nursed a slow ember of guilt in his gut for those who had died at his farm, a subtle, gnawing thing. That small ember had been burning brighter and brighter in him from the moment he had found the child's toy in his house. He had let cruelty pass him over there, in exchange for his life. Here, now, whether he knew the truth of why or not, he could not let it happen again.

He pushed his way through the crowd to the cagemaster; small, young, his skin smeared with dirt around his clan marks. Like most younger people in the bigger towns he did not wear thick make-up. He had three teeth missing and the ones that were left were stained from chewing narcotic roots.

"How much?" Cahan shouted to him over the excited noise of those making bets.

"Bet what you want, Clanless," he said. Filthy bodies jostled him and the smell of the room threatened to fell him. His head spun. "Your money is as good as any other's. But bet quickly, we loose the garaur soon."

"No, not to bet," he said, "to buy the rootling." The cagemaster stopped chewing, his surprise so total that it consumed him. It filled his mind and left him with no room to think of anything else. No space to take the money held out at him by excited men and women.

"Buy it?" The noise of the room receded, like the circle wind dying away and the forest trees calming in their ceaseless sway. He looked at Cahan as if he had appeared from the air before him from nowhere. "This is my livelihood, Clanless."

The forester leaned in close, so he could whisper to him.

"And what do you make from these people, small coins I bet? Little more than splinters. There's, what, one or two fights left in that thing? I will give you ten roundwoods for it." His eyes widened in surprise, and Cahan felt shocked at his own words. Ten roundwoods was almost half the coin he had. The cagemaster cocked his head, lank hair hanging in strings.

"Why?"

"I am clanless, we learn to revere the forest. I owe it a debt." He looked at Cahan, laughed.

"Keep that quiet, Clanless," he spat. "We worship Tarlan-Gig, the forest has no place here, and we care nothing for twisted creatures like rootlings." He motioned towards the cage then leaned back, so he could look at him. It was not hard for Cahan to divine his thoughts: he was thinking of stealing the money. He would have people here who would help. But Cahan was bigger than most, a thick trunk fed and watered well that could stand against all weathers. Those around him were more like saplings on rocky ground, struggling to root themselves and ready to be thrown over by a strong breeze.

"I wish to buy the rootling," he said again. "If I have the money, does why really matter?"

The cagemaster shrugged. "My business partner, I must speak to her." Cahan nodded and the man vanished into the throng. Coming back quickly with a woman as ragged and filthy as himself.

"What will you do with it?" she said.

"Take it out of the town, set it free."

She blinked, twice. "And for this you will pay ten round-wood?"

Cahan nodded. She turned to the man and they exchanged a look, then he raised his voice.

"The fight is off," he shouted, "see Turif for your money. The fight is off!" All eyes turned to Cahan, a blanket of hostility settling across the room.

"We have paid for a fight," said a woman near him, "and we expect blood." A rumble of agreement, a shifting of the atmosphere towards violence.

"And you have had blood," said the cagemaster. At the edge of the room Cahan noticed a man and woman in gnarled and rough barkwood armour appear, clubs in hand. "Unless you want the next blood on this floor to be yours," he nodded at the guards, "be happy with what you have been given." A woman in the crowd spat on the floor and threw a vicious glance at Cahan. The cagemaster waited until the room emptied and turned, holding out his hand. "My coin, friend," he said, the guards watched. Cahan shook his head.

"I do not have it on me." Only a fool would hand it over there. "Meet me outside the walls with the rootling. I will pay you once it is free." The cagemaster did not like that any more than the crowd had liked being robbed of their sport, but had little choice. Cahan looked about him. The two guards were eyeing him suspiciously. He thought it best to leave. Leave the room, the building, the town. Once the rootling was free it would be best to find the crew of the skyraft and sign on. Get away from here.

Outside the city he waited, sat cross-legged before the wooden walls of Harn-Larger. The walls were not so tall close up, but were crowned with sharpened stakes and gibbets, though they were all empty. The walls were a poor defence. If war ever came here a real army would roll over the place and barely realise it. But Harn-Larger was far from any fighting, the red warriors of Chyi had been pushed out of the Northernmost territories many years ago by the forces of the blue and the new Cowl-Rai. It was the south that suffered now, where Chyi had the strongest support.

The man and the woman from the fighting pit came out of the gate, dragging the rootling on a lead. It had a pronounced limp. Behind them came soldiers, not many, only four, but they were armed with spears of hardened wood. Cahan stood, not liking what he saw but knowing that to run would be suspicious and would doom the rootling. The guards might even call on their friends on the walls. He did not want them to look at him too closely, and he did not want them to take the rootling back into town to die.

"I brought some friends," said the man. "To speak to you. Only Turif, my second, she thought it powerful strange that a man would pay so much for a rootling. She worried you were some sort of betrayer, a spy for the red, maybe. Or one who follows forest gods." As he walked nearer, Cahan stood, leaning on his staff. The man was a lot braver with the soldiers behind him.

"Don't seem the way a good man of the blue would act," said the woman, Turif. She wiped a hand across her nose and sniffed. "Paying money for a rootling. No god we know would want one of 'em. We don't put up with forest worship here."

"Brokers give a good reward for traitors," said the man. The soldiers moved behind Cahan. "And we thought, we could get your money, the reward, and keep our forest fellow." He nodded towards the rootling.

Cahan nodded. Looked from the man to the woman, over his shoulder at the soldiers. Shrugged. He could fight. The man and the woman were nothing. The soldiers and their spears a problem but not an insurmountable one. He let his shoulders slump, so that he appeared beaten. Turned to the man.

"This could have been easy," he said to him.

"Seems easy to me." He took a step closer. Brave now. Sure he was in a position of power. Cahan stepped forward and pushed him as hard as he could, sending him stumbling backwards. In his surprise he let go of the rootling's lead. For a second, a moment, it squatted there, like one of the people but not like them. Confused by the world around it. It looked at the forester.

"Run," he said to it. The rootling blinked overly large eyes once, then took off. Alternating between running on all fours in an animalistic lope and running like a person on two legs. Despite the limp it sped away from the town and out of the shadow of the skyraft at a speed no person could match.

Cahan had a moment to watch it. To smile at its freedom. At the sheer joy in its running, its athleticism as it leapt the crevasse. Then the guards approached, spears at the ready. The man was standing now, an ugly look on his face.

The cowl beneath the forester's skin writhed.

You are the fire.

The guards reversed their spears so that they could use the butts to beat him.

And he let them.

Deep in the Forest

You walk forward, you are not forced, you are not struggling and fighting. You are simply doing as they say, robed in gold and red. You are weak and they are strong and they have told you, promised you, that this will make you strong too. Somewhere deep inside you do not want to let them down.

Even though . . .

"Cahan Du-Nahere." She is looking at you, her eyes almost hidden behind the mask. Does she know? Does she know what you really think? "You are here before Zorir to receive the god's blessings."

"Receive the blessings," a hundred voices repeat.

"Kneel before me," a subtle pressure on your arms pushing you down.

"Do you take Zorir within? Do you abide by Zorir? Will you be faithful and true and if you are not do you understand the fire will eat you from within?" You nod. "Speak the words, Cahan Du-Nahere."

And how can you? How can you when they are lies, when you are confused, when you question. But even though those are your thoughts, your mouth betrays you.

"I take Zorir," you say, "and may my tongue turn to ashes if I am untrue." You wait, wait for it to happen as you speak those words knowing you do not mean them. But nothing happens to you. All that happens is a hundred voices intone "and may my tongue become ash".

"Open your mouth, Cahan Du-Nahere," says the Skua-Rai, and a monk steps up behind you and pulls back your head. The monks holding your arms grasp you tighter and panic starts to well up within you.

"Receive the blood of Zorir!" shouts Saradis. And you tense up. Too late to stop now. Too late to fight. The cold of the stone cup crushing your lip against your bottom teeth. You taste blood first. Then a bitterness that makes your whole body revolt and squirm and try to escape. "Drink! Drink the blood of Zorir!"

It burns, this is it, you are paying the price for your unfaithfulness, your tongue is turning to ash. You want to spit it out but there is a hand over your mouth. Another holding your nose. You have no choice. You have no choice and now the world is melting into red and orange, the fire is coming, the fire is coming and you are at the centre of it.

You are the centre.

"He will bring Zorir to us!" shouts Saradis, "and the world will burn!"

You are the fire.

You.

Descend into darkness.

13

The first hour of the early eight, Kirven's eyes sticky with tiredness. She was not an early riser and never had been. She would be glad to leave the skyraft behind. She had not enjoyed the journey, never enjoyed flight, whether on a skyraft or a marant. People were not meant to fly, they were meant to walk on the ground. It was too hot on the skyraft as well; once the great fires were lit to fill the balloons then you could not escape the heat, and even though it was cold this far north the skyrafters went bare-chested and wore only shorts when they were on the main deck. Only the family Archeon went full-dressed, striding about shouting commands. There was always something to do but Kirven did not understand any of it, nor did she want to.

Venn refused to speak to her, in the darkness of their cabin while she dressed her child in their armour she had spoken to them. Her words urgent, almost begging.

"Venn," she had said, "you must understand, once I have left you with Vanhu there is no more I can do for you. You are out of my control. Vanhu answers to the Cowl-Rai, he will do whatever he deems necessary."

"Then do not send me with him, Firstmother," said Venn. Their voice dead, and in the darkness she could not see their face. She paused in the lacing of their chest piece. Her lips were dry, the heat made her head ache.

"I could get a histi, Venn, they have animals on board. Wake your cowl, one small death, and we can go back to Harnspire. Galderin has a marant in the hold." She waited, hoping that they would answer her. That she would feel their muscles go limp, feel them slump and give in. That she would finally win this foolish battle of wills with her own child. Venn did not reply and the only sound was her breath in the darkness. Sweat ran down her skin. She bowed her head and pulled on the straps of the armour, deliberately making them too tight in a way she knew would chafe. "You are not the only one this hurts, Venn," she hissed. "You think I do not feel pain?"

But they did not reply and she finished putting on their armour in silence.

On the deck the fires were out, though the great braziers still radiated heat into the air. The balloons were being folded away and the air was full of the sound of the rafters as they finalised docking the huge craft to Harn-Larger's docking spire. Not a real spire, but a rickety construction of wood that she would not trust for a moment if she were asked to walk up or down it. Already some passengers, laden with goods, were leaving that way, over the gangway and down the stairs around the spire. She was glad she would be going down on the lift.

She no longer wore the layers of wool, instead she wore tight-fitting crownhead leather in brown and blue. Her hair tied back rather than in elaborate braids. She knew that there were those who would not approve, but she did not want to announce her presence here. She had hoped to sneak in and out without being seen. Events had conspired to stop that and now she must meet the Leoric of Harn-Larger, and their monks, though they had been told to keep her presence secret. Her intention had originally been to travel with only Vanhu, Kyik and Sorha but Rai Galderin had convinced her otherwise. She knew that he did not argue his presence was needed only for her safety as he said; most likely he did not want Vanhu to have her ear to himself, even for a few days.

Rather than fight Galderin and risk him becoming resentful she had allowed him to put together an honour guard, with the agreement they would stay on the raft when she went into town. As if to underline to Vanhu who had the power, Galderin had brought with him not only a branch of soldiers but a marant and also some Hetton. She had commanded they must remain in the hold. The Hetton had an unpleasant effect on all who saw them, but the presence of Galderin and the Hetton had ensured her visit could not be kept secret.

Now she stood with Venn, the trion doing their best not to look at her, and the two Rai, one either side of her.

"I must meet with the Leoric," she said. "So we may have to postpone what you have planned, Vanhu." The Rai nodded.

"Are you dressed to meet their Leoric?" said Galderin. As ever his make-up and armour were perfect, as if he had stepped out of his own chambers in Harnspire, not a cramped skyraft cabin.

"I am the High Leoric," she snapped the words out, "how I dress is always correct." Galderin bowed his head. "Besides, it is better if these provincial towns see their High Leoric as someone who is like them, and that is how I dress. Not as some out-of-touch aristocrat in clothes they could work all their lives and never be able to afford."

"Of course, Kirven," he said, as if amused by her ideas.

"A little time is not a problem, High Leoric," said Vanhu. She realised his worn look, someone who put more import on his weapons than his looks, was just as deliberate as Galderin's. "I intend to send Kyik ahead to find a good place and prepare it for the trion's ascension to Rai." He smiled at Venn, though they did not look at him, instead becoming very focused on a rafter doing something with ropes nearby. Galderin tried to hide a sneer but failed. "And I need you to arrange for some suitable material. Three or four prisoners should do."

"I will speak to the Leoric," she said.

"Good. Presuming the materials are ready we will travel to the forest tomorrow, and by the evening our dear trion will know their power and be ready to rule." He looked over at Venn. "Their attitude will have changed then, High Leoric, I promise you." A sharp look from Venn, full of resentment. For a moment she thought they would speak but they did not. Only returned to watching the rafter at their work. Kirven felt an emptiness inside, a scouring. Venn was her child, a part of her. She could not bear them hating her. Not when she acted for their good. To protect them. If only she had a little more time with them.

"I will come to the forest with you," she said. Another sharp look from Venn.

"It is a mistake," said Vanhu, too quickly. But the Rai was not a fool, he realised it as soon as he spoke. As did Galderin, she saw him smile. "I only mean, High Leoric, that what must be done, well, it will be hard. A difficult thing for a mother to watch." She stared at him. Knowing he was right, that her presence would not help. This was a torture she must endure just as Venn must endure whatever Vanhu had planned. A thing she had been very careful not to ask too much about.

"The lift is here," she said, pointing over at the contraption as it rose into view, hanging from cranes. She thought they looked far too thin to take the weight of all the people and cargo waiting. "Galderin," she said, "please escort Venn to the lift." He nodded, took her child by the arm and led them away. Vanhu remained, waiting for her to speak. "I want you to know, Vanhu," she said quietly, "that if my child does not return from the forest, I will have you skinned. Then I will wait for your cowl to grow it back, and have you skinned again. That will be your life." He smiled, let out a low laugh.

"Of course, High Leoric," he said. "It is a pity you do not have a cowl. You would have made an excellent Rai."

14

A headache. A bad taste in his mouth. An ache in his bones. A cell.

Those were the forester's first thoughts on waking. They were not bad thoughts as they were truthful, *"all truthful thoughts have some use in them"*. The gardener, Nasim, once told him that, a long time ago in another life. Strange that memories of that man should wake with him, and have been with him so much recently. He had not thought of him, sitting in his growing room at the monastery of Zorir, forbidden books wrapped lovingly and hidden in the earth, for many years.

The cell was one of four in a dank cellar, separated by bars made of woven and hardened vines. No privacy for the occupants – though he was the only person in there. The place smelled bad, but that had been a feature of every prison he had ever been in, and his temper, the anger within that he had held onto so tightly as a younger man, had landed him in plenty.

"Awake then?"

His jailer stood at the bars watching him as she ate some sort of porridge. The hand she held the bowl in was carved from wood as smooth and shiny as her own skin was pitted and flaky. No doubt the skin condition was the legacy of some battle, for she had the look of an old soldier about her: hair short to her skull, though flakes of skin managed to stick in it. He had seen skin like that on the survivors of a cowl fire. The effects of it lasting far past the initial pain, desiccating skin the way a cowl eroded the spirit of the user that fed it.

"Yes. I am awake," he said, champing his mouth to try and lose the awful taste within. "What am I in here for?" Next to her table his staff was leant against the wall.

"Vagrancy," she said through a mouthful of porridge. He felt a little happier. Vagrants were simply ejected from the city. If he had been jailed for blasphemy the punishment would have been much worse.

"I had money in my purse, and plenty of it." His hand went to his chest. The purse was gone but he was not surprised.

"Not after you paid for the rootling, and paid the fine for setting it free in town." He was about to argue, tell her he hadn't let it loose in the town but decided not to waste his breath. There was no point. They would no doubt have plenty of witnesses among the guards to say he did, the contents of his purse shared between those same guards and their officers. There was little justice for outsiders in places like Harn-Larger, and even less for the clanless. The taxes needed to fund the war in the south squeezed towns hard, people with nothing had little charity or trust.

"You'll let me out in the first eight?" he asked her. She stared into her bowl.

"It's two of the first eight, you had quite the sleep. You'll be gone from here in an hour or so, aye, when the light is full risen," she said, still chewing.

"Is the skyraft still in?"

"Aye, and will be for a while yet."

"Good," he said, and moved hair out of his face. They

had even stolen the small wooden ring he used to tie his long hair back. "I intend to sign on to the crew and get out of here." She shrugged and turned away to sit at the small table with her back to him. Put down the porridge bowl and reached for her bottle with her wooden hand. The fingers creaked as they closed around the neck of it. She must have performed some great service for someone of import: the hand was willwood, and such things did not come cheap. The flesh of Wyrdwood trees fought the carver, growing spines and thorns as they were cut. Wyrdwood resented any that came in to take its bounty.

The jailer ignored him, doggedly drinking her liquor. He tried to find a comfortable place on the hard floor to wait, knowing there was a wealth of difference between being let out and being let go. *"There can be an ocean between what we hear and what is said."* Nasim had told him that too, and he began to think that maybe he had somehow called the man's ghost to him. Once more he could almost feel the small wooden toy that had belonged to the child cut down in his house. Guilt drew ghosts, everyone knew that. The thought made him feel worse. He did not think Nasim would be pleased with what he had become.

His jailer did not feed him, though she gave him a container of brackish water to swill around his mouth, which he did in an attempt to banish the foul taste. It did nothing but teach him where the foul taste had come from. Then he sat and waited quietly for his release. Eventually, his jailer asked him to stand and put his arms through the bars so she could bind him with rope.

"You think a vagrant so dangerous he must be bound?" he said. She did not answer. From the way she swayed it may have been that she did not trust herself to speak without slurring her words in drink. He watched her willwood hand work, it was a beautiful piece, the craftsmanship exquisite. From earning that to becoming a jailer in Harn-Larger, she must have fallen far.

"Come on," she slurred as she opened the cage and ushered him out.

"Will you bring my staff?" he nodded towards it, "it has sentimental value." She looked from him to the staff then shrugged and picked it up.

"Up there," she said, nodding towards a door. She pushed him forward with the tip of the staff and they emerged from the dim jail into a small, bright courtyard that smelled of animal dung. In the centre was a large raft, kept afloat by large gasmaws tethered underneath the wooden bed, and pulled by four crownheads. They needed to have their fleeces sheared or they would soon be too matted to sell. On the raft were four cages. Two were occupied by sad-looking men, shivering, filthy and naked. They paid him no attention, lost in their own misery.

The rafter looked him up and down and gave the jailer a nod. Cahan let himself be loaded into a cramped cage and the jailer locked him in and retrieved her bindings. Then she and the rafter vanished, coming back with a net of bladderweed. They used the bladderweed to counter Cahan's weight, chatting pleasantly in the way bored professional people did. He heard the jailer whisper to the rafter, "Remember, whatever you get, we share", and then she staggered back towards her jail and her bottle. The rafter picked up Cahan's staff from the floor and examined the carving, smiling to himself appreciatively before laying it on the bed of the raft.

Cahan had thought they would lead him past the towns-people, so he could be pelted with whatever filth they had at hand. Such things are popular in the towns and consid-ered a good way to teach vagrants not to return.

He was relieved when they did not.

The raft left Harn-Larger through a back gate, going down a track that headed away from the town and the skyraft he had hoped to escape this place on. He looked forward, watching the path ahead and saw two figures standing either side of it. Still as stone, and as grey. The reborn who had come to him at his farm, watching him, waiting for a signal from him that he never intended to send. He did not trust reborn, fearsome warriors they may be, but from what he knew they were blunt tools. They killed the enemy and anyone that looked like the enemy, lost in battle, joy through death. Besides, he was not what they sought. He would not and could not be what they sought. That was no longer a part of his life. He had failed. Been found wanting. Cahan turned in his cage so that he faced away from the reborn who had her visor up, the same one who had talked to him at his farm. Only to find himself looking at the other, visor down, face orientated towards him, following him in the cart as it passed. He moved again, looking ahead over the shoulder of the rafter. Never pausing to think it odd the rafter had not even turned his head to look as he passed them.

He expected the raft to stop when the town was out of sight and for the rafter who was, or had been, a soldier from his cheap sap-hardened wool, to give him his marching orders and warn him what would happen if he returned to Harn-Larger. But he did not. The raft carried on, turning towards the dark line of Woodedge. He felt like he should protest, but he was strangely tired. When he finally managed to form the words in his mind he sounded more curious than angry.

"Rafter!" he said. "Hey, rafter! Where are we going? When do you let me out? I need work, and the skyraft is where I will find it." The driver ignored him. One of the men in the other cages raised his head, looking at Cahan through bars of dirty hair. He had the eyes of a beaten man and the body of the neglected. Dirt and filth are everywhere in Crua, hunger, too, but these men were too thin, and the dirt on their bodies barely hid a multitude of bruises. The one furthest away, who paid no interest to Cahan, cradled one arm with the other as if to protect it. It looked either dislocated or broken.

Cahan began to think that nothing good awaited any of them at the end of this trip, but he found himself barely caring. How odd, he thought. How odd. As the day passed from the early eight to the middle eight they entered Woodedge on a path that looked freshly cut. It ran like an arrow through the undergrowth, pointing towards the darker, more twisted Harnwood.

Five Rai waited along the path. They were splendid in their war attire, all black, deep blue and purple cloaks and jerkins over wooden chest plates, porcelain chains around the shoulders, arms and chest, skirts of lapped wood protecting their upper legs and solid boots their lower.

"Ho, rafter," said the first among them, a woman who wore the close-fitting polished wood cap of the Rai, smooth and sculpted like the shell of a nut. Unlike the other three she wore her visor up, the better to show the elaborate colours and swirls of her carefully applied make-up. "These are the prisoners?"

"It is so, Rai," he said, though he sounded unsure about the title. Cahan looked more closely at her; he was not so sure she was Rai, though she carried herself as though used to power. She turned to the raft and Cahan looked down. The Rai saw a direct look as a challenge, and he did not want to risk it. With power came cruelty in Crua. Cahan thought it the cowl, though he had heard others say maybe it was true of all of the people. The monks who raised him would have had opinions on that; they had opinions on most things.

The woman, Rai or not, turned away from the rafter to one of the four Rai behind her. A squat man, whose helmet had a plume of treated and stiffened wool and whose make-up looked like it had been applied days ago and simply left.

"There, Vanhu, you have what you need." The woman turned to another of the four, the smallest. They raised their head and Cahan was surprised to see from the markings on their face, the long blue line over their eyes, that they were a trion. He had never heard of a trion becoming Rai. Trion often acted as go-betweens in family groups, the point of pivot, though they were rare now. A trion in a marriage was more a sign of wealth than anything else. They also acted as diplomats, good at finding ways to smooth out problems. The woman straightened. "I will leave you here then." Was there some sadness there? Cahan was not sure. Something felt wrong.

"Go then," said the trion, but too quietly for the woman's liking.

"What was that, Venn? Do not squeak it. Vanhu," she motioned at the stocky Rai with the badly painted face, "tells me you are worthy of being Rai, so you must act like it. Do not be weak."

"I will be strong," they said, louder if no happier sounding. He wondered what this woman, important from the look of her, was doing all the way out here.

"Well, Vanhu," she said to the squat Rai. His eyes were hard from war or cruelty, most likely both. "Do what you have promised and I will owe you a debt." The man, Vanhu, nodded and smiled at her, but there was little warmth there.

"It gladdens me to help you, and to be the one who will bring Venn to their power and to ascend to Rai for Tarlan-Gig." The trion looked away and Cahan found that odd; they were not yet Rai, their cowl not yet activated by the death of another. Most could not wait to be Rai, to take on the power and rule others.

The woman gave Vanhu a curt nod.

"Rafter, leave the raft with them and act as my guard on the way back to Harn-Larger." The rafter bowed his head in assent and jumped down from the raft to be replaced by one of the Rai. Cahan started examining his cage for a way to escape and as the woman walked past she looked into the cages. For a moment, a single count, he thought she paused at his prison. Looked at him a little more intently, then she walked on. The raft rocked, moving forward once more. What was happening here boded nothing good, but his cage was well made and the lock that held the door shut stout. Everything felt twisted, hazy and unreal.

You need me.

That voice, always there when he was weak, always tempting. He pushed it away.

The day went on, they passed through Woodedge, and as the second eight ended, darkness began closing in, they entered Harnwood. They did not go far in, for few people go far into Harnwood, even the Rai, who considered themselves powerful, began to look a little nervous as the trees of Harnwood closed in. The air changed, took on moisture and filled with the fresh scent of green and living things, the earthy scent of dead things breaking down and, maybe, behind that the stranger, headier and more colourful scent of things that were not quite living and not quite dead. Trees here grew thick with hanging moss and creeper, and the undergrowth raised itself around them into hills and walls that hemmed the raft in and steered its path.

Cahan no longer thought about getting free. The only reason for Rai to go into the forest was because there would be no one there to see what they did. So they must plan something awful. Now he worried about surviving, though it was an odd worry, somehow detached from him. As if he worried for someone else.

He watched the Rai. The man who led them, the squat one, Vanhu? He carried a sword at his hip, the other two Rai held spears. The third, the trion, was little more than a child. Venn, had the woman called them? They had no weapon, and trailed the larger Rai the way he had seen children trail adults when they are called to work. Knowing it cannot be avoided but lagging behind to keep back a few moments that they can call their own before a back-breaking day in fields unwilling to give up their bounty.

He wondered if the men in the other cages had guessed what was in store for them? Probably not; the secret ways of the Rai and their cowls were seldom shared with the common people of Crua. Besides, maybe they also felt like he did, as if they barely cared for what was to happen.

The crownheads were brought to a stop and the raft bobbed on the air.

"Are you excited, Venn?" said Vanhu, coming to stand before the trion. "Today is to be a great day for you, eh?"

"Uhn," said Venn, in the non-committal grunt of the young the world over.

"Kyik, Sorha," shouted Vanhu, "open the doors." He walked over to the carts. Stood before the cages. "You are here for a whipping," he said. "Be compliant and you will only have the sentence carried out, ten lashes each. Struggle and we double that. Fight, and we will whip the skin off your back and leave you for the boughry to string up in the trees." The other two prisoners, exhausted, filthy and beaten, only nodded their heads. Cahan sat with his head bowed, teeth gritted.

"Do not do this," said Cahan to the floor of the cage. Within him something stirred and he held it back. Cowl users could sense the cowl in another.

You need me.

No.

He must not.

"Quiet," said Vanhu. He had a hard face. Scarred by war and burned from the use of his cowl. His eyes were pale, often Cahan had seen this in cowl users of an age, eyes as pale and worn as their morals. "Speak again and I will put the lashes on you myself, and I am strong, you do not want that." All he could do not to lock eyes with him, old pride fighting its way up. The cowl writhing beneath his skin.

You need me.

No.

To meet the gaze of the Rai would be death for the clanless. And a whipping? He could take such things, he had borne them before and could bear it again.

It is not a whipping.

No.

He knew it was not a whipping. But that strange fog in his mind. Maybe it really was only a whipping.

It is an awakening.

The other prisoners were taken from the raft to where poles had been dug into the ground. Four of them. The men were tied, hands above their heads. He wondered why they were so passive, so willing to let themselves be led. The one with the broken arm did not even cry out when they yanked his arms above his head.

When they came for Cahan he was ready to fight them. The cage was unlocked, the two Rai, Sorha and Kyik, reached in for him. His mind told him to fight, but his body refused. His limbs, legs, arms, hands were limp.

The brackish water given in the jail. The way the jailer had turned away from him as he drank. He must have been drugged.

Something of his desire to break free, now denied him by his body, must have shown on his face. The Rai named Sorha smiled at him.

"Thought you may cause some trouble, eh, big fellow?" she said with a laugh as they pulled him from the cage. His body would barely obey him, he was in no state to try and run, never mind fight. The Rai dragged him across to a post and bound his wrists above his head.

He felt the forest watching.

It was as if the trees held their breath.

When he was bound the Rai did not strip him, or the others, of their clothes for whipping. They had them trussed and helpless, there was no need for pretence now.

In their drugged stupor the other two men made no noise and no complaint. As Cahan hung there the pain grew in his shoulders. He hoped it meant control of his body might slowly be coming back. For all the good it would do.

You need me.

Closed his eyes. Banished the voice.

The Rai lit a fire, took their time doing it. Once it was going well, crackling and spitting in the cold night air, they took a switch of herbs from a bag and set it smouldering. Then they stripped the trion to an undertunic and passed the burning herbs over their skin, muttering words and incantations as the trion coughed on the smoke. Cahan did not know exactly what they said, could not quite hear them, but he knew words like them, old words that had been spoken again and again over generations. Words meant to awake a cowl and have it lend them power. After every four sentences the oldest, Vanhu, raised the smouldering herbs to the sky and shouted out the name of Tarl-an-Gig. Cahan thought them fools to bring ritual fire into the forest; even here at the edge of Harnwood it was likely to attract the attention of those none should wish to look upon, orit, swarden, greenling or skinfetch. Creatures real, half-forgotten and imagined. Or even worse, the boughry, the Woodhewn Nobles of Wyrdwood. Old gods, with their own agendas, that none could understand.

But worry over the creatures of the forest was driven away by the pain in his arms and shoulders as he hung on the stake, his feet only just touching the ground. The other prisoners did not seem bothered by it, but they were smaller than he was. The drug probably worked better, or they may have had a larger dose. And, of course, they did not have cowls beneath their skin. One of the men groaned and the Rai Vanhu turned to look at him.

"So, Venn, looks like the gullan juice is starting to wear off." He led the trion over to the first stake. The firelight made their walk a jagged, jerking puppet thing. The man tied before them stared vacantly, said nothing. The corners of his mouth wet with drool. "The rituals are done, your cowl is ready. This man," he grabbed the bound man by the hair and pulled his head back, "he has no clan. He is lowborn and follows filthy forest gods if he follows any at all. He is forsaken by the great monasteries. His life, Venn, it is nothing. He is a criminal." He let go of him. Stepped back. "But this flesh before you can be made into something. It can be important. Useful. Everything it is not now."

"I don't want this," those words from the trion, soft and shy as new leaves. "I will not do it."

"Want does not matter," said Vanhu, "you are born to be Rai. You must come into your power. Your strength is needed. The cowl needs death to awake. The more pain you cause, the more powerful you will be in the end."

"Do not do this," said Cahan softly. They paid no attention to him. The drug was still working in his body, the forest on the edges of his vision blurred as if it constantly moved.

You need me.

No.

"Now, trion," said Vanhu. "Fire is the easiest way, and the quickest."

"Most impressive, too," said one of the other Rai, the woman Sorha.

"But, Venn," said Vanhu, "if you worry you may be weak in the face of pain, that the smell of burning flesh may soften your bones, then water kills them quiet, with little sign."

"It is harder to control," said Sorha, "but they do not scream." Behind her the shadowy figure of the third Rai, Kyik, stepped forward, grinning.

"Do not do this," said Cahan, more loudly. They ignored him.

"When you are more advanced," said Vanhu, "there are many things you can do by throwing the cowl, rip a man apart, and I have heard the Cowl-Rai can even bring their warriors back from the dead. I know they can lay waste to entire battlefields. I have seen it."

"No," said the trion.

"But to harness that power, Venn," he said, "you must feed the cowl. It is simple, put your hand on this waste of flesh, give his pain and his life to that which lives within you." He pointed at the man. "This can only be done by touch, you must share the experience with the cowl or it will not feed, it will not grow and increase in power." The trion did not move, they stood frozen in the leaf litter. It is a big step to take a life.

"It is simple," said Sorha, "touch him and will your cowl onto him. You need not even choose a method, your cowl will have a way it favours. But do not let it feast, starve it a little, make it obey you." She took a step nearer, fire flickering over her armour. "It is a good way to know your cowl, then to master it, control it."

"Listen, child," said Vanhu, his voice cold. "These men, they are already dead. They are a burden on all others. You do the blue of the north a favour."

"I don't want to hurt them," those words the trion spoke as they stared fixedly at the ground, so loaded with pain and misery. Vanhu smiled.

"Do not do this," said Cahan. Vanhu looked to his compatriots.

"Sorha," he said to the woman with the spear. "Venn clearly wishes to avoid pain, they care for others. Use the first of these men. Show Venn how it is done."

"Do not do this!" and now Cahan shouted it. Now the Rai turned. Now they saw him.

You need me.

"The clanless fool thinks to order his betters about," said Vanhu to Venn, "see what happens when you are not strong, trion? They think you are weak and you can be sure if they think you are weak then they will try to take what is yours."

"I will not hurt them," said the trion.

"That trion is stronger than all of you," shouted Cahan. Vanhu walked over to him, twigs snapping beneath his boots. Fire crackling around him. He stared into the forester's face.

"We will see if you still like that one," he pointed at the trion, "so much when they are burning the skin from your body, eh? And you are big, you have a lot of skin." He smiled. "Venn will kill the second man, to save him from pain because that is their weakness." He leaned in close. "But then the cowl will have them, they will not worry so much about pain then. I will use you to teach them control." He cocked his head to one side. "You will scream long into the night."

You need me.

"You will regret this," the words forced about between Cahan's teeth. "Walk away from this place." Within him a hoarfrost of panic coated his organs, tendrils of fury slipped around his lungs, making breathing hard. The voice again.

You need me.

The Rai's face twitched. Cahan wondered if he sensed the cowl in the way he could feel it in the Rai. If he did he must have thought it a mistake. Clanless with a cowl? To one like him the idea must be unthinkable. He turned away from Cahan, back to the woman with the spear.

"Sorha, show Venn the way." She gave him a nod, reached out for the first man. He did not cry out, not at first. Unlikely he knew what was happening. The Rai put her hand on the man's arm, turned to the trion.

"Touch, Venn, as Vanhu said, is the only way to feed your cowl." She gave him a small nod. "This moment, between you and him and your cowl. It is sacred, child, it is a communion directly with Tarl-an-Gig. You talk with a god through another's agony. You sacrifice to build us in their power. We are Rai. Iftal broke his body to deny the Osere control of his power. But gave us cowls to do the god's bidding. You will your cowl onto those who will feed it. In this moment, you are as a god. You hold a life in your hand." Cahan heard the forest shift, the wind still. The constant motion of the trees stopped and something he could not shut out screamed and raved and hungered in the back of his mind. "It is like a push, inside your head." The raving became a howl, but one from very far away. It was like the echo of a wild hunting creature, heard by a city man in the centre of a quiet town. Something forgotten and left behind, something that chilled the blood. A memory of an ancient terror that the enclosing walls could never truly shut out.

The screaming began. With it came the stink of singeing flesh. The man on the stake struggling and writhing and crying as Sorha's fire ate into him.

"I will where he burns," said Sorha. She spoke with the same hunger, the same howl, Cahan felt in his mind. "His shoulders." Smoke rose from the tops of his arms, his hair caught and he screamed more, begged for it to stop, for the fire flowing through his veins to leave his body. The pain so deep it tore away the narcotic veil. The trion watched, shaking their head and mouthing "no", again and again and again. Trying to back up but finding the third of their group, Kyik, behind them. Holding them by the shoulders. Forcing them to watch as the man begged and burned. "You do not like the noise of his pain, child?" she said, those pale eyes locked on him. "I will stop it." A fire burned in her victim's mouth, flames shooting out and scorching his lips, ending his cries though not his agonies. His body jerked and spasmed as she manipulated the heat within him. The crying and the hunger and the howl in the forester's mind grew. He fought against his bonds.

"Just end him!" Cahan's words, screamed out as he fought his bonds. "End him quickly, you cowards! Just end him!" A fist against his face, blacking out the world for a moment, bursting his lips and the veins inside his nose. Warm blood running down his face.

"Quiet, filth."

But he would not be quiet, and with every word he spat blood and fury.

"Stop this, take me if you must", and he had dreaded hearing those words from his mouth. He was not strong enough to give in. Knew this could only end one way. "Stop this."

They did not stop, they did not care what some clanless vagrant thought or said. The woman continued to burn the man, talking the trion through his pain as she worked her cowl, letting it feed on his agony and misery as he died. When she had finished, the clearing full of the smoke and stink of charring flesh, he was nothing but a blackened shape hanging from ropes which remained untouched by the fire.

"Now," she said, taking away her hand. "Tarl-an-Gig is pleased. We do this in the name of the god and the Cowl-Rai in rising, Venn. The one who prophecy told of, and who will sweep away the evil of the Chyi's rule, the red flags gone and will bring us plenty." Her words were animated, and carried far more conviction than when Vanhu spoke. "For them, we do this, Venn. For the Cowl-Rai this man died. His life gave me power." She held up her hand and a tendril of fire leapt out, burning through the untouched rope around the corpse's wrist. The body fell to shatter on the forest floor. "My cowl has grown, Venn, a small amount. It grows with every death, makes us stronger. The people think their sacrifice fuels us, but it is nothing compared to death. We are the engine of the blue. We must not falter. We must not be weak. Victory is close." In her eyes shone the surety of the fanatic. He had known monks like that in the monastery. They had always been the cruellest, though he doubted her devotion was to any god. Rai cared only for themselves. "Now," she pointed at the second man, "it is your turn. For Tarl-an-Gig, chosen of Broken Iftal. For the Cowl-Rai in rising. For the High Leoric of Harn. For us all."

"We will burn each one, slowly, Venn," said Vanhu. He stepped forward. "And all of that pain will be yours. On you. And, if by the time the last one dies, you have not woken your cowl," the Rai turned, his back to Cahan. His face towards the trion. "Then I will burn you as a traitor. Do you understand?" he said. "You are not protected here."

The trion stood, breathing hard, staring at the shattered remains of a man on the forest floor.

"No," they said, "I will not do it." And though their voice wavered Cahan marvelled at their bravery. At the trion's age, he had not had such strength.

"These deaths are yours then," said Vanhu and turned away.

"Do not listen, child." Cahan's breath came short, his mind full of colours and stains and blood and death, "What they do is on them. It is not on you, it should not lie on your conscience."

"Quiet!" another fist to the face. Vanhu stood before him again. "I have had enough of you", he spat in the forester's face. "It is not your place to speak before the Rai. You are clanless and less than nothing. The trion's next lesson is now you. I will make this lesson a long one." His washed-out pale eyes met Cahan's.

"Do not do this," said the forester softly, "you can still walk away. I am not as strong as the trion." The Rai laughed, not a real laugh. The laugh of something cold and pleased with itself.

"You are not strong at all," he said, "Clanless." He placed his hand on Cahan's chest, stared into Cahan's eyes. "Tell me this before you die. The rafter told me of your crime. Why does a man with a good amount of money in his pocket, a clanless man who should lie low, throw it all away for a rootling?" There was real confusion in his pale, cruel eyes. Cahan wondered what he could say that the Rai would understand. Realised there was nothing.

"It seemed like the right thing to do."

"Right?" said Vanhu. "That is a luxury your kind do not have." The pressure of his hand on Cahan's chest lessened for a moment. A look of confusion, fleeting, here and gone. "Knowing what is to come. Do you regret it? What you did?" He studied Cahan as if he were some strange new creature that had been born of the forest.

"No", and Cahan found that was true. He did not regret helping the rootling, not at all. The Rai cocked his head to one side and Cahan knew that what he said was as beyond the Rai's understanding as the strange language spoken by the rootlings and the boughry at the deep shrines was beyond his.

"Well," said Vanhu, "you will."

Slowly the Rai pushed his will into his cowl. Cahan felt it, the movement slow, like some gelid liquid as he pushed his power into the forester's skin.

Cahan's vision cleared. At the edge of the clearing did he see two grey figures? Too late for them now.

You

The Rai's face changed. Confusion.

Need

As he found it harder than it should be.

Me.

The Rai's cowl no longer moved in concert with his will. He looked at his hand. Then back at Cahan's face.

"How?" he said, and for a count his puzzled, slightly worried expression made him look like one of the people once more. Cahan heard the voice of the reborn woman who had come to his farm, who waited at the edge of the clearing to be called. "*I can sense death, Cahan Du-Nahere and it is drawn to you. Deny it all you wish, it is still coming.*" He answered the Rai in a whisper that only he could hear. He felt the tendrils of his cowl move beneath his skin.

"They say only one Cowl-Rai rises in a generation." Vanhu tried to pull his hand away. Found he could not. "Rai Vanhu," said Cahan, "that is a lie."

And that was when the killing began.

Deep in the Forest

The word is fire.

Fire through the alleyways, through the doors and windows, over the roofs. Nothing escapes. A vast, hungry, expanding conflagration that sweeps and scours the village, cares not for innocence or guilt or age. When it ends. All that is left is you. Standing in a smoking black circle where once those you had known and passed the time of day with had been.

A boy.

A smoking ruin, and more shame and guilt than any child should ever have to carry.

You are running but you are not running fast enough.

You are running.

Running.

15

He pushed fire upon Cahan.

Cahan knew fire.

If it had been water he knew water. Such things were simple and base, flashy, impressive to the onlooker. Unsubtle. The recourse of those with little but brute strength and anger within them. Rai Vanhu tried to pull his hand away. Tried to stop the fire pouring from him into Cahan. He could not.

The forester would not let him.

Close your eyes, take a breath.

The forest came to life around him.

Feeling each and every tendril of life: gasmaws floating in the canopy, the bladderweeds and floatvine plants climbing through the branches, histi and burrowers beneath the ground, the sheer and almost unbearable weight of the life around him. Behind that the massive, slow and heavy life force of the trees, and underpinning it the vast and delicate web of the fungal mats that touched upon everything on Crua. For a brief moment Cahan knew the terrifying, undeniable interconnectedness of it all. He saw it not as material, not as flesh or wood or anything solid. He saw it as light. Streamers of it, light of every colour, some light blinding some light dark, existing in ways he had no words for, and all of it a flow. He only needed to reach into this man to become a part of it.

Breathe in.

He had sworn it was over, done with, never to be part of his life again but he had underestimated his will to live. The cowl beneath his skin was awake once more.

You need me.

Fire being pumped into his body by Vanhu, desiccating his flesh, driving out the moisture. His blood boiling. Agony coursing through him as the fire bound the flesh he was created from with the air in a slowly growing, dark and agonising crust around the Rai's hand.

He wanted it to stop.

The pain stopped.

The burning stopped.

The power, instead of hurting him, fed him.

The ropes that tied him to the post were in his way. He felt their existence, felt the space between the tough sinews of plant fibre, he pierced their apparent solidity.

Break.

He released a million chained worlds within the bindings and the ropes fell away.

There should have been panic on the Rai's face, but Cahan saw only fury. He was shouting.

"Kill him! Sorha! Kyik! Cut him down!" Vanhu barking out the words, making them orders. It was remarkable, testament to the Rai's powerful wish to survive that he had the presence of mind to recognise a cowl was no use against the man before him.

A spear. A blade of heartwood finely wrought, a twisted shaft with a wirereed basket to protect the hand. Aimed at his head. The Rai Kyik bringing it down in a fine, well-aimed killing blow.

No.

The spear like the rope, an illusion of solidity, a thousand million links hidden from the naked eye. Use the energy pouring into him. Dissipate. Uncreate. The wielder, Kyik, stumbling, denied the balance of the spear's weight. The material, the unlinked, the unneeded now nothing but energy.

Reform.

A handful of darts, sharp and pointed as a garaur's tooth. Sending them back through the air as the spear wielder trips. Piercing their flesh, the heart, the eye, the neck, the groin. Blood, so much blood as he falls. The woman with the spear. Withdrawing it from the other prisoner. She misunderstood Vanhu's order. Killed the wrong one. Too far gone in the service of her cowl to be anything but furious. Cahan can feel her anger like he feels heat from a fire. She looses water at him, heedless of what she was told. It surrounds him, searching for a way into his body. Through mouth, nose, ears, eager to fill and block, to drown, to choke.

No.

Return.

A wave of his hand. A step forward. Pushing Vanhu back a pace. Sending the water back to the woman. It surrounds her head. Panic, her fear bulbous and magnified by the water around her. Trying to rip the globe away but water will not be denied. It slips around her hands. She is drowning by moments. Her cowl fights, pulling air from the water, trying to save its host while knowing her life is over.

In the ground, the web of fungus, hyphae that links everything.

Mine.

Pain. His cowl sending out tendrils, breaking the skin of his feet, shattering the soles of his shoes to find the earth.

Connection.

The web of the forest. From cowl to floor to cowl to woman. Growing around her feet, almost invisible, little more than a haze of waving tendrils as she staggers and struggles to breathe. She lifts a foot, staggers to the left snapping hyphae. More come, forming and reforming, beginning and ending.

Connection.

A sudden strengthening, cracking flesh, a soundless scream within the bubble of water.

Corruption.

He feels her cowl die the same way he feels Vanhu's fire feeding his own cowl. Then it is a moment's work. Her cowl recognises strength, it recognises seniority and it crumbles away. Cahan sees the betrayal on the woman's face, that this thing, this companion that has been with her all her adult life, the font of her power, of who she is, could be gone so quickly and so easily. For a moment she is the same as everyone else. She understands the terror each of her victims felt before they died. Then she is no longer thinking, only drowning. Falling to her knees and dying in increments.

Take.

No.

He does not allow it. He will not be that. Will not suck another's life, feed on it. If he must kill again then at least let him keep that one part of his vow.

Leaves her scrabbling in the earth as she struggles to breathe.

The Rai, Vanhu, staring at him. He cannot accept his death. Even though he must know. He must feel how his strength has come up against something more powerful, so much stronger. Still, he is fighting, pushing fire towards Cahan's heart. Struggling to end him even though the fire is being drawn off, absorbed as quickly as he can create it. The strain on his face. His skin flushing beneath the make-up. This is like nothing he has come across before.

"What are you?" he says, and even those words, they are not said in curiosity. They are said in anger.

"I am Cowl-Rai."

Vanhu's eyes open wide. Now Cahan sees fear. And any hope the Rai had of standing against him is gone. Cahan is no trickster who conjures with elements. At this distance, so near, Cowl-Rai can control energy, the fundamental tools of creation. For a moment Vanhu is puzzled. Cahan sees it on his face, feels it through the link to him.

"But you are not," he says. "I have seen the Cowl-Rai. It is not you."

Cahan makes his point in fire. Burning Vanhu from the inside out. The power flooding into him stops and he must use his own life force now. Vanhu's final scream is volcanic fury, blistering heat.

Then all is quiet. Cahan's burns fixing themselves. Pain, ripping through him. He is a starving man, it is not food he needs. It is life.

Without the flood of power the cowl will take what it needs to survive, will take it from whatever it can. Take it from him if there is nothing else.

The forest silent as if shocked by the deaths. One sound cutting through it. The sobbing of the trion the Rai had brought with them, as arrhythmic as water falling from trees. They must be frightened of what they had seen here. Cahan knows, because he is frightened of what he did here.

You needed me.

It seems right to tell the trion not to fear him. That he will not hurt those that do not hurt him, that he has denied the cowl for more than half of his life. That he does not feed it. Did not feed it. Only used what the Rai Vanhu fed into him.

But it hungers.

And the trion is full of life.

He is weak, he needs to be strong.

Weak, you need to be strong.

A step.
A step towards them.
Be strong.
His hand reaching out.
So much life.
And a darkness descends upon him.

Deep in the Forest

You woke in the dying room. The smell of corpses thick in your nostrils. At first you thought it was pitch black, that maybe you were also dead. Then you saw the light, the faint glow. The shapes of the mushrooms growing on the bodies, tall and slender, spreading caps above them. With a low hiss, you saw them release the spores in glowing clouds. Then another and another and you tried to hold your breath but you could not, you breathed them in.

You.

Breathed.

Them.

In.

The slow unfurling of the cowl within. The meeting. The conduit. The waking of something that had slept since you were so young you barely remembered the Wyrdwood and the creatures there.

16

*S*he hated leaving them.

Hated herself for putting her child into the care of the Rai. Into the care of Vanhu particularly. She forced the guilt aside, lied to herself, told herself that this was the only way. Falnist had trapped her, curse the trion, she would deal with them when she returned to Harnspire, and if Venn was hurt then she would watch the older trion die and make sure it took days. She would not sleep or eat or even blink while their life left them. She wanted to spit as she trudged back to Harn-Larger. She had been manipulated, *her*. And she had known at some level. Falnist had seen her weakness, her need and her cowardice, and used it. She should have been harder on Venn, she had known that, but she was their mother and it held her back. Falnist had taken that knowledge, given her an easy way out that meant she did not have to be the one to brutalise the child into their power.

She knew the truth of Vanhu, even as she had tried to deny it. Why else would she have warned him, told him what she would do if Venn did not survive? She knew, deep down, how far the Rai was prepared to go. That he, in his power and cruelty, would push her child as far as needed, even if that cost Venn their life.

And if that happened? Vanhu would not burn, she would not be able to kill him. He would fall from grace, of course, probably be moved away to fight in the south which would please Galderin. But the Rai were long-lived and she was not. Vanhu had that advantage over her. He did not need to plot against her, only move out of her orbit and wait for her to die naturally.

Sometimes it was hard to think like them. To realise the truth of them.

Kirven wanted to scream, but could not look weak, and the soldier who had driven the raft knew who she was. News of the High Leoric screaming in frustration would spread, no doubt work its way back to Falnist, and the trion would think it some score on their chart against her. A victory. She could not have that.

She almost stopped. Almost went back.

No. For better or worse she was caught in the trap now. Venn was strong, she would trust in their strength. Her family had a powerful desire to live and if it came to it, if Vanhu put her child in that position, she believed they would choose to live. No matter the cost. She believed that. She had to.

They were stubborn, the Ban-Ruhn.

It was a family trait.

So it went, round and round in her head on the walk back to Harn-Larger. The rafter had tried to speak to her a few times, deferential, knowing their place. Talking of the landscape, the new ravine that had opened. The skyraft. The forest. Each time the conversation had died because it always led her back to the raft, and the men who had been on it. What that meant for her child.

Galderin met her at the gates of Harn-Larger; he was more subtle than Vanhu, had only two soldiers with him, did not greet her by name or title.

"It is done?" he asked.

"It is done," she pushed past him.

"The skyraft leaves before the light falls," said Galderin, turning to walk with her, his soldiers running ahead to clear their way. "If we hurry we can be on it." She did not want to leave. She wanted to stay and wait for Venn to return with Vanhu. It would be no more than a few days at most. But that would also make her look weak in front of the Rai. She knew Galderin would leave if it was his child, leave without a second thought. To rule the Rai she had to be like them, them but more; harder, fiercer.

"I take it we are ready to leave?" The stink of the town was more apparent after the freshness of the forest and plain around it. She lifted her hand to cover her nose. "It will be good to be away from this place." Galderin looked across, smiled at her.

"That is often how I feel, too," he said. "Did you enjoy the forest?" He held her gaze for a moment too long, it made her uncomfortable. She did not acknowledge it though it sent a shiver down her spine. Made her worry again what Vanhu had planned for Venn. What he would do. Made her wonder if Galderin knew why she hated the trees.

"Clear the lift for me," she said. "I do not want to catch lice from these people." Galderin nodded, sent his soldiers on ahead.

In the hours it took to get the fires burning and the nets full of gasmaws rigged, Kirven had to stand with Galderin on the deck, watching the skyrafters get the great craft ready. Feeling the heat, listening to the wind howl, the ropes creaking. Not showing her worry or pain. Not thinking about Venn.

Were they there yet? Had they done it yet? Did the cowl kindle within them? It was foolish but she felt like she would know. She would sense them changing. She was their mother after all. Ties of blood were stronger than any other.

She glanced across at Galderin. His face cruel even in repose, an ever-present half-smile on his lips. Sometimes she thought the Rai were barely even of the people.

What had she done?

Kirven took a deep breath.

Strength. She had given her child strength. Was giving her child strength. Without strength you were nothing. The new Cowl-Rai had shown that, binding all together under the one god. Strength. Power. Change. Venn would be part of that, a leader. If they still thought the world unfair once their cowl was active, then they could use their closeness to the Cowl-Rai, the power brought about by the great tilt, to exact change. She glanced across at Galderin again. He smiled to himself as groups of the indentured, those who owed the skyraft family, struggled, naked and back-bent under huge loads of wood.

If Venn still wants change when they have a cowl, she thought to herself. The steerswoman of the raft walked over, a stout woman, Archeon of the family, wrapped in colourful wool and chinking porcelain jewellery, strange symbols of the wind gods. Tarl-an-Gig had no power among those who lived in the clouds.

Not yet.

"Balloons are about ready," said the woman, pointing up at the vast ovals of colourful cloth. "You can give the order to leave if you want, High Leoric."

"Thank you," said Kirven, she knew it was considered an honour, though she would rather be back in her cabin pretending she was on the ground. "What do I say."

"Just shout at 'em," she pointed to a group of rafters at the edge of the craft, "cast off, and heave bellows." Kirven nodded, smiled at the woman.

"Cast off!" she shouted, "and heave bellows."

"You heard!" shouted the steerswoman, her voice louder

by far than Kirven's. "Cast it off, heave the bellows." The order was repeated. A large group at the edge of the raft hauled in the anchor that attached them to Harn-Larger's rickety tower. Then she heard the crack of a whip. Looked towards it and saw the people who had been bringing wood, or maybe others, it was hard to tell when they were all filthy and naked, pulling on huge handles. A cough of air, and the fires roared, flames leaping up. She worried the balloons would catch. With a lurch that made her stomach flip the skyraft moved. Kirven watched for long enough that it did not seem disrespectful, then she turned to Galderin.

"I will be in my cabin, my responsibilities do not end simply because I am travelling." He nodded.

In her cabin she could not work. She could not think. In the end she took to her bed but slept fitfully, her dreams of fire and pain. When she woke the next morning she thought those dreams a good omen. What were the Rai if not fire and pain? Surely this was her blood speaking, her link to her child. Venn, finally stepping up to their responsibilities.

She felt a little calmer for the dream. More able to sort through the papers in her trunk. She had put them away in no particular order. Unable to concentrate. No doubt what she wanted would be right at the bottom, such was generally the way of things. She moved the first set of papers, reports of crops and how badly the farmers of Harn county were doing at growing them due to bluevein, to one side. Beneath it were the portraits of the false Cowl-Rai her hunters had been charged with finding. A face stared up at her: Cahan Du-Nahere, killed by Sorha at his farm.

Familiar, somehow.

She found herself frozen. Horror, reaching out from the drawing and stealing all her strength.

This could not be.

A face staring at her from a cage.

"No," she said it softly. Disbelieving.

Fire and pain.

Then she was up, running from the cabin, her voice raised. "Galderin!" she shouted. "Galderin!"

17

*S*ound.

First he is aware of sound. The trills and calls and roars and hums of the forest creatures. The hiss of something hard moving through leaves.

Then sensation.

It feels as though every part of him is either worn down or rubbed raw. He is desperately thirsty, desperately hungry. His joints grinding as if full of sand. His head throbs. The pain brings with it an awareness that he is moving. But he is not moving. He is lying down. A sharp lance through the throbbing of his head, light hitting his eyelids. Then it is gone. Then it is back. Then it is gone.

He didn't understand. Not at first. To move and to be still. How could such a thing be? But slowly, his mind put together the pieces of the puzzle. The rhythmic hiss of leaves, the movement-yet-not-movement. There was a definite rhythm to it: a flashing of light, bright and dim and bright again.

He forced his eyes open, suppressing a groan, and found himself looking up at the green canopy of the forest. The light above hidden by interlocking tree branches, breaking through them as he juddered a little way forward. Heard a grunt, felt himself dip to one side. Another noise, wordless yet full of pain and frustration and exhaustion.

The angle of the light above told him it was late in the second eight. He had been unconscious for nearly a full day at least, and was being dragged through the forest by a figure unseen. Though why he did not know. He tried to move but could not. He was bound, tied tightly to a travois.

There was his answer. No doubt he had been found surrounded by richly dressed corpses and someone thought him a fine prize to give to the Rai. One that would make them rich. He could not allow that, but he could also do little about it. Not now. He was as weak as a newborn crownhead. Weaker really, for within moments of birth a crownhead could stand and run. Cahan doubted he could do so much. To save itself the cowl had taken as much from him as it could without killing him. Beneath the wrappings his body would be wasted, his muscles like wireweed wrapped around bone in a corpse yard. His face gaunt and shadowed.

Strength and life would return, given time. It would seep slowly from the ground every time he came into contact with it. It was clever of his captor to wrap him in blankets and tie him to the travois. It would keep him weak for much longer if he had to seep life from the air. Clearly whoever it was knew how to bind a cowl user properly. He felt cold within. Fear.

There would be little mercy for him now.

Then whoever dragged him fell again, and this time he heard them swear.

"Osere below," they hissed, "I hate this place." They continued to mutter to themselves as they stood. Then slipped again, this time pushing him against his bonds and he let out a groan, unable to hold the pain in. His captor stopped. He felt them lay the travois down. A face appeared above him, almost hidden beneath a helmet that was actually a little too big for it. "You are alive?" they said. He tried to nod, though if he managed it he was not sure. The world swam around him and he knew it would not be long before the cowl put him to sleep again, to exist in the unspace of the cowl's mind while it did all it could to keep his flesh alive. The Rai, Vanhu, must have been more powerful than he thought if besting him had taken so much. He should have allowed the cowl to take from the Rai's life, only a little.

You need me.

Shame, sudden and strong coming upon him.

So many years he had pushed away the cowl, told himself he would not use it no matter what. But in the end, when pressed, he killed without mercy or thought. His last conscious memory was the terrified face of the trion as he walked towards them. The unbearable hunger of the cowl burning inside, the pain as his body struggled to feed it. His captor should take advantage of him now, while he was as weak as a crownhead kit and kill him. It would be best for all.

You need me.

"Here," a gourd appeared in his vision, "drink. I thought you dead, the whole night you have been out." His captor did a good job of almost drowning him. Water and fire were two of the few sure deaths for the Cowl-Rai, though they were slow deaths. Cahan moved his head. Choking, panicking. His captor moved back, clearly unsure of what to do now he had refused water. The forester tried to speak. It felt like his words were nothing more than the breeze between saplings, something to be lost in the forest. His captor's face wavered as Cahan struggled to focus. Then they pulled off their helmet and leaned in close. Putting an ear near his mouth, while being careful not to touch him. Wise: a touch when he was this weak and his cowl could bleed them dry of life.

"Speak again," they said. "I will help how I can. It is the least I can do after you saved me"

"Saved?" a slow expulsion of the word.

"Oh, Tarl-an-Gig bless you, can you not see? Did they burn out your vision?" Something about the voice, something familiar. "My name is Venn, you saved me in Harnwood." Cahan could feel them looking at him. "Truthfully, for a moment I thought you would kill me too, you had a face like one of the Osere, come from below to take me. But then you fell, and I knew you only wanted help. I was careful not to touch your skin, like they teach, but I got you on the travois. Now tell me, how do I help?"

The trion.

He had not killed them, and he breathed a little lighter for it. He tried to speak again. It took all he had. Forcing each word from his mouth.

"Lay . . . me . . . on . . . the . . . ground." He could not tell if they heard him or not. Everything was become darker, his vision closing in. He felt the trion draw away, felt the world recede, sound melting into one long sigh of wind as he drifted back to darkness.

Deep in the Forest

"Your sister is dead, Cahan Du-Nahere." You, in that moment of pain, became strangely fascinated by the glittering paint on her face. "You are angry, Cahan Du-Nahere, and this is right." The Skua-Rai Saradis raises a hand and a cold breeze runs through the room, the fires gutter and your trainer of arms and trainer of spirit enter. Their sacred white robes are splattered with mud and blood. They are dragging a man between them. "We have the man who killed your sister. All you need do is touch him, and let that within you do what it wishes. Do not waste her death, let it raise you into something more than one of the people."

You are the fire.

18

He awoke in pain, though less pain than before.

They were deep in the third eight, light had passed from the world and darkness replaced it. Beneath him was the comfort of the earth, a flow of life seeping into him the way the water of the geysers in Tilt was taken up by thread-vines and wetvines and passed throughout Crua. A gradual drip of life returned to him through the land, the threat of drifting into cowlsleep forever had passed. He no longer feared being lost to the thing within's desire to continue at all cost. He lay on his back, staring up into the canopy and the patterns of glowing lights there, how they changed and spun, ebbed and flowed with the breeze and the movement of unseen predators.

"Water," he said it out loud, surprised by how well he could speak.

"You're awake," came the reply. Footsteps. The trion above him, their gourd of water ready. Threatening to drown him with eagerness once more.

"Wait," he said, holding out a hand to stop the water. "Help me sit." They paused, then backed off warily. "The hunger has passed, child," he said softly, sadly. He felt no joy in making a child afraid of him. "You are safe, trion. And you wear gloves." They looked down at their gloved hands, then nodded to themselves and helped him sit. A struggle for them both, Cahan heavy and weak, the trion weak and wary of touching him. The forester hated this feeling, this languor within him though he knew it would be there for weeks yet, maybe a whole season. The trion grunted as he took Cahan's weight; they were a slight thing with barely any flesh on them. Despite their own difficulties the two of them managed, with much groaning and huffing, what one alone could not have – to get him sitting against a tree.

He took the water, finding when the gourd touched his lips that he was far thirstier than he had thought. He had to fight to stop himself gulping down water which he knew would only end up coming back up. Slow sips were best for now. The trion stepped back.

"I will light a fire," they said.

"No," oh he was quick with that. The trion recoiled from the word as if struck. "The forest will not thank you if you do," said Cahan more gently, "and I am too weak to gather deadwood and ask permission."

"Oh." He could not see their face in the gloom, they sounded hurt. "But we are hunted," they said. "Something out there follows us," they pointed at the forest. "Fire scares forest creatures away, does it not? I thought . . ."

"Some fear fire," said Cahan, taking another sip of water then placing his hand on the earth, his fingers sinking into the loam. It looked like the hand of a man of many more decades than he had lived, age made plain in fissures, spots and shadows on his skin. "But it can also bring other things upon you, and they are not scared away by fire." He took another drink. Watched the trion, seeing how nervous they were of every noise, every chirp of sound or crack of twig hidden in the darkness of the trees. "This creature that follows, you have seen it? A flash of grey maybe?" They shook their head. "Is it loud when it moves through the brush, like a man?"

"No," they said, "whatever follows, it is not large." They looked embarrassed, though the truth was size meant little in the forest.

"How long has it been following us?"

"Since you . . ." their voice died away in the darkness. "Since the clearing." It seemed odd to Cahan that the trion did not want to talk of what he had done. The Rai of Crua delight in strength and violence, and though they were trion they were Rai. He could feel the cowl, see it in their expensive armour. "Once," they said hesitantly, "I thought I caught a glimpse of the beast in the bushes. Like a slender ghost, that was all of teeth." Cahan nodded and smiled to himself.

"Stay still," he said, "and do nothing." He took another drink, to wet his mouth, and then whistled. Silence, at first. Then a high-pitched bark from between the trees. The sound marked by a flurry of spiralling lights as the noise upset tiny night creatures. A rustling, then a long, furred shape careened across the ground towards him. He heard the trion gasp, but they held their nerve and did not move as the garaur threw itself at Cahan, winding around his body until it lay curled around his neck. Deep rhythmic growls of pleasure passed through his body, warming and comforting him.

"What is that?" said the trion. The tone of Segur's growl changed, became less pleasurable and more threatening.

"Calm," he said to Segur, reaching up to bury a hand in the rough fur around its neck. "Segur is a garaur," he said, "they are used here in the northlands to herd crownheads."

"It has big teeth," said the trion.

"They are predators, and capable of killing a person, but Segur will not hurt you if you do not hurt me or it." The trion said nothing. The return of Segur felt like a gift to Cahan. Though soon after came a crushing tiredness, his body speaking of its great desire to slip into the deep well of sleep and fix what it could. "We are in Woodedge?" he said. "Or Harnwood?"

"I do not know," said the trion. "I know only a fool goes too deep into the forest. I wanted to reach Woodedge but was quickly lost." They looked around. "All the trees look the same."

"My staff," Cahan said, as he would need to walk eventually, "was it left on the raft?"

"Staff?" said the trion, they looked alarmed. Then confused. Then smiled.

"A long stick? Carved with maws on the top?" Cahan nodded. "I did not know it was yours," they said. "But I used it to build the travois I dragged you on."

Cahan felt happier at that, a little good fortune. The staff had been with him a long time and was the last reminder of someone he considered dead.

"We should sleep," Cahan said, though the truth was he had little choice. "Even on the edges of Harnwood it is not always wise to travel at night."

In the morning he still ached, but the terrible, bone-deep tiredness had left and he felt that he would at least be able to walk a little. Segur had brought three histi, the burrowing creatures it loved to hunt and that were also good eating. Generally they were best eaten cooked as the raw flesh was tough, but they had no fire. The trion looked like they had hardly rested at all, their eyes wide and nervous, and they had that odd, twitchy alertness that came from lack of sleep.

"What is your affinity?" said Cahan as he pushed himself up to sit against the tree again. His bones ached, his blood moved sluggishly. The trion looked at him. "Speak, child, I will not bite." They shrugged. "You must have one, you are cowlbound." He could feel it, a pressure on his mind, an invisible presence in the small clearing where they sat. "If it is fire you could cook these for us." He held up the histi. The trion looked away, as though the limp bodies physically pained them.

"I . . ." their words died and they wrapped their arms around their body. "I have no affinity." Cahan took a deep breath. The naivety of the young taxed his patience. Most things taxed his patience.

"You have a cowl, you have an affinity," he said. "It is that simple. When it became part of you, then you would have felt it. Even if it was only a hint of water dripping or the scent of smouldering straw." He laid the histi on the grass, smearing the green with bright blood. "It is no shame not to be strong." Venn shook their head. That was when Cahan noticed they wore no clanpaint. Odd: to have no clanpaint was to be shamed and shunned. The Rai who had travelled with them had been strong, and they had not treated them like a pariah. The trion looked away from him, bringing up a hand to where the clanpaint was usually placed. Suddenly self-conscious.

"They locked us in the death room with the corpses while they bloomed. I felt nothing." They looked away. "The priests of Tarl-an-Gig said the cowl had taken but I have no power. I have never felt any and I do not want it."

"That is why they brought you to the forest," said Cahan, more to himself than the trion as memories came back to him. For most the kindling of a cowl was small, insects, gasmaws, creatures of little will which could be extinguished easily and feed the thing growing within. But for others, those who did not fit well with the cowl, sometimes a harder death was forced on them. A sudden rush of life to wake and bond the cowl. It was not a thing Cahan liked to think about, the pain, the blood of it. The burning. And for those given the "blessing" of the cowl who did not awake at all, well, the Rai of Crua had no time for weakness. They would be slain and placed in the blooming room. "Your name is Venn?" They looked at him. Blinked.

"Yes, Venn," they said.

"And you are a trion?" he said, raising the inflection at the end to make it a question. They nodded. "I have never heard of a trion being given a cowl before." A shrug in return, and they turned away, showing the blank side of their face where clanpaint should be. He wanted to ask about it, but thought it would be unwelcome. Too personal. Now he looked closer at them they looked half starved, their face all hollows and darkness. For someone so young they seemed to carry a great weight. "We should eat," he said.

"But we cannot have a fire," said Venn.

"I do not always need a fire," Cahan replied and turned. Placing his hand against the tree he had sat against. He had discovered once, when wounded, when he was very weak after coming off worse in a fight with a wild spearmaw. Sometimes the trees would lend a little of themselves, but only a little. He did not know why he did this simply to cook some food. It was foolish and the energy would have been better spent on himself. Maybe he needed to show the trion he had some power. He was not used to being weak. He looked up into the branching canopy of the great evergreen. "Lend me a little of your strength, old one," he whispered, "so these deaths do not go to waste." He felt the great life of the tree, the flow of it. Felt it open to him, let a little of its power pass through him, through the cowl and into the histi.

Roasting the flesh was a matter of moments and then he took his hand away the imprint of the bark was left on his skin. A coldness within him; he had not done that for a long time, had forgotten the feeling of it. Forgotten why he so rarely did it. The trees of the forest were conduits of great power, and it required skill to tap it and goodwill on the part of the tree. What passed through them was as deep and dark as any forest, and it was easy to become lost in it. It frightened him, because he knew no cowl could save him from that. Beyond the tree was something so much larger, so much more. He held a steaming histi out and Venn slid forward, reaching out to take it while keeping their body as far from him as they could. Did they notice his hand was shaking? The third histi he threw to Segur, who would have happily eaten it raw but preferred its meat cooked. They ate in silence, until Venn broke it.

"Can you walk now?" they said.

"For a bit. Not for too long, though," Cahan replied.

"I will ready the travois."

"There is no hurry," he said. "We can stay here for a few days. I will regain my strength a bit and then we can move on." Venn shook their head.

"No, we must move, they will come for me. They will never let me go."

"They will hardly be in a hurry to capture one who cannot even use their cowl, trion or not." Cahan slid histi flesh off the bone with his teeth. He was hungry. Ravenous. Could really have done with all three to himself. "Even if they do, they will not know what happened, not until someone finds the bodies. We can take our time."

The trion shook their head, standing, the half-eaten histi in one hand.

"No, you do not understand, they will come. The woman will tell them what happened and they will come for me." They looked terrified, pacing back and forth. "They will send more Rai after me."

"What woman?" Now they had his attention.

"The woman," said Venn. "The Rai woman. She was still alive when I left."

Anger. Flooding through him, as dark and powerful as the flow of the tree. He would have stood, fists clenched if he had not thought his body would betray him.

"You did not finish her?" he said. "Knowing she could wake and tell of me and what I had done?" The trion looked at him. Even in his weakened state he was sure he was stronger than the child. They would have been wise to be afraid of him, and though he saw the fear there they did not back down.

"You think I am weak because I did not kill someone who was helpless?" they said. Answering Cahan's anger with their own. "You know nothing of me. You do not understand. You are no different from them." They pointed back into the forest. "My cowl does not bind to me because I cannot touch it, or hear it." They took a deep breath. "I know it is there." Venn banged a fist against their chest. "It does not bind because I refuse to kill to feed it. I have seen what it does to people. I refuse to kill at all." What they said. To Cahan it seemed outlandish, a madness for anyone living in the land of Crua. He laughed. He could not help himself. For a child to be brought up in this land and think you could live without killing was a joke like few he had seldom heard.

"Not kill," he said, and rubbed his hand across his beard, spreading histi grease through it. "Truly, you are the spoilt child of some Rai. Either that ideal will not last long or you will not." He took another bite of histi. "The cowl will out," he said. "I have tried to stay away from the affairs of men, to live quietly and alone. To deny what lives within me, and look where it has led me. To you, and three dead Rai in a forest." He stopped chewing. The laughter dying in his mouth. "Two dead Rai."

"I have lived fourteen harvests, and never killed." They stared at him, their breath coming hard.

"Have you been locked away in some spire?" said Cahan. "Death is everywhere in Crua." They blushed.

"I will not kill," they said again, fists bunched into tight balls. Cahan raised his free hand.

"And thanks to that we must keep moving." He threw a bone into the vegetation. "You think they will come for you, I know they will come for me." The trion nodded, light sparkling along the make-up on their cheeks. "If you cannot kill, child, can you climb?" Venn nodded, looked puzzled. "Climb this tree I sit against," he patted the trunk, felt a small thrill at the energy running through it, "then, get as much floatvine and bladderweed as you can. Let us make that travois of yours a little easier to move." Cahan struggled up and made a saddle of his hands to help the trion up into the tree. They were light in their wooden armour, but he was not as strong as he had thought and even that small act left him tired. He considered tapping the trees for more strength, but had already borrowed from them once today. The forest did not like those who were greedy. Besides, he could feel the desire of his cowl in the back of his neck, as if someone held a hand there, trying to push him towards the power. He thought that feeling long behind him; a battle already fought and won. But he had awoken the cowl, and now that battle would have to be fought again.

From the corner of his eye he thought he saw a figure, grey, still as a statue at the edge of the clearing. When he turned towards it there was nothing, only a confluence of branch and shadow.

Venn climbed, with much huffing and fuss, as Cahan backed away from the temptation of the trunk.

"There should be plenty of floatvine up there," he shouted into the branches.

"There is," came back. Then he heard swearing.

"What is it?"

"I pull it off and it floats away," they shouted down.

"Well, of course it does, it is floatvine." Cahan wondered where they had been all their life that they could know so little of harvesting something so common and useful. "Pull off long strands, and wrap them about your body."

"How much do I need?" they shouted back.

"Enough that if you jump from the tree you will gently float down to the ground."

"How do I know when that is?"

"You will feel it, a lightness in your body. Like you may

be able to fly." He could glimpse the trion looking down through the foliage at him, solemn, worried, their face that of a child younger than their years. "We will probably need at least two lots, you are small for your age."

It did not take Venn long to gather the weed, though the first time they wrapped themselves in so much vine they almost floated away, and would have, had they not become tangled in the branches of the tree. Once they finally made their way down Cahan untangled the long strands of broad and bulbous-leafed weed from them and wove it into a net. Then he sent them back up for more while he attached the net to the underside of the travois. Though he had mocked Venn for not realising the floatvine would float, he almost made a similar fool of himself, forgetting to tether the travois as it became lighter than air and having to throw his weight onto it to hold it down. Fortunately the trion did not see this and the travois was well tethered by the time Venn returned with more weed.

"See now," he said, when he had attached the second net, "it will hold my weight, and be easier for you to pull." They nodded. "Which way were you heading?" Venn pointed into the trees.

"I followed the edge of Harnwood," they said. Cahan looked up, angling his face towards the light above. "You can see where the brush is thicker, the trees older. I was scared to go in there. I have heard stories."

"East, I think it is," said Cahan and slid onto the travois, relief flooding through him as he took the weight from his feet. He did not tell them they had never left Harnwood. Venn moved to the front of the travois, taking hold of the handles. "The floatvine will be good for a day at least," said the forester. "And I think we will stray a little into Harnwood, it is harder to track people through it." As he spoke the forest around them quietened, the yelps and howls and clicks and chirps that were its normal cacophony fading away. A moment later he heard the same hum he had heard when the soldiers came to his farm. A marant cruising overhead. And he felt something more. The same thing that quietened the forest. A wave of darkness travelling with the beast.

"They have come for me," said Venn.

"Aye," said Cahan, though he thought it more likely him they were after, "we should move."

You need me.

19

They made good time with the travois. Cahan wondered about the trion who pulled him along. So much odd about them; that they did not know about floatvine was something he would have thought impossible for any but the most privileged of Crua society. It was something the youngest child knew from the moment they could walk, floatvine and bladderweed were toys every child played with. Most could balance a weight with floatvine by sight before they were old enough to work in the fields or tend crownheads. It grew everywhere, not just in the forest, but its seeds clung to buildings and it grew so quickly it must be cleared lest it overrun them.

Stranger than that was the trion's lack of fear of Harnwood. They were wary, aye. Had spoken about not wanting to cross into it. But they seemed oblivious to the real dangers of it. They had been scared of Segur only because they felt something followed them. Most people were wary about entering even the relatively harmless Woodedge, but Venn grunted and pulled and barged their way through Harnwood without even looking about them. On occasion Cahan gave directions, to the right or left, so they strayed away from bushes he knew had vicious or poisonous vines. Or he told them to stop and wait when he saw the shadows of larger creatures moving through the canopy, wild maws, and on one occasion the streamlined shape of a spearmaw hunting them.

The people of Crua only wished to use the forest for themselves and that meant they were not welcome and on some level they knew it. They lived on the edges and looked over their shoulders at it, sure that the ancient and powerful Woodhewn Nobles, the boughry, that lived within it were waiting for them, to devour them. Cahan doubted they had the power. The old gods had been dying for a long time, and in many ways the followers of Tarl-an-Gig were only finishing what the followers of Chyi had started.

But if it was not the boughry that frightened them then it would be swarden, or orits, or Forestals, or rootlings, or skinfetch or one of so many possible horrors. In the minds of most the forest creatures were mixed up with Osere, the dark creatures that had once been the masters of the people before Iftal sacrificed itself.

But Venn pushed their way through the thick growth of Harnwood as if they were part of it, not afraid at all. And though Cahan would have loved to believe this was true he was sure it was simply ignorance, that they did not know enough to be afraid.

The cries of the forest quietened and the low buzz of the marant came again. It passed over, once more bringing that unpleasant queasy feeling. Venn slowed, staring into the air, trying to see through the thick canopy.

"Do not stop or worry," said Cahan, "as long as you can hear it they are not coming. And the canopy is too thick for them to see us." Venn turned, looking over their shoulder at him, so young, skin smooth and unmarked beneath the shining wood of their helmet and scant make-up. "They may well give up, Venn, few wish to come into the forest." The trion's eyes were wide.

"They will come," they said, and they sounded both sure and resigned, "they will never rest until they have taken me back."

He wanted to tell them not to worry, that it was him they looked for. He had shown what he was in the wood, and if that woman lived she would have told them. He did not, his life had been spent running from his past. If the trion did not want to question him then all the better.

"Float on," Cahan said, "we must make the best time we can." He wondered what made them think they were important enough to send a whole squad of soldiers after them. Though, truthfully, all Rai thought they were important.

The buzzing of the marant stopped.

"It is down," said Venn, and they leaned into the harness, pushing on harder through the brush, filled with a sudden and painful desperation.

"Wait," said Cahan. "Too much noise, it makes us easy to follow."

"This place is nothing but noise," said Venn, still pushing on at speed. "It never ceases to make noise. It hurts my ears, it buzzes in my veins. I can feel the trees growing." They pushed on harder, as if they could escape from the sound and life of the wood.

"Venn," Cahan turned on the travois and reached out, "stop." He grabbed their shoulder. "What you describe is the cowl, you feel all that through the cowl. As do I. And if we are chased by Rai who are strong enough to feel the forest, then we create a disturbance by pushing through so quickly. We must go slow, we must go careful." Venn stumbled to a stop, breathing hard in the cold air, clouds around their mouth.

"My cowl is as good as dead within me."

"I do not think so," said the forester.

"Well, I do not want it," said the trion. Then they pulled off the harness, getting stuck in it and cursing the Osere below as they struggled out. "Why even run if they can find us?" Panic in the trion's eyes. "Why even run?" They said again as they escaped the harness and slumped into the leaf litter. Cahan slipped from the travois with a grunt. Without his weight it started to rise and he grabbed it. His staff ran down one side as a support and he pulled it loose, letting the rest of the travois collapse into a mass of dying vine and vegetation which he let go. They must travel on foot now and he would need the staff. Tears ran down the trion's face. "I do not want this thing in me," they said, pulling at the wooden armour that covered their forearm. As it moved Cahan saw the arm below, scarred by a blade. They stared at their arm then turned to him, looking hopeful. "What did you do to that woman?" Their eyes searched Cahan's face for some sign of the hope they lacked.

"I destroyed her cowl," he said. They stared at him, then grabbed his arm.

"Do it to me. Free me. They will not want me then." Cahan took their hand from his arm; the hope the trion had, it was something almost physical, a force. Cahan felt it rise and then he felt it die.

"You do not know what you ask," he said. The trion looked him up and down. "The cowl is part of you. You can deny it, and you can bury it," he said. "But to remove it completely is to remove something of you. That woman, she will die, they always do."

"But you can do it," they said.

"I will not."

"Then you are like everyone else," the trion's voice thick with scorn, "you see me as some experiment to play with and . . ." Cahan grabbed their arm, his hand, far larger and rougher than theirs, closing around the smooth wood of their armour.

"I know nothing about you," he hissed, "nothing." Behind him he heard Segur let out a low growl. He pulled the trion close. "All I know is that you let a woman live who you should have killed, and now I am hunted through the forest because of it. If you wish even a chance of escape you will do as I tell you and stop complaining."

"They do not care about you," they said, "they come for me."

"Why would you think that?" As Cahan spoke he was thinking that maybe they were right. Would the woman have had time to get to Harn-Larger? Especially hurt as she would be without her cowl. He did not think so. But if they had expected the trion to return, and they really were important. Maybe a search party so soon made more sense. Even then, it was strangely quick. "Who are you, Venn, to think yourself so important?" The trion stared at them. Looked away, into the forest then back again.

"I am the first trion in a generation to take on the cowl," they said. "And I am the child of Kirven Ban-Ruhn, High Leoric of all Harn." Cahan realised he was not breathing. The trion was right. They were coming for them. Not him. They may not even know he was here. He could slip away, leave the trion and escape.

"Are you going to leave me?" They sounded desolate. Lost. Cahan knew he should. He was hurt, weak, in no state to protect either of them. But he still had the memory of that toy crownhead, could almost feel it in his hand the way he could almost feel pain radiating from the child before him. The guilt burned.

"Listen to me, Venn," he said quietly. "It is called a cowl for a reason. Like a thief may wear a cowl to hide, we can use ours to blend into the forest."

"I cannot use it, I have not woken it. And I will not kill to do so."

"Then I will do it." Venn stared at him, wide-eyed.

"I thought you would leave me." Cahan shook his head. Even though he knew leaving the trion was probably the most sensible option. "They will really not be able to see us?"

"No, that requires more delicacy than I have. What you saw in the forest was the first time I have used my cowl in many years." He licked dry lips. "I had hoped never to use it again."

"Why?" the question quick and sharp. The answer just as bladed.

"What are we? Lovers that you think to know my whole life?" The trion blushed at that. "My past is not your business, and the less you know of me the better for us both." He took a deep breath. "The forest around us, Venn, it is life," he said, "you must know that?" They shook their head. "You told me you felt it."

"For my whole life the forest has only ever been a line on the horizon." Again, Cahan wondered how they could know so little. "Everything here is new to me. I do not know what is normal."

"Well, we are life, Venn, and if we do not act against the forest, and make the life of it too aware we are here we can blend into it." The trion blinked. "These Rai that come with the marant, they will hunt us by feel. By the disturbance we make, if they have the strength."

"I did not know a cowl user could do that," said Venn.

"Most cannot. And if we are lucky those who chase us will not be skilled enough to try. Now, I need quiet, let me commune." They sat back and he closed his eyes, let himself relax. The cowl beneath his skin shivered as, for the second time in as many days, they became closer than he had allowed in many years.

You need me.

A whisper, then another and another and they were joined by another and another and a feeling of togetherness so pure and shining that he could not believe he had fought this for so long. This needed no power, this was simply letting the world around bleed into him, rather than pushing himself into it.

I have missed this.

No.

He forced the feeling away, compartmentalised it as he had been taught to through years of discipline. The cowl wanted closeness, it was a tool for it to use. But he was the master of it, he was the one in control. The cowl must be subservient to his will. The susurrus of its whispers died away. He took a deep breath, imposed his will and felt himself disassociate from his body. He saw the forest as if from above, but it was not green and noisy and colourful. He saw it in monochrome silence, a grey haze against a cold, white ground. Down and down towards the haze. Drifting. He let himself fall. The nearer he approached the more he saw the forest as something else, no longer a haze.

A net.

A web.

A hundred thousand interconnected lines of life. Some moved, some did not. Some were thick and old and some were thin and new. Some were wrong, in a way he had never experienced before and he avoided them. Drifting. Down and down until he found the nexii, the junctures, the meetings, the concentrations of life. In among them a gap. Him and Venn. Around them the constantly changing and twisting net of life. Aware of, and avoiding, these foreign bodies. He pulled his awareness further out to look for the Rai, they were not hard to find. Thin lines withdrawing around hazy grey circles, as if life could not bear to be near them. The blank areas noticeably larger than around Venn and him.

Eight. Spread out in a crescent. Coming their way. Hard to get a sense of distance. He could not tell if they were far away or a step away. A feeling of wrongness. Like these Rai were abhorred by the life that gave their cowls power. Was that what he had felt before? They moved forward and the life of the forest did not so much retreat as fade away, as if they drank it up as they passed. As if they were death moving.

He had never seen the like before. It worried him.

Cahan forced his consciousness away from its place above the forest and back amidst it, surrounded by his own web of thinning life. Whether cowled or not, there was something about the people that stood out as different from the other life. Not the way gasmaws and crownheads were different, unalike but still simple. The people were darker, stranger and not as connected to the ever-moving web of life of the forest. Unwelcome in this place. He let out his breath, sensing the web, calming it, cajoling it. Pulling it around himself and Venn. He imagined his body as a doll made of twigs and attached the web of life at his shoulders like a cloak, drawing it around them. Then he withdrew, taking a moment to look from higher again, seeing the Rai had paused in their pursuit before he slipped back into the world.

"It is done," he said.

"I don't feel any different," said Venn.

"You will not, now, be quiet and stay close to me." He turned fully around and began to creep forward.

"But that is where we have come from," said Venn.

"Yes."

"That is where the Rai are," they said more forcefully. "We would be fools to go back that way."

"It would seem so," Cahan whispered. "But if you think it they are also likely to think it." He heard the voice of the Trainer of War in the back of his mind, *do what your enemy least expects*. Winced at the thought of hard hands, cruel whip. The trion shook their head.

"They will see us." Venn stood. "We should carry on the way we were going." Cahan grabbed their arm, pulled them close and hissed into their ear.

"Listen to me, child, I was taken from my family when I was far younger than you, by cruel people who saw me only as a means to an end. They trained me to fight, to use my cowl. They made me study tactics for hours on end.

What do you know of such things?" They opened their mouth, began to stammer some objection but he carried on. "Nothing. That is what you know." The trion blinked at him.

"But . . ."

"But nothing," hissed Cahan. "They may value you, child, and punish you when they take you back. But I wager they will take you back. Me, they will kill. And if they know what I did to the woman they will make it slow." The trion looked shocked, as if none of this had occurred to them. "The Rai come at us in a crescent," said Cahan, more softly, more gently, "they intend to herd us. They will push us out of the forest to somewhere we cannot hide. No doubt someone waits for us to break from Woodedge. By going towards them we confound them, we are doing what is not expected. If we do it well we may even make it to their marant and we can steal it, leave them stranded here." Venn stared at him and he tried to smile. "Do you understand?" They turned their head away from him and he let go of them, wondering why he wasted his time with a child. "Well, I am going back towards their marant, you go where you will." He turned — better for him if the trion went another way — then he almost stumbled on a root in his weakness. Venn was there, putting his arm over their shoulder to support him.

"Very well," they said. The forester nodded. Leaned his weight on them and his staff.

"Stay quiet, Venn, and stay low. When I stop, you stop." They nodded and moved forward. At first Cahan was bent over, his body complained and when his weakness threatened to overcome him he crawled. All the while he could feel the Rai getting nearer. He could not tell exactly where they were. They were a presence in the forest before him, but they filled him with apprehension.

They stopped for a moment's rest, and Cahan looked around as he had that feeling of being watched again.

Behind them in the forest were the two reborn. The visor-less one staring at him. He could use them, here, now. But if he did, what then? He was beholden to them, and admitting he was something he had been running from for decades. No. He had a plan. Get back, take the marant. It was not impossible. He looked at the reborn. Then very slowly shook his head. With a single nod they vanished into the wood.

As the Rai came closer Cahan began to regret his decision. He felt something he had felt only once before, many years ago. A loathing, as if he had walked into a charnel pit where bodies were thrown to rot down to bone. The nearer these Rai came the quieter the forest became. The creatures that lived here did not want to be noticed by these Rai either.

Cahan reached out and put a hand on Venn's arm.

"Stay." Venn nodded. They crouched in the brush.

As if they had heard him the noises of the forest stopped. A long gargling hiss came from the brush ahead of them, the sound of something diseased. His mouth filled with a vile taste, like some infection in his tongue and teeth had spilled into his mouth. Cahan grabbed the foot of Venn, and they turned to him, face almost green with biliousness.

"They have come for me," their face a mask, caught somewhere between terror and misery. Cahan wondered if he had a similar look. He felt these creatures, their presence squirming in his gut. Worse, he knew it now. Hetton, shock troops. He had only ever seen the Cowl-Rai's Hetton from a distance. They were their elite soldiers, something unique to them the way the reborn had been unique to a long-ago Cowl-Rai. The Hetton were terrible, broken. He had come across them at a small town in Mantus named Vohar-Over-Rise. The place had maintained its loyalty to Chyi and the existing Cowl-Rai. Vohar's Leoric had refused to send its young to war under the blue flag, or pay tribute to the monks of Tarl-an-Gig.

He had learned of the town from a farmer when he had

asked what the smoking ruins he had passed through were. The man had pointed out the camp of the Hetton to him, gaily coloured tents in a small hollow. From it came laughter and in among the laughter came the screams of those the Hetton had kept for either punishment or their own amusement.

The nearer he went to their camp the sicker he felt.

He had left them to it and moved on.

With the palm of his hand, Cahan signalled Venn to lie flat. They would have to stay right there, in the little dell among the trees and keep their nerve while these Hetton passed. So they lay in the leaf litter while the taste of rot in Cahan's mouth got worse and the strange gargling hissing noise moved around them. Cahan did not immediately realise what the noise was. At first he thought the Hetton travelled with some creature. But as they neared he realised it was the Hetton speaking to one another. The more he listened the more he could discern words within the hissing. Broken words, full of menace and desire. As if the appetites of the Hetton were given physical form through their language.

"Where?"

In a gargling hiss.

"Where?"

One word drawn out into something that made his mouth water as if his guts were rejecting the food in his stomach.

"Where?"

Through the thick undergrowth of ferns he saw a movement. A shadow. One of the Hetton. It moved forward, clad in armour much like that of Venn. Darkwood helmet, bracket fungus shoulder guards, the rest of the armour made from the expensive woods of cloudtrees. But where Venn's armour was vital, still living in the way the wood of the cloudtree can when cared for, the armour of the Hetton was dull and cracked. It was like the oils and sap that gave the wood its sheen had been siphoned away. In places it looked splintered as if it had been left out in great heat; in other places it was swollen, as if it had been left to soak in water. The Hetton stepped forward, and even that was wrong, it moved strangely, giving the impression its arms and legs were not connected correctly at the joints. Venn lay by him, breathing heavily. Cahan turned to them, to find they had their head buried in the loam. The trion raised their head and looked at him.

"Why—" they began, but he clamped his hand over their mouth. Looked back at the Hetton. It had stopped moving and turned towards them. Its face strange, as twisted as any rootling's, but lacking the softness. The skin had lost any colour it once had and was dry, flaky, the eyes all whites and its nose gone. It reminded him of nothing more than a cooked fish head. For a moment he thought it had no mouth, then it opened a slit in its face, showing a set of thin, sharp teeth. It made the noise.

"Where?"

He was sure, in that moment and without question, that it knew they were there, that it was calling to its kin. Venn looked at him, eyes wide. Cahan expected to see terror there but it was not what he saw, more acceptance, as if they had always known this would happen. The Hetton took a step towards them. Opened its slit of a mouth again.

"Where?"

Another step towards them. Cahan reached down to his side. Once, long ago there would have been a weapon there. Now he found only the warm fur of Segur. He moved his hand, finding the garaur's head. "Where?" gargled the Hetton again.

Cahan breathed, the air coming out staggered rather than smooth and realised it was fear, pure fear, the like of which he had not felt in a long time. Even the cowl was quiet, something in it knew that they did not have the power to take on this thing, not now, no matter what he tried.

Take a breath. Think.

Segur growled again. He glanced down, the garaur's

mouth open as it panted, its eyes slits. He tapped the garaur twice on the head. With a growl Segur shot out of the thicket where they were hiding and between the feet of the Hetton. In one swift move the creature drew its sword and slammed it into the ground, missing Segur – who was quick as wind when it chose to be – by a whisker. The Hetton turned its head, following the garaur's path into the brush. Then it clicked to itself: one, two, three, four times and turned away, moved on. Venn began to lift themselves but Cahan grabbed them, held them still, slowly shaking his head. He understood their wish to be away from the Hetton, but it was too soon to move. Never had he felt something as wrong so keenly as when the Hetton approached. Worse here than at Vohar-Over-Rise. Stronger.

He felt the need to get away from it, but he fought it. They waited, lying in the earth between the leafy plants, crawling and flying things moving against Cahan's skin and the foul taste in his mouth slowly fading. When it was gone completely he nodded to Venn and they began their slow crawl away from the Hetton. Now, tuned into the forest through his cowl, he could feel the marant in the distance, a huge, warm and comfortingly natural thing. He wondered how it coped with something as unnatural as the Hetton upon its back.

"What were they?" whispered Venn.

"Hetton."

"They were not people."

"They probably were, once," he said. "Having a cowl removed changes a person, but it can go the other way. That is what I have heard said of the Hetton. They are those who the cowl has subsumed. They become something powerful but animal. Single-minded, pitiless, loyal only to whichever thing it is they recognise as strong."

"You are strong," said Venn. "I saw it in the clearing. You could control them." He shook his head.

"I have not fed my cowl in a long time, even then I did

it quick. I think it is the ability to inflict pain that something like the Hetton would respect." A shudder ran through him. "And I do not want to be of them, to share myself with such things."

"Can you fight them?" said Venn as they began to crawl away from the Hetton.

"Maybe once I could have fought one, two at most. But I will tell you a truth," he said to them. "I have learned that the more unnatural a creature is, the harder it is to kill."

"You could fight them, though, if you had to?" said Venn.

"There are eight of them at least, trion," he said. "So, no, I could not fight them." They stared at him, some light in their eye dying away, the way the day was always destined to die. "Come," he said, "we must make it to their marant. That is our only chance for escape."

They crawled on through the wood, pushing their way through the undergrowth and with every movement Cahan felt his strength ebbing. Often they had to stop and let the slow seep of power from the ground give him a little help. All the while he could feel Venn's desire to push on, how they were on the edge of panic. Above the light moved across the sky, relentless in its regularity, and the canopy began to darken. They had been crawling through the undergrowth for hours. When they paused again he let himself drop into a fugue, pushed his mind out of his aching body and let the grey web of life subsume him. It was harder this time, his mind as tired as his body, and what he found gave him no cause to rest. The eight Hetton had turned around and were coming back towards them. He dropped out of the fugue. Despair must have shown on his face.

"What?" said Venn. "What is it?"

"The Hetton have turned back, they must have realised we slipped past them somehow." They grabbed him, delicate hand on his forearm.

"What do we do?" Fear on their face, stark.

"The marant," he said. "We must hurry." He took a deep breath, pushed himself up onto all fours once more. "Come," he said, and they moved on, through the low bushes and around the soaring trees.

They heard the marant first, its breath wheezing in and out of its massive lungs, and at the point he thought his strength would give out he saw the break in the trees where it had landed. Hope, the possibility of escape, gave him the strength to push on.

It was a short-lived hope.

The marant, vast and black and gently buzzing to itself, dominated the clearing. By it stood two more Hetton, and with them were two Rai. Their armour glowing with battle signs and honour paint, showing where they had fought and advertising the acts of bravery attributed to them. The smaller of the two had crownhead horns set into the wood of their helmet.

"Galderin!" said Venn, panic gilding their voice with bright, high tones. They grabbed his arm. "What do we do now?" Cahan did not know. Even if he could somehow get the guards away from the beast, marant were slow to rise, and noisy.

But if they did not act then the rest of the Hetton would return. Cahan searched his mind, going back through their journey, through his life, what he knew of Rai, what little he knew of Hetton. Looking for something, anything, that could help.

The reborn. It was all he could do and yet he could not form the words in his mind. He wanted another way. There must be another way.

One of the Rai, the one without the horns, turned towards the forest, said something and pointed. Cahan turned to Venn, pulled them further back into the undergrowth.

"Venn . . ." he began but stopped. The trion was looking at him, or more looking into him, and had the strangest expression on their face. As if the life were draining from them.

"They will kill you if they catch you, when they realise what you did," said the trion. Their voice so soft, so gentle. "Clanless, with a cowl." They blinked as if what that meant was only now becoming clear. "They will kill you so slowly." Cahan nodded.

"Aye, they will."

"I said I would not kill," they stared at him, "I meant it." They began to stand and Cahan grabbed them. Hands either side of their helmet.

"Move and they will see you," he said.

They reached up and took his hands away from their helmet.

"They will not kill me," they said. "They will only take me back."

"To what." Cahan found himself barely able to talk. "Take you back to what?" They shrugged.

"To a room in a spire. One that I cannot leave. But I will live," they shrugged. "You will live. I will tell them you died."

"Venn, there is another—"

"No," they said. "There is not."

They turned, scurrying away into the undergrowth and left him there, feeling desolate. *The feel of a child's toy in his hand.* Cahan lay between bushes. Watching. Venn appeared from the undergrowth; they had gone all the way around to the opposite side of the clearing.

"Galderin," they shouted, staggering forward out of the bush.

The two Rai and the Hetton turned towards them. The Hetton stared, milky eyes on the trion. They let out a hiss. One of the Rai said something and they bowed their heads.

"Venn," said the taller of the Rai, "your mother sent us, she was worried. One of the men in the cages . . ."

"He killed them," said Venn.

"How?" said the other Rai. Venn shrugged.

"I was knocked out when he got loose," said Venn. "I awoke his prisoner. He was badly hurt, dying. It was not hard to get away."

"Where is he?"

"Dead, I think," said Venn, and they stumbled towards the marant. "That way," they pointed the way they had come. Away from him.

"We are glad you have returned," said the Rai with the horns. "You should have given yourself up to the Hetton. They would have protected you."

"They scared me," said Venn. Cahan heard no reply. He saw the Rai nod.

"Must we bind you?" said the taller one. "I would rather not take you back to your mother in ropes. It will shame her."

"You do not need to bind me," they said. He did not think he had ever heard anyone sound so defeated. Neither had he ever felt so small. He did not think he would ever have done such a thing as this child did here. The horned Rai turned to her partner – Galderin? – and whistled. The Hetton around them climbed onto the marant, as did the first Rai, then Venn. He remained hiding in the under-growth, like the coward he was. Those on the marant made themselves secure for flight and he heard Venn quietly sobbing. His mouth filled with that same filthy taste as when the Hetton had passed him in the forest, and then those that had been searching the wood returned. Cahan counted only seven back. One must have fallen foul of the forest. It would not like creatures so unnatural.

The Hetton did not seem to care that they had lost one of their own. They climbed onto the marant and the Rai with the horns leaned into the goads on its forequarters. With a squeal of pain and a deepening hum, the marant lifted into the air, leaving Cahan with only guilt for company.

He waited.

Watching the marant fly away until it was only a dot in the sky before he felt safe to move.

But he was not safe. Not at all.

"Here," the hissing voice. The sense of foulness. He turned. The last Hetton. Sword coming down. He did not even have the strength to cry out.

Darkness.

Deep in the Forest

They bring him out. The gardener. Your friend. The one who tells you gentle stories of the goddess of the lost, Ranya. You do not know what to do. What to say. Why is he here?

"Let us test this one's faith!" shouts Saradis, and she is talking about the gardener, but she is looking at you and in that moment it is clear to you.

They know.

He is made to walk the fire. He walks and you watch and you hope that the god will spare him. But you know he will not, because the gardener does not believe in Zorir. He does not like Zorir, he tells you stories that run opposite to everything Zorir says.

The gardener is not one with the fire.

And yet he walks.

You watch him walk.

You watch it begin to hurt.

Somewhere, in the back of your mind, you are suspicious, the firewalk is so much longer than any other. Why? Why would that be? As the gardener passes, he looks at you, just for a moment, only long enough to mouth two words at you.

"Remember Ranya."

We can help him.

But you are scared, so very scared.

Then the gardener's face contorts. Pain runs through him. His long robes catch light and he is a pillar of flame. But still he walks. He walks on and on and on without making a noise or screaming or anything. Until he falls and is silent.

But someone is screaming.

Someone is screaming.

20

He woke in the darkness. But there was strange familiarity to it. A sense of knowing the darkness. The smell, the sound.

He hurt.

Cahan tried to move, expecting to find himself bound, but he was not. Moving increased the hurt.

"It wounded you, Cahan Du-Nahere." The voice. He knew it and yet he did not. He opened his eyes. A roof, full of trinkets hanging from the rafters.

Home?

He was home?

"How?" He tried to move. A searing pain in his shoulder.

"Stay still. It cut you. But you are healing quickly."

"How?" Forced his eyes open. The reborn, standing over him. Tall. He must be lying on the floor.

"The Hetton."

"You saved me?" She nodded. "I did not call you . . ."

"No," she said. "You did not." She crouched, coming nearer to him, looking into his face. "You should have." He thought about that, he had been about to call her but had been given a way out by the trion. A coward's way out and a coward had no place ordering anyone to save them.

"I am not what you think." She stared down at him.

"We killed the Hetton. Brought you back here. Heal, Cahan Du-Nahere. Death is coming," she stood again. "You cannot avoid it." She turned and walked to the door of his farmhouse. When she opened it the light hurt his eyes.

"I did not call," he shouted. "I made no agreement with you!"

She stopped, turned. "My sister," she said, "has no hope left. She would have let you die in the forest but I would not allow it, so you live. If you do not call next time," a shrug, "my sister will be the one who decides your fate."

A pause.

"I am not what you think," he said again.

"No, Cahan Du-Nahere, you are not." She walked out into the light, letting the door shut behind her. Leaving him in darkness.

He healed. Slowly at first but when he was strong enough to stand and to eat his body and the cowl within gained strength more quickly.

He went back to farming. He knew the Rai might come for him. The missing Hetton would be noted.

Cahan could not find it in himself to care.

Sometimes, when he closed his eyes, he heard the terrible quietness after the soldiers had been in his farm, after the killing was done. If it was not that then he saw the trion, Venn, walking out of the undergrowth in an attempt to save him.

One child dead.

One imprisoned or maybe worse.

And him to blame.

He moved through a fog.

There was a rhythm to this life on the farm, even if there was no pleasure in it. He rounded up crownheads which had strayed too far, the pink dyes he used to mark them as from his farm had almost run out of their wool. Segur helped him herd them and corral them for re-marking. He had been guilty of the same thing as the man who had taken his farm, letting the crownheads loose without care. He had lost another half of his flock and now only had three. He suspected there would be a crownhead farmer nearby whose flock had grown by three when the traders had returned and Cahan had not.

Days and weeks passed. He ate, but did not taste. He worked, but barely lived.

Cahan cut back where Woodedge was encroaching on his fields, his body continued to heal and grow. He found a place where bluevein was attacking his crops and it was hard work to dig it out. Blood and blisters on his hands. He tried to forget Venn's sacrifice. He tried to forget the feeling of power as he had used the cowl. He tried to forget the soldiers who had come looking for him and killed an innocent family.

Each day he expected to hear the buzz of a marant, the march and call of soldiers as branch commanders sent them forward to take him. The foul stink of Hetton. The numbing embrace of dullers.

He visited the grove in the wood where he had buried the child's toy, visited it often. Sat before the shrine of Ranya and wished he thought it would do any good if he offered sacrifice. He had tried to believe but Cahan had never seen any sign of gods that came when people needed them. This was Crua. The gods took, and they watched as the strongest walked over the weakest knowing that meant more for them.

Every day expecting trouble. Always faintly disappointed when it didn't arrive. Never quite able to admit to himself that he had given up. That he was simply existing and waiting for something to happen to him. It felt inevitable.

When it finally did, it was not from the sky, and it was not the Rai that brought it. It was Furin, the Leoric of Harn.

She appeared at the edge of the wood as he was clearing the ground of unwanted plants and putting them into his rot pile, barely even checking for bluevein. Too worn out for effort.

"Iftal's blessing to you, Forester," she shouted. He paused with his hoe above the ground.

"And to you, Leoric," he said, leaning on the hoe. "Have you come once more to tell me to give up my land?" He felt like he said the words by rote, rather than because he cared. She shook her head.

"I have come to ask for your help." He laughed, unable to help himself. What a fine jest. He was no help to anyone.

"Helping you cost me three of my crownheads. And before that you sent a man to steal my farm. I have little appetite for helping you, Leoric, it costs me dear." She wrapped her blue woollen cloak around herself. She wore her black-dyed hair in elaborate braids, her face painted white and her eyes lined with deep blue.

"I sent the man, aye," she said. "I will not apologise for that, you know my reasons."

"For sending him, aye, but you did not explain why you sent the soldiers for me after." A flash in her dark eyes, anger.

"I did not send the soldiers, and I told you that. I do not lie." She walked towards him. "That family were out of their depth and I was about to have them hand the farm back when those soldiers came. They had nothing to do with me."

He turned from her. Made a dismissive noise and began to dig at the unyielding soil. "But I am not here to plough up old ground, Forester." Only now did he see the way worry marred her features, hear how her voice wavered. "I am here because I need your help, not for Harn, but for me. And there is no other who can help." He dug his hoe into the ground again, worrying at a root.

"I do not know what I can offer you that no other can,

if it is to guide your traders again then the Forestals were quite plain." He looked up. "They offered passage only once. I will not risk their arrows for your secrets." For a moment he wondered whether he should. An arrow to the head was a quick death.

"It is not trade I come about," she said, and stepped forward. "We will not send anyone to Harn-Larger for half a season yet. Maybe more given how deep the bluevein bites." She put a hand on his arm, stopped him as he dug into the ground. "Please, Forester, if you have any pity in you, listen to me." He looked at her, brown eyes on the point of overflowing with held back tears. "My child, Issofur," the words came slowly, hesitantly, "he has been foreststruck." Her voice almost broke and he looked away from her pain. "My firstwife and my first- and secondhusband, and our trion, all went to the war and did not come back. Issofur is all I have."

"You just want me gone," he said, leaning on his hoe and turning to her. "That is all."

She shook her head and he hoped she would leave. He'd had his fill of children, of failing them. Of other's pain.

"I do not care about your farm." She stood straighter. "You know the forest, you go deeper in it than any other." She licked her white-painted lips. He wanted to say no but he had seen her child playing, smiled at him. He told himself children who wandered into the wood seldom returned. He should send her away. Maybe, if he had not met Venn, if he had not watched them give themselves up to save him, if he had never found the crownhead toy, he would have done.

"*The only certain failure is never to try.*" Nasim's voice, too many ghosts.

She took his hesitation for refusal. "I can trade you something worthwhile," she said.

"What?"

"People came to me recently, asking about a man who

sounds like you. Big, long hair, a beard," she said. "There is a reward for whoever turns over the man that killed two Rai. I have kept it from the village as best I can, but secrets never stay secret. Someone will tell the soldiers in Harn-Larger it sounds like you, probably Tussnig. The monk is desperate to curry favour with the forces of the Rai. He thinks he is better than Harn."

"Then," he said, changing his grip on the hoe so it could be a weapon if it needs be, lowering his voice, "would it not be foolish of you to threaten a man who killed two Rai?" She shook her head, opened her arms as if to beg him.

"That is not what I am doing, or what I offer, Forester. Bring my child back from the forest and, should the soldiers come to Harn looking for you, I will make sure you are warned."

"But you won't stop them." She was fighting back tears and he thought losing. But she held herself together until the battle was won, then spoke again.

"You have seen Harn, Forester. The Rai have bled our strength away for their wars, we are not soldiers, we barely have the strength to farm." There was a desperation, but also a dignity in her words. "But I swear to warn you of any danger, swear it on the faraway graves of my family. If I lie may they come back as Osere and slay me in my bed." Now a tear escaped from her eye, running a track through the make-up on her face and exposing the skin beneath. "Please, Forester. I will send no one to your farm. I will never ask you for a splinter in sacrifice or tribute. But bring my child back from the forest. I beg you." He let the air out of his lungs in one long breath, pushed the hoe into the ground so that it stood upright. Closed his eyes.

The silence of death around his farm.

The trion standing, ready to be taken.

The feel of a child's toy in his hand.

"How long is he gone?" said Cahan.

"Today, they say he went this morning as if drawn, like he heard something call him." That was bad. If he had only wandered into the forest it was worrying enough, but to be called was worse. There were creatures in the forest that sang out a song to those who would listen, to bring out those they desired. Most often those who heard were lost forever, and if they came back they were changed. They were the ones chosen by old gods, dark ones cast out and worshipped by none. Only feared.

"A day is a long time in the forest, Leoric," he said. "You know this." She nodded.

"Even if all you can bring back is a corpse for me to bury," she said, unable to look at him, "our deal will stand." Something in her snapped and she let out a sob. Fighting to control her breathing. "He is barely five seasons, Forester, I will beg you if—" Guilt, sudden and strong as the fiercest circle wind. The most intense thing he had felt since he returned. He stepped forward and put a hand on her shoulder.

Froze.

Had he overstepped the mark? It was not done for clanless to touch those above them, but she did not react. He towered above her but felt small and pathetic because he had not offered his help the moment he knew what had happened. He, who knew the forest, could help this woman who had lost the last thing she had in this world that she loved.

"You do not need to beg, Leoric," he said. "I will do my best to find your child and bring him back." Why he made such a promise he did not know. Even if the Leoric believed she would honour him for returning a corpse, it would be unlikely to do anything but fester and come back on him. But in her misery and tears, maybe he felt some kinship. Or maybe he acted only to assuage his own guilt. It did not matter, he had committed now and must gather himself for a trip that would likely lead him into Wyrdwood, somewhere fraught with danger and a place few ever went.

"Will you go now?" she asked. "He has been gone a whole day, almost."

"I must gather myself and a few supplies first," he said. "If the boy has been gone that long a few hours more will make little difference." She nodded.

"Then I will see you in Harn, Forester." He watched her walk away through the frost-rimed fields. He felt different, less numb.

But did not understand why.

21

Kirven sat and listened to Jaudin, the head monk of Harnspire.

The main chapel of the spirecrown was lined with statues of Tarl-an-Gig, the balancing figure. Behind these the eight-branched star of Iftal. As High Leoric she did not have to attend the daily speeches or the small sacrifices. Her presence was not expected and she generally did not concern herself with such things. She felt it gave Jaudin a form of authority over her, they were the mouthpiece of Tarl-an-Gig, though that really meant they were the mouthpiece for the Skua-Rai of all Crua in faraway Tilt.

But sometimes she came here because the words spoken were familiar. The stories ones she knew by heart. Even the walls, decorated with pictures of Iftal for the many people of Crua who could not read, reminded her of her childhood. Of a room in a small white building, of a droning voice she had barely listened to and the close comfort of her mothers and fathers. She needed familiarity, needed to lose herself in it. Because otherwise all she could think about was Venn. Her child, in the forest with a man who should be dead, a false Cowl-Rai.

He could be nothing of course, weak, a pretender, a malicious report from jealous neighbours.

Or he could kill them with a thought.

Her hand tightened on the wood of the bench before her. The porcelain statue of Tarl-an-Gig on a piece of leather threaded through her fingers swung back and forth, the familiar smell of burning herbs filled her nostrils.

"Venn," she said to herself. Closed her eyes. Tried once more to lose herself in the droning of the monk.

The stories had changed since her youth. When she was young the monk had been for a forest god named Caralan-the-Many-Horned, though they did not call them forest gods then. Now the stories were of Tarl-an-Gig. But the meat of them? That did not change. The creator, Iftal-of-the-Tree, made the land and the gods and bade them guard his world from his palace in Great Anjiin, and promised all a paradise found along the Star Path if they did. The gods made the people to help them. But some gods became jealous because Iftal was fascinated with the people. The gods split into two factions: gods, who were wise and good, and Osere who were jealous and cruel. They trapped the gods and Iftal in Ancient Anjiin and hid the fabled city from all. Then they took over Crua where they ruled and the people suffered under them. Worse, the Osere denied the Star Path to the people and this broke the balance, stole the seasons from the world. And Iftal, the great god, suffered in seeing its creation so unbalanced.

All this was familiar, the same as it had always been. But then it began to change. Once, Iftal would have broken itself to break the bond between its children and Crua, banishing all from palaces of Great Anjiin and freeing a thousand gods, strewing them throughout the forest for the people to find. And when they were found the gods gave the people cowls and asked the people to give of themselves in return, to keep the gods alive so that one day they may cause Iftal to be reborn and all would walk the Star Path without need for death once more.

So the people fought the Osere using the cowls, as the gods could not. There were many heroes, many deaths, many sacrifices. Eventually, the Osere were beaten and forced below, where they would never see the Star Path, and even then they had to be promised the worst of the people as slaves and for below to be their land, where they could rule.

In the stories told now there were no other gods, only Tarl-an-Gig. And though most of the Osere were sent below, not all of them were. Some escaped to hide in Wyrdwood where they called themselves gods, ready to trick and lie to the people, ready to betray them once more.

Kirven no longer believed the stories, any of them. Oh, Iftal had existed, she did not doubt it, and the gods gave them cowls and maybe the Osere did live below. But Tarl-an-Gig being the one true god was most likely a lie used to seize power. If there were no other gods no new Cowl-Rai could ever rise, power could be best maintained through ruthlessly suppressing the hundreds of small monasteries that had once littered Crua.

"No roots, no trees." That was what Kirven had been told in Tilt, by the Skua-Rai herself. And here she heard the same, said more subtly maybe, but none the less it was said.

People walked up to the front of the temple, left their tribute and she heard them say, "I do not walk with the old gods of Wyrdwood but in the light of Tarl-an-Gig," then walk away. This, coupled with the rewards, offered for those who reported any who held to the old ways, had proved effective at establishing Tarl-an-Gig as the only god.

She heard the great doors open. Turned to see a soldier, one of her personal guard in a deep blue cloak. Kirven felt her heart speed up as the soldier approached.

"High Leoric," she said softly, going down to one knee.

"Yes, trunk commander Vetar?" She pulled the figure of Tarl-an-Gig into her hand, ran the leather between her fingers. "Why do you disturb me at worship?"

"I am sorry, High Leoric," she said, "but you told us to let you know the moment we saw anything."

"Rai Galderin is back?"

"A marant approaches," said Vetar, "whether it is Rai Galderin or not I cannot be certain. They are still a way off, but there are few marants in Harn." Kirven nodded. She liked this trunk commander, Vetar, the woman was sensible, accurate. That was why Kirven had put her in command of her spireguard.

"No signal, no mention of the trion?" Her mouth was dry.

"They are too far away for light mirrors," said Vetar. "We have time if you wish to finish here and offer tribute, High Leoric." Kirven shook her head and stood.

"Trunk commander Vetar," she said, "my entire life is tribute to Tarl-an-Gig. If that is not enough to put me on the Star Path then I doubt a bowl of fruit will help." Vetar nodded but did not smile or laugh. She was committed to her duty and humour was not part of it. "Let us go to the spiretop, meet this marant."

"Your guard awaits," said Vetar, and they left the head monk of Harn to continue his blessings.

22

It was no small thing to head into Harnwood, and something much larger to venture into Wyrdwood. The people of Harn, despite living within Woodedge, would never venture so far. The people of Crua only entered Wyrdwood en-masse when there was treefall, and greed for the precious hardwoods of the great trees outweighed their fear of the creatures that awaited the unwary in the gloom.

From his farm Cahan took a gourd and filled it with water from the wetvines that fed the crownheads' drinking pool. Sometimes forest water did strange things to the minds of those who drank it, so he would take as much safe water as he could with him. He found his pack and put in it dried meat and some root vegetables from the store behind the house. Then he strapped a knife on; most would also take an axe to cut their way through the undergrowth, but not him. The deeper you went then the less you disturbed it the better. If he could not get through the undergrowth without an axe he would go around. For the same reason he left his fire-making kit behind. He took rope, some hardwood spikes for climbing and a change of clothes in case he got wet. That done, he was ready. He grabbed his staff, left the farm and whistled for Segur who bounded over, climbed up to nestle around his neck. Then they set off for Harn.

The gate guards at the Tiltgate waited in armour which provided more comfort than protection. The Leoric was right about her people, they would not be much use for fighting. Her story of lost family was familiar, the wars in the south had stolen all those with the strength to use a spear. Those left in Harn were too young, too old, too ill, or too maimed to fight. They offered little more protection to the village than the old armour gave to these guards. Still, they crossed their spears and barred him entry as he approached.

"Why are you here, Clanless?" said the woman on the right. She was missing an eye and a scar ran from the socket all the way down on her face. Cahan did not know her but she looked like she had been a fighter once. The man on the right stared at him, he was old and more decoration than use.

"The Leoric asked for me."

"You will go into the deepings of the wood, then?" said the one-eyed guard. "To find the Leoric's child?"

"I will," he said. She stepped forward, smelling of woodsmoke and vost, the soupy alcohol that was as much a meal as a drink.

"I am no coward. That our Leoric should trust clanless like you instead of us shames us in the eyes of our first-mothers . . ."

"Aislinn!" the voice was hard, harsh. Walking towards the gate was Dyon, the Leoric's second.

The guard stepped back. Then looked over her shoulder at Dyon as they approached. He wore a long robe of faded yellow wool that looked like it had once been expensive. His head shaved and face painted white, like the Leoric's. His lineage freshly painted on, in larger signs than usual. He must have been proud of it to go to such effort when most could not read more than their own clan sign.

"We waste our time with this one, Dyon," said Aislinn, stepping away from him.

"Do we?" said Dyon, stepping between Cahan and the guard. "Maybe Tarl-an-Gig has sent him."

"So they are your god now, Dyon?" Cahan asked. "Star knows this place has had enough of them. I remember when you stood in as monk and told all Chyi watched over them, and also tended shrines in Woodedge to a handful of others."

Dyon smiled. "You should be careful how you speak, Forester," he said, taking Cahan's arm and guiding him past the guards. He had never cared much for the forester, but he had always been loyal to Harn and what he considered best for it. "The new ways forgive past mistakes, but punish those who refuse the true god. Bow your head for Tarl-an-Gig and keep your mouth shut." It was good advice, though Cahan did not agree. The smaller someone's world was the surer they became their way was the right way, and the world of most of those in Harn was very small.

"They are not the usual guards," he said, thinking it better to change the subject.

"No," said Dyon, "we were attacked by orits."

"Orits?" He could not keep surprise from his voice, they were Harnwood and Wyrdwood creatures. Not often seen in Woodedge.

"Aye, they had made a nest north of us." He did not look at the forester as they walked through the village. It was far quieter than the last time he had been here. "We had to burn it out. Furden and Duhan led the group that did it."

"They were hurt?" Dyon shook his head.

"Not badly, but the Leoric thought it best they rest." From his tone Cahan did not think he agreed, but Dyon was a hard one to read. "First orits, now the Leoric's child." He drew Cahan to a stop. "There are those that think the forest has turned against us, they blame the Leoric for letting in Tussnig, and him forbidding worship of the old gods. Tussnig in turn blames her as she will not stamp down on those who hark back to older ways." Dyon glanced around, then spoke quietly. "The monk found a shrine to the boughry an eightday past and I thought he would soil his robes. If our people are quiet about it Furin still lets them worship who they wish." He stared at Cahan, then leaned in to whisper even more softly, "If you cannot bring her child back, Tussnig will tell the people it is a bad omen. That Tarl-an-Gig does not want her here. They will not trust her as leader any more." He gave Cahan a hard look. "Without her in charge, outsiders will no longer be welcome." He left that thought in the air where it hung like the stink of the tanning pits. Cahan tried not to hear it cynically, as Dyon telling him how he would rule, but had always been one to think the worst of people.

"I will bring the child back," he said.

Dyon sniffed, then coughed and spat something onto the cold ground.

"Good," he said, taking a step back. "Good, may Tarl-an-Gig bless you for it." He bowed his head. "Now, the Leoric awaits you and she is impatient, worried for her child. Come." Dyon led him through the roundhouses of Woolside and to the market square. It was a sad place now, no stalls on this day, only the shrine with the poorly made star and balancing man.

It was so quiet, so empty, Cahan began to wonder if he had been brought here on false pretences. Had the Leoric set up an ambush? Sold him out to the Rai? He wished he had brought an axe, not that it would have done much good.

"Wait," Dyon told him, "she will be here soon. Furin is making offerings in the privacy of her longhouse." He nodded at the building. Cahan could not help notice he did not name what god she made her offerings to. "It is not good for the people to see their Leoric bleed."

"Where are you going?" Cahan said.

"To keep Tussnig distracted. He is no lover of you, Forester."

He watched Dyon walk away.

"The Leoric wastes her time if she bleeds for Tarl-an-Gig." He turned to find the monk he had given a coin to when he was here last. "That fraud cares nothing for children. Only for themselves."

"And you know more of gods than she does? Yours seems to have left you a beggar and I know few monks who are forced to beg."

She raised herself to her full height, which was not very great despite her spiked hair. Somehow she managed to sound quite haughty, despite that her robe was filthy and caked in mud, the ends of it tattered and soaked. "I am a monk," she said, "I told you so before. I know much of gods." She nodded as though words were enough to prove her point. There was a scar on the side of her nose where it had been slit; punishment for a thief. She saw him staring at the cut and lifted a hand to touch the scar. "A reminder from a previous life," she said. "Before I found my true calling."

"And who calls to you, monk?" Travelling monks used to be common, wandering in hope of followers and the riches such things brought. Now she would be either brave or foolhardy to let any name but Tarl-an-Gig fall from her lips.

Her answer was not what he expected, and it hit him like a hammer blow to the temple.

"Ranya."

For a count, Cahan could not speak. He was a child again, leafing through books in the smoky hut of an old gardener. Hearing tales of a god like no other, of ways of learning that did not involve switches and beatings, or standing for hours on end on one leg, or pain and rules and endless repetition. The filthy little monk was staring at him, a quizzical look on her face.

"What did you say?" It was all he could do to get the words out of his mouth. The monk smiled at him, an odd expression creeping across her face, the way the light creeps across the sky

"You have heard of her." He nodded, and could do little else. Struck with a sense of unreality, of the world bending and twisting around him, of events being out of control. It was not a feeling he liked. "Few have heard of Ranya," said the monk quietly. "I had not, well," she grinned, "not until she spoke to me." She tipped her head to one side, examining him like he was some odd creature she had found in the mud. "Most prefer to put their trust in gods they can see working, and the new Cowl-Rai is sweeping the land in the name of Tarl-an-Gig, truly it seems to be a god-in-rising." She stepped closer to him. Up close she smelled of meadows, a welcome thing in the stink of Harn. "But you have heard of my Lady of the Lost," she sounded puzzled, contemplative. "Maybe my path was more guided than I thought." She laughed to herself, and though he thought her laugh a little touched with madness, there was something infectious about it. He was so used to the people he met being solemn, scared, or disapproving of him. It was strange to have someone be amused.

He was not sure he liked it.

"You are laughing at me?" It came out as a growl.

"I laugh at the world, I laugh all the time." She circled around him until she stood once more before him. "Though laughter seems a little alien to you," she giggled, "you are quite the dour one." Then she hopped from one foot to the other on the spot. Cahan flinched, though why he could not say, she was no threat. "And big," she said. "So big." She moved in closer, her voice falling to a low whisper. "But unhappy, and lost, so very lost." She reached up a hand, as if to touch his cheek. Almost, he let her, then he remembered he had no time for monks.

"What I am is none of your business, monk. Life deals what it deals and we cope as we must." She laughed again, she was a strange, sharp-featured and filthy thing. Not what he thought of as a monk at all. They were generally well dressed and strewn with expensive wooden beads.

"Well," she said, laughing to herself again, "that is a rule to live by if ever there was one." She turned. "The Leoric is coming," she pointed at the longhouse.

Leoric Furin left the longhouse and turned towards the altar of Tarl-an-Gig at the end of the market square. As she backed away she bowed to the effigy of the balancing man and the eight-branched star of Iftal, to show respect. In one hand she held a rag and as she turned she used it to clean the blood of sacrifice from her skin, then held the rag in her palm to cover the wound she bled from. Furin paused and studied at her hand, taking the cloth on and off. When she was sure she was no longer bleeding she walked quickly over to where Cahan stood with the monk.

"Udinny," she said, then she dismissed her from her mind and turned to him. "I was not sure you would come, Forester."

"I said I would."

She grunted, nodded her head. "You have always kept your word, I suppose."

"Show me where the boy was last seen." Furin pointed towards the Forestgate, then turned and walked up through Tanside. He followed, the monk dogging his steps as the Leoric led them out of the village and past the tanning pits, up towards the small fields that were between Harn and the gasmaw farm at the edge of the wood. Beyond the fields rose the great steps of the forest, increasing in darkness as they increased in size. The pale green of Woodedge, the darker green of Harnwood, where old trees reached up for the sky, and in the distance the very dark green, almost black, of Wyrdwood where the tops of the great cloudtrees vanished into the misty sky.

"He was in the field over there," said the Leoric, her voice dull, as if all emotion had been burned from her.

"With the rest of the children of Harn, clearing the land in readiness for planting when Least comes in. They were searching for bluevein in the weeds. It gets worse every season." She stopped in the middle of the field. "The others were not called," she stared at him, "why were they not called?"

"Who knows why someone becomes foreststruck?" Cahan shrugged. "I only know it happens." He walked on through the field. "Where exactly was he standing?" She led him to the edge of the field, where stones had been laid to mark one tenant's ground ending and another's starting. Cahan knew the crops they would grow there were never enough. He thought they would be better feeding crownheads and trading the skins and meat for grain when the skycarts came in to Harn-Larger. That was if the Forestals let them, of course. He stepped over the rocky demarcation line and found where the children had been. The ground had been cleared of old crops and vines. The Leoric had moved forestward of him as he studied the soil and rocks.

"It was here," she said. "Half through the first eight. The children carried on clearing, almost until lightfall so I did not know. They told me Issofur stopped working. He stared at the forest while they cleared, long enough for them to become angry with him. They threw mud at him for it, but he ignored them. Then he walked away."

"He did not say anything?" She shook her head and wrapped her arms around her middle, ruffling up the bright blue wool of her clothes. Cahan used his staff to move the soil about, not that he expected to find any clue there, but her pain made him uncomfortable and he did not want to look at her. "They did not try and stop him leaving? Or come and tell you when he did?"

"No, they did not stop working." She looked away, back at the walls of the village. "Those that do not clear their quota of ground do not eat." She turned back to him. "Before you judge us, Forester, you should know that rule is for all in Harn, not just the children. We cannot all forage in Woodedge for food. The children must learn they live in a community, that we depend upon each other."

"No matter the cost?" he said, and immediately felt small and cruel for it.

"Yes," she replied quietly, bowed her head, "no matter the cost."

"Issofur," Cahan said softly to himself.

"Yes," she looked up once more, "he is a good boy. Works hard for the village." Cahan nodded.

"I will do all I can to bring him back." He moved the pack on his back, making sure it was comfortable. He had padded the straps with crownhead wool but they could still rub. "Leoric," he said.

"My name is Furin. You can call me that."

"Very well, Furin," he said, "I will do what I can for you." He paused in the moment before he headed towards the forest. "You know, if I do bring your boy back, sometimes people are . . ." he searched for a softer word to use, but there was none, or at least his mouth was not used to softness. "They are often changed by Wyrdwood. Not always," he added, "but often." She nodded, more to herself than him.

"Bring back my Issofur, Forester," she said, "and I will cope with whatever that means when I must." She stepped nearer, so she could whisper. "What is your name? I would know the name of the man who would help me." He stared at her, he guarded his name well. It was a danger, not only to him but to any who knew it. To give his name was to trust and he was not one to trust. The Leoric stared at him and he saw the pain in her eyes, the loss. Maybe it was foolish of him, but he felt a kinship with her through it.

"Cahan," he said. "Cahan Du-Nahere. It is not a name I share with many." Did the ground tremor? Did he feel one of those small earthquakes that constantly shook the land of Crua?

"Thank you for sharing it with me, Cahan Du-Nahere. I will hold it close." She stepped back. "Old god's watch you, and Osere stay below where you walk." He nodded as he did not know what to say. It was many years since any had wished him well and meant it.

"I should go." She nodded and he walked towards the forest. Stopping when he heard footsteps behind him, thinking the Leoric had decided to follow. He was ready to tell her she could not come, though a part of him would regret that. But it was not the Leoric; she stood way back in the field, staring at the ground where her son had last been seen. It was the monk with the spiked hair running after him, her robes flapping as she dragged her pack onto her back.

"It is dangerous in the forest," he said to her as she stopped before him. She grinned.

"It is dangerous everywhere, Cahan Du-Nahere," she laughed to herself again. "That is a good name, strong, it suits you."

"I did not share it with you." If she heard the threat in his voice she did not show it.

"But nonetheless I know it." That strange smile again. "I wonder if my Lady of the Lost sent me here, to Harn, because of you." She looked up at him. Her white make-up was only a smattering of powder, and the greasy mud that kept her hair in spikes had melted at her hairline and streaked her face. "It seems an odd coincidence that I should run into another who knows her name so far from anywhere civilised." He thought to send her back, but could think of no reason why she would obey him. She did not strike him as the type who obeyed anyone.

"If you choose to come with me, monk, you must do as I say." She nodded.

"Of course, those people in the village say you know the forest. I think that is why you frighten them." She grinned at him, her eyes sparkled. "So I would be a fool not to listen to you, Cahan Du-Nahere."

"The Leoric called you Udinny?"

"It is as good a name as any other." She bit on her lip. "Not as good as yours though."

"Well, Udinny," he wondered if she could hear how little he wanted her company, "as long as you do as I say, and exactly as I say, then you may walk out of the forest alive if you insist on following."

"You think our way will be fraught with danger?"

"I think," he said, settling the straps of his pack once more, "that the forest took the child, so it may not want to give him back." With that he turned and began to walk towards the forest, trying not to think about how, in only a few seasons, he had gone from a quiet life where few ever bothered him, to venturing into Wyrdwood with a monk for the village of Harn's leader. He felt like he was being forced into the open and looked around, expecting to see the reborn, but they were nowhere to be seen.

He watched the monk as she skipped over the field by him. She served a god he had only ever known to be worshipped in secret, and by one man. Dizziness threatened to overwhelm him again, a feeling of events beyond his control spinning around him.

He turned away from the monk and back to the forest, took a deep breath. Among the trees lay his more immediate worries.

You need me.

23

"It is a long walk," said Udinny from behind him as they pushed through the undergrowth of Woodedge. Cahan grunted. "Your creature—"

"Segur is a garaur," he said as it loped past him. Segur had joined them as soon as they were away from the village. Like all garaur it had an unlimited appetite for running, part of what made them good herders. Cahan's feet already ached, Segur did not even pause for breath.

"These garaur," said Udinny, "do they bite?"

"Segur will not bother you if you do not bother it."

They walked on in silence. Cahan stared through a break in the canopy at the mistline which formed around the tips of the cloudtrees of Wyrdwood, arrogant in their majesty.

"I had heard tell they were big," said Udinny joining him. "I am from Tilt, and people talk of the god trees at the rim of the world, but when they say they are big you do not really understand how big they are until you see them. Even if only from a distance."

"They will get bigger still," said Cahan, "a lot bigger. The trees of Wyrdwood are so massive that they look nearer than they really are. You walk and you walk and they become so big you are sure they can get no bigger, but they do. Eventually their size will steal your breath away, and you will still be far from reaching them. From understanding just how big they are." More words than he had spoken at one time in many years. He picked up the pace a little, hoping it would keep the monk quiet. He had found, as they walked through Woodedge, that the monk talked a lot. He hoped it was not catching.

"I have heard," said Udinny — she had quite a high voice that he was beginning to find annoying — "that there are people in the forest that live forever and do nothing but build towers. And no man or woman can understand the use of them."

"Aye, the swarden. But they are not people."

"I would like to see a swarden."

"Pray you do not."

"Why? I have never heard of them hurting anyone." She sounded a little out of breath so he walked faster.

"Think on that, monk." She was quiet while she thought on what he said. He wondered if she would remain silent.

"Oh," she shouted as they tramped along a path in the scrub. "You mean that only those who are not killed by these swarden ever get to tell about them." He did not answer. He did not think her words needed an answer. "I suppose many of the creatures of the forest are like that, are they not?" He stopped, and the monk almost walked into him. He turned to find her looking up at him, a smile on her face.

"Do you always talk so much?" he said.

"No," she said.

"Good," he turned and began to walk. She followed.

"Mostly I am alone in my travels," she shouted as she ran to catch up. "So there is little point talking as there is only me to talk to. I very rarely have a companion, so I feel I must catch up on all the talking I have not done whenever I have one."

"We are not companions."

"I believe we are, for this journey at least." She trotted along beside him. "It is good for companions to know a little about each other." He began to think he knew why she was usually alone. "I have not always been a monk, for instance. I have been many things. I have lived low in the towers with the rich, I have begged on the streets of Tiltspire I have . . ."

". . . had your nose slit for being a thief." Mention of such a shameful wound would silence most people.

But not the monk Udinny.

"Yes, it is true, an eventful life leaves its scars, and my life has been eventful. I once . . ."

He stopped again, turning to confront her.

"We are on our way to Harnwood, the start of the true forest, monk." She nodded, looking around at the scrubby brush and shrubs that marked the end of where Woodedge was no longer tamed by the village grazing their crownheads and harvesting the trees. The growth here was mostly saplings, thin and wiry, reaching up to touch the light in the few hours they were not in the shade of their greater brethren dotted among them. The trees would become thicker and taller the further in they went. Their way would become harder, the paths less obvious, the wood deeper and darker and more dangerous. "The forest and its creatures have little love for us. There is a reason whole armies go in whenever there is treefall in Wyrdwood, and that is because it is not safe for people." He nodded at the way they would go. The monk only stared at him from wide eyes, still smiling. "Even here in Woodedge, the shallow forest, it can be dangerous. I am sure our search for the child will lead us into Harnwood, maybe even Wyrdwood itself. The best way for us to get in and out alive is not to be noticed." The monk looked at him, blinked twice.

"It sounds like a grand adventure," said Udinny, still grinning.

Cahan shook his head.

"An adventure likely to get you killed," he said, and turned, walking on.

"I understand you," said Udinny, running after him again, "Ranya says, do no harm and do not be harmed."

"Well, in that she is wise," said Cahan.

"She is wise in all things," said Udinny.

"The way will be hard, monk," he said. "We will try and follow the paths even if they do not seem to go in the right direction, so we do not have to cut our way through the forest. A thing we will only do if there is no other choice. We make no fires, and most of all, we make as little noise as we can."

"No talking?" she said, tipping her head to one side as she strode along with him.

"Aye, no talking. Or as little as we can get away with." A flyer landed on the monk's forehead and she went to slap it. He caught her hand, pulling them both to stop again and brushed the creature off her as softly as he could. "We move through the forest gentle, Udinny, monk of Ranya, as much a part of it as we can be." She nodded. "We have been following the child's tracks through the fern, but I have lost it because of your chatter. While I look for it, if you would do something useful look for fallen trees and find yourself a stout staff like mine." He held up his carved staff. "They are good for moving the vegetation out of the way, it disturbs it less than cutting and will ease your way." She nodded at him and went to look for a staff, giving him some welcome quiet while he searched for the boy's path. It was not hard to find, the child was not attempting to conceal his way. Those who are foreststruck do not think to hide their tracks. Cahan found broken branches, a scrap of material caught on a thorn. Then waited until the monk returned. She held two sticks.

"These were just lying there," she said. "I did not know which one was best."

"The forest provides." He took the larger stick from her. "We will leave this one for someone else who needs it." Udinny nodded and weighed the staff he had left her with, finding the place which was most comfortable for her to hold it. She looked very pleased with it. Cahan called for Segur; the garaur appeared from the underbrush with a histi in its mouth and he took the creature from it, gutted and skinned it, leaving the offal for the scavengers. The monk stared, a question forming on her lips. "The garaur is of the forest, it is natural for it to hunt here." He used his knife to cut the fillets from the histi and threw the rest of the carcass to Segur, who jumped into the air to catch it then proceeded to crunch the bones up in its strong jaws. Cahan held out a fillet to the monk.

"What do I do with this?" she said, taking it from him. "We cannot cook it, you have said no fires."

"There are other ways," said Cahan as he sat on the floor and removed his boots. Then he cut the fillet into two thin strips, wrapped them in leaves and placed one inside each boot. "Do this," he said, "the action of walking on the meat will cook it, in a way."

"I do not think I want to eat shoe food," said the monk.

"Then give yours to Segur," he said, "but do not complain of hunger this evening." The forester did not mention the dried meat in his pack. Better the monk got used to trail food now. She stared at him, shook her head, then sat on the ground. She split her fillet as he had and put them in her shoes.

"Let us walk," said Cahan.

"It is unpleasantly squashy to do so," said the monk. "I do not think I am going to like being a forester much."

"You will get used to it," he told her, and they set off down the path.

The forest was a strange place. You could journey for days within it and get nowhere, and sometimes it was only hours and you were further in than you had ever wanted to be. The child had found the most direct possible route through Woodedge, and they made their way through quickly.

Cahan did not generally like entering the true forest; despite what the villagers thought of him he did it rarely. He travelled to Wyrdwood even less. The life of the forest around him made his skin crawl. He was too aware since he used his cowl to help the trion, Venn, and the forest was a temptation. "As we walk," he said, to take his mind off the itch of the cowl, "I will be tracking the boy, but the forest provides plenty to eat. Fruit and berries at a height you can reach can be taken at will. If you see a tree that looks like it has been tapped for sap by people or animal then tell me, and we will bleed it a little. But do not dig up roots, it does not like that."

"What of mushrooms?" she said. "I like a good mush-room."

"They are mostly fine," he answered, "though some types will kill you if you eat them, and others will kill you if you so much as touch them."

"I think," said the monk, "I may pass on mushrooms." Cahan smiled to himself.

"And if you see food high up, or gasmaws, or anything that looks like a gasmaw eating from a plant, avoid that plant. Whatever it is will be poisonous to you."

"Oh," said Udinny and they stood, blinking while Cahan moved on through the undergrowth.

The air became more chill as the light moved through the sky. They neared the end of Harsh. At the start many of the trees lost their coats, dropping them to the earth but now the first buds and leaves of Least began to push through. It was never truly warm in the north, not since the last tilt, but if the new Cowl-Rai could bring all of Crua under their rule then at midyear, when the light was at its highest, the great sacrifice would be made and the world would tilt again. Warmth and glory would come to the north, and the south would be plunged into the cold. Any northerner would tell you they deserved it for stealing the warmth from the north in the first place. And so it went, again and again, each generation feeding on the resentment of the last while the gods waxed and waned and their priests and monks fought for power.

Fools, all of them. Cahan wanted no part in it.

"How deep will we go?" the monk said, at least she whispered now, though there was no real danger in Woodedge.

"The boy has a good start on us." He pulled a branch nearer, the thin twigs on the end broken where someone had passed. The buds were a beautiful pink colour. "We will go as deep as we need to. If you wish to turn back, monk, now is the time. By tomorrow we will be in Harnwood, and it is dangerous to be there alone if you do not know its ways. You will not be able to go back."

"Ranya sent you to me. I will stay with you."

Cahan nodded, and they carried on along the path. Fewer saplings grew, replaced by more mature trees and the ferns and small bushes that grew between them thickened. The air became heavy with the verdant scent of growing things. Mosses and vines crowded the branches of trees and hung from them in streamers, ropes and blankets. Cahan heard forest creatures moving, calling to each other, branches shook as beasts jumped from one tree to another. Nothing of it felt out of place. This was normal and normal in the forest was good. The real danger came from things that were other, they lived by their own rules. The animals were understandable, motivated by hunger or fear, the other less so. But here in Woodedge they were unlikely to find them, even though orits had been found near Harn. That worried him. They were beasts of Harnwood, natural ones, but to be out of Harnwood was not right for them.

Cahan used his staff to move aside branches loaded with moisture which fell in a pearlescent rain. He pushed through undergrowth as they headed down a run worn by the forest creatures, passing through arching tunnels of fern thick with cloying pollen that dusted their clothes and made Udinny sneeze. Such paths were mostly made by wild crownheads, smaller and faster than the domesticated version, and shy, as together with the stilt-legged raniri they were hunted by almost everything. The trees grew taller and he stopped looking only in front of them, but now looked above, too. Through the canopy he could see the dark green lines of floatvine twisting round trunks and branches until it reached the tops, and from there it grew straight up to wave in the circle winds, bulbous bladder leaves on either side holding it in the air. With the floatvine came the myriad creatures that fed on it, and the creatures that fed on them – all some type of gasmaw, bladder-backed and tentacled. He stopped, putting out a hand and stopping the monk also, then crouched down among the ferns.

"What is it?"

"Gasmaws," he told her quietly.

"They are harmless," she sounded confused. "I have seen them in towns and . . ."

"They are not harmless," he said. "You have only seen them domesticated, made safe." Eight gasmaws came into view, floating between the trees. They were large, much larger than the juveniles bred in the pens, their stinging tentacles removed.

They were the same shape as the domestic ones; a large lozenge-shaped gasbag made up most of their bodies, covered by almost white skin that could change colour to hide them within the vegetation. Tentacles grew from their heads, four for manipulation and four that hung down, trailing through the air. Behind the tentacles were the gasmaws' eyes, one facing down, one up, and two forward, though the number of eyes on gasmaws varied wildly.

"Made safe?" said Udinny.

"The trailing tentacles you see." He pointed at the tentacles hanging lank and limp beneath the gasmaws. "They are removed on domesticated ones as they are poisonous." The monk looked alarmed. "They would probably not kill us, but they hurt, and they scar, and can make you sick for days on end." He pulled up his sleeve to show a thick line across the skin of his arm. "That is a gasmaw burn."

"What do we do?"

"We wait," said Cahan, "see how round they are?" Udinny nodded. "It means they eat plants, we are of no interest to them if we do not bother them. They will pass on." One of the gasmaws stopped at a tree, its tentacles searching the trunk for food while the rest of the herd moved away. After a while of searching and finding nothing that interested it, the gasmaw floated away, the faint hiss of air from the vents on its back driving it forward. It left a floral smell in the air that was faintly narcotic and made the songs of the flyers in the trees sound sweeter. He turned to the monk, less used to such things, and found her eyes had glazed over.

Something shot out of a tree, like a gasmaw but sleeker, skin mottled in light and shade. Its stinging tentacles shooting forward, piercing the grazing gasmaw, which made a strange, high-pitched bleating sound. Manipulatory tentacles fought the attacker, but not for long, and the predator pulled it close, sharp beak grinding into the body of the dying creature.

"A spearmaw. The poison of that one," he said to Udinny, "that would kill us. And it will hunt us if it sees us." He grabbed her arm and pulled her on further into the wood. She was still wide-eyed from the gasmaw narcotic, or maybe in shock from the sudden violence they had witnessed in the canopy.

"It would eat us?" said Udinny.

"Aye, given a chance," said Cahan.

"That it can eat us, but we cannot eat it seems unfair," said the monk.

"They cannot live off our flesh," whispered Cahan. "They simply enjoy the hunt."

"Such is life in Crua," said Udinny, and they moved on.

They spent the day following the boy's trail. He went in an almost straight line where the wood allowed him; when it did not he tracked back and forth along paths until he was going in the direction he wanted. Always north, always towards Harnwood and Wyrdwood.

Cahan stopped them in a clearing where four trees had been brought down by something. Whatever it was it had done it long ago, two years at least from the size of the saplings growing in the gap and the bright fungus and waving ferns growing over the fallen trunks. The forest glade was dappled with light from above, grassed with dense, short grass that was spongy underfoot. Whether it was an illusion, because the break in the trees let in more of the slowly dying light than when they had been under cover of the wood he did not know, but this place felt good. Safe. Most places in Woodedge, Harnwood or Wyrdwood left him feeling nothing; they simply were. But some felt oppressive, dark, and he had quickly learned to avoid them. However, he liked it here and that was enough for them to stop. Walking round the clearing he found he was not the only one who had felt that way. There was the remains of a nest in the grass, the faint shape of a small body and around it the stones from some of the fruit hanging heavy from the trees.

"Something lives here," said the monk. She sounded nervous. Cahan shook his head.

"No, the boy slept here, that is the shape of a child in the grass." Udinny crouched down and stared at the nest.

"Or it could be a rootling," said the monk.

"Maybe, but I think it was the boy. Either way, they would not stay here if it was not safe."

"A mystery to me how you can tell, Cahan Du-Nahere, but I believe you."

"We should sleep here," he told her. "I think our journey will be long and the light will die soon. Tomorrow we will be in Harnwood." He looked up. "It seems the fruit of these trees is safe to eat."

"I have been waiting for you to say we should stop," the monk said. She looked at the fruit suspiciously then sat, cross-legged. "I do not think I have walked so far in such a determined fashion in my whole life." She began to pull at her boots, seemingly untroubled by news of how close Harnwood was.

"Get used to walking, it will only get harder." He sat a good length away from her and whistled for Segur. The garaur came bounding out of the forest. If it felt any tiredness it did not show it.

"I think my feet may fall off," said Udinny, finally pulling off her boot and almost falling over backwards. Cahan's boot slid off easily and he reached in and took out one of the meat fillets. It was soft and warm to the touch, but the action of walking on it all day had made it palatable. The monk watched as he took a bite then she reached into her boot and took out one of the fillets he had given her. She sniffed it and made a face.

"It need not smell good to fuel you," he told her. She took a small bite. Her eyebrows raised and she nodded to herself.

"This is surprisingly tasty for something that smells of feet. I have eaten worse." She took another bite and then said, through a mouthful of meat, "I do not like how your creature is staring at me." The garaur was indeed staring intently at her, strings of saliva falling from its jaws.

"Segur is hungry."

The monk ripped a bit of meat off the fillet and moved towards Segur, stopping when it let out a low growl.

"A fine way to react to someone who is bringing you dinner," the monk said. Segur stood taller on its stubby legs and hissed. The monk raised her hands. "Very well, you are as antisocial as your master." She threw the meat to Segur and it was snapped out of the air. "Cahan," she said, "I have some sweetcakes in my pack," the monk pointed at it, "will you growl at me like your beast if I offer you one?"

Despite himself, he found he could not suppress a smile.

24

He was woken by the sound of movement.

The light had not yet risen, the air was thick with darkness. Years of spending time in the forest had sharpened his senses and now the slightest out-of-place sound brought him instantly to wakefulness.

For nothing.

It was the monk, Cahan snorted in annoyance.

She had left her bedroll and was wandering towards the edge of the clearing, each step slow, as if she was not yet truly awake. Cahan gathered his blanket around himself and rolled over. As he moved something in the forest, past the monk, caught his eye. He sat up.

Something in the light. A million glowing points lit the forest; plants and creatures of every colour filled the night. Most were normal, harmless; but not all. Within the chaos of soft and shimmering light existed all the life of the forest, prey and predator alike: the panicky flashing despair of dying things, the throb of pleasure from creatures that knew they would not go hungry. The staccato excitement of creatures trying to attract a mate. In among the riot of organic illumination Cahan recognised another, fainter, but far more dangerous glow. A limpid green amid the bright primary colours, something flashing rhythmically against the trunks of the trees. He threw off his blanket and scuttled across the clearing until he was behind the monk, keeping her between him and the glow. Udinny remained unaware of him, unaware of anything but a pattern of light against the trees. Cahan reached around her, placed a hand across her eyes and pulled her close, shutting his eyes tight as he did. She struggled, fought, but was little match for the forester's strength. He knew her fight would not last long. It was not the monk that fought him, it was the thing she walked towards. The thing that had put into her mind the need to leave the camp. And though its draw was powerful, it was short-lived without constant interaction. When the monk stopped struggling he dragged her back to the centre of the clearing. When she started struggling again, this time trying to speak, he let her go.

"What are you doing?" she said. Pushing herself away from him, pulling her ratty old robe tighter against her body as if he was the threat.

"Saving your life," he said, picking up his pack and reaching in for some of the berries he had picked on the journey. As he did the monk turned away from him. "Stop!" She did. The warning in his voice shrill, hard. A memory of someone used to being obeyed.

"Why?"

"What is the last thing you remember?"

"Needing to pass water," she said, "and I still need to pass water so if you would allow me to . . ." she gestured towards the edge of the forest. He sat on his bedroll and put his hand out, stroking Segur's fur. The garaur let out a low, comfortable growl.

"You walked to the edge of the forest, Udinny, and then what?"

She frowned at him. "Well, then I pulled up my robe and . . ." her voice tailed off. "I . . . saw . . ." Her face twisted, and she scratched at the base of one of the tall spikes of her hair. "My older brother? But he has been dead many years . . ."

"Do you remember the lights?" he said.

She blinked, nodded. "Yes, he was surrounded by lights, they felt warm."

"It was a golwyrd." She looked blankly at him. "I will show you, in the morning when the light has risen. But for now, pass your water with your eyes down and your back to the trees." The monk sat down. Then she let out a screech and stood again, pulling up her robe to show her scrawny legs. Attached to one was a small black creature, four tentacles around a hard black body that stuck out of her flesh. The monk raised a hand to kill it. Before she could he grabbed her arm with one hand, using the other to pluck the creature from her flesh, making her yelp again as he did so. "As little harm as possible, remember? This littercrawler," he held up the thing, it waved tentacles vainly in the air, "was simply doing what it does." The monk stared at him.

"I think I may hate this place," she said.

"It has no love for us either, and it will not get easier." She looked away, shrugged.

"So, you are saying that if I kill some awful biting creature a hoard of monsters will come out of the trees for us?" He stared at her.

"If you had killed the littercrawler," he told her, "the mouthparts would have stayed in you and festered. I would have had to cut it out, you would have been unable to walk and I would have had to leave you behind while I searched for the child."

"I really hate this place," said Udinny.

"Maybe if you eat, you will feel better?" She stared at him.

"More foot meat," she said. She vanished behind a tree to pass water, then returned to kneel by her pack, sorting through it until she found some food. They ate in silence, Cahan sitting on his bedroll and the monk standing, occasionally moving to one side or the other of the clearing. He presumed she wanted to avoid another tangle with a littercrawler. By the time they had finished their food the light had risen enough for them to see and the display of the forest had faded. Cahan packed his bedroll, the monk did the same and they started to walk again.

He found no signs of the child, but knew the direction in which he was heading. Before they set out he wanted to show the monk how close she had come to death. They walked in the direction she had been trying to go in the darkness. Down a thin path, Cahan pushing aside the vegetation, causing a flurry of petals to fall from above as he struck a pipvine. Not far along the path he stopped and brought the monk forward.

"This is what you saw in the night," he said, pointing with his staff. "A golwyrd."

Udinny stepped forward carefully. He heard her swallow. The golwyrd was a pit, no wider than the outstretched arms of a tall person. If Cahan had stood in the pit it would only have come up to his hip. But in the pit the golwyrd grew sharp spikes, and from them leaked a pale green liquid that was as poisonous as it looked. Among the spikes were the bones of many animals. It had not occurred to him until that moment that they might find the child in there, but there was nothing of the people among the bones. Around the edge of the pit he could make out the tips of the tentacles that, at night, would extend and dance their hypnotic dance in the darkness.

"Ranya help us. It is not even safe to look at this place," said Udinny, staring into the pit.

"It is, but you must be careful. The draw of the golwyrd gets stronger the more you look. You will recognise the feeling now, and know to look away." He turned, and started to walk in the direction the child had been heading. "But be careful not to simply blunder into their pits, of course." The monk did not follow him immediately, then he heard her crashing through the brush behind him.

"And what of that other thing, the littercrawler?"

"Littercrawler bites are simply part of being in the forest. You must learn to live with them, it could be worse."

"Worse?" she said, but he did not answer. They still had a long way to go and he would save his strength for walking.

They carried on through Woodedge, it always struck him as odd that the deeper into the forest you went the easier the walking got. The hardest part to get through was always Woodedge, for the tree cover was not as complete and that led to exuberant growth on the lower levels of the wood. As they passed from Woodedge to Harnwood the thick carpet of fern remained, vines ran from tree to moss-hung tree and floating or flying creatures zipped around through the air, but the way became a little clearer, there were less of the strong woody shrubs. The child had not kept to a path here, which made him easier to follow, the history of his journey writ in broken stalks and bruised leaves.

Cahan would have liked to enjoy the journey; the light was clear, the air crisp but not too cold. However, the monk was incapable of silence despite his warning them that sound brought the forest creatures. If she was not talking to him about inconsequential things she was trying to befriend Segur, who wanted little of her. The garaur had always been sensible.

"Segur will bite you if you do not leave it alone," said Cahan.

"So will every other thing in this place. It seems unfair to deny your pet the opportunity." The monk continued trying to tempt the garaur with dried meat.

After they stopped for food he noticed the monk was sweating, despite the brisk air, and scratching at her leg where the littercrawler had bitten her.

"The bite itches?" She nodded. "Show me." She lifted her robe to show her leg. The littercrawler bite was red and angry looking, a large raised circle of flesh around it. "Wait here," he told her and walked back a little along the path until he found a patch of wide, dark green leaves, surrounded by bright yellow mushrooms that looked like fingers reaching from the ground. He picked some of the leaves and some of the mushrooms and took them back to the monk. Giving her two leaves and one mushroom. "Chew these into a paste," he said, "but do not swallow. Spit out any liquid." She nodded, and placed them in her mouth, making a face a moment later.

"This tastes vile," she said.

"That is why I am not doing it," he told her. Udinny looked around.

"I think I am starting to get bored of green," she said, while chewing and scratching at her leg.

"You should get used to it, there will be little else until we find the child." He left her to her chewing and scratching, then went to find and cut some flatleaves; common enough in the forest. When Cahan returned the monk still chewed.

"Ma out ist umb," she said. He nodded.

"Your mouth will be numb for an hour or so, maybe more. Numbing is one of the properties of the Allbalm leaf." He held out the flatleaf. "Spit the paste into this." She did, looking quite miserable. Then he wrapped the leaf around her leg, making sure the paste was up against the bite. He secured it with vine; tight enough not to slip but not so tight it hindered the flow of her vital fluids. Then they set off once more. One of the more pleasant effects of Allbalm for Cahan was that the monk was quiet for a time. They walked in silence for most of the afternoon. Segur hunted, bringing back four histi which Cahan gutted and skinned. As before they placed some of the fillets in their shoes. Eventually the monk got her voice back but she stayed quiet. He thought the walk was beginning to tire her, but she did not ask to rest, which was good. Cahan had no intention of stopping.

"What is that?" she said. He turned, expecting her to have asked a foolish question about something obvious, and have to say once more, "it is a tree" or "it is a bush". But this time her question was not foolish. She was pointing at a construction, three or four sticks about as long as the forester's arm. The sticks were arranged as a pyramid, the points coming together at the top. Within the triangle of sticks was a small pile of rocks. Udinny blinked. "Is it the work of swarden?" Cahan stepped past her.

"No, if it was the work of swarden we would be hiding. This is a shyun marker, no one knows why they leave them, but it means we are in their territory."

"Shyun?" repeated the monk.

"You may have heard them called forest children?"

"They murder travellers," the monk sounded alarmed.

"The shyun will kill if they are threatened. But they are more likely to hide than attack us."

"You are sure of this?" He shrugged. The Shyun were unpredictable but there was no point in giving the monk more to worry about. He kept his eyes open for more signs of the forest children, but did not see any. Truthfully, he felt a little calmed by the shyun marker. Since they had entered the forest he had not been able to shake the feeling they were being followed. He did not feel a threat from it, only a presence, though not one he was sure enough of to mention. His suspicion that it was the reborn made him not want to think about it. It would only mean more questions from Udinny.

An hour later the forest children sprung their trap.

They were passing through a clearing. The ferns driven out by short grass as thick and luxuriant as Segur's fur. When they reached the centre of the clearing, a shriek went up and a wooden spear pierced the ground in front of

Cahan. He stopped, the monk turned to run but he grabbed her by the scruff of her robe, pulling her back.

"We are attacked!" she hissed.

"Maybe," he said, looking round the clearing. Thick ferns walled them in where the grasses ended at the treeline. "We're most likely surrounded. Run and you run to them."

"My doom is upon me," Udinny fell to her knees. "Ranya, hear your servant—"

"Quiet," hissed Cahan. "That was not thrown to kill." He waited to find out if the spear was a warning, or simply badly aimed. Nothing happened. Nothing appeared. He waited, studying the weapon.

It was not a large spear, more like a toy for a child, and it did not look like it could really hurt. Unlike the spears used by the people of Crua it had not been hardened in fire, it was simply a sharp stick. But he had heard the shyun used poisons, and if so all they needed to do with their weapon was pierce the skin. The size of it did not matter.

The shrieking started again.

It was not constant, never coming from the same place twice. Quickly changing position in the ferns around them, and at the same time the plants began to shiver and shake. The forest around them coming alive with noise and movement, as if it waved its plumage at them in threat. Surrounded, as he had thought. Udinny continued her prayers, albeit quietly.

Cahan knew little of the forest children, having seldom come into contact with them. Always choosing to avoid their places when he had seen the signs. They existed in the between place of nature like the rootlings, neither intelligent like people, nor simply working off instinct like an animal. Segur knew what it thought of them: the garaur's teeth were bared and it let out a constant low growl. "Down, Segur," he said, and with a final hiss it sat at his feet. He placed his pack and staff on the ground, motioned for Udinny to stop praying and do the same.

The first of the shyun emerged from the bracken.

Calling them forest children made sense when you saw them. The creature was no larger than a child. From a distance it could easily be mistaken for one, though up close there was little chance of confusion. It had grey skin with an unpleasant oily sheen. Its head was elongated when compared to a person's, completely hairless and it had three long, black, lozenge-shaped eyes, one on each side of its head and one on the top. For a mouth it had a nest of tentacles that moved constantly, and within them a sharp beak opened and closed. Its body was clad entirely in large green leaves and Cahan could not see if they were attached as clothing or part of it. In one hand it held another of those short spears.

The shyun moved towards them in half-crouch, a few steps forward, pausing to sniff the air, another step. As the shyun's mouth tentacles moved Cahan realised it was making a noise, a low hiss like the wind passing through the branches of the trees. He felt Udinny move closer, her hand closing around his bicep.

"Chyi's breath," she said, "kill this monster before it brings its fellows down on us." She crouched, letting go of him and reaching for her staff. He grabbed her arm and slowly pulled her back to him.

"How many times must I tell you," he said quietly, "we do not act against the forest unless given no other option."

"There is a monster with a spear," hissed the monk, "I think our options are limited." Behind the first shyun two more emerged. The sound of the wind became louder, passing around each of the forest children, out into the ferns and moving around them. The lead shyun had its head angled towards Cahan. Whether it was staring at him or Udinny it was difficult to tell as its eyes were fixed and did not move, they were simply black stripes on the skull.

"Udinny," said Cahan softly, "do you have any of those sweetcakes left in your pack?"

"This is not the time for . . ."

"I once heard that the forest children liked sweet things, so go in your bag, gentle and slowly, and get out any cakes you have left." Udinny looked around. More of the shyun were emerging. There was little to tell them apart. Cahan only knew which of them had been first to leave the forest as it stood a little further forward than the others. It appeared to be considering them. The others stood quite still, heads raised to the light as if breathing it in. Udinny opened her satchel and the lead Shyun moved, fast, spear pointed at her throat. The monk shrieked but did not move. Cahan raised his hands, showing them as empty. The shyun moved its head towards him. Cahan pointed at Udinny and mimed eating.

"Do not tell it to eat me!" said the monk.

"If that is their wish, monk, there may be little we can do."

"Little I can do anyway," said Udinny, glancing up at him. He wondered if she knew more about him than she had let on. Then she found the sweetcakes, wrapped in cloth, and passed them slowly across to him. "Save some for me," she said, "they are hard to come by." He took them from her, there were six of the sticky buns wrapped in the package. He took one out and held it towards the leader of the Shyun. It took a step forward, the tentacles around its beak opening and waving. Then the sound of whistling wind around the clearing became momentarily louder and it hopped backwards. Pointing with a three-fingered hand at two other shyun. They vanished into the ferns.

"Is that good or bad?" whispered Udinny.

"We will soon find out," he said. They waited, surrounded by unmoving shyun, until the two who had gone into the bracken returned. One held sticks, the other rocks and they quickly constructed one of the small pyramids Udinny and Cahan had seen before. Then they backed away, making the noise of a gentle breeze. The first shyun whistled, a soft up and down noise, and nodded towards the shrine. Cahan stepped over, slowly and deliberately, then placed the cakes on the rocks beneath the pyramid of sticks.

"Oh no, not all of them," said Udinny mournfully. He stepped back, looking around him at the other shyun. There was a moment of excitement, the wind of their voices rising to a crescendo, then silence. The shyun vanished into the ferns and, shrine and sweetcakes aside, it was as if they had never been.

"Come," said Cahan, picking up his pack and stick.

"What was that about?" said Udinny.

"I do not know, but if it was a test it seems we passed." He walked towards the edge of the clearing and heard Udinny follow, then her footsteps stopped. She stood in front of the shrine.

"Do you think they will leave them there?"

"It is not our concern."

"What a terrible waste," said Udinny. He walked back, took her arm and pulled her away from the shrine before her sweet tooth overwhelmed her good sense.

Deep in the Forest

You remember a room, close and claustrophobic with heat. Voices, some high, some low, calling and singing across each other in a twisting intermeshing cacophony as you are brought forward. The atmosphere is both celebratory and funeral. You are elated and frightened.

Colour and darkness. Flickering light. Four great fires lit in the name of Zorir, the god's name spoken by a hundred mouths and each speaker dressed in finery, robes and cloaks of shimmering fungal colour. Before them all, on top of the three stone steps before her throne, is Saradis, the Skua-Rai, in her bearded mask, and she sings in a high discordant voice that hurts your ears. You should be enjoying this, this should be a momentous moment, a waystick on your path to greatness. All you feel is fear.

All you feel is fear.

They have put all they are into you, and all you feel is fear.

The singing and drumming and cymbal crashing reaches a peak, the monks holding your arms grip you tight because no matter how brave you say you are, they know the truth, they recognise the weakness, the fear in you. They know that you may run at any moment. That here, before Zorir-Who-Walks-in-Fire, before a god whose voice you have heard echo round the throne room, you are all too aware of your betrayal. Surely, here and now is when you are revealed, that your utter and complete unsuitability ignites you, that your doubt and your lies will doom you in the eyes of a creature that burns those who disappoint it in fiery walking pyres.

25

"Do you not find it oppressive?" said Udinny as they pushed on through the ferns.

"Find what oppressive?"

"This, the forest, it is like walking through a never-ending cave." He looked up. The trees of Harnwood were huge, some further around the trunk than two big people could reach, and tall enough they made you dizzy when you looked up. But above he could see light; the canopies of the trees never quite touched. It was as if they could feel one another. Between the treetops ran a million cracks, letting in a light that fed the ferns and small plants of the forest floor. Vines encircled trees, floatvine waved lazily as it reached upwards, moss fell in soft rivers, creatures flew or floated or crawled or ran around the great trunks. Brightly coloured mushrooms and strange fruiting bodies were everywhere, on the floor, the bark, the branches and a fair few of the animals. Through his cowl he felt the web of life stretching out around him, not through trying; it was simply a constant, an awareness of the world.

You need me.

He locked the voice away.

"Caves are dark," he said, and carried on through the ferns.

"But the weight," she said, "can you not feel it? And the eyes, everywhere, watching us. I do not feel welcome in this place."

"You are not," he said, "neither am I. It tolerates us."

"You talk like it is aware of us, what nonsen—" He turned to see Udinny had tripped over a vine of some sort and was picking herself out of the fern and leaf litter.

"Maybe it is more aware than I thought," he said. She frowned at him and he turned away to hide his smile. It was coming to the end of the second eight and the light was beginning to wane. He knew they should find somewhere to camp.

"When will we find the boy?" asked Udinny. "We seem to have been walking forever." Cahan nodded.

"I had hoped to have caught up to him by now," he said. They had been three days in the forest.

"A child with short legs should not be outpacing us." Udinny sounded out of sorts, still sulking about her sweetcakes being gone.

"The forest does not work like the land, a straight line for one is not for another." Udinny stopped. He heard it as a ceasing of the hiss of dead leaves she trailed through. He turned. "What?"

"You have made me dislike this place even more," she looked around. He shrugged but it had not escaped his notice that, since they had encountered the shyun, the monk had become less bright. As if until then she had not truly understood that they were alien to the forest, and the forest was alien to them. "It is like the forest is some vast creature, and we are travellers through its guts," she said.

"It is not such a bad way to think." The monk stared at him, and he realised how scared she must be, this woman who was so unlike him. Small where he was big, not used to this place, born in a town where the great forests were only stories told to scare people. Raised with tales of Wyrdwood gods and their dark deeds, or, worse, stories that here the Osere of below had found a way out of their confinement and hid between the trees, waiting for prey.

"I have no wish to be eaten by the forest, Cahan Du-Nahere," she said.

He had no belief in old evils; what lurked in the forest was strange, unnatural to them maybe, but it was part of this place. It fitted here, it was not some creature bent on enslaving the people to a dark will. Udinny had left her life behind in the name of a god. One who he thought all but he had forgotten, one as dead and powerless as a fallen tree. Yet, the monk had come with him, walked into the forest with only the faith of Ranya as a guide.

Brave or foolhardy? He was not sure.

Ranya was for the lost, but she told people they could be found. As he stood there, watching the monk shrink into herself and the forest begin to glow as the night creatures filled the air with their calls, words rose to his lips. "Though you think you are alone, I walk by your side, and guide each step." The monk looked up, blinked.

"You really do know her," she said quietly, "she spoke those very words to me. We are chosen, Cahan Du-Nahere. You and I." Her words made him uncomfortable. He had been told that before, and it had ended up as nothing but lies.

"Come, Udinny, let me show you how I track the child," he pointed forwards. "It may take your mind off the presence of the forest." Because she was right, it did have a presence, one he had been aware of it all his life. Even when he had been locked away in a monastery, far from the forests of his childhood, he had dreamed of these green and gloaming spaces. They had existed in his mind as somewhere to run to when the rigors pushed upon him by the trainers of Zorir became too much.

The monk and the forester walked through the breath

of trees, their presence disturbing the interconnectedness of the place, even while they tried to be a part of it. Crua had once been a land of many gods, though few that ever did anything or showed their faces. And yet here, Cahan could not help but believe they were in the presence of Crua's one true deity, the forest.

The monk stared at him, the spikes of her hair had wilted in their travels. Cahan pointed. "If you look you will see some of the fern leaves glint silver in the last of the light." She nodded. "That is where the leaves have been turned by the passage of the child."

"How do you know it is not an animal?"

"Partly because we have been following his trail. But also, animal tracks tend to weave through the undergrowth, they are looking for food and they do not move in straight lines like the boy does. And," Cahan reached out and took a tuft of wool from a thorned vine, "every so often I find material torn from the child's clothes. Animals do not dye their fur." Udinny took the wool from him and stared at it.

"How long does this silvering last?" It was a good question and she looked brighter than she had done since they met the shyun.

"About a full day, but after that the broken leaves will begin to die so you can still follow the path."

"And have some idea of time, how long it is since your quarry passed?"

"Aye," he said, and knelt, finding a broken leaf and showing her the broken stalk. "See, the sap is forming a hard crust? For this type of fern that takes about half a day."

"It is different for all plants?" She looked at him.

"Yes, and I do not know how long it takes for all of them, only the most common. To study the forest is a lifetime's work." She nodded, looking at the broken stalk. "Why don't you lead for a while, Udinny?"

"Me?" said Udinny.

"You see the path, do you not?" She nodded. "Well, follow it until you find a place that looks like we should camp there." The glow of the forest was brightening while the light from above was dying.

"I will," she said, "thank you, it is good to feel useful." They walked onwards into the gloom. Being given a purpose had filled the monk with a new energy. She strode ahead, using her stick to push through the undergrowth, not even stopping to eat berries from the trees and the few bushes they passed. He let her walk further in front of him than he was comfortable with, hoping to make her feel like she truly led. Udinny walked up a gentle incline and when she reached the top she turned and shouted back. "I see a camping place! And I long to rest!"

She ran.

"Udinny!" he shouted, for it was foolish to run towards anything in Harnwood. He chased her, reaching the top of the crest as she reached the beginning of the clear ground she had seen. His blood froze. It looked like a perfect camp, a wide clearing of undisturbed leaf litter between tall trees. The monk running towards it as fast as she could, lifting her robe so it did not impede her legs. Cahan shouted again, "Udinny, stop!" But she was not listening, only running. There was something joyful about her.

She did not know she ran towards her death.

He could not stop her.

A spear did.

Cahan did not see the thrower, only saw Udinny fall as the spear pierced the ground before her. The sudden appearance of it shocking her. She tried to stop, but was going too fast and tripped, rolling in the leaf litter. Quickly up and scuttling away from the spear on all fours. Another spear fell in front of her, forcing her back up the hill. Cahan continued running towards her. Another spear drove her towards him. When he reached the monk she was babbling. Her eyes wide with fright.

"Shyun," she said, voice slick with panic, "it is a shyun spear! They took my cakes, didn't even eat them. Now they try and kill me!"

"Come away, Udinny," he pulled her up by her arm, and backward at the same time, away from the clearing.

"They tried to kill me, Cahan!"

"No," he said, "they saved your life." Her brow furrowed, puzzled.

"By throwing spears at me?"

"By stopping you," he said. "That is not a clearing." He pointed at the leaf litter. "That is a littercrawler nest." He helped her up, walking her away.

"I have been bitten by them before," she said, "and I know how to make the Allbalm poultice, it is not—"

"Remember how we saw the plant-eating gasmaws, and the spearmaw that ate them? How they were the same creature but different?" The monk nodded. "Well, there are different types of littercrawler, Udinny." She stared at him, still confused. The spikes of her hair drooping at the ends, making her look comical in her confusion and sadness. "I will show you." He looked around and found a large rock. It took all his strength to throw it as far as the clearing and it splashed down into the centre of the large pool of leaves before them.

A moment of silence.

As if all the creatures of the forest knew what was to come and quietened in anticipation.

The centre of the lake of leaves erupted. Huge, thick tentacles as long as four or five people in a line, shooting out of it. Following the writhing tentacles a massive, black-carapaced body. Within the tentacles Cahan saw the beak of the littercrawler opening and closing, making a sound like wood shattering. The huge creature cast about with feeding tentacles as thick as tree trunks. Black ropes reaching in every direction, waving madly as if each had a mind of its own. Running along the edges of the leaf lake, twisting up and round the trunks of trees. Hungry, trying to find whatever it was that had disturbed it. When it found nothing it let out an ear-splitting shriek.

"Ranya's sore feet," said Udinny, staring as the creature continued to churn up the leaf litter in frustration. "It would have eaten me and I would barely have been a mouthful. Truly this place hates us."

"No, Udinny," said Cahan quietly, "it does not hate us. It does not care about us at all." As if to show how little it cared, the littercrawler gave up its search for food, the vast black form slowly vanishing from sight under the leaves until once more most would never know there was anything but a clearing there.

He thought he heard something behind him and turned. Nothing.

"They saved me," said the monk, standing and brushing leaves from her robe. "The forest children saved me." Then she raised her voice. "Shyun!" she shouted. "I apologise for thinking badly of you! I will never eat sweetcakes again without asking Ranya to bless you!" There was no reply but the gentle sigh of the wind between the trees. Udinny looked about, licked her lips then nodded to herself. "Maybe, Cahan," she said softly, "you should lead for a bit."

"The child's tracks led right towards that," he said, staring at the leaf litter. "You were going in the right direction."

"Our search is over then?" said Udinny sadly. He shook his head.

"No. We will camp here on the rise. In the morning when the light is better we will go around the other side of the nest. See if the child made it past."

"Past the creature?"

"The forest called to the child, Udinny." He pulled his pack off his back. "It may not care about us, but it wanted him. It has its own purposes and I doubt it was to feed the boy to a littercrawler. Though I suppose only a fool thinks they know what the forest intends." The monk took her pack off and rolled her neck to get out cricks.

"Will we be safe here?"

"I think so," said Cahan, looking around, "it seems the forest children are watching over us."

Deep in the Forest

Where are they?

Where have they gone?

The building is empty. No one is here. Yesterday the place was full. The monks were everywhere, they were watching you. They were always watching you.

And today they are gone. Everything is gone. No one is here.

No one is here?

How can that be?

Have they left you?

They cannot leave you.

You are the Cowl-Rai, chosen of Zorir. You are the one who will tip the world. You are the one who will lead the forces of Zorir.

But they are gone.

There is no one here.

And you are all alone.

26

The landing balcony for the marant was two-thirds of the way up the central spire and Kirven's legs ached from the stairs. Her guards had not come into the balcony with her, they waited inside the spire. If an assassin was committed enough to climb all this way up the outside of the spire then Kirven thought they probably deserved the kill. The spires were notoriously slippery.

But she was not worried about assassins. No one would climb up the spire simply to kill her, there were far easier ways. Even thinking of it was a flight of fancy; she was generally not given to such flights but she needed to occupy her mind with something. Otherwise she would ask the signaller behind her if the marant had returned their flashes yet and she knew very well it had not.

Before her were two spires, and between them the marant, making its leisurely way towards her. Beneath it Harnspire town, the stately circles of the spirecrown and the dirty squares of the city, the mazes of the streets, dotted with trees, dirtied by vines and partially obscured by smoke. It was better up here, she thought, fresher, the air clearer.

"Have you . . ." she began, tailing off and then restarting, "been a signaller long?" The woman behind her was surprised by the question, and Kirven wondered whether it made her appear as soft as if she had asked if they had signalled yet.

"All my life," they said, "learned it from my second-mother, can read a mirror flash the same way some would read a scroll."

"Good," said Kirven. "I like that we have the best on the spire."

"Would you like me to signal again, High Leoric?" She would, she absolutely would.

"No, it will be here soon enough." The signaller said nothing, not that sending a signal mattered as she could not ask what she really wanted to know. "Did you find my child?" The most she could ask would be, "was the mission successful?" Even a yes on that was not a definite answer telling her Venn lived. Quite like one of the Rai to tell her the mission had been successful because they had found corpses, knowing full well what she meant. Cruelty thicker than blood. Even this, their refusal to return a signal, was a sign of it. No doubt Galderin ignored her because he could and no doubt he would have some good excuse for it. A small cruelty, but one that reminded her how she must rule them, and never make the mistake of thinking them her friends or allies. They were her enemies as much as the forces of Chyi in the south were.

Though she needed the Rai on her side, some of them at least.

The marant was nearer now, she could make out passengers. Galderin, next to the goader, flanked by two Hetton, more behind him and there, bundled up, so familiar in their miserable posture, was a shape that made her heart leap. Venn. She knew them as well as she knew herself. Whatever had or hadn't happened, they were coming back. She stepped to the side of the balcony as the marant came in, so she was not accidentally pushed off. Realising as she did that this was how she would kill someone if she had to up here. A "marant accident" would be far easier than climbing assassins.

The beast came down, filling the air with its buzzing and the warmth of its body; the nausea of being near the Hetton quickly followed.

She had no eyes for the marant. Only for Venn. They looked tired, and dirty. Keeping their eyes down, not looking at her, at the Rai or Hetton around them. What had they been through? What had been done to them? The signaller tied the beast down as Rai Galderin stood and pushed a small ladder over the side, climbed off. Followed by the Hetton, she noted one was missing, then Venn struggled down the ladder and she thought of nothing else. They looked barely able to walk and she wanted to go to them, to help them, but she did not. She could not show weakness. She could not make Venn look weaker than the Rai already thought them.

"Rai Galderin," she said. "You did not answer our signals."

"Forgive me, High Leoric," a small bow of his head. "We lost our signalling mirror." Was there a smile on his face? So hard to tell through the make-up. "We did, however, bring back what you care about most." She heard a noise from the other Rai, the one still on the marant, possibly a laugh, or it could have been a cough.

"Hetton," she said, "return to your barracks." Her words met with hisses, in among them she was sure she could pick out the word "return" repeated multiple times. The Hetton trooped past, her mouth filling with saliva, her stomach threatening to rebel at their presence. They revolted her, but they answered to her and were part of her strength. Even the Rai were wary of them.

"The trion," whispered Rai Galderin as he closed with her, "will not talk about what happened, and what they do say is not the truth." She nodded. "Venn walked out of the forest unharmed, while Vanhu, Kyik and Sorha died. It seems, unlikely."

"The false Cowl-Rai?" Galderin glanced back at the trion standing behind them, not looking at her. "Venn says they were badly hurt and they escaped, that he is probably dead. I left a Hetton behind to find the truth of it."

"You do not believe them?" Galderin's face creased into something dark, something cruel.

"The details, I think they are true. But they do not tell everything." Galderin scratched his cheek. "I can find out, if you wish." She ignored that, instead stared at her child.

"What of their cowl," she whispered to Galderin, "was Vanhu successful before he died?" Galderin blinked, very slowly, and there was something deeply unsettling in the way he did it, something that reminded her Rai were no longer people in the way she was.

"Something has changed," said Galderin. He looked at her, and then he did smile, a real smile as his eyes flicked over her. "They are no longer helpless," he said. If she had ever doubted that she was right in not trusting her ally, that settled it. His opinion of her clear in that moment. She was not Rai which meant to him she was prey. The smile vanished. "But they are not Rai as I know it." He was thoughtful then. "Though I have never met a trion with a cowl before, maybe it is different for them." Kirven nodded.

"Thank you, Rai Galderin," she said. "You may go now."

27

In the morning Cahan was first to wake. There was still
the faint glow of the night forest in the air as the light
was not yet strong enough to banish it entirely. In a way
he thought himself lucky to be here, seeing displays of
beauty few would ever witness.

He scouted around the campsite, finding more of the
stick shrines of the shyun. They looked new. The forest
children had been watching over them during the night,
though he did not know why they would: Udinny had no
more sweetcakes, but Cahan had some dried meat left, which
he put on one of the shrines. Segur would have taken the
meat had he not rebuked the garaur when it made an
attempt steal it. It slunk away to hunt in a way that made
him sure it would not be sharing its catch with him today.

When Udinny awoke they made their way carefully
around the littercrawler's leafpool, giving it a wide berth.
They had witnessed how long the reach of the beast was.
More signs of it were apparent in the light, scars on the
thick trunks of trees where it had lashed them, wounds
where low-hanging branches had been ripped away. When
he felt they were opposite the bank they had set out from,

he started to look for signs of the child's passage, carefully probing the ground with his staff to make sure it was hard beneath the leaf litter and he did not stray into the crawler's pool. Udinny did the same, she learned quickly.

In the end it was her, not Cahan, who found the child's tracks.

"Here, Cahan," she said softly, "there is a scrap of wool on this thorn." She was right, and from there he could see the child's tracks going straight as a thrown spear, deeper into Harnwood.

"We should catch him soon," he said, though more through hope than surety. They set off down the track following the child. When they stopped to eat lunch he found a patch of mintwort, and showed Udinny how to weave it into a chain to wear around her neck that would keep away the smaller littercrawlers. He should have shown her that on their first night but, like all people, sometimes he knew he could be small and cruel, and though Udinny could have rebuked him for it, she did not. She only thanked him for sharing his knowledge and they sat together in silence and ate while Segur watched intently, awaiting its turn to be fed. Cahan gave the garaur some of his food and it curled up around his feet, the disagreement from the morning forgotten.

They did not stay for long, and were soon on their way once more.

Udinny let him lead.

"I had been to many places before Ranya found me," said the monk as they walked through a field under huge, bright purple mushrooms with equally bright yellow gills. The monk had come up behind him so quietly he had not heard her, "and Ranya has walked me to many places since. But nowhere has been as beautiful or as terrifying as this place."

"And we have barely seen a hundredth of it, monk, it is like the trees." He stopped and knelt down, clearing a patch of ground before him of leaves and disturbing a whole world of small creatures most barely gave a thought to. "We see the trees above us, and these mushrooms around us and we think of them as massive." Udinny nodded. "But that is barely half the forest. Most of it," he traced a root as thick as his thigh across the ground, "is hidden beneath our feet. It is the roots that create the gaps between the trees. There is a constant hidden war for water and food going on beneath the ground. We consider trees peaceful, but they are not. They are warriors, fighting a very slow war."

"I did not know any of this," said Udinny. "I see a tree and think it is simply a tree."

"It is all connected," he covered the root back up as best he could. Udinny was staring at the ground, deep in thought. She scratched at the base of one of the drooping spikes of her hair.

"Ranya's web," she said quietly to herself.

"What?"

"Years ago, when I first heard her call, I searched for knowledge of her. At first I used what money I had, books that mention Ranya are rare and expensive. Hush money had to be paid also, the wrong books and beliefs, even then, could get a person in a lot of trouble."

"Did you get in a lot of trouble, Udinny?" She nodded and grinned.

"Oh aye, my family were bottom of the spire types, rich as you can imagine but even their money could not save me." Her usual playful demeanour fell away. Something must have shown on Cahan's face and she raised a hand. "My firstmother, firstfather, trion and the rest put up with a lot from me. I spent my youth chasing excitement, and found it. Mostly in drinking, fighting and thieving."

"That is how you got your nose slit?" She nodded, her smile entirely gone.

"My friends, those who fought and thieved with me, they died screaming as the Rai took them. My family's connections saved me. They wanted me to become Rai once, but that questionable honour went to my younger sister and brother. It was their cowls my friends fed while I watched." She was staring deeper into Harnwood, but no doubt seeing somewhere else. "When I found Ranya I was quiet at first. Kept it to myself, but I could not contain my knowledge, my joy." Her smile was back. "I shouted of her on the streets of Tiltspire, and, well," she traced her staff through the dirt, the smile falling from her face and voice, "I suppose you can imagine how that went. My family gave me up rather than be shamed. Locked me in my room to await the Skua-Rai of Chyi and her troops. It was Chyi then in Tiltspire, not Tarl-an-Gig." The monk looked up at him, shrugged. "The skills I had learned as a thief saved me. I escaped by unlocking a window, then spent many years travelling, trying to find what I could of Ranya. Sometimes I would begin to lose faith, to think myself mad. Then I would hear her, this voice that brought me a peace like no other I have ever known." She sniffed her necklace of mintwort, smiled at the pleasant aroma, but when she spoke again she sounded distracted. "I found a book once, dusty and old, in the house of a rich merchant who collected things purely for the sake of owning them. In it I found mention of Ranya's web. It said, 'Those who know of Our Lady are never truly lost, for her delicate web touches all things.'" She sat down next to him, and picked up a twig, using it to flip a tiny crawling thing that was stuck on its back onto its legs. "Few are those who know her name, Cahan Du-Nahere." He knew she wanted to hear from him how he knew of Ranya, but he was not ready. Did not want to talk of the old times, before he knew the great lies people told each other. Besides, it was not the name of a god that had sent him into the forest. It was the promise from the Leoric to look after him, and the guilt he felt at failing people he should have tried to help.

"The child is making better time than I thought, monk,"

he said. Did she look saddened that he did not share his confidence with her the way she had with him? A little. "I had hoped to catch the boy before he made it to Wyrdwood." He looked up and into the canopy. The light was up and a mist hung between the trees, obscuring the way forward. "But that is not going to happen." He sighed. "I feel that somehow the forest slows us and speeds him." Cahan gently flicked a creature off his face. "There is real danger in Wyrdwood, Udinny. I had hoped to avoid it."

"Unlike the pretend danger we have faced here in Harnwood," said the monk, a smile in her voice.

"Wyrdwood is different," he said. "I do not want you to think you have to come with me."

"You think I wish to stay here alone?" The monk grinned. "You made it plain to me it was dangerous to be alone in Harnwood. That once I had committed I could not go back."

"The shyun are watching," he told her, "I found their shrines."

"They threw spears at me," she said.

"Their spears saved your life. If you stay here you should be safe enough. I will leave you some spikes so you can climb one of the trees if you need and—"

"Stop, Cahan Du-Nahere," said Udinny, raising a slender hand. "It is good of you to worry about me, truly." She turned to look out into the mist. "Ranya led my feet to you, so I will go where you go and trust to my lady to keep me safe." She grinned. "You also, Cahan, I trust you to keep me safe. Our Lady works in you."

He said nothing. Venn had also put their safety in his hands and he had let them walk back into the hands of creatures that scared even him.

"Pick up your pack then, monk," he said, "the day is wasting."

28

They walked for half a day, following the tracks of the child through Harnwood and, though it made no sense, it felt as though the forest was getting warmer. He put it down to exertion, to pushing through the leaf litter and constantly having to watch your step so you were not tripped by hidden roots or vines. Occasionally he would find the bodies of histi, caught in the snares of trapvines, and if the corpses were fresh enough he put them into his bag to deal with later.

Harnwood throbbed with life and the further into the forest they went the more life there was. Or maybe it simply saw less of people here, so was not as scared of them. The air was full of flying and floating things: clouds of biting creatures that looked like tiny marant, huge herds of gasmaws, of all different sizes and colours and shapes, a hundred shy climbing things only glimpsed in a moment. He noticed that the different types of gasmaw did not mix. The more he saw of them the more certain he became they were not the same creatures, they differed so wildly in shape and size and colour. In turn that made him wonder if the small littercrawlers that fed on blood were not juvenile forms of the large ones that hid in leafpools, but something entirely different. Though how one could know if this was true he had no idea.

Udinny was strangely quiet that morning. He let her lead again and was sure that they would soon catch the child. The signs were becoming much fresher, broken branches still leaking sap, leaves only recently turned.

The monk was in a good mood. Her constant feeding of Segur with scraps of food from her pack had begun to pay off. Now the traitorous garaur rode on her shoulders as they walked. He had never thought to see the garaur so familiar with another but, curiously, he was not as offended by it as he thought he would be. It did not stop him frowning at the creature whenever it looked his way, making Segur whine.

It was not upset enough by his displeasure to leave the comfort of the monk's shoulders.

"The garaur should walk," he said to Udinny, "it is a lazy beast and will get fat and slow otherwise. And it will weigh you down."

"I do not mind. Though the air here is warmer there is a cool breeze and Segur is keeping my neck warm." Cahan would rather his own neck were warm but did not say anything. Udinny stopped. "Cahan, do you hear something?"

"Of course," gruff words, "the forest is never quiet."

"No, something new." He stopped and listened. Heard what Udinny spoke of. A strange noise on the air, a babbling like one would hear in a market though he could make out no words and was sure that, this near Wyrdwood, they would not stumble across a market.

"Over here, Udinny," he said, keeping low and moving behind a barrier created by a fallen branch. Fungal brackets with bushy, bright orange and yellow fruiting bodies sprouting from it covered the shaded side. They squatted behind the trunk. The fruit of the brackets oozed a clear liquid that attracted flying creatures. The creatures became stuck in the liquid, then the stalks gradually curled up around them, becoming prisons for slowly dying animals. They let off a pleasant, sweet smell.

"What is it?" said Udinny.

"I do not know. That is why we are hiding."

"It sounds like people," said the monk, alarmed, "is it Forestals, do you think? They are murderers and robbers."

"I do not think so." He was trying to listen harder but could only make out the same hubbub. He tried to move aside the globes of the insect-trap fungus but succeeded only in covering his hand in sticky liquid. "Ruins of Anjiin," he said, trying to rub it off with leaves from the litter, getting his hands covered in rot and dirt.

"Look!" said Udinny, "there! Something moves!"

Through the forest came a riot of creatures, familiar, taller than the forest children, but not as tall as people. They walked in pairs, holding hands like children at play, each pair almost close enough to the one behind to be touching. Uniform from a distance but as they came closer he could see they were not the same at all. Some were furred, some were bare of skin, some had horns, some had long hair. Some were bent, some straight. They, like the gasmaw herds, were of many colours and shapes. They had adorned themselves with things of the forest: leaves and flowers, the shells of crawlers, bones and the wings of flying creatures. As they walked they kept up a constant babble, it was not language, though it was definitely communication. They moved constantly, changing partners often, babbling to each other and filling the air with a sound that could only be described as joyous. Like the fire of life bubbling over. When Cahan looked across at Udinny she was smiling.

"Rootlings," he said, unable to keep the smile off his own face.

"Happy little fellows, are they not?" She smiled. "I have only seen them miserable, caged in the towns for sport. Or in Woodedge. A fleeting presence, there then gone into the underbrush." The monk grinned at him. "I feel like joining them."

"We shall let them pass, Udinny, they are happy because they are undisturbed. It is best not to spoil that."

Udinny stared at the glad parade of creatures. "I was scared until I saw it was only rootlings." She stood before he could stop her.

The rootling procession stopped. The creatures stared at her. One began to growl. Then another, and another. Udinny stepped back. Cahan stood, the rootlings knew they were there now. No point hiding.

"Back slowly away, Udinny," he said. The growling of the pack became louder.

"But they are only rootlings," she said, unable to understand what was happening. Her mental image of the beasts as shy, hunted things running up against this mass of growling creatures before them.

"And I have told you, the deeper you go into the forest, the more dangerous it becomes." The mass of rootlings began to advance on them. "We are in their place, not they in ours." The air filled with the sound and scents of aggression. Cahan stepped back. He had never before noticed exactly how sharp rootling teeth were. How long their claws were. Here, and now, they were no longer the vaguely comical creatures most thought them. They were dangerous. Lethal. Of the forest.

Something crashed out of the brush behind them, frightened Segur from its perch on Udinny's shoulders. Before Cahan could turn he was barged out of the way by another rootling as it rushed between him and Udinny. It stopped before the mass of rootlings, favouring one leg as it stood. The rootlings studied this new arrival as it chittered and danced and chattered before its brethren.

"What is happening?" said Udinny softly. "Where did that one come from?"

"I cannot be sure," said Cahan quietly, as confused as he was amazed, "but I think that is a rootling that I saved in Harn-Larger. Maybe it has been following us." The rootling continued its dance, and as it danced the growling of the rest lowered in volume, the aggression began to leave the air and then the rootling, without looking back, joined its fellows. With that they continued on their happy way, as if Cahan and Udinny did not, and had never, existed.

They waited until the last rootling was out of sight and it was strange, when the threat was gone from the rootlings, how difficult it was not to feel the joy of them, just as they had done when they had first seen the crowd. There was something of the festival about them. It left them both in a better mood than they had been in when they first saw them.

Cahan's good spirits did not last long. The sticky sap from the trap fungus made his skin itch and turn red. He tried to keep this from Udinny, but the itching became more and more intense, eventually becoming a burning pain that felt as if he had dipped his hand into scalding water. When he looked later the skin had turned an even brighter red and his fingers had begun to swell. They walked on and he began to sweat profusely, his breathing became difficult.

He stopped.

Unable to go any further, he could not even hold his staff. Segur whined at him.

"What is it, Cahan?" said Udinny.

"It is nothing, an irritation is all." He sat heavily, sweat pouring from him, and knew what he said for a lie. Though he had pushed the cowl back in his mind it should be healing him. Something as simple as a skin irritation should not affect him. Even consciously pushing the cowl away could not stop it working on his body, it was a part of him like his skin or eyes.

Udinny squatted in front of him. He noticed she had got the sap on her, too; leaves were stuck to her hands but she did not appear to be affected in the same way. The world swam before his eyes. Udinny seemed to grow in size, her body swelling into something round and misshapen, though oddly benevolent. Her voice filled his mind. The forest scents lifted the hairs on his skin, his eyes would not stay open, the colours before him were too loud. He heard the wind scream as it was split by the trunks of trees. He started to laugh, sure he was dying. After all he had been through in his thirty and more seasons, he would die because he had moved a plant out of the way to watch some rootlings pass. It seemed a great jest for life to have played upon him.

Deep in the Forest

"Zorir!"

With that shouted name the Skua-Rai cuts her hand across the noise, stopping it dead. In the silence you have never felt so alone. You want your sister but she is not welcome here, not allowed within the inner circle, not worthy of the mysteries. You know that was where the doubt started, for is she not more than you in all things? Better scholar, better fighter, better tactician and no matter how many times you hear "but she is older, that is all". You know it for the lie it must be.

But if that was the case, then that would mean the Skua-Rai is wrong and she is infallible, she is the vessel of Zorir. She is the container of the furnace. She will be the architect of the future of Crua and she will bring the fire, put things back to how they should be.

You should not be afraid.

You should be sure and you should be confident and you should be righteous.

All you feel is fear.

"They who walk in fire!" the chant begins. "They who walk in fire! They who walk in fire!"

Forward, one step at a time with a slight sway to the walk as you have been taught. The robes of the monks shimmer and twist and change in time with the words. The crackle of the fires fills your ear, the smell of woodsmoke fills your nose, the heat makes you think you will burn. You want to run, to scream and to cry and tell them you are not ready for this, you are not the right one for this. You are a clanless boy from a farm in the north. You are nothing.

The fire that should warm you within and without only scares you because you are all too aware of the damage that fire can cause.

But still you walk forward, you are not forced, you are not struggling and fighting. You are simply doing as they say, robed in gold and red because you are weak and they are strong and they have told you, promised you, that this will make you strong as well. Somewhere deep inside you do not want to let them down. Even though . . .

Even though.

"Cahan Du-Nahere," she is looking at you, her eyes almost hidden behind the mask. Does she know? Does she know what you really think? "You are here before Zorir to receive the god's blessings."

"Receive the blessings," a hundred voices repeat.

"Kneel before me," a subtle pressure on your arms pushing you down.

"Do you take Zorir within? Do you abide by Zorir? Will you be faithful and true and if you are not do you understand the fire will eat you from within?" You nod. "Speak the words, Cahan Du-Nahere."

And how can you? How can you when they are lies, when you are confused, when you question. But even though those are your thoughts, your mouth betrays you.

"I take Zorir," you say, "and may my tongue turn to ashes if I am untrue." You wait, wait for it to happen as you speak those words knowing you do not mean them, but nothing does happen to you. All that happens is a hundred voices intone "and may my tongue become ash".

"Open your mouth, Cahan Du-Nahere," says the Skua-Rai, and a monk steps up behind you and pulls back your head. The monks holding your arms hold you tighter and panic starts to well within you.

"Receive the blood of Zorir!" shouts Saradis. And you tense up. Too late to stop now. Too late to fight. The cold of the stone cup crushing your lip against your bottom teeth. You taste blood first. Then a bitterness that makes your whole body revolt and squirm and try and escape. "Drink! Drink the blood of Zorir!" It burns, this is it, you are paying the price for your unfaithfulness, your tongue is turning to ash. You want to spit it out but there is a hand over your mouth. Another holding your nose. You have no choice. You have no choice and now the world is melting into red and orange, the fire is coming, the fire is coming and you are at the centre of it.

You are the centre.

"He will bring Zorir to us!" shouts Saradis, "and the world will burn!"

You are the fire.

You.

29

"Cahan!"

He heard his name. His head ached.

"Cahan! Do not leave me here!" Water in his mouth, tried to swallow and got it wrong. Coughed, choked. "Oh, thank Ranya! You are alive!" He opened his mouth to speak. Udinny tried to force more water down him, pushing the gourd against his lips. He looked at a hand to stop her. It was covered by a large leaf.

"What?" he coughed again and it sent shards of pain through him, "what is this?" He looked at his hand. It wasn't only one leaf, it was many, formed into a large and ugly glove.

"Well, when you passed out—"

"I passed out? How long?"

"It is the same time now tomorrow of yesterday in which you passed out." He tried to make sense of that but it eluded him.

"Do not speak in riddles, monk."

"A full cycle of light and dark." He could not see the sky. They were in some sort of structure.

"Where are we?"

"I built a hut, out of broken branches and fallen leaves."
He was about to admonish her but she shook her head, spikes
of hair wobbling comically. "I did not disturb the forest, just
like you say I should not. I simply found what it had discarded
and used that." Cahan pushed himself into a sitting position.
Within the glove of leaves his hand moved. It felt unpleasantly slimy. "Your hand swelled up," said Udinny, "and I
remembered the Allbalm you used on me. So I made some
more from what you had in your pack. But it would not stay
on your hand. So I found some leaves and sewed them
together to make a glove. I know you said not to go off alone,
but I had to get more leaves and fungus. For the Allbalm."
He slowly pulled the leaf glove off his hand to see it
caked in Allbalm mush. It no longer looked swollen.

"You went into the forest alone, for me?"

"Well, I did not fancy going all the way back to Harn
without you to watch out for me. Besides, I had Segur to
protect me." She smiled. "Truthfully, the garaur is an easier
companion than you . . ." He stared at his Allbalm-caked
hand.

"Thank you, Udinny," he said.

"What is a foul taste and a numb mouth between friends,
eh?" She smiled. "I suppose we have lost the child, though?
A whole day gone." He thought on that, then shook his
head. The world wavered and deformed. He breathed in,
waiting until his surroundings correctly constructed themselves before he spoke.

"Maybe, maybe not. It could be that we were catching
the child too quickly and the forest sought to slow us."

"You really think it makes decisions like that?"

"No, I think it is more like a nest of vutto." She looked
confused. "They are tiny shelled things that live in their
thousands below the ground. They build mounds and carve
out intricate patterns on tree bark, they hunt and even
grow food within their nest. But they are not clever, they
simply do."

"Like tiny orits?" He nodded.

"Yes, exactly like tiny orits. I think the forest is like them. Sometimes it simply does. We cannot understand why and maybe it does not know either."

"Maybe, to the forest, we are the tiny orits?" said Udinny.

"That could be." He did not like that thought much, but he did not have to think any more as Segur bounded into the shelter and threw itself at him, hissing and growling in pleasure at seeing him awake. He sunk his non-Allbalm-covered hand deep in its fur. "We should go," he said. "I would like to make Wyrdwood before the light is gone."

"You are well enough?" He nodded, then winced at the pain it caused him.

"Yes, we are not far from Wyrdwood now, I can feel it."

"I have never been there," said Udinny.

"Few have."

"Though I had never been to Harnwood before you brought me," she smiled and stood, leaning on her staff, "and now I am quite the forester." He smiled at that, and she did, too. Once he had cleaned his hand, which he did slowly to give his head time to clear, they set off once more.

Life grew thicker with every step, and louder, too. They saw many of the four-legged creatures of the forest, the crownheads and raniri that made good eating. But they were not hunting and these creatures were all too aware of them, their presence ghostly and transient. Large structures grew between the trees, like pillars of yellowy white wax. Another one of the many forms of fungus that grew in the forests. These ones were long-lived, and the waxy outer coating could be peeled off and melted into an oil that would burn well. Smaller forms grew in Woodedge. Like a lot of Harnwood, they were both familiar and unfamiliar.

The light began to wane and the trees of Harnwood become sparser, not because they were victim to some sickness, but because they were simply bigger and blocked out the light for smaller trees. Far in the distance Cahan could see a line of black. After another half-hour Udinny also saw the black line. To her it looked like a massive wall running as far as she could see in either direction.

"Look," said Udinny, sounding excited. "Is that treefall?" She ran ahead a little, the sound of her feet in the leaf litter a rhythmic crackle. "Treefall would be good news for Harn, it would make each and every person living there rich, bring in artisans from all over the north. It would rejuvenate all of Harn county." She stopped and turned to him. "We could take this gift back in the name of Ranya, she would rise again. I am sure Tarl-an-Gig would not mind if they got such a great gift. And maybe Ranya's gentle path may become one well-trodden." Cahan smiled to himself as he caught up with Udinny and stared at the massive black wall, though there was little real happiness in him as he knew he must ruin her excitement.

"I am sorry, Udinny, but that is not a fallen cloudtree, that is only the root of one." She stopped dead.

"A root?" she said.

"Aye, prepare yourself for Wyrdwood, monk," he said to her, and shifted the straps of his pack, "it is a humbling experience to meet the true gods of Crua."

30

The change between Woodedge and Harnwood was a gradual thing, like falling into a slumber; it moved from the familiar to the unfamiliar gently. The common Woodedge trees, burnwoods, shadewoods, bladewoods, the harks and the fretberries, slowly vanishing. A gradual softening of the light, a slight darkening of the air. A thickening of the trees as they became more aged. The bracket fungus getting bigger and more gnarled and old, the vegetation stranger, moss thicker, until eventually Woodedge was gone and you were in Harnwood, which was like Woodedge but in a dream where you are a child. Everything is bigger than it should be, and it makes you uncomfortable.

To move from Harnwood to Wyrdwood is more like being plunged into icy water and half drowned, waking on a strange riverbank where nothing is as you knew it and you are constantly aware you are not of this new place. There is no gradual change of the plant life, no gradual expansion of the girth of trees, no slow move from gentle dapple to gloaming. One moment you are in Harnwood, feet constantly fighting for balance against the roots and trapvines hiding beneath the leaf litter.

Then you are not.

Harnwood simply stops, as if there is some barrier where the great cloudtrees, the forest gods of Crua, have said: "No further, this is our domain," and Harnwood has bowed down to these giants of wood and leaf and done their bidding. The ground of Wyrdwood is free of leaf litter, it is a vast and ongoing plain. Studding the plains, separated by up to a day's walk, are the great trunks of the cloudtrees which reach up and up and up until even some of the lowest branches are lost in the clouds that obscure their canopies.

It is never day in Wyrdwood, apart from in those few places where treefall has scarred it. Wyrdwood moves between a darkness so total it feels physical, and a pale imitation of day, more like the moment in the second eight just before the light dips under the horizon, a golden-brown dimness.

It is easy to look upon Wyrdwood and believe nothing could live there. But, of course, this is an illusion that quickly fades. What looks like a lack of leaf litter is not, only that the cloudtrees, these monuments of wood and bark, have the smallest leaves of any of Crua's flora, more like tiny silvery pins than actual leaves. They cover the floor in a thick carpet that smells vaguely of mint. Cahan had heard the dead leaves could be brewed to make a pleasant tea, though he had never tried it. Plants grew there, of course. They looked like small things, creeping out of the litter, low to the ground. Mushrooms, everywhere – it seemed there was nowhere on Crua they did not grow – and then in the dim light were the shadowy shapes of bushes with large, flat, drab-green leaves that grew far taller than any person, but looked diminutive in the setting of Wyrdwood. Cahan knew from experience that those large, dark-green leaves were defended by long and wicked thorns.

Sound faded, no chirps or howls, only the occasional mournful low "hooo" of some beast he was unfamiliar with. But the more you listened the more you heard. It was not that there were no creatures living here, it was simply that they were quieter, as if awed into hushed tones by the great trees.

"I feel strange," whispered Udinny, "as if I have shrunk."

"It is normal," he told her as they walked slowly towards the vast wall of the cloudtree root.

"Do we go around that?" she said, pointing at the root. Cahan shook his shaggy head.

"No, there is no telling how far it runs."

"What do we do then?" said Udinny as they approached the root, its wood black, the bark smooth and warm to the touch. It was as tall as five people standing on each other's shoulders.

"We go over." He went down on one knee and let his pack fall to the floor. Removing rope and a small grappling hook.

"This does not look enjoyable," said Udinny.

"There are old nubs, from where side roots have broken off," he pointed at the wounds on the root, "you can use them as footholds while you climb."

"I suspect our speed is going to slow to a stop if we have to climb roots all the way through the forest."

"We will not," he said, "most cloudtree roots are buried deeply. The tree this is attached to," he pointed along the root, "must have moved a little, pulling the root out of the ground."

"How did the child get over this?" Cahan shrugged but Segur answered the monk's question, growling and hissing at a spot at the bottom of the root where there was a tunnel, dug by some animal.

"He didn't," said Cahan, "he was probably small enough to go under it. Orits will have dug that, they are plentiful in Wyrdwood. They nest in the bracket fungi."

"I have heard orits eat people," said Udinny, staring at the hole as Segur vanished into it.

"Given the chance, but they are slow and only prey on

what is easily caught." Udinny hmmed to herself, evidently displeased with his answer. He whirled the grapple around his head and threw it up and over the great root. Once it had caught he tested it, leaning back and putting his full weight on it to make sure the hold was good. "You go first, Udinny."

"Why me?" said the monk.

"Because it will be easier for me to catch you if the grapple does not hold, than for you to catch me." She nodded at that and took the rope. Usually he had found that skinny, wiry people were good climbers but Udinny was the exception to the rule. She made climbing the root look like an impossible task, one of the great labours of the old ones. Finally, with much grunting and the odd yelp, she was standing on top of the root. Looking proud of herself, though he had no idea why.

It took him only a few moments to get up onto the root. The monk squinted at him. "I thought you had been a thief?" he said to her.

"Yes," said Udinny, "but everything valuable in the spire cities is on the lowest levels. There was little climbing involved." She stared out into Wyrdwood. "I did not expect it to look so empty," she said, "or to be so quiet."

"It is quiet," he told her, "but not empty." She turned back to him, looking a little alarmed. "Can you get down alone, or do you want me to go first so I can catch you if you fall?"

"I am not entirely incapable, Forester," said the monk. She threw the rope over and, before he could stop her, began to lower herself down. The grapple, still set for a rope on the other side, came loose and Udinny fell to the ground, landing with a thump and a groan, knocking all the air out of herself.

"You are a little incapable, though, monk," he said from the top of the root. He was sure Udinny would have liked to come back with some retort but she was struggling to breath. Segur helped her by licking her face as Cahan climbed down. By the time he was at the bottom the monk was standing again. "Are you hurt?" She shook her head.

"Only my pride," she dusted the tiny pinleaves off her robes. "Let us get on, unless you wish to bask in my humiliation further."

"It is tempting," he said, "but we have a child to find." With that they set off into Wyrdwood. As they walked through the gloom signs of life became more apparent. The strange constructions of the orits, angular, soft-looking towers. Though they were not soft, they were hard to the touch. Orits made them by chewing up dead wood and then regurgitating the pulp, slowly building these towers over many years. What purpose they served no one knew. He watched Udinny marvel at them, then marvel even more when they came to their first cloudtree trunk, and how long it took for them to walk around the base.

"Does this thing never end?" she said.

"I measured one out once," he told her, "over three thousand paces to walk all the way around."

"That is half the distance from your farm to Harn," said the monk. She stopped and looked up. The huge trunk was ringed with giant bracket fungi that stuck out like steps. The bark itself was thick, prized by carvers throughout Crua. It grew upon the trunk in creases and whorls, almost like writing. It was not hard to imagine the cloudtrees had been graffitied by some ancient and massive race. Their size made them seem impossible, and it fired the imagination. Udinny was looking up the trunk, and stepped back, fear on her face. "It is falling!" she shouted, starting to run. Cahan grabbed her.

"It is not. It is an illusion created by looking up at it. The cloudtrees are so tall your mind cannot understand, it makes you dizzy and because you know your feet are on the floor and you are not moving, you think the tree is falling. We are quite safe." The monk did not look convinced, but they carried on their way and the tree did not fall and it was not mentioned again.

They saw their first orits later that day. Strange-looking creatures. Four legs, encased in hard shells, extended from the round, gleaming shell of their body. They came in every colour you could imagine, reds and blues and blacks. These ones were a deep purple. Their sensory organs, a ball of tentacles located on top of their round shells, were never still and the four tentacles beneath their bodies were just as restless, picking up objects from the leaf litter and transporting them to the hard mouthparts hidden beneath the shell. They moved in an odd, stumbling way. Almost like they were constantly falling and trying to keep their balance. But Cahan knew they could move efficiently if they wanted. Should they choose to pursue they were relentless, not quick, but never tiring – though they were seldom interested in people unless you interfered with them.

They decided to take a wide route around the orits.

"They do not look dangerous," said Udinny. "They are no taller than your knees. I had thought they were bigger."

"Some are," Cahan told her, "these are gatherers, the protectors are larger but I don't see any of them. Even gatherers' legs end in sharp spikes and the shells are hard as rock, they can spray a liquid which burns the skin." There was a strange noise, like someone playing a horn badly, and Cahan pointed at a group of orits attacking one of their own number.

"What are they doing?"

"That one must be wounded, they drive away the wounded and the sick. Those ones are often dangerous, stumbling lost around the forest and striking out at anything close."

"You are very talkative, today," said Udinny as they carefully made their way around the foraging orits, making sure they went the opposite way to the wounded creature. It was true what Udinny said, he was speaking more than he had in years. Partly because he was becoming used to the monk, but also because this deep into the forest his cowl was more apparent to him. It had lain almost dormant in Woodedge and Harnwood, but now it felt like it was moving beneath his skin, trying to escape. Its voice a constant whisper on the edge of his perception, words he could not quite make out. The orit in particular seemed to set it off, and they saw many more of them in many different colours. At one point Udinny stopped to watch a line of them walking straight up a cloudtree and vanishing into a hole in one of the huge brown and white bracket fungi. As they stood there the whispering in his mind became louder, clearer.

. . . *need you need you need me* . . .

So he talked, spoke of the orit, of coming to Wyrdwood to hide when he had felt unwelcome in the world of people. Not only because he was clanless, but because of the cowl, though he did not speak of the cowl to Udinny.

Night came.

So sudden and complete, it was as if someone had put a bag over their heads. Udinny, who was a little ahead of Cahan, stopped dead. He did the same.

"Cahan?" she said, her voice trembling.

"Here, Udinny," he told her. In that moment they could have been the only two living creatures in existence, the darkness was so total, and so silent. It was not hard to imagine that the creatures who lived here, and experienced this every time the light set, were still surprised by the totality of each night.

"I am scared, Cahan," said the monk. "It is too dark. I do not know how or where to move. This is what it must be like to be dead."

"Wait a moment, Udinny," he smiled to himself, for unlike the monk he knew what was to come. "You are about to receive a gift few will ever have."

"If you mean the forest will glow, I have seen it in Harnwood, every night."

"Not like this, Udinny," he said, and smiled in the darkness, "not like this."

The forest exploded.

It was the lightshow of Harnwood, but amplified by a thousand. Light running up the trunks of the cloudtrees, light running across the forest floor. Flying creatures zipping through the air leaving bright lines that slowly faded into the black. Huge clouds of flying things gathered together, only to erupt into great flowers of colour when disturbed by predators. Far above larger creatures floated, bright tendrils hanging down, either as warning or as a lure. So much life that had been hidden during the gloom of the day was now before them, a pulsing, twisting rainbow of constant effervescence so bright they could see the wonder on each other's faces.

"Truly, though I have met with a fear on this journey like few other times in my life," said Udinny, staring up, "I think Ranya blessed me when she placed my feet on the path we share, Cahan Du-Nahere."

"Well, it is beautiful right enough, and look," he pointed ahead of them. Running through the leaf litter as clear as if they had been painted onto the floor, was a line of footprints.

"We are not camping yet, then," said Udinny, the grin on her face distorted by the ever shifting and changing colours of the forest light.

"No we are not, we follow the child and sleep when we can walk no more."

31

Cahan woke to the dim light of day in Wyrdwood. A light dew had settled upon everything and soaked into his clothes, making him both cold and damp. It was not the cold and damp that had awoken him. Cold and damp was simply part of life. It was Udinny's snoring that had pulled him from the depths of sleep. He prepared food, dried meat, nuts and berries, while he waited for the monk to wake. Udinny continued to snore so loudly he thought every creature in Wyrdwood must know they were there. With a wave he sent Segur over and the garaur woke her with its rough tongue. The monk's spluttering and gasping had him turn his head away to hide his amusement.

"Away, cursed creature!" spat the monk, sitting upright. "I was in the midst of an excellent dream where I was the rapt attention of a first-, second- and thirdwife, and the required amount of husbands waited in case they tired." The garaur whined and cowered down before Udinny, hiding its sharp face beneath small paws. "And two trion," added the monk. Then Udinny scratched between Segur's ears. "Well," she said, "I suppose I cannot blame you for finding my face attractive as well. It is a very fine face."

"Food, monk," he told her. She came over and picked up the leaf he had placed her food on.

"Ah," said Udinny, "feet meat and nuts, I have been looking forward to this." She began to eat. "Do you think we will find the child today?"

"Today? I hope so," she looked at him as she shovelled nuts into her mouth with one hand, "we have been catching up with him quickly since we entered Wyrdwood. I think the forest wants us to find him now."

"It makes me uncomfortable when you talk like that," said Udinny. The cowl shivered beneath his skin. Did he see a grey figure out of the corner of his eye?

"Best not to think, then," he told her, threw his empty leaf away and combed fingers through his beard to remove any food that may have been lodged there.

They set off once more. The first part of the journey much the same as the last, trekking onward, avoiding the ever-present orits as they scavenged the forest floor to build their strange towers. Segur took delight in baiting the creatures; the garaur would run up to them, growling and hissing. If they did not react it would bite at their legs until the orit raised itself up on two legs, exposing the pulsing mouthparts and feeding tentacles on the underside of its body, then slammed down the sharp points of its feet. The garaur was never in any danger from them; it was far too quick, and they never followed it when it ran away.

It was also never foolish enough to bother the larger, protector orits. Nevertheless, Cahan forbade the game and Segur chose to go and sit around the neck of Udinny, occasionally giving him baleful looks from its big brown eyes.

"Light!" said Udinny, pointing ahead at a faint glow. As they approached it became almost blinding. Their eyes had become used to Wyrdwood gloom.

A clearing, far ahead of them, where at some distant point in time one of the forest gods had fallen. Cahan could not imagine the violence of such a thing. When a tree is so tall it took you most of the morning to walk around the base came down, the destruction and noise of its fall must be apocalyptic. The fallen cloudtree was long gone. It had probably come down many generations ago and was no longer even a memory. Certainly, Harn no longer showed any profit from it. As far as he knew, once a cloudtree fell it was gone forever; nothing ever grew in its place and he had never heard of anyone seeing a cloudtree sapling. There was something melancholy in that, to know even these gods of the forest may die.

He squinted as he approached the bright clearing. A meadow had sprung up where the tree had once been. Long grass swayed in the breeze and the temperature dropped now they were no longer insulated by the cloudtree canopy.

"Ranya bless me, but I have missed the light above," said Udinny, raising her face to bask in the brightness and reaching out to grasp a handful of grass. "It is good to be between land and sky once more."

"Come, monk," said Cahan, "and keep watch, the grasslands of Wyrdwood are dangerous places."

"Is any place here not dangerous, Cahan?"

"No, monk, it is all dangerous."

"And what horrors await us here?"

"Swarden, among other things." Her eyes widened and she hurried after him.

"I have heard tell of swarden," said Udinny, staring across the grassland, "and hope you will say they are 'not really dangerous', like the orits."

"No," he said. "If we see swarden we hide in the grass until they are gone. They are not like the orits, not at all."

"What are they like, then?" said Udinny, hurrying to keep up.

"Something other, something unnatural." He grasped his staff more firmly and they carried on walking until Udinny pointed out a shape rising from the grasslands ahead. The monk had sharp eyes. What rose from the grass was not unlike the towers of the orits, but it was built from branches and bits of wood and bush rather than chewed-up matter. It resembled a spire of the spire cities in its shape. A central tower that was tall, maybe as tall as five people, and he thought there must be a good view from the top, though no one in their right mind would climb it. There was nothing of it that spoke of permanence or skill in the building. Around it a ring of smaller towers, half built and seemingly forgotten midway through construction.

He pulled Udinny to a stop. It looked like something moved on the structure.

"Down," he said quietly. "That is a swarden tower, they do not put up with intruders. We will use the grass to mask our passage and go as far around as we can." The monk nodded, her face drawn and worried-looking. He no doubt wore a similar expression.

He had seen swarden in action once; he did not want to see it again.

It was backbreaking, to crawl around the tower with their heavy packs. At the halfway point he could see the figures on the tower more clearly, not enough for detail. They were only shapes moving over the scaffold of branches. Unlike people they did not stay upright, but climbed like animals, head facing whichever way they were going, up, down, left or right, and he found it disconcerting, uncomfortable to see. Cahan counted eight swarden. They frightened him but he kept it to himself as they crawled on.

Udinny remained blessedly quiet.

They stopped at a track in the grass, one that had been flattened by the passage of feet, though not the feet of people. Udinny crawled over to him and was about to move through the wall of grass and across the passage when he stopped her. She looked at him and he shook his head.

"Listen," he said. She frowned. A moment later she heard what he had, a sound like leather clothing squeaking as it rubbed against itself. Rhythmic, coming closer. "Swarden," he said softly. "We wait here and hope they pass."

The gradual approach of the swarden was like a growing weight on him. If he closed his eyes he heard the screaming of a warrior he had once seen them capture. Saw them hacking at them, no thought to killing swiftly, their actions mechanical and unthinking. It had taken the warrior a long time to die.

When the swarden came it was in another group of eight, walking in single file. He thought of the swarden as the soldiers of the forest, brought into being for some unknown purposes. Perhaps they, like the reborn, were the work of some long-ago Cowl-Rai. Certainly, the presence of swarden was something he felt as much in his cowl as he saw with his eyes. Some still held swords in their skeletal hands.

"The dead walk," said Udinny. Terror in her voice. He shook his head for it was not true: the swarden were no reborn who retained what it was that made a person real. They were only remnants, skeletons animated by Wyrdwood. Where people were moved by muscle and flesh, the swarden were moved by forest grasses wrapped around their bone frames. It was the vegetation that made the leathery sound, the squeak of grass against grass as the group of swarden marched past. Moss-clad bone glimpsed through layers of dying greenery. Few of the swarden still had their jawbones, they had been lost long ago. Most were clearly old corpses, the bones browned and splintered with age. One was white-boned. New. That fascinated him; whatever it was that created them was clearly still working.

The line of swarden marched past, the last of them limping and had fallen behind, the grass around its hips frayed and broken. It stopped in front of them, sightless skull moving from side to side. Took a step closer. Cahan covered Udinny's mouth lest she squeak in fear and give them away. The mouldering skeleton stood, sightless eye sockets looking into the grass, and he found himself holding his breath. The swarden stood there for a long time. Then a bony hand reached out and grasped a handful of long grass, ripped it from the ground and pressed it against its leg. Cahan watched as the grass, like a living creature, wrapped itself around the swarden's hip and thigh, joining with what was already there. Then it turned and continued on its way, the limp gone. They waited, hidden, his hand clamped around Udinny's mouth until he was absolutely sure the swarden would not come back.

"Well," he said quietly, taking his hand from her mouth, "I seem to remember you wished to see swarden, Udinny, are you glad you did?" She nodded, a sheen of sweat across her brow.

"Ranya tells us no experience is ever wasted," she whispered back. "But at the same time I am not sure it was the best-considered wish I have ever made."

"I will not disagree," he said, then glanced down the path of grass. "I think it is safe to continue now."

When they were far enough from the swarden tower to stand again, the line of dark forest between the huge cloudtrees looking no more than a pace away, such was their size, they stopped. His back ached from constantly being bowed over and his head ached from keeping alert to the possibility of more swarden. Udinny's face was covered in small bites from the creatures that lived in the grass. No doubt his was the same.

They continued through the meadow, enjoying the light until they re-entered the gloom of Wyrdwood. They walked without incident until late in the second eight when Udinny grabbed him, pulling him to a stop and raising a trembling hand, pointing back the way they had come.

"A giant," she whispered, "hiding in the bushes at the base of the cloudtree." He turned, slowly and carefully. Her words may have sounded foolish but in Wyrdwood all was possible. He stared at the cloudtree trunk, a soaring wall of living wood, and at its base he saw Udinny's giant and smiled.

"Some call rootlings forestmen, Udinny," he said, "but that is a real Forest Man." The figure would be, if standing, maybe as tall as three people standing on each other's shoulders. But it did not stand, it remained slumped where it was as if it had fallen asleep against the vast tree. "It is only a statue," he said. "Would you like to look at it more closely? It is quite safe." The monk nodded and they walked over to the Forest Man. Up close it did not appear as much like the people it did from a distance; its carved armour was of an old design, long lost to them. Its face strangely stretched and the beard stylised, in a way that reminded him of the mask that Saradis, Skua-Rai of Zorir, had worn when she was about her official duties. The Forest Man's hands were odd also, having only two fingers, and those fingers shorter and thicker than looked right.

"Who carved this, all the way out here?" said Udinny, staring up at the Forest Man. "And why?"

"I do not know, nobody does. They are ancient, but there are plenty of them and all different." He touched the wood of the Forest Man; it was cold. "They are of an older time, from when the spire cities were raised and Iftal ruled in Great Anjiin. Or that is what I was told. Some are so old that the cloudtrees have grown over part of them, and they appear to drown in the wood." Udinny stared at the statue.

"We should go, Cahan," she said, "it makes me uncomfortable. People should not be so large." She shook herself, like Segur after a rain shower, and turned to walk away. "It is unnatural," she shouted back and he hurried after her before she got too far away, so he could point her in the right direction.

It was not long after they came across the Forest Man that they found the child.

32

It began with a light.

Not the harsh light of the treefall meadow. Not the bright multi-coloured lights of night in Wyrdwood. This was different, a suffused glow in the distance, a warmth within the gloom. The broad, dark-green-leaved bushes crowded the light, and grew thickly, some no higher than Cahan's knee, some far higher than his head.

They approached carefully, warily, using the bushes as cover until they had a better view. At first the light was like a hearth fire seen from outside a house after a cold day in the field, it promised warmth and welcome, drew them in. Though Cahan knew Wyrdwood well enough to know such feelings could not be trusted. Then it became brighter, more intense as they neared. No longer the glow of a fire, more constant, and rather than flickering or shining it seeped out into the air as if it were alive.

Closer.

Night fell. The abrupt darkness of Wyrdwood. As if in response the light changed again, almost painful to look at now. Cahan heard a hum, a sharp and painful noise, cutting into his head. Then it was gone, and once more the light was soft, gentle and warm. Some property of it blocked out the spectacular lightshow of the forest. He wanted to walk towards it, and within him the cowl ceased its shifting and aching that had been his constant companion. In the light he found a peace his life had been sorely lacking. He felt, for the first time he could remember, no fire within.

Had it not been for Udinny, standing and blindly stumbling towards the light, just as she had when they encountered the golwyrd, he would have done the same. But her actions disturbed him. He remembered the dangers of the forest. How nothing here was his friend. Grabbed her arm. Pulled her back.

"No," she said, "my home. I want to go home—" He covered her mouth, for a moment she fought. Then her eyes cleared and she stopped struggling. He let go. "Was it a golwyrd?" she said. "I fell for it again?" Cahan shook his head.

"No," he whispered, "this is something different. Stronger." He felt the draw of the light, the offer of peace within it, but the distraction of Udinny had broken the spell and he could stand against this feeling now. "Be ready to grab me if I act strangely," he said to the monk. Then he looked around the side of the bush towards the glow in the forest. Felt the same peace, the retreating of the furious heat of anger that lived deep within him, but he did not feel like he would lose himself this time. It felt more like a test. He slipped back behind the bush. "I think it is safe to go nearer. If you feel drawn, tap my arm." Udinny nodded her face stricken, as though she had suffered some deep and profound loss.

They moved closer; he was impressed by how silent the monk could be when she put her mind to it. When they were near enough to see the glow directly, a lance of fear passed through his body, as white and cold as if he were pierced by an icicle. The brightness obscured most of what was before them, but it showed enough. Three figures in the night, sharp-edged, impossibly tall, heads topped with branching horns.

"Iftal help us," said Cahan. "The boughry have him."

"Boughry?" She looked at him, frightened.

"Look," he said, moving a branch so she could see, as that was easier than explaining.

"Osere below!" Her eyes opened wide. "We should get away." To tangle with the boughry was death, and a strange and slow death at that. Why the boughry did the things they did none knew. They skinned people alive and left them screaming, hung from trees in Woodedge. They hacked off limbs and left bodies squirming. Put out eyes and returned the blind to their villages. And no matter how mortal the wound, those taken by the boughry lived longer than they should, died only slowly. It was not foolish to be frightened of the boughry. When the monks of Tarl-an-Gig talked of old gods, and the terrible things they did it was the boughry, the Woodhewn Nobles of Wyrdwood people thought of. They were not of the people, and their ways could not be understood. He moved a branch aside once again, looked harder, trying to pierce the light.

"The boy is there," he said, "the boughry are gathered round a taffistone with him before it." He breathed deeply. They should go, he knew that. Maybe not too long ago he would have turned around and done that. But in his mind he saw the face of Venn, braver than he was, giving up their freedom for his life. In his hand he felt the remembered shape of a toy crownhead. And also something of his journey with the monk would not let him leave: it had changed him and he did not understand how or why.

Maybe it was that the monk thought him brave, when all his life he believed he was only angry, scared or selfish.

He looked around, expecting in this moment of danger to see the grey shapes of the reborn women. At the same time, knowing they would not be there. Not because of the warning given to him when he was hurt and sick in his house. But because this was not their place, something else ruled here and they were not welcome.

He took a deep breath.

Sometimes there was no real choice. He could act or run away, forever pursued by a guilt more persistent than any dead, grey warrior.

"Wait here, Udinny." He let out a low whistle to call Segur and the garaur came bounding over, its jaws slightly open as it panted. Cahan ruffled its fur, then picked it up and put it in Udinny's arms. "Hold on to Segur and do not let it go, no matter what. If the boughry take me, then you run and take Segur with you. Do you understand?" She nodded. "Tell the Leoric we did our best but the child was dead, the body eaten by beasts."

"Not that the boughry took him?"

"It is kinder not to let her know." Udinny nodded, then glanced back towards the glow.

"Can we not wait for them to leave?" said the monk. Cahan licked his lips and tried to still the hammering of his heart.

"No, Udinny. Who knows what they may do to the child. I have heard no kind stories of the boughry."

"But still, you will go to them."

"The forest has led us here, Udinny. It has played tricks, slowed us and sped us on. I must believe that is for a reason, not simply to make me a game for its darkest creatures." Wise-sounding words, but they both knew by now that Wyrdwood could not be understood. Had others thought the same, before meeting their end with the boughry? The monk stared at Cahan, the spikes of her hair wilted by their journey, her face drawn and sad.

"Ranya brought us here, Cahan," she said, "it is for a purpose, not simply to sacrifice us. I believe that." She reached up to take hold of his arm but he moved away, looked towards the light once more.

"Do not worry for me, Udinny." He put a hand on her

shoulder, tried to look more sure of himself than he felt. "I am better able to handle these creatures than you may think." Beneath his skin the cowl woke.

You need me.

She looked at him, smiled to herself.

"You mean your cowl, Cahan Du-Nahere." He stopped then, completely still.

"You knew?" She nodded.

"I met many with cowls when I lived in Tilt," she said softly. "The Rai often visited, there is something unmistakable about cowl users that you learn to recognise." She smiled to herself. "You are different from the Rai in many ways, gentler, but it is still there."

"And yet you never asked me to use it to save us from danger."

"You did not volunteer to, and I presumed you had your reasons. Ranya says follow your path, but do not force others onto it." He let go of Udinny's shoulder, and touched her on the forehead, leaving a small muddy mark in the centre of it. He did not know why.

"Ranya guide you, monk," he said.

"And you too, Cowl-Rai," she replied.

"That title is . . ."

"A mark of respect, once, in the old books," said the monk, "and, renegade that I am, that is how I use it, in respect." For a moment, he wondered how much she knew. Then decided it did not matter as, for the first time in as long as he could remember it did not feel bad to hear that title from another's mouth. He gave her a small nod. Then turned and crept out past the edge of the bush they had hidden behind, moving from bush to bush towards the light. The boughry remained obscured; he saw only shadows cast by the light. Glimpses of movement.

Silhouetted in the light emanating from the large, egg-shaped taffistone, was the boy Issofur. Sitting on the floor, playing with the leaf litter and laughing to himself.

You need me.

It was tempting to listen to the voice of the cowl in that moment. Cahan felt very alone. He could let the life of the forest flow into him. Here in Wyrdwood, near the taffistone, he could feel life flowing around him in a way he never had before. Strength and power and life filled the air. It was as if the great trees were conduits for it. He could open himself and the cowl to the energy flowing around them and they could go together against the boughry in fire and water and power. He could take apart these creatures. Burn them away with a thought. What better reason to use the cowl than to save a child? What better reason to become the fire?

He wanted it.

He hungered for it.

It burned within him, a core of anger and fury and resentment that was so much a part of him he could not imagine life without it. An end to fighting his past, and for the best of reasons.

You need me.

And yet.

And yet and yet and yet.

What had he said to Udinny when first they entered the wood? That to move against the forest was to wake its ire. *Harm not and you will not be harmed.* And, throughout their journey, he had been unable to lose the feeling that they were led, slowed and speeded as needed. In pursuit of the boy, yes. But led. He had talked of the forest as something alive.

Was this a test?

Like the light?

You need me.

For what and why he did not, could not, know.

The boughry moved before him, sinister shadows within a strange light. Great rays of it pierced the air.

You are the fire.

Breathe, slowly.

In and out.

In and out.

He laid down his staff.

Stood.

Walked out before the Woodhewn Nobles. Held his arms out to show he brought no weapon. Imagined he heard Udinny gasp behind him as he walked forward. Became another shadow within the boughry's light.

"Woodhewn Nobles of Wyrdwood!" he shouted. It felt like screaming into the fiercest circle wind.

Then it didn't.

Life stopped around him. The constant noise of the forest paused. The light, up until then its rays shifting and spinning, became still. He saw the boughry, truly saw the boughry, for the first time. Three of them, standing around the taffistone. Impossibly thin. Taller than him by half of his own body, and he was tall for the people of Crua. Each of the boughry, head and hands aside, was covered by a long robe and whether the robe was moss, or some material or even part of their body, he could not tell. Their hands were bundles of twigs, yet smooth and supple, like the willwood hand he had seen on the jailer in Harn-Larger, in what felt like a lifetime ago. The boughry had no eyes, or ears or nose, instead they had skulls, long and slim like those of crownheads. Instead of curling horns, branches strewn with moss grew from the skulls. Not one of the boughry was symmetrical. Each the same but different from the other, as each reaching branch on their heads was different from its counterpart. One boughry was bright, as if made of light, another was gauzy, barely there like the finest of mosses hanging from a tree bough. The third was tall, and thick and strong, like a trunk. The air around the forest nobles smelled of loam and leaf and flower, thick with the fecundity of the forest. And though they towered above him, and though he had heard so many dark stories of them, he felt no threat. At the same time he knew he was not safe. He was in the presence of something more powerful than he could understand. His idea of pulling power from the air and destroying them had been childlike and naive. They were as immutable as the cloudtrees, and just as old, maybe older. If they wished to crush him, they could do it without a thought.

"Crua," a voice in his head: crackling leaves and cold breezes. "What brings you before us, Crua?"

It was not a question, though it also was. It had something of rote to it, like a litany, like the words he had heard the monks intone before the altar of Zorir when he was a child.

"The boy," he said. "His mother asked me to find him, and to return him." The boughry, as one turned to look at the child, as if they had not noticed him until that point.

"Have you killed and burned in our realm?" This time it was a question. "Have you left the paths and taken without permission?"

"Not knowingly," he was shouting again, caught in the gale of their attention. His hair whipping round his face. "Or meaningfully." Silence. The light began to turn again. The atmosphere hung heavy with danger.

"You would take that which we have claimed." Rocks falling down a cliff edge, water escaping a wetvine. "And to what reward?" He did not know if they meant what reward he would get, or asked for something in exchange. He hoped they did not require some gift, he had nothing to give.

"I receive only goodwill for this," he said. The boughry considered him, the smooth domes of their foreheads focused on him. "And offer it in return."

"A worthy champion," said the voice in his mind. "But what is taken must be replaced."

"Then I . . ."

"Take me." He turned. Udinny stood behind him.

"Monk," Cahan hissed, "I told you that—" She stepped forward, addressing the boughry, not him.

"I have lived a life," she said, loud, but he could hear the fear there, "the child has not. I have followed the path, hoping for purpose where I have had none." She stepped forward again. "I see now, there is no purpose without sacrifice."

"Udinny . . ." He tried to step forward, found himself unable to move. With a hiss like a branch breaking the nearest boughry, the one that was like gauze, moved. One moment near the taffistone. The next in front of Udinny, towering over her. Its form shimmering as though seen through great heat.

"You know of what is done to those we take?" the boughry's voice as brittle and foetid as a rotting log. Udinny nodded.

"You offer yourself of your own free will?" said the voice of another, sharp as an icicle hanging from a tree.

"I do. My lady Ranya led me here. I will continue to walk the path." Did he imagine it, or at the mention of Ranya did the whole forest shiver? Did even the cloudtree shake a little? He was not sure, he knew only that he shook. That he shook for Udinny, for what might happen to her. That he shook in fear for himself as he stood before creatures far more powerful than he. That he shook in fury, as even his tongue had been stilled and he could not demand they take him.

"We accept," came the voice in his mind. Udinny turned to him, gave him a small, sad nod and small, sad smile. Then she turned back to the boughry towering above her. He did not know what he expected. Death? Blood? Screaming?

There was none of it.

The boughry stretched out its hand and touched Udinny on the forehead, on the spot of dirt he had left there. In that moment she changed, she did not look frightened or lost or sad. She looked full of wonder. "We know your name," came the voice, "and we will call." The light of the taffistone went out. The boughry vanished and the utter darkness of the forest enveloped them.

"Cahan?" His heart leapt at Udinny's voice.

"You are alive?"

"Aye, you also?"

"Aye." Then the child let out a cry and the forest lit up with its explosive display of life. He saw Udinny before him, the child in her arms. He found himself unable to do anything but laugh, full of sudden and fierce joy, so glad that the boughry had not taken this woman who, he had only realised on the point of loss, he called friend.

Deep in the Forest

You are running but you are not running fast enough.

You are running through the monastery, running from room to room. You cannot see for tears. You cannot breathe for panic.

Where are they?

Where have they gone?

They have gone.

The building is empty. No one is here. Yesterday they were here. Yesterday the place was full. The monks were everywhere, they were watching you. They were always watching you.

And today they are gone. Everything is gone. No one is here. How can that be?

Have they left you?

They cannot leave you.

You are the Cowl-Rai, chosen of Zorir. You are the one who will tip the world. You are the one who will lead the forces of Zorir.

But they are gone.

There is no one here.

Escape.

You cannot escape. You have a destiny. There is a prophecy. You are a thing of power. They will come back. They must come back. You run up to the tall tower. From the tall tower you can see everything, you can see the edges of the world and the slowlands where people die for forever and a day.

You can see smoke.

You can see fire.

You can see soldiers. Soldiers making their way up the front path to the monastery. They hold flags of blue. They hold banners that name a god you have never heard of, "Tarl-an-Gig", and in that moment, you knew something terrible had happened. That despite all you had been told, you were not what they said you were. They lied to you. You are not the one to tip the world. Zorir will not lead the world in fire.

The Cowl-Rai has risen. That is why the monks have gone. How often did you hear them say that those who worshipped other gods, who would not bow would die. And Zorir would never bow.

The monks have run.

The soldiers are coming.

They are coming for you.

Run.

You run.

33

Kirven's legs ached. So many stairs, and her head also ached from walking through the upper chambers of the spire. She rarely did it more than once in a day because she knew how it affected her, but on this day she had been unable to stop herself. Once Venn had landed they had spoken to her only to ask to return to their rooms and she had let them. Watched them walk away while the Rai spoke to her and she spoke to them, but what they talked of she could not remember.

She had returned to her workroom as if in a daze. High, as if drugged, astounded that her child, her precious, wonderful child was back and alive after coming so close to a creature as dangerous as Cahan Du-Nahere. She did not generally read of the false Cowl-Rai, for they were of little interest to her. Let the hunters do the work. She was only there at the end when they were effectively neutered and awaiting their fate. Hetton or duller.

But in the time between recognising his face, and Venn coming back, she had read what they held on Cahan Du-Nahere. At first she was comforted by it. That he was a known quantity. Then tortured by it. Torturing herself with it. The sensible part of her saying there was no reason to worry, Vanhu was strong. The mother in her unable to stop herself, exploring every awful possibility.

In her workroom she could not concentrate. Could only think of her child and eventually she knew that she would remain distracted and confused unless she spoke to Venn. Not only to know whether they were well, but to know if Vanhu had been successful before he died. If Venn had risen to be something else, something new and wonderful that would assure their survival in the world of the new Cowl-Rai. She stopped outside Venn's room, Falnist sitting on their stool, head in a parchment while she ached in leg and head.

"Are they asleep?" she said. Falnist shook their head.

"I heard them moving about." They blinked at her. The whites of their eyes were bloodshot.

"How do you stand being in the heights?" she said, waving a hand at the walls, and her robe of the lightest, thinnest wool, moved strangely, as if she were in water. "Does it not make you ill?"

"I read," said Falnist, "and when I must walk about then I keep my eyes on the floor."

"And it stops the headaches?"

"Not really," they said, and returned to their scroll. She waited a little, in case they said more but they did not even look at her.

"You can go," she said.

"But who will . . ."

"I will call if you are needed," she said. Falnist waited a little, and she had no doubt the trion was annoyed. Good. She had not forgiven them for manipulating her and would not have them listening in to her and Venn talk. They could not disobey her, not openly.

"Very well, High Leoric," they said. She waited, watching them walk away down the disquieting corridor, her head throbbing. When they were gone and she heard the gentle tap of feet going down the stairwell she opened the door and walked in.

Venn stood by the window. Staring out over Harnspire, and north towards the faraway Wyrdwood. They did not seem aware the door had opened, and she took a count, a moment, to stand and watch her child. Were they different? She thought so but was not sure why. Maybe they held themselves a little straighter? Maybe it was something ineffable that she could only sense in the back of her mind, the animal part. The same place that revolted when the Hetton were near, though there was no sense of revulsion here.

Maybe they had grown up a little.

"Venn," she said softly. They turned. Clean, white make-up and blue stripe newly applied, short, black hair damp.

"Mother," they said.

"You still do not wear your clanpaint."

"No," they said.

"I was frightened for you, Venn." She stepped forward. It felt odd not to be locking the door behind her, but she did not. There had been a change, she knew it even though she did not know what it was. "As soon as I realised, as soon as what the man in the cage was registered, I sent you help, Venn."

"He would have killed me," said Venn softly.

"I know, he is . . ."

"Not the prisoner," said Venn, "Vanhu. He made it quite clear. He would have killed me."

"I gave him orders, Venn, he was not allowed to hurt you. He was trying to scare you." Her child walked up to her. They were as tall as she was now.

"You may have given orders," they said. "I looked him in the eye while he threatened me." Something in her cracked at that, at the expression on their face. The ache left by terror was never forgotten, it remained for a lifetime and in a bid to erase it, rubbing at its tracks, she knew the scars were only made deeper.

"Venn, do you remember Madrine? The Rai?" Venn stared at her.

"Your firstwife? I remember everyone was frightened of her. You were frightened of her." Kirven nodded.

"She used to say she would kill me, came close more than once. Drowning was what she liked, Venn. When she said she would kill me, I did not doubt she meant it. Never once, not until she was dead did I realise she never meant it. It was the fear she enjoyed, it let her control me, all of us. The act of hurting me, bringing me close to death, that was simply so I believed her."

"But she killed her firsthusband, thirdwife, and my first-father, you told me."

"They acted against her." Kirven was losing Venn and knew it. Could feel a moment of empathy slipping away. "But that is not the point. What I mean is the Rai are very good at frightening people to get what they want. I would not have sent you if I truly believed Vanhu would hurt you."

"You put me in the blooming room," they said. She didn't answer. Not at first.

"I never doubted you, I know you are strong."

"Twice, you have been happy to let me die."

"No," she shouted it. Calmed herself. "Never that. The moment I realised what sort of creature they had imprisoned on that raft I sent Galderin for you."

"Creature?" said Venn. "He was only a man."

She shook her head. "No, he was something else."

"What?" She stopped. What she knew she was sworn to keep secret. It was a thing not shared, not spoken of. But one day Venn would rule with her, would know anyway. And she needed their trust. Venn was staring at her, intense, as if they could steal what she knew from her eyes.

"Before the new Cowl-Rai, Venn, there was chaos. A

thousand dark forest gods, all mostly the same, rising in the north, the south, the east and west, everywhere. Every monk of some filthy little copse claiming they had the Cowl-Rai, all lies, of course. Most were tricksters. Many, many people died because they believed their lies. My whole family among them." Venn's brows creased, as if they were letting what she said sink in. "But sometimes, and none know how, they would manage to raise a cowl user. They are mostly weak, these false Cowl-Rai. But with surprise, well, you saw what they could do in the forest." Venn blinked. Said nothing. Let her continue. "These forest cults simply misunderstood the words of Tarl-an-Gig, that is why they were so similar. But not the one of Cahan Du-Nahere."

"What is different about him?" said Venn softly.

"He came from a monastery of a god called Zorir. They were different. They did not believe the Cowl-Rai came to better the people of the north."

"No?" said Venn. Kirven shook her head.

"No, they believed that Crua must be destroyed, burned, that fire should rage across the entire land and only by every man, woman and trion being sent to the Star Path could our land be set to rights." She bowed her head a little. "All the false Cowl-Rai are dangerous in their way, Venn, all of them. But this Cahan Du-Nahere? He would kill us all given the chance, and think it to our benefit." Venn did not speak, not straightaway.

"He did not kill me," they said eventually. "And never spoke of killing others."

"The best killers, Venn, are never suspected. It could be he saw you as important, as a way towards his goal, whatever that is." She wanted to know what had happened in the forest, but did not want to push the trion. They were talking to her, it felt like a healing of their relationship. "You saw him die?"

"When I left," said Venn, "I thought it unlikely he would

survive." For a moment, a single moment, she wanted to scream. How could her child not know about the way the cowlbound healed? How hard they were to kill? They were surrounded by Rai. But she bit it back. Held it in. Gentleness, now, at this moment. Heartwood hardness later if it was needed. There were more important things for now.

"Good," she said, "good." Looked away, knew there was no simple easy way to phrase what came next. "Before Vanhu died, Venn. Did you . . ." her voice tailing off. Venn's face hardening. Then softening. Were they remembering what they went through? Were they remembering fighting it? Had all her worry and fear been for nothing? She could see a war going on in their features, as if they had some secret. Defiance there too. She wondered if Venn was aware they bunched their fists, bit their lip as they thought. Then they bowed their head.

"Yes," they said. "Yes, I did it."

"I knew you were different," she said, and embraced them. Felt them stiffen for a moment then relax and it was as if something unwound inside her. Like some key she did not know needed turning was twisted and a pain within was released from its cage.

"Am I still confined, Mother?" they said. She stood back, keeping her hands on their upper arms. Looking at them.

"To the room, no, the spire is yours, Venn. Go where you will. I will arrange a guard, and I imagine Rai Galderin will want to teach you in the use of your cowl—"

"No."

"No?"

"I do not understand the cowl," they said. "But I know I am different, I am trion after all. I must find my own way." She stared at them, taking that in, weighing it up.

"Well, of course," she said. Then smiled. "Of course. I will still assign you a guard, Venn, you are too important not to be guarded." They nodded.

"I am tired now, Mother," they said, "I would like to rest."

"What about your clanpaint, Venn," she said. "Will you wear it again." They looked away.

"Maybe when I have earned it, Firstmother," they said.

"I understand," said Kirven, and she backed away, standing in the doorway for a moment before leaving. Looking at them. Proud of them. She had waited so long, so very, very long for Venn embrace their power. That they had finally done it filled her with such joy that she did not once consider they might lie to her. Or, that in exchange for their freedom, her child might only be telling her what they knew she wanted to hear.

34

The child fell asleep in Udinny's arms and they camped before the taffistone, where the boughry had kept court. The forester and the monk felt no fear or worry and neither could explain it, except to say that it felt as though the boughry had accepted Udinny in some way as "theirs". They laid their heads down amid the riot of light in Wyrdwood and slept as deeply and peacefully as the child, as if they had not a care in the world.

Cahan awoke to the daylight gloom, movement in the corner of his eye. He felt no need to jump from inaction to action. He let himself move slowly from sleep to wakefulness. Only then realising how the days of venturing through the forest, always having to stay alert, had weighed on him. When he woke fully he found that nuts and berries had been scattered around him, so thick he only had to reach out and his hand was full. He sat eating the berries, letting their juice quench his thirst.

Udinny, had woken before him, a rare thing in itself, and she stood by the taffistone, running her hands over the egg-shaped rock. It was taller than her, taller than him, and she could not reach the top, though she was trying — her thin body stretching, showing her scrawny ankles as her robe lifted. Then she stood back, inspecting the monument. Segur watched her intently, head cocked to one side.

"There are many of them dotted around Crua," said Cahan, "surely you have seen them before in Tilt?"

"I have been at sacrifice, like everyone, Cahan. Given of myself and felt the malaise that follows, but I have never really looked at them." She put her hands on the smooth grey surface. "It is warm to the touch, did you know that?"

"Aye," he stood and went over to join her, "some of them are in the north. When the snows fall it never settles on the taffistones."

"And there are handprints on it," said Udinny. She pointed at one and he leant in to look.

"I have seen things on the others that I thought may be handprints," he said, "but never so clear as that." Udinny put her own hand on the rock handprint, splaying her fingers.

"How does someone leave a handprint in rock, Cahan? Were the ancients so strong they could press their hands into stone?" He shook his head.

"The cowl, Udinny, for those few who are blessed, or cursed, depending on how you see it. That is how it is done."

"And you, Cahan Du-Nahere. Was I right? Are you so blessed?" She was looking at him, thin face, wide eyes, hair spiked once more. No judgement, only an honest question.

"I am cursed so, yes." She smiled at him.

"Do you know the story of the Leoric whose fields were constantly eaten by virin?" He shook his head, he had not been raised in a place where folktales were told. "Every day, Cahan, the Leoric came out and cursed their luck, that the crops of their people should be so blighted by virin. They did everything they could to destroy the virin, sent children out to scour the plants and squash them on the leaves, burned their nests whenever they were found. But the virin were like water, and they flowed around their efforts, blighted the crops until the villagers eventually left. But the Leoric remained, full of hate for the virin and vowing to fight them. They died alone, cursing the virin, who ate their corpse never understanding they were hated. Then a new Leoric came, bringing people from far beyond Tilt. These people had been raised a different way with different customs. At first they were scared, looking at this tumbledown village that had been abandoned apart from one old corpse, chewed on by virin. They worried that some terrible fate may have befallen this place, and might await them here if they stayed. But their Leoric was different, and recognised the signs of what had chewed on the corpse. Where this Leoric and their people came from they regarded virin differently. They knew virin could be eaten, mashed up into meal, or fried as they were and they were considered a great delicacy." Udinny grinned at him. "The new Leoric looked upon the blighted fields and said to their people, look at this bounty that has been provided for us, and the Leoric and their people thrived." She sat down among the berries and nuts. Leaning on one hand.

"Are you saying I should eat my cowl, monk?"

"Sarcasm, Cahan, is not clever." Udinny popped a nut into her mouth. "I only mean that, curse or blessing, sometimes it is in how you look at a thing." He nodded. She smiled but it fell away, one of her hands on the forest floor. She was staring at it, as if she had never seen a hand before.

"Maybe," he said, though he did not believe her. She did not know how a cowl weighed upon you, demanded you feed it. Still, he did not want to argue with her and he remained strangely relaxed.

"There is so much life here, above and below us, Cahan," she said.

"And we must move on," he replied, "return the child."

They constructed a travois for the child from their staffs, and then harvested floatvine to go beneath it. Cahan lifted the boy onto the travois and laid him gently on a bed of the soft, dark leaves that grew on the bushes. "Should the child not be awake by now?" he said, staring down at him.

"He will sleep until we leave Woodedge," said Udinny.

"How do you know that?" She shrugged.

"I only know that I know it." She scratched at the base of one of her hair spikes, spoke in a softer than usual voice. "Maybe it is something to do with the boughry."

"Doesn't it worry you?" He put the straps of the travois around his shoulders. "That they may take their price from you?"

"It should," she said, "maybe it will later but it does not now. I will not borrow trouble." She looked up. "I heard so much about the forest before I entered it, Cahan. But it is a place of wonders as well as danger. Maybe the boughry are not what we think either?"

"I have seen their victims," he said. "If they call you, ask and I will do what I can to protect you." She put her hand on his arm and smiled.

"Cahan, despite your size, and what lives beneath your skin, I am not sure you could help me against them." She looked back at the stone. "Besides, I walk Ranya's rambling path, I must go where it leads, it often surprises."

"Why, Udinny?" he asked as they began to walk away from the stone, Segur dashing about around them, "why follow a god most have forgotten? What do you expect from it? Followers? A temple? Is there some prophecy that guides you?" Even to talk of such things as prophecy left a bitter taste in his mouth.

"I want nothing, Cahan," said the monk, "I have already told you, I simply heard her voice and I answered her call." He paused and she walked ahead, whistling softly. He wondered if he should tell her of his past. If she was someone he could really trust. Ranya had once intruded into his life, and if she had not then he would not be the man he was. He would either be dead or something terrible.

For many years he not been sure whether he thanked the intervention of Ranya or, rather, her acolyte, for the way her teachings made him feel. But something of Udinny reminded him of the man who had taken time from his duties to speak to a small and frightened boy and, like Udinny, that old man had done it selflessly, knowing what the cost might be.

What it would be.

He felt he should tell her, and resolved to do so when they camped. If not everything of him then some of it. It would be good to share and Udinny had proven herself trustworthy.

"How do we get out of Wyrdwood, Cahan?" asked the monk. He glanced up, looking for the glow of light far above but the mist that gathered around the lowest branches of the cloudtrees hid everything. He scanned the floor, looking for the disturbances they had made on their way but he found nothing. The forest floor was as pristine as if they had never passed by.

"Truthfully, Udinny, I have never been this far into Wyrdwood before." He looked across and did his best to smile. "I had hoped to follow our tracks back but they have vanished."

"What do you suggest then?"

"We walk until we find a cloudtree," he said, "moss always grows on the northern side, so we head in the opposite direction to the moss. Then we should, eventually, find ourselves in Harnwood. Once there I can get us back easily enough." Udinny nodded, pleased with his answer, and they headed towards what looked like a tree trunk in the distance, but proved to be only a bank of the dark-green-leaved bushes. They continued walking; the bushes were easy enough to push through if you were careful to mind the thorns.

As they left the bushes an arrow halted their progress.

He heard it first, not the whistle of its passage through the air. That was lost in the constant sound of Wyrdwood;

whistles, whoops and howls. He heard the "thud" of it landing in the earth, digging in. An unmistakeable noise to anyone who had ever shot an arrow. He must still have been in the strange fugue brought on by the boughry as he did not run, or tell Udinny to do so. If the archer was good there would have been little point anyway. Instead, he simply stopped, staring at the arrow buried in the earth as if it was a new thing to him; a strange creature he had never seen before. The fletching was of high quality. Whoever had made this arrow was skilled in an art that would get you killed in most of Crua.

"Come no further!" came the shout.

"We mean no harm!" Udinny shouted back. Cahan felt a hard dig in his ribs as the monk used an elbow to shock him from his torpor. "Armed people, Cahan," she hissed, "maybe the bigger one of us should deal with them, eh?" He nodded. Stepped forward. Another arrow. This time he heard it cut through the air. It landed no more than a handsbreadth from his feet.

"We mean no harm," he shouted, "and if you intend to rob us we have little but you are welcome to it, we request only passage." He waited, expecting another arrow. Maybe this time in his chest.

"Who are you? To enter Wyrdwood?" The voice that came back was soft, though it had something of heartwood in it, strong and unbending. Familiar also, he was sure he had heard it before.

"My name is Cahan, I am a forester. This is my friend Udinny, a monk of Ranya."

"And why are you here, Cahan the Forester, and Udinny, monk of Ranya? Disturbing my forest?" Cahan undid the straps of the travois and pulled it round to bob in the air before him.

"I only wish to go, and leave your forest undisturbed," he shouted back. "This boy was foreststruck. His mother asked me to come here and bring him back."

"Brave, to venture so deep," came the reply.

"We did not expect to, or want to. The forest brought us here."

"And what damage did you do, Cahan the Forester, and Udinny, the monk of Ranya, forcing your way through this green realm where you are wholly unwanted?" By now, Cahan was sure he knew which of the green bushes hid the speaker. If he had wanted to he was also sure he could get to them. A jagged run would spoil their aim. He considered it, then decided against. This must be Forestals, and they never hunted alone.

He remained still.

Waiting. Thinking.

The forest paused around him.

"We caused no damage," he shouted back. Voice echoing between vast trees. "Harm not, and remain unharmed, is that not the rule here?" He felt there was an edge of desperation to his voice.

A long gap, no response.

"We did no harm!" He shouted again. "We ask safe passage, Tall Sera." As he shouted that name, of the man he was sure he spoke to, the forest woke once more. Gasmaws moved far above, and a thousand different creatures trilled and called in the gloom. He wondered if he had made a mistake, if the voice he heard was not the man that he had met in Woodedge on his way to Harn-Larger.

A figure left the bush, and more appeared from the foliage around them. Men and women dressed in clothing that was the same greens and browns as the forest, twigs and leaves woven into the material. Skin beneath painted with the same colours and their camouflage was so perfect Cahan realised they could have been following them for days and they might not have seen them. But now he knew they were there he could feel them in his cowl; they were part of the forest but not. Like he was, like Udinny had become.

"Forestals," said Udinny quietly. Cahan nodded. The other creatures of the forest, the orits, gasmaws, rootlings and even the swarden, they were understandable in their way. They acted the way they did because it was their nature, they were dangerous, yes. But that was simply the way they were, and even with the worst of them, the swarden and the skinfetches, if you kept out of their way and did not disturb them about their business they were unlikely to act against you.

But Forestals were a different matter, they were people and there were few things as dangerous and unpredictable as people.

The leader pulled back their hood. His eyes were bright and he held a bow taller than himself in one hand. His followers also had bows, though unlike him they held theirs at half-draw, ready to act should they need to.

"You are a long way from where last I saw you, Forester," he said.

"I could say the same of you." Tall Sera stared at him as he spoke. His eyes shone with amusement.

"We are of the forest, we are its protectors. This is our place."

"We have caused no harm."

"Take off your packs," he said, "and throw them over here. Do it slowly or we will loose our arrows, and not at the ground this time." Cahan nodded and began to slide off his pack, Udinny followed his lead. They tossed the packs towards the Forestals. Tall Sera sent two of his people, looking like shambling two-legged bushes, forward to root through their belongings.

"You will not find much of use."

"Take it all," said Tall Sera.

"At least leave us our water gourds," Cahan pointed at the gourds tied to the packs, "wetvines are spare in Wyrdwood."

"You speak like you think I will let you live," he said with a laugh. "What on earth gives you that impression?"

"You let me live before." Tall Sera nodded.

"Ania had given her word," he said, and took an arrow from the quiver on his back. "No such thing protects you now, Forester. You should know what happens to those who stray into the territory of the Forestals." He nocked the arrow. "And that child, if it was foreststruck it is not yours to take. It belongs here now." He lifted the bow, drew the cord back.

"The boughry gave the child to us," shouted Udinny, putting her body between Cahan and the bowman, "and they let us walk away with this child unharmed." The Forestal leader relaxed the tension on the bowstring, trying to pretend that what Udinny said was nothing strange to him. That he was not surprised, but he could not hide it.

"The boughry," he said, "you met them?"

"They had the child, at a large taffistone," she said. "We asked, and they let us take him."

"Just like that?" a small smile and he raised the bow again, drawing and aiming over Udinny and at Cahan in one smooth motion. The rest of his people did the same.

"No," said Udinny. "Not just like that. I offered myself in exchange."

"And yet you stand before us," he laughed, it died away slowly and then he spoke very seriously. "We do not like liars in the forest. And we like those even less who take the name of the Woodhewn Nobles in vain." Cahan thought them dead at that moment, he thought them lost. Udinny shivered, as if a cold breeze had found her. She stilled, the forest fell out of focus, a faint light whorled and twisted around her and she spoke in a voice that he barely recognised as hers. Udinny's posture changed, she had somehow become taller.

"I am Udinny Hac-Mereward of Tiltspire and I am given to the boughry of Wyrdwood." Out of the corner of his eye he saw movement, barely there, but he was sure it was rootlings, peeking from the bushes all around them as if made curious by the sound of Udinny's voice.

Tall Sera let out a gasp and fell to one knee, the rest of the Forestals did likewise.

"Forgive us and take your gaze from us, Noble," he said, "we did not know." Udinny shivered again, then looked about her in confusion.

"Why are they kneeling, Cahan?" the light gone, her size normal.

"The Forestals no longer consider us liars." He wondered what the boughry had done to her. Tall Sera looked up, then stood once more, though the rest of his people remained kneeling. He walked over and retrieved their packs, taking Udinny's to her first, putting it in her hand. Then he walked over to Cahan and dropped his on the floor. Up close Tall Sera smelled fresh and clean, like the needle-leaved trees that were good for burning and grew quickly in Woodedge. He glanced at the travois, a look of confusion passed over his face.

"All this way for a child. Are you brave or stupid, Forester?"

"A little of both, maybe," he said. He turned to look at the boy, sleeping on his bed of leaves.

"You waste your time," said Tall Sera. "Those chosen by the forest, they always come back, but I suppose you know that." He walked away, stopping at the edge of the bushes. "You cannot continue along the route you are taking." He took a breath and bowed his head. Let out the breath. Stood tall. "Truthfully, because your friend is chosen by the boughry I cannot stop you going where you will, and my people would not even if I asked." Cahan nodded. "But I request a favour, Forester, and Udinny, monk of Ranya, and then in turn I will owe you the same one day."

"I have no wish to trespass in places secret to you if you do not wish it," Cahan said. "And would not, boughry or no, you need only have asked." Tall Sera nodded at him. "We came in this direction because we are lost and know only that if we head generally southward then we will reach

Harnwood." The Forestal leader reached into a pocket of his clothing, amid much rustling of leaf and twig. He found what he was looking for, throwing it to Cahan. He caught it one hand. It was flat, smooth, and very dark brown. One end rounded, the other coming to a point.

"What is this?" he asked.

"A walknut. The moss on the cloudtrees this far in is not always like the moss in Harnwood, you are currently heading north-east, and deeper into Wyrdwood."

"Oh," he said.

"Toss the walknut into the air. It will always come down pointing north. Do not ask me why, none know. It just is." Cahan nodded. "Go east from here," said Tall Sera, "until you can go no further. Then turn and head south, that way you will come upon nothing we would rather you did not see."

"Thank you," Cahan said. Tall Sera nodded and, together with his fellow Forestals, vanished into the bushes. Had it not been for the walknut in Cahan's hand, it would almost have been as if he had never existed.

"What do you think he meant by 'until you can go no further'," said Udinny. "Are there slowlands in the forest?"

"I do not know," Cahan shrugged, "but I suppose we shall find out." He tossed the walknut into the air and it came down pointing towards his feet. He picked it up and did it a few more times in case the Forestal was playing some trick on him. Each time it fell it pointed in the same direction.

"Onwards then," said Udinny.

35

They walked east and he let Udinny take the walknut. She took a childlike satisfaction in throwing it into the air and seeing it come down pointing north each time.

"This feels like I should have it in my hand," she laughed, throwing it again.

The journey was far easier than the walk that had brought them to the boughry. It felt as if the forest breathed around them, opening up and letting them travel with as little disturbance as possible. The child slept, his breathing soft and regular as he lay on the floating travois. Udinny and Cahan passed across the soft carpet of cloudtree needles in comfortable silence. As they walked, Cahan became more and more certain that they were being followed and indeed, as time passed, their followers began to show themselves. Rootlings, peeking out from bushes then vanishing behind them. Cahan turned to reassure Udinny that he sensed no threat from them, only curiosity, but she had seen the rootlings and was smiling at them.

"They are gentle souls, are they not, Cahan?" she said. He nodded, and they continued onwards followed by a train of rootlings as the light moved across the sky and the forest dimmed. "I see light, ahead," said the monk, pointing eastward. He looked and could see a faint glimmer, like the moment the light began to emerge but was still well below the horizon.

"A break in the canopy," said Udinny as they moved through the gloom.

"Seems so," said Cahan, though this was not the same as the one they had seen before. Where that had been painfully bright, this one was more diffused. Nearer to it, the light was cut and sliced into beams, shooting through the forest. Cahan began to understand what he was seeing. There was something massive and sharp, huge and black, and from a distance it almost appeared furred. Its true size only started to become apparent as they walked on and it barely got any bigger. "Treefall," he said, more to himself than to Udinny, though she answered, and her voice held all the many colours of wonder.

"I thought, from the base of them I understood the size, but I did not."

She was right, it was something that defied all logic. Cahan had seen a fallen centre spire, in the city of Storspire; so huge it had brought down two of the outer spires as it fell. When it had happened he did not know, and the spire was little more than a skeleton when he saw it. But still, it had a size that he found difficult to understand. The cloudtrees dwarfed it. Even the tallest spire did not vanish from sight. The true, immense, mind-breaking size was brought home when they were near enough that they could see the wall of darkwood blocking their path was as tall as ten or eleven people on each other's shoulders. From it sprouted smaller, though still massive, branches.

"It is huge, Cahan," shouted Udinny and she began to run towards it. "I had never imagined that a tree could be so massive!" He watched her running and only as they approached did he realise the truth.

"Udinny!" he shouted, and she came to a stop. Her body

dwarfed by the giant wall of black wood, still a good half-hour walk away. "This is not the cloudtree!" He saw the puzzled look on her face, then the disappointment. He let her feel it, but only for a moment. "That is only a branch from it." It was hard then, not to laugh at her expression as she tried to understand how vast the actual tree could be that had shed such a massive piece of wood. "It must have fallen off the main trunk when it came down."

"But," she turned back to the branch, then back to him. "How can that be? Nothing can be so huge."

"A cloudtree is, Udinny."

When they finally reached it, they could see what had given the branch a fuzzy effect from a distance: the pinleaves. He had always imagined the cloudtree needles would be green, dark green like the wide leaves on the bushes that grew on the floor of Wyrdwood, but they were not. He reached up, touching the end of a branch and the silvery green needles that clung on to it. They showed no sign of death, even though he could see where mosses and lichens were growing on the branch, where bushes had taken root around it, and guessed there was at least a year's growth there, maybe two or three. He marvelled at the life the great tree must hold that it could keep its leaves fresh for so long past death. To the touch the pinleaves were soft and smooth, unlike any other leaf he had come across, and he had spent much time in the forest.

"It is beautiful," said Udinny, "and sad."

"Sad?"

"That something so great should die."

"Everything dies, monk," and as he said it he thought about the two reborn women – looked around for them but saw no sign – and knew it was not entirely true.

"But that something so great should?" She pulled a leaf from the end of the branch and looked at it, it was as long as her finger. The needles on the forest floor were no longer than Cahan's nail. "Can you eat them?" she said.

"I have no idea." Udinny shrugged, then put the leaf in her mouth and bit on it. She struggled to get her teeth into it. When she managed it clearly did not taste to her liking. She pulled it from her mouth and spat out what she had bitten off, it remained attached to the leaf in her hand by long shiny veins.

"Maybe it is better cooked," she said.

"This must be where we turn, Udinny," he pointed, away from the branch.

"Do you think a whole tree has come down, Cahan?" said the monk. "The last treefall was generations ago. If a tree has fallen this could make the villagers of Harn rich."

"Aye, I think a tree may well have fallen," he said. "All the stories of treefall I have heard start with a found branch, then it is followed back to the trunk. I have heard people say the last treefall took four generations to collect and is what made Jinneng the true power of the south."

"Well, it may not be that much longer."

"Treefall up here will be the last nail in the coffin of the south," he said softly as she walked over to stand by him.

"You do not sound pleased, Cahan Du-Nahere, and you being a son of the north and all. Surely you should be?"

"It will bring Rai. And Rai are a poison," he said, "and the Cowl-Rai the worst of it. Believe me, I know what they are capable of." He turned from her and then felt her hand upon his arm.

"What haunts you, Cahan Du-Nahere?"

"Power, Udinny, and what can be done with it." He took a breath. "But it is not something I would speak of now, I have spent so long not being that which I was raised to be that it is painful to even think of it."

"What were you raised to be, Cahan Du-Nahere?" said Udinny softly.

"The end, Udinny. I was raised to be the end. To hold power in my hand and sweep those who opposed my god away before me."

"Ranya?" said the monk, "she would never wish for . . ."

"No, Udinny, I was raised for Zorir-Who-Walks-in-Fire, by those who yearned to make their will real. You called me Cowl-Rai, as a mark of respect, but I was raised to be terror and death."

"How did you find Ranya?" said the monk, staring at him.

"The man who tended the gardens of the temple, he spoke to a sad and homesick young boy of a gentler god, and a different way of life."

"The web of Ranya is fragile, Cahan," said Udinny softly, "but it is everywhere, and will always find those who need it."

"It found me," he said.

"And brought you comfort, if not happiness. Ranya brings us the way, but you must follow it to find what you need." Something within him wanted to strike the monk for those words. The anger at his core heard what Udinny said as criticism even though he knew they had not meant it. He deserved criticism and held his anger within, denied it the way he denied the power within his cowl. Cahan took a deep breath of the cool forest air. It felt clean and real and it cooled the fire burning.

"No, Udinny, Ranya brought me nothing but strife and misery." He was holding his hands in fists so tight it hurt his knuckles. He lifted his hand, unclenched his fist. "I was sculpted for violence, Udinny, and Ranya allowed me a way not to become what was intended. Eventually. Though she has brought me no happiness, I try to find solace in the fact I have not wrought the chaos the followers of Zorir wished for."

"And rather than Zorir, now we have Tarl-an-Gig." Cahan shrugged, he had no answer. Would he have been better or worse than the Cowl-Rai who rampaged through the south? He did not know, and in the end he did not think it would have mattered. Rai destroyed, it was what they were. To be Cowl-Rai was the same but worse.

"Let us return to Harn," he told Udinny, "the child should be returned to his mother." The monk nodded, and she did not ask any more, for which he was glad.

They walked until the gloom switched into night, and then the forest lit their way. It seemed at every bush there were berries and they filled them with energy. Neither he nor Udinny felt a wish, or a need, to stop.

Before the light rose they were in Harnwood. They took a little sleep there, but only a little. They woke to the light and the warmest day for a long time. The path was easy, no roots tripped them or trapvines grabbed their feet. By the late afternoon they were already entering Woodedge.

"Cahan," said Udinny, "I know the way is easier, but does it seem to you that the distance is also less?" He did not reply as much as grunt; the same thought had been running through his head. "How is that possible?"

"I do not know, but if it is easier on our feet I think it best not to ask." Udinny stood, her finger against her chin as she thought about it.

"You may be right," she said, and started off walking again, a new stout stick she had collected along the way swinging in her hand. Woodedge, unlike Wyrdwood and Harnwood, did them no favours. They struggled to pass through the undergrowth the same way they had when they entered it, but he knew Woodedge well and this was a familiar struggle.

"If we camp when the light falls," he said, "then we will be breaking out of the forest by mid-morning tomorrow, and in Harn by the afternoon."

"It will be good to sleep in a real bed," said Udinny as she watched Segur vanishing into the ferns in pursuit of something. Heard the chattering of rootlings hidden by the brush. "And to eat meat not cooked by my feet will be pleasant. One never really gets used to the taste." Cahan laughed, and Udinny grinned at him. They set off again.

His estimate was a little wrong, it was the afternoon when

they finally broke from Woodedge. As they did the child finally stirred, sitting up on his travois.

"Where am I?" he said.

"On your way home, Issofur," Udinny told him, and pointed towards the shadows of Harn's walls on the horizon. "Sleep, and we will be there before you know it."

"It will be good to be home," said the child, but when he said it, he was looking back at the trees of the wood, not at the walls of his village.

36

Cahan did not know what he expected as they approached Harn with the boy.

A fanfare? Flags? The people running out to greet the returning heroes?

None of these things happened of course, though the gate guards did not bar their way and demand a bribe. Tussnig, the monk of Tarl-an-Gig, stood in his headdress of sticks and watched them pass, he glared but did not speak. Maybe this was the nearest to a welcome Cahan could ever expect from Harn.

Within the walls the people had gathered, quiet, distrustful, staring. Cahan and Udinny walked towards the Leoric's house and Cahan thought it would not matter what he did for the village, he would never belong here. Never be welcome here for want of a little paint on his temple. He would always be clanless. If he helped them they would think they were entitled to it, if he did not help them it would only confirm what they thought of him.

"He lives," Cahan heard it whispered from behind him. Then another whisper.

"Lost Anjiin! He brought the child back!" A babble of

voices, the door on the Leoric's longhouse was pushed open and she appeared, followed by her second, Dyon, who wore a conical yellow hat that he had pulled so low it almost covered his eyes.

"Issofur?" said the Leoric, she said it to Cahan. Her face frozen in fear. He realised he blocked her view of the travois.

"Here," he said, removing the straps and pulling the travois round so she could see the sleeping child.

"Issofur," she said again, and she caressed his cheek, smiling and cracking the white make-up over her face. The boy's eyes opened. He looked up at her.

"Firstmother," he said softly. "I am tired. I had a strange dream."

"Sleep, Issy," she said softly, "you have been on a great adventure." He nodded.

"I made new friends," he said, then laid his head back down and returned to sleep.

"So you are friends with my son, now?"

"He does not know us, Leoric, he slept all the way back," said Cahan. Her face twisted in confusion. "We should talk." Worry, on her face now.

"Come into my longhouse," she said, "Dyon!" Her second nodded and held the door open while she picked up the child and led them into her longhouse. Inside it was smoky, the fire burned in the centre and over it was the same bubbling pot of broth Cahan had seen before. "You must be hungry," she said and walked into the back to lay down her son, reappearing a moment later.

"Yes," said Udinny before Cahan could speak, "we have eaten only our shoes for the entire journey." The Leoric, Furin, gave her an odd look and then took some bowls off a shelf and spooned broth into them. It was thick with gravy and vegetables, and even had a little meat in it. Cahan sat on one of the stools around the fire and took a mouthful.

"This is good, thank you," he said.

"It is better than good," said Udinny. "I have travelled

the length of Crua and I swear to all the gods who have been and those who will be that Furin makes the best broth in the entire land."

"Thank you, Udinny," said Furin. The Leoric looked tired, worn out as she joined them to eat.

"It is the herbs," said Udinny through a full mouth.

"What happened in the forest?" she said, turning from the monk. Cahan raised his eyes from his bowl, glanced at her second, Dyon, standing behind her.

"Dyon has been with me for years," she said. "You may say anything before him you would say to me."

"He does not seem to like me much," replied Cahan.

"Forester," said Udinny, "I thought our journey through the forest had cured you of surliness." He stared at her until she shook her head and returned to her broth. "But it appears not." The forester turned from the monk and back to Furin.

"Your son was foreststruck, Furin," he said.

"I know that. We are not entirely unaware of the ways of the wood, we live within it after all."

"He was chosen by the boughry." She froze, spoon halfway to her mouth. Then she placed the spoon back in the bowl and put it on the floor.

"But you returned? How? They let none return, not with their lives." Her voice wavered, quietened. "Not for long anyway." She stood. "My boy, is he——" She began to move and Cahan raised a hand, stopping her.

"Udinny offered herself in the boy's place." She stared at him.

"They did not hurt Issofur?"

"No," he said. She turned from him to Udinny who was still gulping down broth.

"And you, Udinny?"

"I am not hurt," she said, "but I have a fierce hunger." She held out her bowl and the Leoric stared at her, so many questions on her face. Udinny pushed the bowl towards her again. Furin hesitated, for only a moment, then took it and refilled it.

"They let us leave, Furin," said Cahan as Furin passed Udinny the full bowl, "but said they will want their price paid at another time." The Leoric picked up her own bowl, stared at it then poured the food back into the pot. Her appetite was gone but food was too precious to waste.

"I do not have the words to thank you," said Furin quietly.

"You do not need to," said Udinny. "We had a fine adventure."

"They freed your boy, Leoric," said Cahan, "but few are ever the same once they have been in Wyrdwood."

"Udinny seems herself. Unchanged," she said, pointing at the monk as she spooned food into her mouth. The monk of Ranya looked up.

"Oh, you are wrong, Leoric," she smiled and wiped broth from her mouth. "I have seen much, my eyes have been widened by my journey. My faith in Ranya strengthened." Cahan could not help but notice that the Leoric's eyes flickered to her second when the monk mentioned Ranya. He wondered if Dyon was stronger in his faith than her. And the idea that Udinny was unchanged, well, he did not think that true either but if it helped Furin to believe it, then he would let her.

"Good," said Furin softly. Then she sat straighter. "You are still not intending to preach of your god?" her eyes flicked to her second again.

"That is not Ranya's way," she said between mouthfuls. Dyon stared at the monk.

"You intend to stay, though?" said Dyon, and from his tone Cahan was sure he would rather she did not. The monk nodded.

"Well, we owe you. A place to stay is the least we can do," said Furin. "It is good to have you to look after Issofur, as well." She glanced at Dyon again and then leaned forward to say more quietly, "But stay out of Tussnig's way."

"Is there more broth?" said Udinny. The Leoric smiled and shook her head in amusement. She clearly found some small joy in the familiarity of Udinny's appetite.

"Help yourself, Udinny, and you too, Forester, you have done me a great service." Cahan nodded, though he did not take more broth. The people of Harn were not rich and his farm provided enough for him. All that he wanted was to return to his solitude. Udinny's company had been good, but to be around the people of Harn once more, and to see the way they had looked at him only reminded him why he avoided them. But, as he sat there, among their poverty and saw how freely the Leoric offered her food, though she had little, he felt he must share what else he knew with her before he left.

"There is something else we discovered in the forest," he said. The Leoric looked at him in a way that confused him. As if she feared what he would say as much as she feared the boughry. "There has been treefall, in Wyrdwood."

"Treefall!" This from Dyon behind her, and for the first time since Cahan had known him he smiled. "Furin, this is wonderful. We will be as rich as Harnspire! Truly, Tarl-an-Gig has chosen to bless us."

"Speak quietly, Dyon, less the Osere hear and grant your wish," said Furin, "life is not as simple as you imagine."

"But treefall, Leoric," he said, coming forward, "it will provide all we could need for generations, it is what made Jinneng rich, it is . . ."

"Forester," said the Leoric softly, "did you come across this treefall by accident, or were you directed to it?" She cocked her head to one side, a question in her gaze, and he thought about what she said. About how the Forestals had sent them towards the branch.

"Directed, I think."

"By Forestals," added Udinny, "they were not the monsters we have been led to believe either, they gave us a wondrous thing called . . ." her words tailed off at the look the Leoric was giving her. Then Furin turned to Dyon.

"This is not the gift you believe, Dyon," said the Leoric softly. "The Forestals have been raiding our caravans though there is little enough for them to take. Do you not wonder why?"

"What does this have to do with treefall?" said Dyon.

"It is a trap," said the Leoric softly. "Treefall will bring riches, you are right. That is what the Forestals want, a better class of person to rob. Riches, merchants." She let out a long breath. "The Rai."

"Let them try and rob us," said Dyon, with an unpleasant laugh. "With the money from treefall we can hire professional guards. The Rai will protect us."

"You have never dealt with the Rai, have you?" Cahan said to Dyon.

"I have seen them many times," he said. "When I performed the duties of the gods, before Tussnig came, I even held a ceremony for one. We gave the lives of three of our best crownheads to Tarl-an-Gig."

"They will come here," said the Leoric, no emotion in her voice, "see what we have and take it."

"But it is ours," said Dyon.

"Rai do not care," said Cahan.

"Maybe not about you, Clanless," said Dyon, he did not even look at him. "But we are people," he touched the clanpaint on the side of his face. "I have ten generations' claim on this land."

"The forester is right, Dyon," the Leoric stood. "We are poor, and we are not of them. The Rai care nothing for your ancestors or mine or anyone else's. They will simply roll over us and take what they want." She let out a sigh. "It is better we do not talk of the treefall to others, Dyon. Better we pretend we never heard of it." He stared at her. His face changing, make-up cracking.

"You knew," he said. "You knew about the treefall?" She

nodded. Cahan felt the anger within burn a little brighter on realising he had been used. Not by the Leoric, but by the Forestals. He knew now what message he had been asked to send when he escorted the traders through Woodedge. Why they had sent Udinny and him eastward in Wyrdwood. They wanted the treefall found, so they could prey upon those it would bring.

"Yes, I knew," she said. "Have known for well over a year."

"Well, I . . ." began Dyon and she cut him off with a slash of her hand.

"Will do as I say, if you care at all for our people," she hissed.

"I think," said Cahan, standing, "I should leave now. I have missed my home and would like to get back."

"Very well, Forester," said Furin, turning away from Dyon, "and thank you."

"I will see him to Woodedge," said Udinny and she escorted him out, helped him retrieve his staff from the travois they had made. He passed villagers, some of whom were cordial, others contemptuous; like the butcher Ont, who stood with Tussnig and a little gaggle of villagers. They stared silently at him as he passed, though Tussnig's attention was focused on Udinny. Cahan did not care. Let Harn sort itself out, let its monk bleed them dry, let the Leoric and Dyon fight over treefall. It was of no consequence to him. He would never be welcome there.

At Woodedge Udinny stopped. She squatted and put her hand on the floor.

"Ranya's web," she said. He did not know if she spoke to him or to herself. She sounded lost. "I never knew . . ."

"You can come with me if you want, Udinny." She looked up, as if woken from sleep.

"I must stay here," she said. "I think the Leoric is right about the treefall. Maybe I can help her convince Dyon not to speak of what we know. He is not unreasonable, just distrustful." She put her hand on the ground again and sighed. "They used us, didn't they? The Forestals?"

"Yes, they did." He leaned in closer. "Watch Dyon. I do not think he cares much for your god, he wears the trinkets of Tarl-an-Gig on his clothes."

"He does, most people do now, Cahan." She smiled at him. "But Ranya speaks to all in some way." Cahan glanced back at the wooden walls of Harn. "You look troubled."

"Only thinking, monk."

"Of what?"

"The treefall, she knew of it but ignored it. I did not bring the Forestals' message to her. Then the child is taken, and we bring news of treefall again." He scratched at his beard. "It is almost like the forest wants these people to know of it."

"The Forestals sent us to the tree, not the forest."

"They live in Wyrdwood, Udinny," he said, "there is no telling how it has changed them, or how it uses them."

"But why?"

"For nothing good," said Cahan.

"I will tell her," said the monk. "She will be wary, well, more wary." Cahan nodded and whistled for Segur. The garaur came bounding out of Woodedge to scale him and wrap itself around his neck.

"Ranya's blessings to you, Udinny," he said to her.

"And you, Cahan Du-Nahere," she said and he turned and began the walk back to his farm, though he could not shake the feeling he was not done. The great forests of Crua were huge, eternal, and if they wanted a thing they did not give up.

It was a pleasant walk through Woodedge. These paths, unlike those Udinny and Cahan had walked, were kept clear by use, both by animals and by hunters and foragers from Harn. The fringes of Woodedge that surrounded the village had always felt friendly to him in a way Harnwood and Wyrdwood did not. Segur was happy to be in a place that was familiar to it and left his neck. He could hear the garaur thundering around through the undergrowth around him. He felt a happiness like nothing he had felt in as long as he could remember. Behind him he left Udinny, who he thought of as a friend, and a good deed. It could never be wrong to save a child.

He even felt that he shared some common ground with the Leoric; her wish to have nothing to do with the treefall, despite the riches it could bring, seemed sensible to him. He had written off her and the villagers as fools obsessed with nothing but themselves, like the Rai, but it was not true. Her concerns appeared to be for her people.

Though the way it seemed the forest wanted Harn to know of treefall bothered him.

He made a decision then and there that surprised him: going forward his farm would contribute to the tribute Harn must pay. It did not matter that he cared little for the Cowl-Rai's war, the truth was by withholding from the village it was only them he hurt.

When he broke from Woodedge and saw his farm in its clearing he could not stop smiling. It would be good to sleep in his bed, eat food cooked by his own hand and tend to his crownheads.

Cahan spent the following morning with Segur, rounding up his animals, and found that those animals that had vanished had been returned. Together with a fine male that he had not bought, but had been marked with a pink dye very similar to his. It left him with a warmth inside that was entirely new. He found himself looking forward to a life where his relations with the villagers were of cooperation, even if it was grudging from some of them. If he had earned himself a little goodwill then he intended to keep it.

There was a saying among the people of Harn: "No good tree goes uncut." He did not know it then, in those hazy, warmer days of Least that followed, but the axe was already coming down.

Many would fall to it.

37

It had been a shock when Kirven was told the Rai Sorha had returned. Her Rai, Galderin, loudest among them, was adamant she must die for failing Kirven in the forest, for allowing a prisoner to outwit her. Curiously, none of them were willing to do it themselves. There was much talk of how this was the High Leoric's responsibility, justice was hers and she must see it done.

It was not how they usually spoke, and that made her curious.

Kirven had gone away to look into Sorha, researched the woman's family in case they were powerful, likely to want revenge for a fallen child. They were not. It seemed that she was all that was left of them.

Something was wrong but Kirven did not know what. She had the woman Sorha moved to the taffistone cell under the watchful eye of the silent guards of the Cowl-Rai while she considered her fare. And now she visited.

Sorha was a very different woman from the one Kirven had seen before. She looked broken, sat in the back of the cell, clad in nothing but a thin woollen shift. Too dejected even to shiver. Her red hair streaked through with grey.

"Rai Sorha," said Kirven, the woman looked up. Her face drawn.

"High Leoric," she answered. Even here, at the lowest she could possibly be, Kirven was sure she detected a hint of sarcasm.

"You have failed me, Rai Sorha. You have failed me twice." The Rai shrugged. "But I have come to give you a chance to redeem yourself." Still the Rai did not look at her. "I want to know what happened," said Kirven, raising her voice. "What happened after Venn made their first kill." Sorha looked up.

"First kill?" she said. Kirven nodded.

"Yes, once my child had woken their cowl, how did this man, this Cahan Du-Nahere, best three of my strongest Rai?" Sorha smiled, an odd, fleeting and twisted thing. She stood and approached the taffistone.

"What is it worth to you?" said Sorha. "What will you do for me?"

"A quick death."

"Oh, I want more than that. I want to live."

"I hardly think you are in a bargaining position."

"All Rai know secrets, High Leoric," that smile again. Kirven wanted to smash it off her face.

"Your failures almost cost my child their life." Sorha's smile remained and she sat back down.

"After your child made their kill," a short laugh. No humour there. "Well, this man, Cahan, you called him?" Kirven nodded. Sorha did not even seem to remember she had been sent to kill him in Harn. "He had been shouting, screaming. Threatening. Vanhu decided to teach him a lesson. Burn him slow."

"And?" said Kirven.

"It did not work out well for Vanhu. For any of us."

"Explain." Sorha looked up.

"I have hunted false Cowl-Rai for, what, two years?" Kirven nodded. "Found mostly people disliked by others.

Or weak with barely a sniff of a cowl in them, easy to subdue." Sorha stopped, looked down, took a breath. "I think we had become complacent, High Leoric. This man, this Cahan, he took us apart. I have seen nothing like it. He did not use fire or water, he did things I cannot even understand. And that was before . . ." her voice died away, all her sarcasm and surety vanished. Sorha sounded like nothing so much as a woman deep in the throes of grief. She looked up. "Before he did what he did to me." Kirven studied her, she felt little pity for the woman. Whatever had been done was her own fault.

"Venn says they escaped because this Cahan was wounded. They think he lies dead in the forest." Sorha shook her head.

"No, not dead. Not with strength like that." She sounded almost desperate, and Kirven wondered why. Then realised this woman was Rai.

"You hate him, don't you?"

"I am nothing because of him." The words sharp and full of hate.

"Why?"

"He took my cowl." Kirven had no reply to that. She did not even know it was possible. Suspected Sorha of some trick. But she knew a way to test her.

"I want you to swear fealty to the Cowl-Rai," said Kirven.

"I have already sworn loyalty."

"And failed them, twice."

"I have been most thoroughly punished for that mistake, High Leoric."

"Swear it again. On the taffistone before you, in the name of Tarl-an-Gig."

"Why?"

"I will let you live." Sorha looked at her. "You will be banished, but you will live." The Rai stood. Walked to the taffistone and put her hand on it.

"I swear allegiance to the Cowl-Rai and Tarl-an-Gig, Osere

take me if I lie," she said. Kirven waited, nothing happened. She had expected something, for the taffistone to have some effect on her. "You look disappointed, High Leoric, did you not think me loyal?"

"That stone," said Kirven, "it turns cowl users into either Hetton or dullers. I did not expect you to still be standing." Sorha looked at her, her face changing from outrage at being treated so, to amusement. Then she started to laugh. A real laugh, from her stomach, shaking her body.

"Your own Rai," she said, "who you think to trust, and they did not tell you the truth of me, did they? Why they are not here?"

"What do you mean?"

"Do you know what Cahan Du-Nahere did to me in taking my cowl? He made me a duller, Kirven Ban-Ruhn, a living, walking duller. Not just a barely conscious corpse in a box. That is why they will not kill me, they cannot. Their power does not work around me." She shook her head. "I am tired of this, my life is a miserable one so if this was a trick and you want me dead, hurry up and do it." Kirven was no longer listening to her. She was thinking. A woman with all the martial skills of the Rai, but able to neutralise their powers. She would make a formidable bodyguard. But more than that, who better to hunt down false Cowl-Rai?

"I promised you your life if you swore allegiance," said Kirven.

"In an attempt to kill me."

"Tell me, Rai Sorha, what is the first thing you will do if given your freedom?"

"Find Cahan Du-Nahere, repay him for what he has done to me," she said, no thought, no question. No doubt in Kirven's mind that this woman cared of little else but vengeance.

"Where?"

"I would start at his farm, the village of Harn." So she did remember, that failure must fester within her now. "He may have gone back there if he thinks we believe him dead." Kirven tapped her foot, thinking.

"Thirty troops, Rai Sorha, I will give you that. Find him. Kill him." Sorha stared at her.

"I want to take the trion as well."

"No," said Kirven. Sorha walked around the taffistone, came right up to the bars.

"In the forest, High Leoric, this Cahan seemed more bothered about Venn being forced to kill than he was about himself. He is weak, he cares for others. He will not hurt Venn and that will allow me to get close to him." She grinned but there was nothing pleasant there. "Then he is only a man. Easy prey." Kirven stood, thinking. She could not keep Venn away from the world forever. And if they went with Sorha, and killed this false Cowl-Rai, it would make them far stronger in the eyes of the Rai of Harnspire. But no. Venn would not want to, she was sure. Even if they did, she did not want them to go.

"I will speak with them," she said.

"And I will need time, to train. Get my strength back." She took a breath, looked away. "And to come to terms with what I am." Kirven stared at her, she did not want to give this woman time. She wanted Sorha out there, finding him. "The longer he is left alone, the more complacent he will become, High Leoric."

"Or the longer he has to vanish into Crua."

"If he is going to hide," said Sorha, "he will already be doing so." Kirven thought about that. If she sent out the woman weak she was sure to fail.

"How long to build your strength?"

"Two seasons," said Sorha.

"A year? No, you have until Mid-Harsh." Sorha stared at her, smiled.

"Well, that will have to do."

"Now, Rai Sorha," she said, "I must go about finding you troops to train with."

38

"Forester! They are come! Forester! They are come!"

Least had passed and the cold of Harsh had begun to bite, binding the land in ice. He had spent the evening before with Segur, bringing the crownhead flock in nearer to the farm so he could feed them from hay put aside for the ice months. So cold now it made their wool crackle when he touched them. He had been up late into the night fixing their pen so they did not wander again.

At first he thought he dreamed the voice.

He had been plagued for weeks by dreams of Rai and their troops coming out of Harnwood for him, or coming over in a marant and dropping onto the roof of his farm. Always waking to another day where he was simply a forester and a farmer. As Least had passed he had begun to believe that was all he was. A man with friends, like Udinny and the Leoric, Furin. A man who could live at a farm in Harn Woodedge with few worries. Especially since the Leoric had managed, he did not know how, to convince Dyon that they should have nothing to do with treefall. Though the man continued to dislike him, and he was not the only one in Harn who felt that way. But Cahan had decided to ignore those who disliked him, and enjoy the company of those who did.

In those days, as the warmth waned and the cold returned, the Cowl-Rai and their war seemed very far away.

He batted the disturbance of the voice away and tried to push himself deeper into his furs, but it was not to be. The voice continued and it was joined by a hammering upon the door of his farm.

"Forester! Forester! Leoric Furin says to warn you. They are come! The Rai have come!"

He had a moment, a single moment between wake and sleep when he knew the voice was real but still fervently wished it to be a dream. He tried to lock the world and its darkness out.

Of course, the world cared nothing for what he wished. It simply was and he must exist within it.

More hammering.

"They are come, Forester! They are come for you!"

Life would not be denied. It was not the way. He pushed away the furs, shivering as the cold bit. Moved to open the door. As soon as he had done knew it was foolish. Whoever was shouting could have an army of Rai behind them.

Only a child stood before him, dressed in rags, shivering.

"They are come," she said, looking up at him with wide eyes, "the Leoric says they are come for you and to run."

"They are in Woodedge?" he said. "Behind you?" She shook her head.

"In Harn," she said. "Leoric sent me."

"Come in, child," he said, "before you freeze," she did and he pointed her towards a stool before the banked fire in the centre of the room. He set about the embers, waking the fire to give the child some heat.

"Leoric sent a message," she said, "she says you need to run and hide. Don't come."

"Well, run and hide is exactly what I mean to do." The child watched him as the first flames licked around the wood and a growing warmth crept out of the firepit. "Are they following you, child? Did they see you escape?"

"I were sent," she said. "No one followed." He paused in the laying of wood, wondering why he was doing this as he would have to leave. Should have left already. Then, in that moment of stillness, he thought something the child said did not fit right.

"When did they come, child?" He handed her some hard bread, she looked half starved.

"Yestereve," she said, took a bite of the bread. Odd, that they had been in Harn all night but had not moved against him.

"How many of them, child? How many Rai?"

"Two Rai," said the girl, "lots of soldiers, and some big boxes." He scratched his beard, thinking about what she said.

"Any Hetton?" He could see from her face she did not understand. "Strange people, they look like us from a distance, but their faces are not right up close. They move wrongly."

"Is only people," she said, talking as if he were a fool and taking another bite of the bread. She would not look straight at him and he wondered if he frightened her.

"What is your name?"

"Gillet," she said.

"You did well to escape, Gillet." She nodded, eyes on her bread.

"Didn't escape. I were sent."

"By the Leoric." She shook her head, dark braids twisting like serpents.

"No, Forester, by the Rai." He stared at her, wondering if she was somehow confused.

"But you brought me a message from the Leoric." She nodded. Dark thoughts of betrayal began to gather in Cahan's mind. The fire within burned. The cowl beneath his skin itched.

You need me.

"I were frightened of going into Woodedge by myself," said the girl, gnawing on the bread, "lest the trees take me and turn me into a rootling." She nodded to herself. "The Rai, she were angry, but the Leoric said to her that her way weren't the way to get me to do as is told. Said to send her boy instead." She glanced up at him. "Issofur likes the forest," a shiver down his back. "But the Rai would not have it. Said he were needed, and he is important as he is the Leoric's boy even if he is touched in the head." She gnawed more on the bread and continued to speak. "Then the Leoric spoke to me. Said I were brave and were to tell you to run, and to take me with you. And that I were not to give you the Rai's message." She picked some grit out of the bread and threw it on the floor.

"Well, Gillet," he said softly, moving back from the fire and sitting on a stool opposite the girl. "You have done your job admirably and given me the message sent by the Leoric." She was looking around his room now; her eyes stopped on one of the grass dolls he made from bits of hay when he had nothing better to do. He had planned to sell them in Harn at the coming Mid-Harsh. He took one from where it hung with a bundle of others. "You like this?" she nodded. "I am curious," he said, "what was it the Rai asked you to tell me?"

"Leoric said I wasn't to . . ."

"But you have given me the Leoric's message, and I intend to run as she said. But it does interest me to know what this Rai said to you." He turned the doll, so delicate in his large hands, until he was looking into the blank face made from a thick stalk looped over and tied at the neck. "If you share it with me, then I will give you this." She stared at him, frowned, pouted a little as she thought about what was more important to her: the doll or doing as she had been told. She licked her lips, looked at the bread then smiled to herself.

"Rai said you should come to Harn before the light were high. And she did not call you Forester, so I do not even think she even knows who you are." She nodded, quite succinctly, as if that had entirely answered his question, but he kept hold of the doll when she put out a hand for it. "Gimme it," she said.

"What did she call me, child?" She stared at the doll.

"Something silly, Carn the hair."

"Cahan Du-Nahere?" The girl nodded, put out her hand for the doll again. The cowl rippled beneath his skin.

You need me.

A coldness settled on him. "What else did she say?" The girl stared at him, defiant, then her desire for the doll overrode that defiance.

"Were silly," she looked away, "said if you did not come by lightfall Harn would pay the price." Gillet laughed. "I thought she don't know nothing about Harn, cos everyone knows we are poor as dirt and can't pay nothing." Then she stuck out her hand further. "Now give." He passed over the doll which she cradled like a baby and pretended to feed with some of her bread. He stood.

"Are your family back in Harn, girl?" She shook her head.

"Ain't got none, had a firstfather but he died when the orits came last, got bit and it went bad." He stared down at her.

"Stay here then, girl. If you see soldiers coming, hide in the wood. If you do not harm it then it will not harm you." She looked up at him, very serious for someone so young.

"Can I take my dolly?"

"Aye. If I do not come back this place is yours."

"It smells funny."

"You will get used to it." He took his winter coat from by the door, wrapped it around himself, took his staff and stepped outside.

He knew what he should do, head into the forest and

keep going. Head south, avoid Harn-Larger, avoid people throughout Harn and the whole of the north. Maybe he could find somewhere quiet in Tilt. As the powerbase of the new Cowl-Rai few would expect him to go there.

But in Crua new people are always talked about, and his lack of clanpaint would attract attention, none of it positive. He could lie, of course, paint it on. But it only took one person to ask a question he could not answer. His only real chance would be to catch work on a skyraft, but even they needed their crews to go into the towns and villages.

And this Rai knew his name, like those who had come to his farm before. That was not good. The only ones in Harn who knew his real name were Udinny and the Leoric. He did not believe Udinny would betray him, and if the Leoric had, why would she warn him?

Who knew his name? Who had told them where to look?

He must see what was happening in Harn.

No, he should run. By leaving he was saving them. Eventually the Rai who was looking for him would get bored and leave the villagers alone.

A lie. He knew what talk of "a price" meant. Rai are ever cruel and the cowl always hungers. They are even more cruel when they are thwarted.

You need me.

It was possible the girl was wrong, that there were only a few soldiers and to her that looked like a lot. He had always been good at lying to himself, but found it hard this time. There would be a cost here: one life, his, or that of an entire village.

A whistle brought Segur bounding out of the crownhead shed to wrap itself around his neck and bring some much-needed warmth in the darkness.

"We are going to Harn, Segur," he said, scratching its head so it cooed gently, "and I think we will find nothing good."

Woodedge was somehow fresher and sweeter in the cold

of the night, the plants and trees rimed with frost, the glowing creatures quieter as if they feared their voices may damage the delicate filigree of ice that coated every twig and blade of grass. Cahan did not take the well-worn paths, instead he moved through the wood like a Forestal, stealing between bushes to mask his silhouette, moving so quietly that even the shy nocturnal gasmaws floating through the cold air failed to notice him. These were not skills he had been taught in his youth at the monastery, these were skills learnt since, or echoes of a time before he went away, a time he had forgotten. He enjoyed them in a way he had never enjoyed violence, or the power of the cowl, because the skills of the forest had not been forced upon him. They were his.

He reached the edge of the wood around Harn as the light was rising above the treetops. It made the walls of Harn into a flat, black silhouette. Usually torches would burn above the gates, but not today, and he heard none of the bustle he expected from the village as it awoke. There was something else too, something that felt wrong. Not Hetton, but not far from them.

The gate opened, creaking and sticking. Someone shouted and soldiers of the Rai appeared, their wooden armour painted with bright blue lines and Tarl-an-Gig's balancing figure. He watched the guards from within Woodedge, studying Harn. There was no way to approach the village without being seen. Good sense told him to go back to the farm, pick up what he needed and to leave. Instead he knelt within a bush with Segur wrapped around his shoulders for warmth, observing.

Through the gate he could see into the village. More soldiers stood around and behind them were the boxes the child had spoken of. On seeing them he knew them for what they were, the strange feeling made sense. He could no longer lie to himself. They were here for him, they knew who and what he was. The boxes were dullers, the shiny domed devices used to stop the workings of a cowl. The Rai commanding the soldiers walked out of the gate and he wondered if this was a punishment assignment for them. It was unpleasant for Rai to be around dullers.

This Rai wore much finer armour than their soldiers, more colours painted on it, bracket-fungus shoulder guards, a smooth helmet of dark heartwood. They checked over their soldiers, then looked up at the slowly rising light and stared into Woodedge.

"Any movement," he heard the Rai say. He was sure he had heard that voice before.

"No, Rai." They nodded at the soldier, then looked back into the wood, kneading one gloved hand with another.

"He should have the message by now. You are sure the girl made it?" In the still cold air voices carried. He wondered if the Rai was aware of it.

"Scouts ensured she was safe, and returned here when she was in sight of the house as you ordered," said the soldier. The Rai nodded again and then turned to the forest.

"Tell me if you see any movement," they said. Then vanished into the village. He waited and the light moved across the sky, slowly making its way to the highest point when the message said he should appear. At the moment before the light touched its highest point, and the shadows were shortest, the Rai appeared again. They walked a little bit out of the gate and removed their helmet showing red hair in a tight braid. The ice within him shifted. A crack in his stomach. He knew this Rai. She was the one he had burned the cowl out of when he had been taken as a vagrant.

It made sense, the dullers would no longer bother her, though he could barely believe she had survived. Most did not, madness consumed them.

"Cahan Du-Nahere!" she shouted "Come out, Cahan Du-Nahere! You have murdered two of the Cowl-Rai's servants, you have offended the god-in-rising, Tarl-an-Gig! Come out, and we will make your end quick." She stared into Woodedge. Looking for him.

He did not move.

"Do you think he will come?" said the soldier. Among the blue lines he could see the glistening white paint marks on his chest piece that marked him as a branch leader. The Rai turned back to the village and he saw another figure dressed like Rai, smaller than the woman.

"Will he come?"

"He believes himself a good man," said the smaller figure. "He will come."

That voice. Venn! He felt their betrayal like a physical pain, and at the same time could understand why they would turn against him. He had let them return to imprisonment, and with hardly a fight.

Though even from this distance, their voice sounded thick with misery.

"Branch leader," she said, "bring me a villager, an old one." The commander walked back into the village and returned with two of his troops dragging a man with them. Gart, the fur trader. His long grey hair free and falling round his face. He tried to fight them, but they were younger, stronger, more numerous and he was bound at the wrists. He was shouting, at first Cahan could not make it out but as they pulled him through the gates his voice became clearer.

"I fought for you! I fought for the Cowl-Rai! Why are you doing this? I fought for you." Behind them, Venn stood, head bowed. The Rai stared out into the treeline.

"Silence him," she said. The branch leader punched Gart in the stomach and the man's legs gave way so he slumped in the arms of those holding him. The soldiers dragged him over to the Rai. "Make him kneel," she said. They did, roughly forcing Gart onto his knees where he stayed. The Rai walked around behind him, drawing her sword of black hardwood. She pulled his head back, then placed the sword against his neck.

"I fought for you," he said again. Even from Woodedge Cahan saw the glisten of tears in the man's eyes, heard how confused he sounded. He could not believe this was happening. "I fought for you."

"Cahan Du-Nahere!" shouted the Rai. "Come out or this life will be upon your head! This blood will be upon your blood!" Behind them, Venn turned away.

"I fought for you."

"Come out, Cahan Du-Nahere!" She was looking towards where he hid. Not exactly at him, but in the right direction. He wondered if she knew he was there. No, she could not. He was sure.

"I fought for you," said Gart again. Cahan thought the man was no longer there. That fear had stolen his wits. Or maybe he only told himself that to feel a little better that he did not move.

"Come out, Cahan Du-Nahere, or I will kill the whole village one by one." With that she cut Gart's throat, ran the sword across his flesh, opening the arteries. Gart began a shriek. The sword silenced it. The Rai continued to stare into the forest, holding the fur trader by his hair as blood poured from the wound. She let him go. Let him fall into the mud as if he was nothing. Leaned over to clean off her sword on his clothes and stood once more, blade in hand.

Everything was silent, entirely still.

"This death," she pointed at the twitching body of Gart with her black sword, stared out into Woodedge, "is on you, Cahan Du-Nahere." Within him the cowl writhed and his anger burned, hot and fierce. But he could not, would not, loose it. Even if he did use his cowl, he would be denied it the moment he stepped within range of the dullers.

To attack the village was a fool's errand. He should come back at night, then he may be able to get the people out. It was not impossible. He had seen no more than thirty soldiers through the gate, not even a full trunk. Most would be sleeping. The Rai turned to her branch leader. "Bring the girl with the spikes," she said. "The village monk said he had some connection with her." The branch leader saluted, hand over his chest, then turned and marched into Harn with two soldiers. The Rai stared out into the forest.

"Cahan Du-Nahere," shouted the Rai again. "I understand, from what Tussnig and Venn have told me, that you are a difficult man." She let the words echo over the fields. "But you seem to have made a friend in the forest worshipper, Udinny." Her words gathered around her in clouds as she shouted, as if the cold air did not want to let her spite loose. "The moment that unbeliever steps out of the gate, she is dead. You know I will do this." She pointed at the corpse of Gart with her sword. "You have seen my will. I will not waver or change my mind. Your friend lives while she is within Harn." Behind her soldiers were pulling Udinny from one of the roundhouses. "Is this monk worth something to you, Cahan?" The soldiers brought Udinny on, and the Rai continued to stare into the forest until Udinny was only five, maybe six paces away from the gate. She did not struggle. She walked with them, head held high. Her spiked hair sharp and stiff. Her eyes locked on the treeline.

Thoughts raced through his mind. Osere-cursed monk, fight them! Delay them! Give him time to think. "She dies," shouted the Rai, "the moment she steps outside the walls." The words echoed over the cold fields. "Unless you give yourself up." A name on his lips. The thought of the reborn. A flicker in his eye. Two grey figures.

"*I sense death, Cahan Du-Nahere, and it is coming to you.*"

A step away. She was only a step away. Oh, Udinny. It would have been better for her if she had never met him. But she looked fearless. Proud. Ready to die. Her gown was filthy, but her head was held high.

"A follower of forest gods, as you know," shouted the Rai, "deserves a slow death."

Udinny, on the threshold of the gate. The Rai lifting her sword once more.

"*Death, Cahan Du-Nahere, and it is coming to you.*"

He wanted none of this.

But he had brought this here.

The world became as grey as the reborn. He saw his future, chased around Crua by servants of the Cowl-Rai. Never knowing who to trust. Bringing death wherever he went. No respite, no peace. The right path now obvious.

"Stop!" he shouted, and stood. A smile spread across the Rai's face. Udinny, right on the cusp of the gate, slumped in the arms of her captors. She had been prepared to die to keep him safe. "Ranya watch over me," he said beneath his breath. The oddest thing, he felt light, as if a weight had been taken from him. He let his staff fall into the bush, he did not want them to have it, and looked down at Segur, hiding by his feet.

"You have been a good companion," he said softly, "now go, live wild and enjoy your freedom." Segur looked up at him. "Go," he hissed, with a last whine the garaur vanished into the undergrowth.

"Come to me, Cahan Du-Nahere," said the Rai and triumph flushed her skin, for she knew that once he was within range of the dullers he was only a man and his cowl would do him no good. This Rai had outwitted him, and now he was lost.

39

The cage they placed Cahan in was too small, which was no doubt deliberate. It was set in the centre of Harn, at the edge of the market square where he had come to sell produce from his farm. The stalls stood empty, and one, Gart's, would never be filled again.

The cage sides were open to the wind and the bottom of his cage sat in freezing mud which had soaked through his clothes. One of the soldiers had taken his winter coat, remarking upon its sturdiness, and left him cold and shivering. Bunched up in the cage he had no room to move. His muscles cramped painfully with no way for him to relieve them. He gritted his teeth rather than cry out when he was wracked with cramps.

The people of Harn were not free to walk about as they wished either. They had been gathered earlier before the shrine of Tarl-an-Gig. Tussnig had harangued them from beneath the badly made effigy of the balancing man. Preaching of their place in the world, and how it was their duty to obey and sacrifice for the Rai. The monk of Tarl-an-Gig seemed well pleased with his duty, full of joy even, though the people of Harn did not seem to share it and their attendance at the sermon was not voluntary. One woman, a farmer who had been brought into Harn by the soldiers, complained that she must tend her animals and the soldiers beat her viciously. After that none complained, they simply stood in silence and listened.

When the sermon was over Tussnig helped the soldiers choose some of the villagers to work, the rest were shut within their roundhouses. Cahan did not see the Leoric, or Udinny, and hoped they were not dead. That his sacrifice would not be wasted. Occasionally, he would see the trion, Venn, skulking about between the houses and avoiding him. But they were never there for long, always called away by the soldiers or the Rai.

Tussnig's chosen workers were brought to the marketplace of Harn where a pyre was being built before his cage. A stake had been set in the ground and wood was being stacked around it. First a stack of light-coloured burnwood, on top of that the darker harder woods that would burn more slowly and not as hot. The soldiers laughed as they oversaw the construction. Cahan had no doubt this was the means of his execution but they did not speak to him, not even to taunt him. Maybe it had been revealed to them that he had a cowl and they were wary. Maybe it had even been said that he was a failed Cowl-Rai, though he could not imagine it.

The soldiers took great joy in the building of the fire, and in lording it over those who worked for them. They were not slow to use the butts of their spears when they did not think the villagers worked fast enough. They knew their work though, had clearly built such pyres before. Cahan was generally a man who could find delight in seeing work done by people who cared about what they did. But not in this case, fire was a slow way for a man like him to die. The cowl holds onto life to the bitter end.

All of this pain, physical and mental, was deliberate. But

it was not the worst of it. He had told himself, again and again over the years, that the cowl was barely a part of him. That he could push it away and forget it existed. But now, in this cage, he knew without doubt that was not true. The dullers, those three strange and shiny domed boxes set about the walls of Harn, were doing their work. Whatever connection existed between the cowl and him was not only dulled, it was severed. It felt as if he had lost an arm or a leg or his sight. Everything was wrong, everything was strange: colour had faded, he could hardly see beyond ten steps because past that all was blurred. Worst of all was the emptiness, the feeling that he was no longer himself. Even in the forest, after expending the cowl's power and letting it use the life within him, he had not felt so lost, so bereft.

He once thought that he would rid himself of the cowl, this thing willed upon him by priests of a violent god. Even though he had told the trion, Venn, otherwise. But now he knew that could never be. Whatever it was, however it had come upon him, it was part of him. And here, denied it for the first time in his life, Cahan knew only sorrow and pain. The cowl was as much him as the blood that ran through his veins.

A little late, though, for such a realisation. His blood would not continue to run for long.

The troops had a fire going on the Woolside of the market and were roasting a whole crownhead. Cahan had little appetite, and the smell of singeing flesh made him feel ill. One of the troops rapped on the wooden lintel over the Leoric's door. The Rai pushed the door open.

"There is a skipper coming, Rai," said the soldier. The Rai nodded. She left the Leoric's longhouse and walked to the centre of the square, staring out past the growing pyre and through the village gates. He stared in that direction. But could not see the skipper, only a blur. He tracked its arrival by sound. The Rai strode forward and as the skipper neared he began to make out a blurry form, the messenger approaching in huge, bounding jumps.

The Rai waited. When the skipper was brought to her it was near enough that Cahan could see it had made a long trip. The gasmaw tethered above it had died, its bag so thin it was almost translucent. Its eyes had been eaten by something and the decaying remains of its tentacles hung limply from the bulbous body. The skipper's face and body were swathed in dirty blue cloth. The Rai passed them a message.

"Take this straight to Harnspire and put it into the hands of the High Leoric, no one else." The messenger replied with something Cahan could not hear. "My seal is on the paper, that will get you access. There is a gasmaw farm north of the Forestgate, take what you need."

The skipper nodded, put the message in their bag and immediately turned around and headed out of Harn to find a new gasmaw. Time was money to them, they were paid by distance and message. She watched the skipper leave and returned to the Leoric's longhouse. She did not look at him, neither to smirk nor enjoy her victory and Cahan wondered why. Maybe she did not care about him despite what he had done to her. He was clanless, she was Rai. She probably took victory over him as simply the way the world should be. Saw him killing two Rai and stripping her cowl from her as an aberration, maybe as luck on his part. If she had survived the death of her cowl she must have a formidable will.

He spent the rest of the day in a daze, trying to fight off the fog of the dullers and to grab some sleep between bouts of excruciating cramps. He slept little. The only disturbance in the afternoon when two of the Rai's troops brought in the girl who had come to his farm to warn him. She still clung to the straw doll he had given her, and stared at him with big eyes as she passed his cage. She looked angry, disappointed, and he wondered if that was because he had not listened to her message. She had told him to run and he had come here and been captured instead.

Even to a child, his actions must seem remarkably stupid.

The rest of the day passed slowly and in misery. Without anything else to do he tormented himself with thoughts of what he could have done differently. How he could have saved Udinny and not ended up in a cage. But in those thoughts he was someone else. A man he believed long dead. He had weapons and armour and was not a simple forester from the farthest reaches of Crua. In those thoughts he was a warrior.

The edges of the world wavered in time with the cramping of his muscles. The blurry vista before him changing as his agonies became unbearable. Pain, and the lack of his cowl, began to play tricks on his mind. Twice he heard himself call out. Names he barely even knew he remembered. Sometimes he no longer saw the muddy, brown and humble houses of Harn. Instead he saw walls, brightly painted walls that told the stories of Zorir. He watched the vast burning star of Iftal break apart to sever the gods and Osere from the land. He saw Zorir caper across whitewashed stonework in a wave of blood, remaking the world in fire and sending his chosen to paradise along the Star Path. He heard Saradis, Zorir's Skua-Rai, as she told him of the god, of his part to play in her plan. He hurt. Inside and outside.

He deserved the pain.

The beatings.

No, this was not real.

Always letting people down.

"Cahan Du-Nahere," Saradis' voice so loud and clear, "you have let us down again."

Boys who did not listen to the monks were beaten, and though his sister, Nahac, did her best to soothe the bruises, his world was one of constant hurt.

He was cold and he ached. He was hot, fire all around him. He was man, not a boy.

"Cahan Du-Nahere!"

In his moment of pain, and cowl-lost delirium, he thought it the voice of his sister. She had always wanted something from him towards the end. To know the words in the books that he could read and she could not. To know the training the monks had gone through with him, she made him show her even though she would never have a cowl. Always determined to learn what he knew even though she had no need to. She was not chosen. She had her own training, her place was to stand by his side. It was written so in the book of Zorir. What-was-to-be danced across the walls. A world soaked in blood and pain and fire in the name of righteousness.

You are the fire.

Blood and pain.

I am the fire.

"Keep me from the fire."

She was blood of his blood, and so they would shed blood in the name of Zorir. Together, to cut a swathe across Crua and bring down the false Cowl-Rai of Chyi. He the general, she his bodyguard. Together forever.

But she died.

He didn't want to die.

"Cahan Du-Nahere!" sharper, harder. Something hit him in the ribs. He opened his eyes. For a moment he expected his sister. But it was the Rai that stood before him, a stick in her hand which she had used to wake him. The light was gone. Night.

"What do you want?" It was a struggle to get the words out. His mouth dry for want of water.

"It hurts," she smiled at him, but there was nothing there, as if she was empty of emotion, "to be disconnected from that which you are. I imagine you are discovering that."

"Water," he said. She nodded and produced a gourd, held it out so he had to stretch his arm out of the bars to get it. He drank deep. When he had finished she came close, so close he could smell the earthy fragrance of the oil used to keep her armour shining, but not close enough he could reach her. She stared into his face, looking him up and down and her presence made him nauseous, maybe because of the obvious hate. It radiated from her.

"Tell the truth, Clanless, are you blue or red?" she asked. "Tarl-an-Gig, or do you cling to the old ways of Chyi?"

"Neither," he said. "I want no part in the wars of the Rai, my only wish was to be left alone on my farm." She stared at him, her eyes a deep brown. She looked old, wrinkles at the corners of her mouth and eyes, and across her brow. Grey in her red hair. She probably was not that old, a cowl aged you, while at the same time lengthening your life.

"This is not a world where you have the luxury of standing apart," she put a hand on the hard wood of the bars, the other on her sword, "not that it matters for you. Your days of standing are done, but I suppose you must have realised that." She wet her lips with her tongue. Stood back from the bars and looked over at the pyre then back to him. "I am from Stor, originally." Smiled to herself. "My family were powerful, close to the High Leoric, one of the Rai then, as it should be. We lived low in Storspire with the best of our people." She stepped away from the cage and sat on a cutting block, used by the villagers of Harn to chop wood. "We were loyal to Chyi and the Cowl-Rai in Tilt, we upheld the north for them. Like many, we had heard rumours that the cult of a new god was growing."

"Enough I should die," he said, "now you choose to bore me with your life story." She let out a laugh.

"They said you were a surly one." She leaned a little nearer. "But you should listen, Cahan Du-Nahere, my story will be instructive." She used her stick to poke him again. "Not that you have a choice." She looked around, as if worried someone else might be listening but the square was empty. The only guards on the gates. "We heard of this Tarl-an-Gig, some war god of the far north, but we did not worry. Another forest god, who cares, eh? They may rise a little, then we would crush them, as we had many times before with many gods." She batted at some small flying creature that floated around her head. "Small gods fall and rise and only those few who worship them notice. We took little interest in Tarl-an-Gig. We had the Cowl-Rai, after all." She was almost smiling as she spoke, digging the end of her stick into the mud — which he preferred to her digging it into him. Her face became serious. "We never saw them coming, and by the time they had moved on Storspire it was too late, we were cut off. The blue flags of a new Cowl-Rai were flying." She let out a sigh, looked up at the night sky. The night was cold and clear, though it was all a blur to him. "We expected this new Cowl-Rai to come to Storspire in some great show of power. Thought they might tear down our walls like the Cowl-Rai of Chyi had done to Tasspire long, long ago." More digging with the stick. "I saw the Cowl-Rai in rising. They stood on a hill with their generals, the most powerful Rai they had. There were not even that many of them. The Cowl-Rai could have tapped their life if they so wished. Cast some great cowl working. It was what we expected and our Rai were ready to fight. The High Leoric resplendent, his armour dyed in the red of Chyi, telling us blood would flow like water and our god would feed us the lives of the enemy." She smiled at him and as she spoke he saw her story unfold like the murals of Zorir on the white walls of the monastery. "'They will be the crops, reaped by our scythe in battle', he said, I remember that. I could not wait to fight, to drown those who stood against us in spears and sword and fire." She stared at him. "Do you know what happened?"

"I am not interested in your war stories," he said. Pain ran through him.

"The Cowl-Rai of Tarl-an-Gig never needed their cowl,

they only wished to distract us. They had been smuggling troops into Storspire for months. Their monks had been among our soldiers spreading the word of their new god. Telling of a time when the north need no longer be cold. Promises of plenty for all, not just the Rai. It had been going on for years." She caught the creature that was flying round her head, her hand darting out to imprison it. Then she stared at it in the cage of her hand before crushing it, wiping its body off her hand on the side of the cutting block. "While we watched the Cowl-Rai on the hill, those we thought of as our own people were quietly killing any troops still loyal to us. Then they opened the gates. The fighting in Storspire lasted a few hours, and as far as I know the Cowl-Rai never even stepped into the city. Only their generals came in, Dashan Ir-Vota and Istil Maf-Ren. They pushed us back to the spire and brought in dullers to surround it. It was the first time I had experienced being without my cowl. I do not need to explain the panic it caused among the Rai, to be stripped so. No one had heard of dullers then. No doubt you are feeling a similar sensation now." She smiled, all teeth. "They gave us an ultimatum: come to Tarl-an-Gig and be forgiven, or die at the hands of common soldiers."

"So you rolled your log over to the new god." She nodded. "Well, thank you for this history lesson, but I fail to see why you felt the need to share."

"It is not for the history I tell you this," she said, turning back to him. "It is for what happened after. My second-father, a stubborn man, one of the generals of Storspire and cowlhard all his life, refused to turn. Even when the trion of our family, Sabjin, told him this was the correct way, that it would bridge the way forward for his wives, husbands and children, he would not give up Chyi." Cahan stared at her. "The generals of Tarl-an-Gig made a fire," she pointed at the pyre her soldiers had been preparing all day with her stick. "They let it burn down to coals, and then they suspended my father over it and made us watch him die. He was powerful, could rip the life out of his enemies and feed his cowl from a distance. I had seen him do it many times. But the dullers stopped that. So the cowl used his life to fight death. He burned on the outside and it ate him away from the inside." She stood. "It took him two days to die and he never stopped screaming." She shrugged. "I simply wanted you to know what is in store for you, Cahan Du-Nahere." He stared at her. She had a peculiar expression on her face, as if she had more to say but she was struggling to do it. Then she stepped close, not close enough for him to reach, for what good it would have done, but close. "What you did to me in the forest," she hissed, "undo it. Give me my cowl back and I will kill you now, quick and clean." He could see the hunger in her eyes, the need.

"How can you want that, when you know the truth of it?"

"What truth?" She looked confused.

"You saw your secondfather burn, die screaming while the cowl tried to live. You know who the true master is between you and the cowl." She shook her head.

"Give it back," she said, each word hard as heartwood. "Give back what you stole." He shook his head.

"I cannot," his throat dry, "even if I wanted to, it is not possible." Then she was near, hands on the bars, face against them. All caution gone and her features twisted by need and anger.

"You must!" she said. "I am nothing now, a pariah. Unwelcome among my own. I am Rai without a cowl, I am cursed. How do you think that is?"

"Be thankful you have your sanity," he told her, "few who are stripped of the cowl hold onto it."

"I wish I had not," she said, "it would be better not to understand what I have lost. How I am regarded."

"You have been freed," he told her. She stepped back,

picked up her helmet from the floor and put it on. Used the action to give herself space. Compose herself.

"Tomorrow morning we light the fire," she said, "it will burn well, and when it is coals we shall place you over them. Few here know it, but you are far more powerful than my secondfather was. You will last much longer and I will make sure you are not alone in your pain, Cahan Du-Nahere," she spat the words. "You seem to care for the people of this village—"

"You do not need them, they are nothing to you," he said it too quickly, betrayed himself. Betrayed the people of Harn.

"You are right, they are nothing to me." She took a deep breath. "But they are something to you, Cahan Du-Nahere." She glanced back at the village. "The trion said you were soft, that you hid it but you cared for people." She spat. "It is unfortunate for them. You will die a slow death over the fire, and while you die you will hear these people curse your name and curse that you ever came to their village. It will be a chorus so loud it will bring the Osere from below to claim you." She stepped back. "The monk you like will die first. I will burn her with you."

"I cannot give you what you want." He must have sounded broken, it was what he felt.

"That is a pity," she said, "if you could, I would have left these people to grub about in the dirt to their hearts' content."

She turned away from him and as she did he screamed, rattled the bars and tested his strength against them. But the cage was well made, and he was well trapped within. He fell, deep into despair, expecting to hear a familiar voice slithering into his mind.

You need me.

But for the first time since he had been dragged unconscious out of the blooming rooms by monks of Zorir, his cowl was silent.

40

His existence that night was febrile, half-alive. The combination of pain and the dullers twisting his mind. Sometimes he watched the pyre as it grew. Other times his pain was so great he thought himself already on it, skin burning while his cowl consumed him from within. Between these times he found himself existing in another place.

A boy crying over his bruises in the corner of a monastery garden among the snowflowers.

The heat of the day oppressive.

Nasim the gardener making a poultice of Allbalm. Telling him to calm himself.

"Cahan Du-Nahere! Cahan Du-Nahere!"

"Nasim?"

He was freezing, shivering. The voice was not the gardener's. Was it the Rai, come back to ask once more for the impossible? He did not want to see her, kept his eyes closed. An animal in a trap refusing to see the hunter closing.

"Cahan!" a harsh and urgent whisper.

"Go away."

"I cannot."

The voice. Not that of the Rai.

He opened one eye. Pain rushing in.

"Cahan Du-Nahere, are you alive?" Snow falling, hard and fast. A blur of the air. He did not recognise the face before him, dressed in heartwood armour, of a very expensive sort, painted with the god marks of Tarl-an-Gig, great blue whorls on the cheeks and around the eyes.

"It is me, Cahan, Venn. Do you remember me?"

"Venn?" he said. The face snapped into focus. "You told them where to find me, I do not blame you." He could hear self-pity in his own voice. He did not like it, preferred anger.

"What?"

"You were talking to the Rai. Telling her what to do." He closed his eyes again. "I do not blame you," he said again. He wanted nothing more than to fade away.

"Sorha," said Venn, "that is her name."

"Yes," he said, "I think I remember." His teeth were chattering, a movement beyond his control. He had never needed to worry about the cold before, his cowl had protected him. Venn stared through the bars.

"She was coming here anyway," said Venn. They sounded tired. "I had no choice but to help her." Cahan's head ached and the world spun.

"Why?"

"I lied to my mother, in Harnspire," whispered Venn. "Told her I had done what she wished, woken my cowl." They held up their hand, pointed at it. "Sorha knew it was a lie. But said it wasn't in exchange for everything I knew about you." Cahan tried to move in the cage, find some comfort and failed.

"So you exchanged my life for yours." He opened his eyes to look at the trion. Found bitterness welling up where there had been magnanimity a moment before. "It seems your principles did not last long. Maybe you really are Rai." Venn recoiled at his words, as if bruised by them.

"I came here to save you," said Venn. "I fought my mother,

she did not want me to come. I had to pile lie upon lie. Confront her before her most powerful Rai so she would look weak if she did not send me." Venn looked away. "She hates me for it, I am sure." Then they spoke again, their voice thick with desperation. "We have to get away."

"The village—" began Cahan.

"Sorha is obsessed with you, and if she loses me my mother will never allow her back," they spoke softly and urgently. "When we go she will follow. She will forget all about the village. I stole the key." They moved forward, unlocked the cage. "The gates are guarded, so we will need to go over the wall." Cahan more fell out of the cage than climbed out. To go from being enclosed to free should have been a welcome sweetness, but all he knew was a pain in his muscles, growing until it was almost beyond bearing. It became a battle not to cry out.

"Get up," hissed Venn, trying to pull him upright. "We have to go."

When the pain had subsided he stood, let Venn lead him away. Round the back of a building, through Tanside and over the wooden wall. They made for Woodedge. He felt the moment he left the influence of the dullers. The pain and the cold sloughed away, it was like leaving the ghost of an old man back in Harn and he ran, free of cold and pain; young again. Clarity returned to his mind, focus to his vision. All those years he had been telling himself he did not rely on his cowl. What a lie that had been.

You need me.

"Where do we go?" said Venn. Despite their armour they did not wear a sword, and they were not well dressed for the cold, already shivering. Wrapping their arms around themselves to keep warm.

"To my farm." Cahan let out a low whistle and a moment later Segur appeared from the undergrowth. He pointed at the trion but they shied away from the garaur.

"Friend," he spoke to them both. Venn's eyes widened.

"Segur will not hurt you unless I tell it to," he said, "let it climb your body and sit around your neck. It will share its warmth with you." The garaur whined, and Venn looked nervous, but gave a nod of their head and the garaur twisted up around them. The trion continued to look worried, but when the garaur made no attempt to do anything but be warm they relaxed a little.

"Why go to your farm?" they said. "We should escape."

"We will," he said, "but we need supplies, and you need warmer clothes." He looked back at Harn. "First, I must retrieve my staff," he said.

He found the staff where he left it and the feel of its wood calmed him, providing a strong sense of something that was right. From there they made their way quickly through Woodedge, staying alert for any noise that did not fit.

They heard nothing.

He was not surprised. Sorha and her troops were from the towns. Townspeople were even more superstitious than the villagers who lived on the edge of the wood. But with every step Cahan found himself struggling; not physically, but mentally. A surety within him growing. Venn might believe what they said about Sorha chasing them, Cahan was sure they did. But they were young, innocent, ready to believe what they wanted rather than what was. Cahan knew better. Sorha would not leave the village alone when she discovered his escape; even without her cowl she was still Rai. When thwarted others would pay the price.

"Come on, Cahan!" Venn shouting from in front of him.

They stopped before the fields his farm sat in. No tracks in the snowy grass around it, no lights burned in the building. He walked and Venn ran ahead.

"Hurry, Cahan!"

Harn: the monk Udinny, the Leoric, her child for whom he had been through so much to save. The girl and her straw doll. The returned crownheads and many other small kindnesses he had been gifted.

"Come on Cahan."

Venn would never know they were wrong. They would never come back here. Would have no guilt to carry.

Stop this, he told himself.

He was not a warrior. He was a simple forester. He had been nothing else for many years.

You need me.

"Cahan?" said the trion, "did you speak?"

"No," he said, walking quickly, taking the lead. Pushing open the door to his farm. "There are packs under the bed. Grab food and warm clothes."

Who are you?

"Cahan?" said Venn, they looked confused. He felt the same. Those were not the usual words he heard.

"It is my cowl, that is all."

"I hear a voice but no words, what does it say?"

"Nothing you need bother yourself with, child." They gave him a look he suspected was common to children everywhere when told to mind their own business. "Now pack quickly before they know we are missing. They will come here first." They continued to pack, memories of Harn gnawed at him.

"Cahan? Cahan?" he shook his head. Rubbed his temples.

"What?" the word coming out overly gruff and he saw the trion's eyes widen, as if he had insulted them.

"I only asked what else I should bring, I have hard bread, dried meat and some cheese."

"There is a coat, take that," he pointed at a coat by the door.

"What of you?"

"I will be all right."

"Are you worried about the villagers?"

"No," said too fast, almost barked. "You said yourself, Sorha will follow us." Venn nodded, keeping their head bowed as they went to get the coat from the door.

What was he doing? What had been true before the walls

of Harn when they were about to execute Udinny had not changed. The villagers would die, Udinny would die. The fact he would not be there to see it happen would not change it.

They left, trudging through the snow towards Woodedge. The Rai would never stop coming for him. Never. No matter where he went.

Except Wyrdwood.

None would follow them there. Even Udinny, who was the most infuriatingly curious person he had ever met, had been wary of entering Wyrdwood. There they could live as hermits, make no contact with others.

But Udinny had come with him to Wyrdwood, partly because she thought her god asked it of her. And partly because she did not want to let someone go alone into danger.

And now she would die.

Hard, too, she would die hard. Marked as a traitor for following Ranya, a god most had forgotten.

They would all die.

"Cahan," said Venn, somehow the trion had got well ahead of him again. "Why have you stopped? They could come at any minute." He rolled his head back, closed his eyes and let the snow fall upon his face. He had lived alone for a long time. It was no life.

"I need something else from the farm," he said.

"What?" they asked.

"A shovel," he said, and turned back.

"Why?" shouted Venn.

"To dig something up."

Deep in the Forest

"I do not want it, Nahac." You say this and you are sobbing, sobbing, always the crying little boy. "I do not want their wars or their cowl. I want to go back to the farm."

"I would gladly take it from you," she is angry with you, she was always angry with you near her end, "but it is not to be."

"I never wanted to be special."

"But you are special, Cahan," she told you. "So you must be brave."

More and more angry with you as the years passed. As you grew into what they planned. You still see her, the only image of her left is her sneer as you are taken, sobbing and begging for it not to be, into the dark hole of the blooming room. The stench of the corpses so strong you can taste it, decay, as all things decay. As you will decay. All that will be left after you become the fire is decay. A world rotting down to nothing as its people depart for the Star Path. You are hammering on the door, begging to be let out. Trying not to breathe in. The pain wracking you. Days of pain. You are surrounded by death.

You never wanted her to be angry. Never. You wanted

to be together, but Crua cares nothing for what you want. It is a wild land, and it takes and it takes and only the strong are able to stand against it.

It took Nahac. Your sister.

She was not chosen. Her fate was not danced across the walls, not painted on a world soaking in blood and pain and fire.

And you wanted to run.

But you could never run fast enough.

They always caught you.

You are the fire.

41

Cahan knew every contour of the ground and every plant and tree that grew between his farm and the shrine to Ranya in Woodedge. He knew the tracks of every animal that crossed it on the ground, the air, or through the trees. It was the place where he had left the carved animal belonging to the child, murdered by the Rai at his farm. It was the site of the grave of someone he once knew. The place where he buried the expectations of priests and monks and sought to leave behind a life forced upon him by others.

It was where Cahan Du-Nahere died, and a clanless forester, scratching a living on the edge of society returned to his home wishing he could live as though he had never left.

But Crua was a hard land, and it cared little for what a person might think or want. In Crua, the dead might rise and so it was to be here. In the darkness. In the forest.

He moved the shrine of sticks built into a semblance of a hunter's net. Showed Venn where the ground was disturbed from digging up his coin what felt like a lifetime ago. Gave them a shovel and told them to dig, then thrust the blade of his own shovel into the ground.

"What are we digging for?" said Venn, looking at the shovel.

"For the lives of others," he told them, and levered out a spadeful of soil. The trion looked confused, but pushed their shovel into the ground, straining and standing on the blade to add weight to it.

"The ground is hard," they said.

"It will get softer the deeper we go." Venn managed to scrape a thin layer of earth from where they were digging.

"How far down must we dig?" they said.

"Far enough."

"How will I know how far is enough?"

"You will know. Now dig. I do not want to lose the darkness." Venn stared at him, plainly confused, then began to dig once more. He was about to join them when he felt a prickling on his neck. A sense of being watched. He turned, two grey figures in the wood. "I will be a moment," he said to Venn.

"Why are you—"

"Dig, I will not be long." His voice harsh, no room for argument. Venn frowned, turned away and continued struggling to break ground. Cahan made his way through the brush, following the shadows of the grey figures away from the clearing until he came to the edge of the wood. The reborn stood there waiting, his farm a shadow in the distance behind them.

"Thirty-five against one, Cahan Du-Nahere," said the reborn, her visor muffling her voice.

"I have a plan."

"Call on us. You will not survive otherwise."

"My plan is for the villagers to escape," he said. "That is all. I do not intend to fight."

"You mean to die."

The reborn stood quite still, their entire attention focused on him. He expected them to say more, to argue with him. Instead they simply turned away, walking back towards his farm. He watched them, wondering what they thought. If they considered him brave or foolish, or if they were simply angry at not getting what they wanted. It did not matter. His mind was made up. He would free Harn even though he knew the cost would most likely be dear.

Venn was still digging to little effect when he returned. Cahan picked up his shovel and joined them. It was hard work, but honest. Before too long the spade hit something with a solid "clunk".

What he had buried there was not as deep beneath the surface as he expected, not as hard to reach as he thought it should be.

"Help me clear this box of soil, Venn," he said, and they set to work. Digging around it, brushing off dirt until it was fully revealed. A box of darkwood as long and as wide as a person. The withered floatvine he had used to transport it still lay across the top. The fine carvings, that he had watched a woman do, wondering at her skill as her hands moved, had not been touched or spoiled by years in the soil. "Help me lift it," he said. Venn stood on the box, trying to get their hands under the edge of the lid. "How do you reckon to lift it if you are standing on it, child?" They gave him a resentful look. "Come here, to where I am. There are handles." He used the spade to clear the area and then they squatted at the edge of the grave, reaching down to grab the box.

"It is heavy," said Venn.

"Aye, it contains an entire life. Now lift." Together they strained, though Cahan felt he did a lot more work than the trion. He gave one final grunt of effort and the box came free of the land. Venn falling back into the grass, almost causing Cahan to lose his balance. It had been hard, the digging and the pulling, and he took a moment to get his breath back. Venn was the first to sit up and crawled over to the box, shuffling through snowy leaf mulch.

"Beautiful," said Venn, rubbing some of the dirt off the

carvings of trees, and faces hidden within the trees. "It looks like it was meant for a High Leoric." They looked puzzled. "How does it open?"

"It is willwood, Venn, it will open only for me." Cahan placed his hand on the top of the box. It shuddered. For a moment he thought nothing would happen. That somehow the land had leached its magics away and it had forgotten him. He hoped it had, then felt shame at thinking that, at wishing for an excuse to run.

But the box had not forgotten, the carvings of branches and roots that ran down the side and over the top withdrew. They twisted and curled around until they became ornate handles, allowing him to lift the top off. He heard Venn's sharp intake of breath as they saw what the box contained.

Open, it looked even more like a coffin than before. A fine red cloth filled the bottom, and laid out, as if it were the body of some great ruler, was a set of armour and matching weapons.

"These are yours?" said the trion, their voice a whisper. "I have never seen anything so fine. Who are you?" They stared at him, wide-eyed.

"Not the person those who made these for me thought."

The trion was right about the beauty of the armour. It was a full-body piece, made of dark cloudwood connected to willwood by a process known only to the armourer. It was carved with leaves, strange, serrated leaves, and he had never seen them growing on any tree. The helmet was crowned with the same sort of branching horns he had seen on the boughry in the forest, but unlike them it was symmetrical.

Laid, as if held in the scaled gauntlets, were his axes. Each made of one piece of cloudtree heartwood, their form curved and flowing from the sharp tips of the handles to the wide blades of the hatchets. By them a quiver full of arrows, and in a pocket on it a number of bowstrings.

"You are not running away, are you?" said Venn. Cahan shook his head.

"I have run a long time, child," he told them. "The people of Harn are in danger because of me."

"You cannot stand against all those troops."

"Do not need to," he told them. "I only need to distract them. I want you to go in and lead the villagers out of Harn and to Woodedge."

"Me?" Venn took a step back.

"I will not force you, it will be dangerous," he said. They stared at him, blinked twice. "You are free to go if you wish." Venn took another step back. "But if we are lucky, Venn, they will not even know we are gone yet. You can simply walk back in, and if they do know I am gone you can say you were trying to capture me. That I am at my farm." The trion still stared. "Or go. I will not hold it against you. I will understand. Find a skyraft, not even the Cowl-Rai dare interfere with them." Venn looked down at the armour in the box. Then back at him.

"You are a warrior."

"I have never wanted it."

"Why are you doing this?" Confusion on their face. "Why don't you run?" He did not answer straightaway.

"Sorha, Venn, she will leave no one alive behind her."

"No, she will chase us, she will——"

"That is not true. She is Rai, she will want revenge," said Cahan. "That is how they think." Guilt flooding through him, as familiar as it was hateful. What was he doing? Venn was a child. "You should go, Venn. Leave here. I can sneak in, get those most in danger away and . . ."

"You really believe we can save them?" Cahan breathed, thought about it. About what he planned and, to his surprise, he found he did.

"Yes," he said. "If luck is on our side."

"And Tarl-an-Gig."

"I do not believe in gods, Venn." The trion stared at him, nodded to themselves.

"I will help you," they said. Cahan felt as if he wilted

within. Then he told himself, whatever it took he would get the Trion away this time. Even if it all went wrong and he could save no other, he would get Venn out.

"We need to get the armour from the box, and you will have to help me dress."

As Venn helped him put the armour on, part of him thought it should have felt strange. He had not worn it in longer than the trion had been alive.

It felt like the touch of an old friend.

The armour was part of him, literally. As each piece was fitted he felt his cowl react. Binding with it. Changing its shape so it fitted the contours of his body; how it was now, not how it had been when he buried the box. When they were finished Venn stared at him.

"You look resplendent." He nodded. The armour was meant to be seen, the bracket-fungus shoulder guards had been impregnated with colour that glowed even in the day. Designed so the troops of Zorir would know their Cowl-Rai had taken the field. It was the only thing he had taken from the monastery. Dug in the ashes and ruins to find it. Surprised it had not been stolen. Wanting its protection as he ran, looking for a place to hide. Discovering that the lessons in killing his trainers had given him had stuck. That no matter how he might hate it, he could fight. And he fought well, found in it what he thought was solace. Sold his skills and, somewhere on that journey, lost himself.

"Resplendent is not what will serve us tonight," he said, and willed the armour to be less. It changed: the horns on the helm melted away, the colour subsumed, the carving vanished until he was as smooth and dark as the night. Fighting armour.

"Chyi's feet," said Venn, "I have never seen the like."

"Pass me the axes," he said. Venn lifted the weapons from the box, plainly surprised by how light they were. Cahan watched them study one, then stop when they came upon the marks on the handle, the many scratches and cuts. They looked at the other axe, and found the same.

"Is this from battle?" they said. He shook his head.

"When I was young and angry," he told them, "I named these weapons Truth and Justice. When I finally understood the foolishness of that act, I scored those names out."

"What was foolish about that? They are good names." He took the axes from them, pushed them against the thigh pieces of the armour which held them tight without need for holster or scabbard.

"That is because you are young," he said quietly. "Those words are lies, Venn. The only truth someone with a weapon and the strength to use it hears is that which they want to hear. The only justice they can bring is that which they believe is right. Truer to call these axes tyranny and fear." Venn nodded, though Cahan was not sure they really understood. They picked up the quiver and passed that across to him. This they did not comment on. Like most, the trion was suspicious of arrows.

Cahan walked over to where he had left his staff against a tree, picked it up. Removed the sleeve from the bottom of it. He took a string from the pocket on the quiver, mawgut, still strong after all these years. He tied the quiver at his hip. Then he took the staff and tied one end of the string on. It took all of his strength to bend the staff so he could tie on the other end and his staff became what had been denied it for many years.

A beautiful, deadly arc.

"A bow," said Venn, "all this time you carried a bow around with you. You could have been executed for it."

"The bow has always been my favoured weapon." He tested the tension of the string, found it familiar. "This weapon I named Loss," he said, "that name I kept."

"Why?"

"It is what it causes," he said, and thought, though did not add, "and it is what I went through to get it." Venn stared at him, but did not press him any further. "We go back now," he used the bow to point towards Harn.

"What happens when we get there?" they asked. "I could have the villagers destroy the dullers and . . ."

"No," said Cahan. He would have to speak straight to the child, he owed them that. "Do not believe what you hear in stories, do not believe what you hear in songs or in taverns from soldiers. There are no heroes who take on armies by themselves. It does not happen, and untrained villagers, like those of Harn, cannot fight soldiers. If they try and destroy the dullers, the guards will kill them. It is that simple. You get as many of them out and over the wall as you can, that is all I want from you." Venn blinked, then nodded and pulled their helmet down a little tighter on their head.

"You could win, though." Cahan froze. "Without the dullers, you could," they said. "I saw you in the clearing. Sorha told me what you . . ."

"No," he said. "You also saw what it did to me in the forest." Venn bowed their head. "The cowl requires the lives of others, Venn. And with each life taken, it gets a little easier to take. And you become a little crueller."

"But it is for a good—"

"That is how it starts, Venn." They blinked. Nodded. "We should go."

It felt as if every step he took was longer than the last. As if he had more strength and stood straighter. A trick of the armour, of his cowl being linked to it, of familiarity.

"How long were you a soldier for?" asked Venn. He had forgotten how inquisitive the young were. Almost as bad as Udinny.

"I was never a soldier." Silence then, for a few steps.

"You look like a soldier." Cahan did not reply, only grunted. "So the weapons are for show?" The forester continued to walk, not looking back, and tried to keep the growl out of his voice.

"The people who trained me thought it important I knew how to fight." He pushed his way through ferns, heavy with snow. "And then, well, it was the only thing I knew how to do."

"So you *were* a soldier." He did not reply. "Did you fight for the Cowl-Rai?"

"Sometimes," he said.

"Were you not worried they would recognise what you are? You are Cowl-Rai, aren't you?"

"How can I be?" He did not look at the trion. "We have a Cowl-Rai. One a generation, is that not the truth of it? All others are pretenders, and no more will come now, if you believe the monks of Tarl-an-Gig. I was always careful to keep myself as far away from the centres of power as possible so my cowl was not recognised. Just another spear in the wall." He walked on. Felt the moment when Venn was about to ask more. "This is not a part of my life I wish to discuss, child."

"Oh," said Venn, and Cahan hoped then for some quiet. He was to be disappointed.

"Is it frightening?" they said.

"Is what frightening?"

"To be in a battle."

"Yes."

"You must be very brave." He stopped again. Pushed the heel of his hand into his forehead in a bid to drive his frustration away.

"Bravery is a lie," he said. "We do things because we must, because we have no choice."

"But this," said Venn, "going to free Harn. You have a choice not to, that is brave." He stared at them, and felt envy at their worldview, at how simple it was.

"No, Venn," he said. "I do not have a choice."

"But you may die."

"If I walk away now, I will have the weight of Harn upon me. All those who die because I did not act, they will be mine to carry. It is a slower death, that, but still death. I realised lately I have been dying for years and have had enough." Venn stared at him, their brow wrinkled in confusion. Then they nodded. Cahan hoped they could walk on in silence but the child spoke again.

"How come you have a bow? Bows are banned."

"It is a secret of the clanless."

"And the Forestals," they said, "are they clanless?"

"No, they are Forestals."

"So what is the difference?" He stopped again. It was clear he would have no peace until the trion had at least some answers.

"What weapons are the clanless allowed, Venn?"

"They are not." His answer was rote, said as if Cahan's question was foolish, and to most it would be.

"Exactly, but everyone else in Crua is allowed a weapon, most carry a spear, maybe a long knife if they are better off." Venn nodded. "Do you know what it is to be hated, Venn? To be seen as less simply because of some accident of birth?" Cahan could see the thoughts working through Venn's mind. "It was how I was brought up, for the first six years of my life. To know that I was less. If someone wanted what I had, I must give it up. If violence was threatened, I must run or bear it."

"That is not right," said Venn.

"It is the way it is," he said, and continued to walk. "A staff," he lifted the bow a little, "well, you cannot forbid someone to have a staff. It is needed for walking. But it can be used as a weapon, it has no edge but you can knock someone's brains out with it." The trion watched him, as if fascinated. "At some point, someone realised there is no huge difference between a staff for walking and fighting and a bowstaff, if the right wood is used. My mothers took me into Wyrdwood, where they knew none would come. There they trained me in the bow. I could hit a target at fifty paces by the time I was five," he pushed on through

the snowy underbrush and barely felt the cold, odd that
Venn did. From there they walked on in silence and Cahan
found he was, for the first time, uncomfortable with it.
"How did the dullers affect you, child?" In the quiet
thoughts of the violence to come were beginning to crowd
his mind and now he wanted the trion to speak, to push
them away.

"Nausea, mostly," said Venn. "And a strange feeling with
it. Like I felt some things more keenly, the cold, pain." They
slipped, almost falling into the brush but righting themselves at the last moment. "And other things, sight, hearing,
my strength, they all felt lessened. Was it like that for you?"

"Aye," he said. "But more extreme, I expect." He stopped.
"I thought you had not fed your cowl?"

"I have not. I will not kill," they told him. "My mind is
made up, that is why I must leave before my mother finds
out the truth. She will not forgive me, ever. She will force
me somehow and I am not sure I am strong enough to stand
against torture." Cahan nodded but it set him to thinking,
all his life he had believed a cowl only wakes when its user
makes their first kill. But if the dullers affected Venn, either
the trion lied to him or what they were all told was wrong.
Maybe Venn could not juggle fire, or drown someone in
their own water, but they had a bond. Looking back, they
had felt the life of the forest. The trion was cowlbound
without need for death. "Cahan," they said. He looked over
his shoulder as Venn ran to catch up with him, plants and
bushes shivering off their blankets of snow as they passed.

"Aye?"

"How can you intend to fight them with the dullers
there? They make you weak. I still think I could do something . . ." The trion looked so earnest.

"Venn, they would kill you. Maybe you would manage
to destroy one duller, but the other two would still be in
place. It would be a waste of your life and any who helped
you." He reached out and put a hand on the shoulder piece

of their armour. "Your job is to get the people out. Do not underestimate the importance of it." He touched the axe on his right thigh, drawing their attention to it. "If I find myself in a position where I must use these, then I am already lost." He tried to smile at them, but it was not something he did often, and he was not sure it comforted Venn. "Dullers or not, if I have to set foot in the village I will be overwhelmed."

"Then how . . ."

"This," Cahan held up the bow. "It is a far better weapon than an axe, sword or a spear." They furrowed their brow, distrustful of it. How could he expect them to be anything else? All the people of Crua ever heard was that a bow was for cowards. He lifted it up, so Venn could see the carvings. "Have you ever seen a weapon like this before?" The trion shook their head. "Ever seen a bow?" Venn shook their head again. "This is a forestbow, banned throughout Crua. See how one end is sharp and the other is flat?" They nodded. "So it can be passed off as a staff. There is no finer weapon of war than the forestbow." The trion cocked their head to one side.

"A bow is no use against Rai," they said. Cahan passed it over and Venn held it gingerly, as if it could taint him somehow.

"That is what they would like you to think. Up close, Rai are formidable, with the power of a cowl it can take, what? Ten or so men to kill a strong one?" Venn nodded. "This," he took the forestbow from them, "well, it can hit an armoured target in Harn from Woodedge. Even at such a distance the arrow will punch straight through them and kill whoever stands behind." The trion stared at him. "It is a leveller, Venn, it destroys the Rai's advantage. You can shoot them down before they even see you, their cowl is of no use."

"I thought fighting was about honour," said Venn. Cahan shook his head.

"That is another lie they tell you to control you. Fighting is about one thing and one thing only." Venn was focused on him, like they were drinking up his words. "It is about being the one who walks away alive."

"But you are only one man with a bow." Cahan nodded.

"I am," he said, then spoke again, more to himself than to the trion. "But give me a hundred, trained well in the use of the forestbow, and I would break any army the Rai of Crua can throw at me." Venn continued to stare, and Cahan wondered if they thought him mad. "We head for Harn, Venn. You will see. I will kill the gate guards and, arrogant in the power they are so used to, the Rai and her soldiers will come rushing out to find me." He held up the forestbow again. "Not one will get within a spear throw of me."

"I have never heard of such a thing being done," they said.

"Of course you haven't, they do not allow such stories." They walked on towards Harn, Venn thinking through what Cahan had said. Cahan thinking, too, knowing he had promised the child more than was possible. He had not used his bow for a long time, and it required constant practice to be quick enough to take down groups of attacking soldiers. But he did not need to kill every soldier in Harn, he only needed to get them out of the village. Then he could vanish into the wood, that was his best chance of living. The wood was his element, not theirs. He would move around them silent as death, picking them off until it became too much and they ran back to Harn, only to find it empty.

That was the plan, at least.

42

Harn, a silhouette in a wooded clearing. Torches burning around the wall illuminating the two soldiers at the front gate. Venn and Cahan moved around the edge of the clearing until they were opposite the wall between the Forestgate and the Tiltgate.

"Are you ready?" Cahan whispered. The trion, wide-eyed, breathing shallow, nodded. "Try to breathe slowly, it will help." They licked their lips, nodded again.

"Cahan," said Venn, "staff fighting, you can do it without killing?" He nodded, thinking it an odd question to ask at such a time. "When this is over, will you teach me?"

"Of course," he said, though somewhere within he thought it unlikely. The truth of this; him, alone, against the Rai and her soldiers? He was unlikely to leave this place. He had dug up the grave of who he had been, but Harn was likely to be the final resting place of who he had become.

The trion smiled at him.

"Good," they said, and then they were gone, into the darkness and heading for the walls of Harn. He watched them, keeping low over the cleared ground between the village and the trees. Venn reached the wall and pressed their body against it. He had told them to stand and wait and listen before going over. If it sounded like there was commotion, as if either of them were missed, then they should come back and he would cover their retreat with his forestbow.

So he waited, only realising he had been holding his breath when Venn turned and, rather than going over the wall, which he had expected, worked their way along it until they found a place they could go under.

Listening in the darkness.

Hoping not to hear shouts. Not to hear the voices of soldiers calling out as they saw Venn appear.

Nothing.

Cahan worked his way back around Woodedge until he was looking at the Tiltgate and the guards before it. Now it was his turn to control his breathing. Long, slow and calming breaths. It did no good to loose a bow when worked up. Target shooting was an exercise in concentration; a place where the rush of battle served you poorly, quick reactions were all well and good close up, but not for an archer. It was a cold, deliberate and considered thing, to kill from a distance.

He felt his heart slowing.

Stood.

Hidden.

Clothed in the darkness of Woodedge.

He tested the bow. It had been many years since he had drawn the forestbow, and though it was a skill never forgotten, it was still one that should be practised, for strength, if nothing else. But also because an archer must know their bow, how it felt, how the tension of it was transmuted into distance. How the arrows would act in the wind or lack of it. A bowstaff changed over time, with damp and heat and use, and those changes could only be felt through loosing arrows. He had been confident in front of Venn, as the trion was young and needed his confidence to feed their own. But he was less confident when he was the only audience.

It was getting harder to lie to himself.

He heard a rustling, felt something by his feet and looked down to see Segur looking back at him.

"Hide, Segur," he said. "This is none of your business and you will only get hurt." The garaur whined and stayed exactly where it was. Such was the way of animals, they could not be forced into doing what you wished them to do; they could only be asked. And often, they knew when they were needed. He drew comfort from the garaur's presence even as he drew the bow.

Felt the burn in his arms and upper body.

Relaxed.

He had not drawn it as far as it could be drawn. Even with the help of the cowl beneath his skin his strength had lapsed. Still, he was sure that he had enough range to hit the guards on the gate. The first he would kill. The second he would wound. That should bring out the rest. Then he would show himself and draw them into the forest to play a deadly game of garaur and histi while Venn evacuated the villagers. From the quiver at his hip he took five arrows and stuck them in the ground so they could be easily accessed. Then he nocked the first arrow, drew back the bow and looked along it at his target.

Let out a breath.

The world became his line of sight. All other things disappeared from his conscience.

The arrow :: The target.

Muscles burning as he held the bow at tension.

The string digging in against his fingers.

The soldier in his sight.

Slowly, he let the tension fall from the string.

Who was this person he aimed at? Did they have a family. Were they expecting trouble? They had no idea they were about to die. Would have no chance to say their goodbyes. What gave him the right to do this?

He thought of Sorha, the Rai, and how she had described the way he would burn. A slow and painful death. Whoever this guard was they would no doubt have watched without any sorrow for him. They would have laughed at his agonies, made jokes with their fellows. To them, he was simply a threat to the blue and the Cowl-Rai. A clanless non-person who deserved no better than to die painfully for Tarl-an-Gig.

Nock pull and loose.

One swift motion, drilled into him in his earliest years. Barely a moment to look at the target. Let instinct rule. Not as fast as he would have been once, when his body was at one with the bow. A moment of hesitation as he checked his sighting.

The arrow flew.

He watched and waited with the fascination of an artisan inspecting their work. Did not hear it hit the target. But saw them fall. They dropped their spear, stood for a single breath and then collapsed backwards against the wall of Harn. The second guard did not even notice.

He drew again, a little slower this time as he aimed to wound, and that was harder. To kill was the main body mass, to wound was a smaller target. A leg was always good.

Nock. Pull.

And loose.

The arrow flew. He heard a dull thud and saw the guard turn. Missed. The arrow had hit the wooden wall behind the guard. They saw their fellow, lying against the wall. Walked over, unsure of what was happening.

"Tanhiv, are you drunk?" the words echoing across the clearing.

Nock pull and loose.

This arrow flew true. The guard screamed out in pain. A shout from another, behind the wall. "We are attacked!"

He waited for troops to come out of the village, angry as disturbed orit.

Nothing.

The only sound the wounded guard calling out for help.

He took up another arrow, nocked it.

Wait.

No one came.

Wait.

Had the troops gone, left only those two guards?

Wait.

Surely not. It made no sense.

Wait.

Had Venn been right? Had Sorha really left the moment she knew they were gone?

The Tiltgates of Harn began to close. The wounded guard had managed to crawl to them and was pulled through by some unseen hand.

The gates shut.

No.

A voice from the village, cutting through the cold air of the night.

"Cahan Du-Nahere!" Sorha. Her voice echoing around the clearing. "A bow is a coward's weapon, I thought you better." He did not answer. No doubt she thought to find his position from his voice. She let time pass, and then when she was sure he would not answer carried on. "We have the trion, caught them coming under the wall. It was foolish of you to come back." The cold, which he had not felt until that moment, once more gnawed his bones.

"Let the trion go, and the villagers," he shouted, "and I will come to you."

"I think not," she shouted back. "How odd that we find ourselves in the same position as before, Cahan Du-Nahere. All you are good for is endangering your friends. But I am generous and my offer remains the same: give yourself up and I will let some of this village live. Don't and I will start killing villagers again. The monk first." He heard laughter. "This time I am not coming out to let you watch, of course. Not when you brandish that coward's weapon, but you will hear them screaming as they die. And I will throw the heads over the wall so you know which ones have given their lives for you."

He had failed.

As swift and simple as that. She had seen through his tactic, been waiting for him. Now he was no better off than he had been when they caged him.

You need me.

He would not listen to the voice. Would not.

You need me.

The cowl lied, of course. As soon as he was in range of the dullers, it would be no help at all. In fact he would be weaker because of it. He would fight poorly, his strength and will abruptly sapped.

But.

He did not need to fight well. All he needed was a distraction, and if he created enough of one then maybe Venn and the rest of Harn could escape. Maybe Sorha and her troops would be so occupied with him they would not notice them leaving. The bow might be of no use now, but he had his axes. Even without the cowl he was well trained in their use.

He looked down at Segur, sitting on its rump, staring up at him.

"Well, Segur," he said, "I never really expected to walk away." The garaur whined at him. "Now you really must hide." He knelt so he could scratch between its sharp ears. It opened its mouth, showing equally sharp teeth. "You have been a good companion, but I free you again. Hunt well, though you will have no one to cook your histi for you." The garaur whined. Pushed its head against him but did not leave. Only sat there. Maybe it did not believe him.

He rubbed its ear. "Very well. But do not follow me into the village." A short whine in response.

"Sorha!" he shouted back. "Stay your blade from the villagers. I am coming."

"We are ready for you, Cahan Du-Nahere. The fire is built."

He looked about. Most of the trees around Harn were small, not much more than saplings, but there were a couple of big bladewoods. He walked to the nearest. Touching the tree with his hands, feeling the ancient life, its slow growth through his gauntlets. "Old one," he said, "lend me your strength, I will take only what I must." Then he pushed his hands against the bark, felt the ebb and the flow of life. He was asking for not a drop, or a mouthful, but for enough to fill him. Tapping the tree was not like taking life, you could not do it through killing the tree. You needed permission. There was danger in this. He intended no slight touch as he had done before. He wanted to drink deep. The tree was of the forest, and he had always known the forest could swallow up a single man in the stream of its life quite easily, cowl or no. But he could not afford fear. Or doubt.

"I must ask this," he whispered. "Give me enough power or Harn is lost."

He cast his mind far out into the stream of life.

Such hubris, but born of desperation.

Strange, at first.

The vastness of it, the great flow of life. More powerful than he could truly understand. At first, it shied away from him, this vibrant and cool flow. He needed it, but it defied him. He chased it, but it danced around him. Frustrated, he tried to force his will upon it.

And it noticed him.

A voice.

So loud it deafened him. No other could hear it.

A light. So bright it blinded him. No other could see it.

He would have fallen to his knees but could not take his

hand from the tree. Figures danced around him, tall and thin, twin branches growing from skull heads. There and not there.

"Have you killed and burned in our realm?" a question. "Have you taken without permission?" The boughry. His body wracked by pain. Plants impaling him. Vines strangling him. Roots ground his bones to dust.

"No," an unbearable pressure in his mind. Stronger than any fear, crushing his senses.

"You would take that which is ours." Boulders crashing down a sheer rock face. A geyser exploding from the earth. "And to what reward?"

"I would stop those who come to kill and burn."

He screamed the words. No sound left in his mouth.

Silence.

He felt a pulse. As if something reached out into the land. Touched everything around him.

It reached out and toward.

It reached backwards and before.

Deep in the Forest

You are in a village. At the bottom of a path. The one that leads from the monastery.

You are lost, weeping and frightened. Staggering forward, looking for comfort and answers and explanation. Still dressed in the embroidered robes and colourful woollen clothes of the monks. A moment of relief, on seeing a face you know. The stallholder, Kiessis, who makes colourful toys out of off-cuts of material, and dolls woven from grasses. Their stall one of the few places you have found genuine pleasure in life. The dolls and forest beasts they made, taken and hidden in your room. Food for endless games, a place in your imagination where you can play, where you have never left your family, where your sister never died and you were not alone and trapped within the harsh regime of training. Where you do not have to be a man, and strong, and hard. Kiessis's eyes opening wide on seeing you. You will never forget this moment. That shout.

"It is the false Rai!"

You do not understand. You are not false. You are the one? The one, the foretold. The beginning of change and the step to the Star Path for all. You are the chosen of the

Terrible Lord, Zorir-Who-Walks-in-Fire. You are the salvation of these people.

But the monks, they are all gone.

Kiessis grabs you, powerful arms around you, imprisoning you.

"I have him!" she shouts. Her body is soft against you, while still being unyielding. Her voice is full of glee and you are screaming.

"Let me go! Let me go!" And in your fear and your panic the fire is there.

And then you are free and Kiessis? Kiessis is gone from the world, and you are strong. Strong enough to run, but not strong enough to fight off the horror, the taking of life. This is not a bandit who murdered your sister. This is different.

But you have no time to think.

Her shout brings a crowd, villagers and soldiers. They pursue you. You run, head first, not thinking or looking, careening through narrow alleys, at every turn another villager. The shout of "the false Rai!" echoing between the whitewashed buildings, bringing a heat to your cheeks that the light above cannot. Little by little your escape is cut off. Your routes, up walls, over buildings, are cut off. Then they are beating you, forcing you into a corner of the courtyard, spear butts and fists and voices full of hate and you cannot stand it any longer. Can not stand it, can not stand it.

In one.

Crystal clear.

Moment.

You feel the connections, the silvered lines of power that run through every living thing. How they are stronger in among the crowd where they touch. How the power within is inflamed by emotion, like when air was blown into a fire.

All they taught you, in pain and shame, suddenly understood.

Do not.

You take.

Take everything. Suck it out of them, a great, hot, seething ball of life and power and you feel as if your cowl opens a great mouth and howls. You howl.

The crowd simply stops.

One moment there, angry, hot and furious. Then not.

Empty flesh.

Lying on the ground.

And a feeling inside, both pride, at doing what the monks had trained you for, at proving you are what they said. And shame, that you killed so many so easily. But in that moment, you did not understand those feelings, you were only a child, and they were quickly subsumed by fear. More were coming, more villagers. And soldiers. Soldiers in armour and with spears and swords. And they brought something else with them. Not just anger, but something black and vile. Hate. All you wanted, in that moment, was to escape. To run. To be left alone.

All that desire balled up and expressed in one word.

"Stop!"

The word is fire.

Fire through the alleyways, through the doors and windows, over the roofs. Nothing escapes. An expanding conflagration that sweeps and scours the village. When it ends. All that is left is you. Standing in a smoking black circle where once those you had known and passed the time of day with had been.

A boy.

A smoking ruin, and more shame and guilt than any child should ever have to carry.

You want to run from the horror of what you are, but you can never run fast enough.

You are running.

Running.

Deeper in the Forest

You are in a forest glade dappled with light from above, grassed with dense, short grass that is spongy underfoot. A place that feels good. Safe. Curled up in a nest of grass. Desperate to be alone. The smell of smoke in your nostrils. Safety in among the trees. You do not remember how you came to be here.

Deeper in the Forest

The world is soft and bright and more beautiful than you can imagine. More full and magical and there is sound and light and voices. Around you a ring of mushrooms. Music, laughter. You are waking. *We are waking.* A woman above you. So happy. You know her. You know her.

Firstmother. A barely remembered face.

But you know her.

She is lifting you up.

"Cahan!" she says, and laughs and spins you round in the air. "You are of the trees now, my beautiful boy, they will keep you safe!"

Spinning, spinning, whirling.

Shallow in the Wood

"We accept." A bell tolled in his mind. "A sacrifice will be needed."

"No," whispered into cold air. He wanted it back. He wanted the warm wooded glade back. He is in the cold night outside of Harn.

Cool, vibrant life flowing into him. Not enough to hurt the tree, and only enough for what he wants. So different from taking life, the power is not raw, not furious and strong and red and stolen and hate filled. It is cooler, like dipping his hand into a pool of sweet water. He is not in control, the tree lets him take, but only what it wishes him to have, like draining sap through a wound in the bark. When it was judged he had enough, the tree healed itself and cut off the flow.

Enough. He stepped away, leaned his bow against the tree. He would not need it.

Ready for me, Sorha? he thought. *No. I do not think you are.* And was it his voice or the cowl's that spoke? Was the vicious glee, the excitement, from him or it? He did not know.

The old anger, the fury at betrayal, the desire to hurt, welling up.

Had Sorha and her soldiers been less proud. Less arrogant in who and what they were then they would have thrown their spears, finished him as he ran up to Harn.

You are running.

But they were proud, and they were arrogant, and they thought themselves sheltered and invulnerable beneath the cloak of the dullers.

They were none of those things.

Much of a cowl's power is through proximity. The nearer you are the more their power can affect you, but beyond a few, five, maybe six arm's lengths away there is little most Rai can do. They are taught their skills in schools, of fire and water. They believe them fundamentally different, fire is heat, blood and anger, water is thought, spirit and reason.

It is all lies.

Water and fire, there is no difference, they are the same, simply different ways of expressing energy. It is energy that the Cowl-Rai controls. The Rai look upon the surface of a pool and see the reflection of their world in it, the Cowl-Rai dive below, and knows the pool is deeper and more complex than most will ever understand. In the clearing, when he killed the Rai, burned the cowl from Sorha. It was energy he used. Up close, such control was easy for him, the further away he was, the harder it became. He could not use a fine knife on an enemy across a field.

But he could throw a hammer.

Cahan broke from Woodedge, the energy lent to him by the tree throbbing beneath his skin.

You needed me.

The cowl within vibrating. The link to the armour he wore stronger than ever. As he ran it changed, spikes extruding at elbow, knee and wrist. The axes at his thighs grew wider blades from the hilts, and from the rear of the blades came curved, sharp hooks. The world around him aglow with energy, the deep and strange and infinitesimal net that Udinny called Ranya's web. Within it Harn: a null, a place of darkness where he could not see, could not sense and could not know. The edge of the dullers' influence was as plain to his cowlsight as the walls of Harn to his eyes.

He ran faster. And as he ran he gathered around him the power lent by the forest.

Not to be eked out this power.

Not to be expended little by little through battle as logic and tactics would dictate. When he reached the dullers it would no longer be of any use to him. He would simply be a man then.

So he took all of the power within, all that would not leave him a husk. Gathering it in the air before him. A huge, invisible hammer of energy, a ball of air as hard and as strong as any boulder. In the moment before he stepped across the dullers' line he threw all he had against the gates of Harn. The roar of his voice drowned out by the crack of air, the shattering of the wooden gates into a million splinters, the screaming of soldiers pierced by flying wood.

He stepped from one world to another.

From being Cowl-Rai, to being a man.

His armour weighed upon him.

His eyesight blurred.

Nausea burned in his stomach.

His strength was measured in eighths, not days.

Still he ran.

Not stopping.

Pulling the axes from his armour. Screaming something unintelligible at the shocked faces staring at him.

"Bring him down!" Was it Sorha? Or was it some trooper or branch leader who shouted? He did not know. Did not have time to care. A figure came from the right, jabbing with a spear but it was ill-judged. He knocked it aside. Twin axes sweeping low, biting into the lower leg, jarring his arm as the soldier went down. From the other side two more coming, spears out. The one on the far left of the pair wounded, a spike of wood in their arm. They thrust their weapons at him and he knocked the wounded soldier's spear away with his left axe. The spearman stumbled. Creating space between the two warriors. He moved in and brought his right axe down on the wounded soldier, between helmet and shoulder, cutting into the neck. A killing blow. Pulled the axe loose. Sweeping the weapon across in reverse. The spike piercing the neck of the other warrior.

A spear, well thrown, hit him in the chest. Bounced off his armour but the impact jarred him. He slipped in the mud. Down on one knee, an awkward position. A soldier came in at him, bringing a two-handed axe down in an overhead swing. Cahan threw himself to the ground. Rolling away. Coming up as the axe bit into the mud where he had been. His own axe coming down on the soldier's wrist, cutting a hand away. They screamed out their agony.

Cahan up and moving again.

Running. The only way to survive.

Can you ever run fast enough?

No plan except to attract the soldiers to him. Fight long enough to give Venn and the villagers a chance to escape. Vague shadows in the edge of his vision. Act and react. Block and slash. The impact of weapons against his armour. The scream of pain as he hit back. Again and again until he brought his axes up.

Ready for the next opponent.

No one there.

Had he won?

Had he done it?

Was it over?

Ranya make it so. His breathing laboured, harsh in his throat. Hurting his lungs. His armour weighed hard on him, heavier with every step. Legs shaking.

"You are a fool," the voice of the Rai, Sorha, "to come here like this."

Of course he had not won.

Of course it was not over.

Sorha stood at the other side of the village square, beyond the pyre and in front of the statue of Tarl-an-Gig. Sword in one hand, shield in the other. A wall of spears and shields in front of the Leoric's house, stopping any chance of escape for those within.

He had barely made it past the shattered gate. Six lay dead around him, soon to be seven unless the axeman was treated for his missing hand quickly. Five more lay about the gate, pierced by splinters.

"I am not finished yet, Rai," he shouted back. He needed to bring the spear line forward. "What are you waiting for?" He held his axes out. "I am here! Do you want me or not?"

"Oh, we do, Clanless, we do want you." She spun her sword in her hand. "Me most of all." She walked forward. "Do you think you can best me without your cowl?"

"Come and find out," he shouted back, though he knew it unlikely. She was a warrior, her whole life given over to martial skills. He had spent at least half of his running from them. He may have looked impressive, even felt it while he cut down those first soldiers, but his wind was already gone. Without the cowl he was weak. His breathing coming like bellows, his muscles aching. But if he could get her and her troops away from the Leoric's longhouse maybe the villagers could escape. Maybe Venn could get away, and Udinny, and Furin and her boy, Issofur, and the girl with the grass doll.

His life would be worth something then.

"Come and find out indeed." Sorha walked forward, spinning her sword again. As she got closer he could see it was blackwood, with an inlaid hilt. An expensive weapon, the sort given to a skilled warrior. Her armour was inlaid with many woods, abstract patterns, whorls and spirals. Cahan tensed his muscles, altered his grip on the hafts of his axes. Felt sweat within his gauntlets. Usually the cowl would absorb it, a reminder he did not need of his weakness. "It is a long time since you have fought, Cahan Du-Nahere," she said. "I could tell by watching you. You were probably a good warrior once. Not great, but good." She smiled, stepped nearer. "But I? I am a great warrior." She lunged, the sword coming at his midriff. He jumped back, avoiding the point even though it could not have cut through his armour.

She knew it.

Only testing him.

"Good reactions," she said, and began to walk around him. "But you will slow as you tire." A smile, another lunge, this one he tried to bat away with an axe but she pulled the strike so he swiped at nothing. Continued circling. Continued smiling. "Maybe you were something worthwhile, when you were younger." He turned to keep her in sight. Had to finish her quickly. Now. A warrior like her would have ample strength to draw on. "I'm not going to kill you, Cahan Du-Nahere," she said, her words for him only, "you have ruined me, made me nothing." She spun the sword again. "I will watch you burn." She came in again, this time leading with her shield, jabbing with the sword from behind it. He swept a thrust away, brought his axe down. She caught it on her shield and his blow bounced off. She moved in close. Used the shield to shove him backwards. As he staggered she thrust with the sword. A strike to his chest. Jarring him through the armour.

She backed away. Lifted her visor and smiled at him. Behind her, the troops coming forward to watch. Behind them, at the door to the Leoric's house, he saw a face appear. Venn. Trapped.

"Could have opened your groin," said Sorha, "could have gone for the neck." Smiling as she circled. Pulled the visor back down. "But I will watch you burn." She moved in close again, bringing the sword up as if to swing it. He moved into a defensive position, ready to catch the blade with the hooks of his axes. At the last moment she changed her attack. Stepped left of him, dummied a thrust with the shield. When he moved to answer it she brought round her sword. The flat of the blade crashed against the side of his helmet, making his ears ring and the world swim. "This is not even a challenge," she said. She dummied another thrust, and she did it again and again and again. Wearing away his strength, tiring him out. Belittling him, and always coming back to that one phrase. "I will watch you burn."

When he was done, when he could barely keep his axes up, she stepped back. Lifted her visor.

"What do you have left, old man?" she said. "Nothing, you have nothing. You are nothing." She backed away. "Nothing!" she shouted. Then looked over at her troops. "Beat him until he cannot move," she said, "break his legs so he cannot run. He only need live until the morning, then we will burn him and take his shrivelled head to the High Leoric."

The troops came forward, their spears reversed to use as clubs. He tried to fight, but Sorha had drained him of his strength.

They beat him mercilessly, until he could barely move, and all the time one word going through his head. "Failure." They forced him to kneel in the mud. Held him when Sorha came forward again. The world wavered, it was all he could do to hang onto consciousness.

"No one escaped." She leaned in close, so she could whisper to him. "You took from me, and I will take from you. I will kill each villager in front of you, but first I will cut out your tongue, so you cannot cry out or beg their forgiveness." She straightened, stepped back. Looked down upon him then took a knife from her belt. "If you have any last words. Then say them now." She spat on the floor. "Who do you think you are, to go against the Rai?"

What was he?

Those words bounced around his tired mind. A joke.

That was what he was. A fool who would die here, in the armour he had buried as belonging to a dead man. After using the power he had sworn never to use. After putting himself in a position where the lives of others depended on him.

"*I can sense death, Cahan Du-Nahere,*" the reborn woman had said, "*and it is coming to you. Deny your nature all you wish, it is still coming. Death cannot be stopped.*"

He had thought he was ready to die. Maybe if he had saved the villagers he would have been. But he had not. He had thought to sacrifice himself here, and in the final moments he regretted it. To die for nothing. To have accomplished nothing but to bring death to others, those few he had found himself caring about in a life lived with so little to care for. What a fool.

"Any last words?" said Sorha.

He did not want to die.

He did not want the villagers to die.

He looked up at the Rai.

"Nahac," he said, his dead sister's name unfamiliar on his lips. "I call on you." And as if in an echo, he heard a voice answer.

"*Call my name and we will come.*"

43

He did not know what he expected. Something immediate? That did not happen. The Rai, Sorha, turned to her soldiers.

"Bring pincers and something to seal the wound," she said. "I do not want him bleeding to death or drowning in his own blood." She backed away, watching him with a sneer on her face. No doubt she enjoyed his fear, his panic. The soldiers held him tighter. One came forward with a pair of large pincers, blackened by fire, and a knife. He lifted the pincers, showing them to him.

"What I will do with these is . . ." he began.

"Get on with it," said Sorha. "I want him to hurt." The soldier looked over his shoulder at her, nodded. Someone grabbed his head, pulled it back. The guard came forward. Cahan tried to struggle, tried to clamp his mouth shut but had no energy. No strength at all and it was nothing for them to force his mouth open. The man smelled of mud, and alcohol, and he grinned as he forced the pincers into Cahan's mouth.

In the moment as they clamped around his tongue, he saw the footprints that he and Sorha had made in the snow while they fought. An infinitely complex pattern: a thing of great beauty and he thought if he could study it long enough he would find some meaning there.

"Someone bring a hammer," said Sorha, "to break his arms and legs so he does not run again." The man with the pincers in Cahan's mouth paused. Grinned down at him.

"More attention than someone like you deserves, all this, Clanless," he said. Then pulled on the pincers, crushing Cahan's tongue, making him bleed as he drew it out. Bringing up his knife to start cutting.

Behind the pincerman came a soldier with the hammer, a huge, two-handed thing of the type you would use to drive in tent pegs. They were laughing. Cahan knew his life was about to be reduced to one thing: agony. Nothing but agony; and that was only a precursor to what he would feel on the pyre.

The pincerman's smile vanished.

A look of confusion on his face.

The grip on Cahan's tongue fell away.

From the guard's chest protruded a spear. The hold on Cahan's arms and legs and head, gone. Soldiers were shouting, running for weapons they had dropped to watch the fun. Dying before their hands touched shield, axe or spear.

The devotees of Our Lady of Violent Blooms had answered his call.

A whirlwind of violence blew through Harn. The dullers had no effects on the reborn. They did not tire, their muscles were not subject to the whims or weaknesses of life. What animated them was other, they were other. They had no fear of pain, or death, they had passed beyond that. He saw one of the two reborn take a spear to the gut and she simply slid down it and knifed her attacker through the eye. They fought like none he had ever seen. The last masters of a lost artform. Moving in circles and in spirals. A spear in one hand, a shortsword or shield in the other.

Rarely ever facing one opponent for more than a moment. Acutely aware of each other. They did not bother with defence. Only attack. Had the soldiers of the Rai had time then a shield wall might have saved them, but they did not.

They were not ready.

Cahan was not sure anyone could be ready.

Half of them were cut down in the first moments. The slaughter was terrible, like the end of a battle when one side runs in panic and the other goes mad with killing.

Blood.

Blood and screaming and meat and death until there was only Sorha left. The Rai backing away towards the Tiltgate. The reborn warriors did not touch her. Cahan thought it because they were busy finishing off the soldiers. But when Sorha reached the Tiltgate she turned, running for Woodedge. He wanted to shout, to scream for them to follow, but his mouth was broken, tongue swollen.

One of the reborn walked over to stand before him. Her armour and weapons red with the blood of others.

"The Rai," he managed to say, though they were misshapen and swollen words. Pointed at the Tiltgate, "kill the Rai or she'll bring others."

The reborn, the one who he had named for his sister, turned and lifted her visor.

"I see no one," she said.

"There," he pointed again at the woman running across the fields towards Woodedge. He wished for his bow, though he could not have killed Sorha with it then for he was weak as a newly hatched garaur. The reborn continued to stare.

"I see no one," she said. Then Sorha was gone, into Woodedge and it no longer mattered. He was too tired to wonder how it could be that the woman could be right before his eyes and yet invisible to the reborn warriors.

"We need to leave," he said. But if anyone replied he did not hear them as the last of his energy fled and darkness took him.

He awoke in the Leoric's longhouse, the familiar smell of her broth filling his nostrils. Behind it he could smell roasting meat and he wondered if the villagers had slaughtered a crownhead in celebration of his victory. If they would bring him fresh meat, still bloody as the people round here liked. He hoped not, he had no more appetite for slaughter.

"The sleeper awakes," said a familiar voice. He opened his eyes to find Udinny sitting by the cot he lay on. She grinned at him and lifted the bowl in her hands. "You are welcome to the rest of this," she said, "or I can get you a bowl of your own." He was about to pass, then realised he was wrong about his appetite. He was starving. The nausea brought on by the dullers had gone. He knew peace. Then panic seized him.

"The Rai, did they catch her?"

"Did who catch her?" said Udinny.

"The villagers, anyone," he tried to sit, "if they did not stop her then—" Udinny pushed him back down. The wiry little monk was stronger than she looked.

"You have slept for a day and a half and none could wake you. The Rai is long gone." The nausea returned.

"She will come back, and bring more soldiers, more Rai."

"I thought I heard voices," Furin the Leoric came around the divider holding a bowl of stew. "I am glad to see you awake, Forester."

"I should leave, Furin," he said, trying to sit once more and this time he was ready for Udinny's push, and did not let her stop him. "I brought all this trouble to your village, no doubt you and your people want me gone and . . ."

"Peace, Cahan," she said. "The village does not blame you. Tussnig was quite vocal about his part in helping the

Rai when they first arrived, while they were here to protect him anyway. When they came he was quick to tell them that you lived, that they killed the wrong people." Anger, burning deep within him.

Kill him.

"I would speak with Tussnig," he said, and stood.

"You cannot, he is gone. The village rejected him for what he did, especially after those women you brought destroyed the dullers."

"The villagers worship Ranya now," said Udinny, a grin across her face.

"They do not," said Leoric Furin.

"Well, no, not yet, but I have high hopes." Furin shook her head.

"They will come back," said Cahan. Paused. "What is this about the dullers?"

"They had people in them," said Udinny quietly. "Living people, though it was no life. They looked tortured."

"You did not know?" said Furin. He shook his head trying to understand. "We thought you had been Rai, that you might be able to tell us why."

"I was never Rai," he let his words tail off. "The dullers were a new thing the Cowl-Rai of Tarl-an-Gig brought, the few times I saw them we were not allowed near them." He squeezed his eyes shut, rubbed his forehead. "People?" Udinny nodded.

"They were tied in, men and women. Filthy. Piteous. But there was something wrong with them, they did not answer if you spoke to them. They looked," Udinny paused, "wrong. I have no better way to describe them. The reborn took one look and killed them." Cahan thought of the Hetton, how they had looked wrong.

"The Cowl-Rai twists what is right even further than the Rai," he said.

"The villagers dug a pit for the corpses of the soldiers," said Furin, "but they have burned the bodies of the dullers." She took a breath. "The people did not want their corpses in the land, they looked like they had bluevein, even though it is only a disease of plants. I hope they are free of torment now and walk the Star Path." They were quiet then, and a little of the nausea returned when he realised what he had thought was roasting meat was burning bodies.

"You should have sent people to catch the Rai when she fled."

"Cahan," said Udinny, "they are villagers, not warriors."

"It does not matter," he began. Furin stopped him saying more by putting a bowl of broth into his hands.

"Eat," she said, "and listen." He wanted to argue, but he was also hungry and all too aware of what he had brought down on this village. A little silence was a small thing to be asked for. "As Udinny says, my people are only villagers. Some of them saw you fight the Rai, Sorha, through the gaps in my walls. They saw what she did to a man in fancy armour, who knew how to fight. It is too much for you to expect them to go up against someone like that, and you must know she would cut them to pieces." What she said was true, he could not deny it.

"Leoric, the Rai cannot leave an insult unanswered. They will return." He started to eat the broth. It was still very good.

"What do you think we should do?"

"The forest," he said, "it is the only safe place."

"You think they will not come after us there?" said the Leoric.

"I think it is easier to hide there." Furin nodded.

"There are a lot of good things to eat in the forest," said Udinny. "Though you cannot cook them except with your feet, which I do not personally like."

"There will be a village meeting, Cahan," said Furin, ignoring the monk. "There are those among us who have their own ideas of what should be done." She watched as he spooned down more stew. "I would like you to speak to them."

"Why would they listen to me?" he said. "I brought this down on them." Furin stood.

"Do not be so quick to self-pity, Cahan," her face stern, and he felt small. "They choose you over their priest, they cast him out for betraying you. Admittedly, partly because it brought the Rai to their doors. But for a village to do such a thing for the clanless, it is a huge thing. You are part of them now." He felt an odd warmth within, though he tried to hide it, and maybe it was the broth. "Now, there is someone outside who is desperate to see you. Are you strong enough?" He nodded, ate more. Furin looked at Udinny.

"I am staying," she said. Furin nodded and left. He heard voices, then Venn entered. They no longer wore their armour, instead they wore a woollen jerkin and trousers in a muddy brown. They looked like cast-offs from others as the clothes were well worn and bulged strangely around the neck, but the trion was smiling. In their hands they held his bowstaff.

"I got this for you, from where you left it." The trion's smile fell away as they realised Cahan's hands were full and he could not take the staff. Then their face became serious. "I am sorry, Cahan, that I failed you." Udinny watched, an odd look on her face. Almost a smile.

"Failed me?" he said. As the trion turned he saw what caused the bulge around their neck. Segur, the garaur, was nestled in there.

"They caught me as soon as I came in," they said.

Cahan sat up a little straighter and stared into his bowl. The gravy was thick, full of vegetables and bits of meat. "You did not fail me, Venn," he said quietly. "I failed you. I should not have sent you in alone."

"What else could you have done?"

"I cannot forgive you, Venn," he said, shock on their

face. "There is nothing to forgive. And if there was then Segur has made that choice and already forgiven you. They are far harder to convince than I ever was." He saw Udinny hide a smile. "Can you forgive *me*, Venn, that is the question?"

"Why?" The trion looked genuinely confused.

"For sending you into the village. For letting you go back to your mother in the forest."

"You had no choice," said Venn, they sounded confused, laid down his bow by the cot. "I have to go," they said, "the Leoric said you needed peace and I am meant to be watching Issofur." Cahan nodded, and watched Venn leave. When they were out of the building Udinny turned to him.

"I like them," said the monk with a grin, "they will make an excellent follower of Ranya." She stared into her bowl, looking comically disappointed it was empty. "Unlike your other friends, who I do not think will follow anyone."

"The reborn?" She nodded. "They are not my friends." Udinny put down her bowl and the smile fell away from her face. Silence slowly settled between them.

"This meeting the villagers want," said Udinny. "They think to make amends with Harnspire somehow, but the Rai will not let what happened here stand, will they?"

"No."

"It feels, Cahan, like things are coming to a point." He nodded. "Let us hope that Ranya's web is cast over us." It was as if she spoke to him from very far away. He thought that maybe it was fear he heard in her voice.

"Aye," he said. "Let us hope it is."

44

There was no building large enough in Harn to hold the entire village, so the meeting was held in the square with Tussnig's poorly constructed statue and the eye of Tarl-an-Gig watching over it. Furin and Dyon stood before the shrine. Udinny had decided not to come, she had told him she thought the whole thing doomed. He did not know why she thought that, and did not ask. It was rare to see the monk of Ranya so negative and he did not like it. Instead she had gone with the boy Issofur to play in Woodedge.

The villagers gathered and he saw Venn, standing at the edge of the crowd away from others that he knew or recognised: Ont, the obnoxious butcher, huge in among the rest of them, bigger even than him. Gussen and Aislinn, the gate guards, Sengui, the gasmaw farmer, the tanner, Diyra, Manha, the leader of the weavers, and next to her Ilda, the woodcarver. By the Forestgate the two reborn stood, still as statues. If he had not been looking he would not have seen them.

A gentle snow fell on the crowd and though the air may have been cold in the square the atmosphere was not; the people of Harn knew the trouble they were in. Maybe they had put it aside until now, but the calling of the meeting had brought their fear and worry bubbling up.

"Listen!" shouted Dyon. "Listen to your Leoric! The Leoric wishes to speak and so the people must listen!" The crowd quietened, apart from a little mumbling. Furin looked around herself. Nodded thanks to Dyon.

"We live in strange times," she said, standing before the statue of the balancing man. "Even the weather is strange, last week we had the warmest day of Harsh any could remember. Today it snows once more." She put out a hand, catching a flake of snow. The crowd murmured general agreement. Cahan had heard it said in the monastery that as the new Cowl-Rai rose the weather became unsettled, as if the great changes happening in Crua confused the seasons. "We lost one of ours, Gart, who was respected by all." More murmuring. "We were made afraid for our lives, by soldiers of Harn county, of our High Leoric, of our Cowl-Rai. People we thought we trusted. Those we have fought for, and believed were meant to protect us." Only silence in the square. "We were saved by a man many of us scorned." Discomfort in the crowd but Furin did not stop. "We must decide, now, what we do. Who we are. Where we go from here."

"It is done," shouted someone from the crowd. "They lost, they will not come back. Why would they care about Harn?" Murmurs of agreement, mostly from those few who had been here all their lives, never left the place. But others, the ones who had fought, or visited other towns in trade or wandered, as some did, they did not say anything.

"The Rai are proud," said Furin. "They rule with that pride, they are used to that pride." She looked around the crowd of villagers. "They will not let what happened here stand."

"Then what do we do?" this voice quiet. Cahan thought it was Ilda, the woodcarver, who spoke. She was not well liked, considered unlucky. Her work required wood from

Harnwood and she had lost two wives and three husbands to the gathering of it.

"I will let the forester speak. Come up here, Cahan," said Furin.

Hearing his name used before all, making his way through the crowd was a strangely hard thing. He felt every pair of eyes upon him. They were frightened, and they wanted strength and reassurance. Once he had been the forester, a clanless outsider. Slowly they had come to accept him, and now he stood before them a warrior, in armour finer than most would ever have seen. He had thought it odd that the Leoric asked him to speak but as he came to stand by her he understood why she wanted him. The people of Harn were used to looking up to the Rai. To obeying them and expecting them to lead, and in his armour he echoed what they knew. He looked like someone powerful and of means.

He had never spoken before many people at once. He tried to speak into the expectant silence. Failed. Cleared his throat and started again.

"You must leave here," he said. Then stepped back. Happy to have said his piece.

Uproar, immediate and loud. People shouting at him. At each other. Furin shook her head, stepped forward.

"Quiet!" she held up her hands, raised her voice. "Quiet!" The crowd quietened, a little. "Let the forester give you his reasons," she glanced back at him, and it was not a friendly look though he did not know why. "He will tell us why we must leave, and where we must go. He will not simply tell us what to do." She turned to him. Spoke softly to him, "Won't you, Cahan." He took a breath, nodded. Understood her anger a little. Stepped forward once more. Cleared his throat before he tried to speak.

"The Rai are proud as Furin said," he looked at the crowd. So many faces. "What happened here," he waved towards the village, "they cannot stand for it. It is a wound to their pride. They will come back, and they will come back stronger."

"This is your fault!" shouted Ont. "They came for you! You brought them here!" He pushed through the crowd until he stood at the front. "They want him!" he shouted. "We should give him to them!" Something slow and ugly moved through the crowd. He felt it before they did. He felt their fear as if it were a littercrawler's tentacles, wrapping around its prey, grasping it. Ont had given them something to hold onto in a moment of desperation. And they were pulling it close. The idea transmuting their fear into anger, toward violence.

"Stop this!" shouted Furin. "Stop this now!" The crowd were pushing forward. Beneath Cahan's skin something writhed.

You need me.

He could make them stop.

"You saw him fight!" shouted Furin. The jostling lessened, though the atmosphere still felt ugly. Ont stepped out to the front of the villagers.

"We saw him and that Rai," he said, "she beat him easily. He has no power, not like the Rai." The butcher was all threat, all anger, and Cahan knew this man did not know what he had done to the gate. None of them did, and that made the crowd more dangerous. To him, and to them. "There is only one him," said Ont, pointing at Cahan.

You are the fire.

"And what of them," shouted the Leoric, and she pointed towards the Forestgate where the reborn stood. "Did you forget them? They butchered every guard in the village and never broke sweat. You think you can stand against them, do you?" Silence, the crowd looking at one another.

"Then the forester should leave," this from Ilda, the woodcarver. "We cannot fight him, and we should not wish him harm. But he should leave here." Agreement in the crowd.

"Leave!" shouted another voice.

"Aye, leave us, Clanless," shouted another.

"It will do you no good!" This shouted from the back. The words stopped the crowd. They turned. Venn, standing against the mud wall of a roundhouse. "It will do you no good to banish Cahan, and it is not his fault either, past being born who he was and none can help that." Their voice quietened a little towards the end of their words.

"And what would you know of this?" said Ont. "You are just some child of the Rai, brought along for their first blooding."

"Child of the Rai," said Venn softly. "Yes, I am that." The trion wiped at the blue line across their eyes, smearing it over their face. "I was there when the orders were given to Sorha by the High Leoric. They did not only want Cahan," Venn looked around them at the crowd. "They were sent here to kill him, yes, him and anyone who had known him, or talked with him or seen him. They were to wipe all trace of you from Crua. Cahan's farm, your village, everything around it. All of you."

Silence.

Into that silence came a voice, a question. Spoken quietly, unbelieving.

"Why?"

Venn wrapped their arms around themselves, avoided the gaze of the gathered villagers.

"I do not know. But it was the order she gave."

"The High Leoric wanted us all dead?" That from Ont. Venn shook their head again.

"Not the High Leoric," said Venn. "The order came from the south. From the Cowl-Rai in Tilt." The villagers looked at one another.

"What do we do then?" said one, the weaver, Manha. "Where do we go?" Cahan stepped forward.

"The forest," he said. A collective gasp. "I know it scares you, but to stay here is death." Upset, discomfort, none wanted to hear it.

"He is right," said Furin, the Leoric. "He is right."

"We cannot," said Ilda, she sounded broken. "The forest is death, and I well know it. Besides, this is our land, where we have lived for generations. This is our place in Crua. We cannot leave."

"We must," said Furin. "I travelled here from far Jinneng," she said, "I followed my secondmother's bloodline back to Harn. I made a new life. We can do that." She looked from face to face to face among the crowd. "We can make a new life in the forest."

"Become Forestals?" said a voice from the crowd. "Outlaws?"

"No," said Furin. "Not that, we will be us. The same village but in a different place. We will rebuild."

"This land under our feet," said Ont, "is what we are. We move somewhere else, we betray our ancestors. We become clanless."

"It is that or death," said Furin.

That silence again. The sound of people confronted by something they could barely comprehend. By a choice that, for them, had no favourable outcome. To be clanless was to be nothing, a form of death to them.

"Maybe there is another way." This from Dyon. He stepped forward. "Maybe we can offer the Rai a trade," he said. "Maybe we can make ourselves worth keeping to them. Make Harn worthwhile to them."

"How?" said Ont. "We have nothing that they cannot take."

"I think we have," said Dyon. Furin turned to him.

"Do not do this," she hissed the words. Cahan's heart fell. He knew what Dyon was going to say, he knew how it would sound to the villagers and he knew it would do them no good.

"It might work," said Dyon to her. Furin turned away, her anger barely contained. She could not look at her second, but it did not stop Dyon.

Cahan felt no anger.

Only a terrible sense that events were out of his control. Of knowing where this path ended, and that there was nothing he could do to change it. "There has been treefall," said Dyon, "in Wyrdwood."

Silence. This time of a different timbre.

"Treefall," said Manha, the weaver, she scratched her head. "Here? In the Northern Wyrdwood? Are you sure?"

"Yes," said Dyon.

"And you kept this secret?" said Ont.

"You do not understand," said Furin. "Treefall will bring them here, in the same way news of Cahan did. It is not a bargaining tool. It is another cut that will lead to us bleeding to death."

"I have thought on that," said Dyon. He had the crowd now, they were desperate for hope. Any hope, and Dyon was giving it to them, false and foolish as it was. "We send people to them," he said. "But no one who knows where the treefall is. Wyrdwood is huge, they could waste many years looking for it. We get them to agree to leave Harn alone, in exchange we will show them where it is. We will work with them, help them."

He had the crowd, or most of them. Those who had served, who had been soldiers and met the Rai? They stayed quiet. But the others, the ones to whom this small place was their entire lives, they were desperate to believe what Dyon said. Furin moved closer to Cahan.

"He is killing everyone here," she whispered, "and does not know it." Cahan nodded. Whispered back.

"You, me, Venn, Udinny and whoever else will come. We must leave here, Furin." She pursed her lips. Took a deep breath. Shook her head.

"They are my people, Forester, I cannot leave them."

"Then you will die, the Rai will roll over this place as if it does not exist for treefall." She stared at him.

"Maybe not," she said, and Cahan wondered if Dyon's

idea was a madness that was catching. Furin used one hand to massage the other. She was looking at Cahan, a terrible sadness within her. "If they will not save themselves, Forester, someone must stay and save whatever can be saved."

"But you know . . ." he began, she cut him off. Moving forward holding her hands up.

"Listen to me," she shouted, "and let us see if we can find some way forward."

"What do you suggest, Leoric?" this shouted by Aislinn, the gate guard who had lost an eye fighting for the Cowl-Rai in the south. She knew more of the world than Dyon and was one of those not taken in by his words. It did not pass Cahan by that she was careful to use the Leoric's title, to remind the people around her of who they had trusted to lead them for so long.

"I say we use the forester's expertise. He knows how to fight." Furin gave him a nod. "We fortify the village. We strengthen the walls. We learn what we can of arms and when they turn up we look like we will be hard for them to take. It will be easier for them to make a deal with us then, especially if Dyon already told them that only we know where the treefall is. The Rai respect strength." There was some talk among the villagers. Then one stepped forward, Cahan did not know them.

"Will it not annoy the Rai," they said, "to get here and find us standing against them?" Furin smiled. Shook her head and managed to look so sure of herself it amazed him.

"No," she said. "If they are thinking of hurting us then it will make them think twice, and if not, we will simply say we have fortified the village to protect it from Forestals, knowing the riches that will come with treefall." The villager nodded, and with that it seemed the crowd were satisfied. No matter how strange it felt to Cahan that they could be so easily swayed. Dyon walked away from the shrine, not looking at his Leoric as he knew he had betrayed her confidence. Furin stood by the forester.

"I cannot make your people into an army, Furin," he said. "They are not warriors."

"I know," she replied. Stood nearer, looked up at him and put a hand on his arm. "We need only hold them for one day, Cahan. Then these people will know the truth of the Rai, and what they face. They will be all too happy to escape to the forest then. We can spirit them away in the night."

"Even one day may be more than your people can manage. And that one day will be bloody work."

For years he had thought of the Leoric as little more than an annoyance, focused on nothing but collecting taxes and tithes, but to look at Furin was to know himself wrong. He was not sure that ever, in his life, he had met a person as brave as her. She gave him a small smile that made something painful flip over inside his chest. Nodded.

"Then let there be blood," she said.

45

Venn and the child Issofur slept curled up on a bed, as if they had nothing in the world to worry about. Udinny spent the night sitting cross-legged in quiet contemplation of Ranya, staring at a plant the Leoric kept inside her longhouse. Cahan had thought he would be happy to be free of the monk's constant chatter but he was not. Something had changed in the monk since they had ventured into Wyrdwood. He could not place it but she was different. He wanted, for the first time in as long as he could remember, to talk.

His mind raced. Thoughts of the village, where it was, how such a place could be defended, ran in circles like the winds around Crua. He wanted to give voice to those thoughts, as if by doing so he could empty his mind and sleep. Or at the very least, he could sort the jumble of ideas through in some way he was currently denied.

So Cahan spent half the night staring at Udinny as she sat, in silent communion with a plant, her hands flat on the earthen floor of the longhouse. He became annoyed with her, and hoped she would somehow feel his gaze upon her and speak to him.

She did not.

It seemed even in silence the monk of Ranya could find ways to irritate him. Maybe she had not changed at all.

There was a conversation he could have joined. Beyond the partition Furin sat with Dyon, trying desperately to convince her second he was making a mistake. Dyon could not see it. He lacked her knowledge of the world outside; in some ways Cahan thought his ideas strangely childlike and innocent. Give the Rai something valuable and they will treat you well in exchange. He saw the world like a trader, as trade was his world. He imagined the world outside to be like Harn, where the people worked together and looked out for one another. In a way Cahan pitied Dyon, the shock of what was to come, when he found out that the Rai were ruthlessly selfish and they considered people like him as little more than tools, to be used until they were broken and then thrown away.

From the urgently whispered conversation he could tell there would be no changing Dyon's mind, though the Leoric did not give up and their whispers were the background noise of the night while Cahan worked through all the ways he could think of to defend Harn. Again and again he came to the same conclusion.

He could not.

Not alone.

Sleep, when it eventually did come, was not restful.

In the morning he woke to find himself unrested and alone. Udinny, Venn and Issofur were gone and the Leoric's room was quiet. He walked through and took a bowl of broth, eating in the gloom and listening to the comings and goings of the village outside. It was odd, he thought, that they could know the threat they were under and yet they went about their business as normal, as if nothing wrong was happening. As he finished the broth Furin walked in. She looked tired, like a woman who knew that her doom was upon her and there was little she could do about it – and a woman who had been up all night.

"How long do we have, Cahan?" He shrugged.

"It is difficult to know."

"Looking at you, in that armour," she said, "I feel that maybe you will be able to make a better guess than anyone else here." He could not fault her reasoning, and stared morosely into the embers of her fire. "Do you sleep in your armour, Cahan?"

"Yes. It is not like clothing, more like a second skin. Difficult to describe." She sat opposite him.

"So how long do we have, your best guess?" He chewed on a rubbery piece of meat, giving himself time to think.

"Sorha was on foot, she will make for Harn-Larger and from there she will go on to Harnspire." The Leoric stared at him. The make-up that covered her face was still the previous day's and had begun to flake away. He had never seen her without the white clay, her clanpaint and the black whorl of the Leoric carefully applied. Her eyes begged for what she would not ask, that he give her some hope. "The circle winds blow away from Harnspire at this time of year, so unless the skyraft is in . . ."

"It is not," she said.

"Then in that case it is quicker for her to make direct for Harnspire on foot, rather than ride the skyraft to Stor and cut across."

"Won't she send a skipper?" Furin poked the embers with a stick, coaxing a little life into the fire before adding a log. "They can make that journey in an eightday if they are fresh." Cahan shook his head.

"She has failed here," he said. "The Rai do not like failure so she will not want to tell them of it in a message. She will want to explain it herself, show it in the best light possible. Beg them for a chance to redeem herself."

"Then what?" The Leoric was not looking at him, she was staring into the fire.

"They will put together a punitive force. A full trunk of soldiers at least," he found he had lost his appetite, "and five or so Rai to command them."

"They must want you a lot."

"This is not for me, Leoric, not any longer. You heard Venn. The Rai will most likely think I am gone, with the trion. Because that is what they would do." He hoped they would think that at least. If they did not, if they thought that either he or Venn were still here then he felt sure they would send Hetton. They might send them anyway, but he did not want to think about that. "They want Harn gone. Because you know about me." She stared at him. For a long time. "What?"

"I was going to ask," she said, "what makes you so important that you feared others knowing your name. But I do not think I want to know."

"No, you do not." They sat, sharing the warmth of the fire. Listening to it crackle and spit in an almost companionable silence. The Leoric was watching him and he did not know why. Eventually she nodded to herself.

"How long to put this force together?" she asked.

"The Cowl-Rai in rising has their forces spread out over Crua, so it depends what they have close," Cahan said. "Anything from a quarter season to a full season." She nodded to herself, still staring into the fire. "A force that big," he added, "I do not think they have the marants for it, and the skycarts are wary about transporting large military forces, so they will have to walk. Armies move slowly. A quarter to get here at best."

"So," said the Leoric, "we are about to enter Least, we can expect them as Harsh begins to bite again."

"Aye," he said, "and that bite will be deep."

"Can we do it in that time, Cahan?"

"Do what," he said quietly, though he knew what she meant. He wanted to create time to think, though he had thought about little else all night and still had few answers.

"Have the village and the people ready, to defend ourselves."

"We will have to." He rinsed his bowl in the water by the fire. Looked up. "One day," he said, "one day of fighting and they will realise the danger and we will flee to the forest?" She nodded.

"One day, that is all we need."

"I think I can do that." They were interrupted by noise from outside, a babble of voices.

"That will be Dyon," she said, standing. "Getting ready to leave." She began to walk away and he stood, took her arm. She looked up at him, almost smiled, but when she saw the look on his face any happiness fled.

"I worry that by being here I make things worse. If I am here they will—"

"Never stop? Keep coming?" she said, and looked strangely disappointed. "If you feel you need to leave before they arrive then do. I will not stop you. I know Dyon's idea of them treating us well because they want our knowledge of treefall is a nonsense. I know the idea we can make them respect our strength is even more foolish. But they are coming whether you are here or not, Cahan Du-Nahere." She put her hand on his. She was warm, soft. He was not used to being touched. "I would rather face them with you by our side than not, but it is your choice." With that she walked away, leaving a whirl of confused feeling within him.

A count later he followed her outside to find Dyon, standing with three others. He recognised Furden and his firsthusband, Duhan. The woman with them he had seen about the village but did not know, she gave him a look that left him in little doubt she blamed him for her troubles. They had packs ready for their journey. Dyon looked happy, peaceful even. Villagers were handing him bread and dried meat for his pack. Wishing Tarl-an-Gig to accompany him and look down on him. There was an air of celebration about the village.

"We go," shouted Dyon, "to bring peace and prosperity back to Harn. Yes, mistakes have been made. We lost Gart who was dear to us." He looked at Cahan, but did not mention his name or blame him. He wondered if Furin had made sure he did not. The crowd became quiet. Dyon raised his hands. "But I will bring back enough to make up for that, and we will give a piece of our new wealth to Gart's family, and we will make good his loss to them." A chorus of agreement. "And now we go!" he shouted. His words greeted with applause and shouts of "Iftal bless you, Dyon!" Cahan let him walk away, then went to find Udinny and Venn. They were squatting in the mud, playing a game that involved a circle in the dirt and some pebbles.

"We need to go with them," he said. Udinny stood.

"Gladly," she said. "I long for adventure."

"She was losing," said Venn.

"It was a tactical retreat," said Udinny, then kicked the pebbles out of the dirt. Moved a little closer to the forester.

"Are you leaving, Cahan?" whispered Udinny, "because without you these people . . ."

"No, Udinny," he said. "I am not leaving. I think I must stop running. But I need some things from Woodedge, and Dyon may end up being glad of my company."

"Why?" said Venn.

"You will find out," he said. Then looked for Furin in among the crowd of villagers watching Dyon and his party leave. He took the Leoric aside. "I am going to accompany Dyon a little of the way."

"You are going?" Worry, further cracking the mask of white on her face.

"Not for long."

"How long is not long?"

"Could be a few hours, could be a few days, but I think it will be worth the time." She stared at him, and must have been wondering whether he was running and too cowardly to say so. She looked to Udinny.

"You are going with him?" The monk nodded and this seemed to calm the Leoric a little. She turned back to Cahan. "Is there anything we can do while you are gone?"

"Yes," he said, "the stakes that are around the village, move them closer together."

"How close?"

"Close enough that you would need to turn sideways to pass through them."

"We do not have enough stakes."

"Then cut more," he said. "In fact, clear Woodedge around the village to do it. The more clear ground between the wood and the village the better."

"I have heard that the forest does not . . ."

"The forest will understand," he said, "and Woodedge is hardly the true forest. More like cutting its nails or hair." She nodded. He began to walk away then stopped and turned back. She smiled at him.

"Cahan, I . . ." she said.

"And dig a pit," he added, "in front of the wall, as deep as the tallest villager, more if you can. Wide enough you would struggle to jump it. After that, dig another before the stakes. And strengthen the wall, too." She looked disappointed and he did not understand why. If she wanted kinder words or assurance he was not the person for it. Maybe what he said only brought home what was to come, the inevitability of it.

"It will be bad, won't it," she said softly.

"Yes," he said. "It will."

46

It took longer than he had imagined to leave Harn.

His instructions were not enough for the Leoric and her people. Where he had a clear idea of what he meant, about stakes and ditches, they did not. Fortifications, tactics, these were alien to them, they were farmers, and traders and artisans, not fighters. He should have known that. Instead Udinny had to stop him before he walked away and get him to explain his plans in more detail. Then he had to walk them through the placement of ditches and stakes. Exactly where to dig the rings around the village, how deep, how wide. Where to put the stakes, what wood was best to use, how far apart they should be. How high to make the wooden wall, how to build a platform running around the insides. In a way he should have been heartened. That when they realised what needed to be done the villagers committed wholeheartedly to it. He thought, in a way, that building was understandable to them, and the strengthening of their village made sense. The idea they would have to fight their own Rai was still an abstract one, something Cahan felt sure they did not really believe.

But treefall? They understood that. It was treefall the

Leoric used to convince them to build, telling them that if it brought riches it would bring the Forestals. She barely even mentioned the Rai. At first he had wondered why she spoke of Forestals so much but eventually understood; they were a known threat.

In an effort to leave he tried to convince the villagers that they should let the reborn guide them in their building, but they were suspicious and frightened of the grey warriors. The reborn in turn had little patience with the villagers, at least one did not, the other never spoke. Neither was pleased that he was leaving them behind.

"We should come, to kill your enemies," she said.

"I hope not to meet any."

"But if you do," she said, "we must be there to kill them." He stared at the reborn, her grey face blank. What he intended would require diplomacy, and he was sure the reborn were not in the least diplomatic.

"The best way to keep me alive is to help fortify this place." He pointed at the walls but she did not look, only stared back at him.

"Do you order it?"

"Yes." With that she nodded and walked away.

The light had dipped below the horizon before the villagers were finished with him, the beginnings of the first pit were being dug and there were plans to construct a way of running the tanning pits into it. The clearing of Woodedge had started; there were many things he could accuse the villagers of Harn of, but being scared of hard work was not one of them.

Despite the coming darkness, Cahan, Venn and Udinny set off to catch up with Dyon and his small group. Soon they were joined by Segur, who bounded along with them. As they moved from the clearing into Woodedge, he had the oddest sensation, as if the world paused, as if something touched his mind.

A soaring figure, its head topped by branches.

Then it was gone.

"Why do you want to catch Dyon?" said Venn. "Do you intend to stop them? Because if you are going to kill—"

"Cahan is not going to kill them, trion," said Udinny with a laugh. Then she became more serious. Looking up at him in the dim light. "You are not going to kill them, are you?"

"Of course I am not, monk, what do you think I am?"

"Pragmatic," she said, "surly and—"

"Enough, Udinny." She shrugged and turned to pet Segur who had come to sit at her feet.

"Why are we going after them then?" said Venn. "I do not understand."

"Because if we do not they will never leave Woodedge."

"They are hardly in danger here," said Udinny. "Even I could make it through Woodedge, and they have lived here all their lives." She looked across at him. He continued to walk, using his bow as a staff and trying to ignore the monk's chatter as he followed the waysticks that set out the path. "Though I suppose there have been orits reported in the forest."

"What are orits?" said Venn.

"Strange creatures, of many colours that forage and build," said Udinny, who sounded like quite the expert, despite only having recently seen them herself.

"They are dangerous?" said Venn.

"Well," said Udinny, "not if you do not disturb them, the workers anyway . . ." She left her words hanging. Segur whined. Venn looked across at Udinny and the monk smiled. "But the protectors," she said, "oh, they are fierce, and they will follow you for great distances if you—"

"It is not orits," said Cahan.

"What about swarden?" said Udinny.

"What are swarden?" said Venn.

"It is the Forestals," Cahan said before Udinny could once more show their questionable expertise. The monk nodded sagely, as if they had known this all along.

"But Dyon has taken nothing to trade with him," said Venn. "Why would the forest bandits be interested?"

"The Forestals want something from Harn, and Dyon carries it but does not know it." Udinny looked at him, a cloud of puzzlement on her painted face.

"Is this a riddle, Cahan?"

"No," he tried not to sound too surly. "The Forestals want treefall to be known, they cannot send someone to the Rai, they would be killed out of hand. They want Harn to send the message."

"Why not just start a rumour in the towns?" said Venn.

"There are always rumours," said Cahan. "No one would listen."

"So if Dyon is doing what they wish," said Venn, "why does he need protecting?"

"Because he does not know he is doing what they wish. And relations between the village and the Forestals have never been good. There is a gulf between them, and in that gulf is space for much misunderstanding."

"I can see how that could be," said Udinny.

"And I wish to speak to the Forestals also," Cahan said. Once more the monk looked confused. "Now save your breath for walking, I want to catch Dyon and his group before they talk themselves into an arrow." They walked through the night, occasionally catching glimpses of the bright Cowl Star through the canopy. By the time the Star was starting its curving journey down towards the horizon Venn and Udinny were beginning to falter. They camped in among the bushes and Udinny showed Venn how to make a necklace of mintwort to keep away the tiny biting creatures. As they worked on their necklaces Cahan placed a hand against a tree trunk, feeling the power beneath. A ripple of excitement ran through him. The strength of his cowl would be a comfort when they came across the Forestals. If he reached in just a little further . . .

But when he tried to tap the power of the tree, it squirmed

away from him. Shame flushed through him. Was he not good enough now? A deep breath. Another. Calming himself. The boughry had lent him the power of the forest when he needed it, and now, in this moment, maybe he did not. Who was he to expect another to lend him their life just so he felt a little more secure? He was more than most people even without giving his cowl power. He would have to be content with that.

Besides, he was sure it was the boughry he had felt as he entered Woodedge. Touching his mind, checking his intentions. Or maybe as a reminder that they watched? Uncomfortable thoughts, and as if sensing his disquiet Segur came to lie by him. He buried a hand in the garaur's thick fur and the garaur let out a satisfied growl.

The next morning they walked on, it was pleasant, the light moving through the eighths of the sky and spearing through the new growth of Woodedge trees as Harsh loosened its grip.

"We are followed," whispered Udinny after a while. Cahan did not stop walking. If they were being followed he did not want to alert those who did it. Though Venn rather spoiled it by immediately looking about them. Segur growled, picking up the sudden change in atmosphere.

"You are sure, Udinny?" he said. The monk nodded. "You have seen them?" She shook her head.

"No, but I know they are there," she said. "Rootlings, all around us."

"Rootlings?" Udinny looked confused for a moment, as if what she had said was obvious.

"Yes." The monk shrugged and they continued to walk. But now Udinny had spoken of being followed Cahan knew she was right. A shuffle of bushes, an out-of-place noise. A shining eye, a furred elbow or leg vanishing into the undergrowth.

"Rootlings," he said to himself. He felt no threat from the forest's creatures. "We need not worry about them."

Udinny nodded and smiled, though Venn did not look as sure. He saw them crouch and touch a hand to the forest floor when they did not think he was looking. When they stood they looked less worried about the rootlings that followed, calmer. They walked on, the light passed further across the sky.

"Do you hear that?" said Venn. Cahan stopped. Udinny stopped. They listened, but apart from the usual noise of the forest heard nothing.

"What do you hear, trion?" said Udinny.

"Voices," they said. "Some raised in anger." Cahan took off his helmet, the better to hear but still there was nothing. He placed it back on and turned to Venn.

"You reached into the forest, Venn, when Udinny heard the rootlings?" They looked away, then nodded.

"I touched Ranya's web," they said, and he wondered at that, they had never used those words before. He glanced at Udinny, who was finding a nearby tree very interesting. "Only lightly," added Venn.

"You should not," he told them, "not without letting me know what you attempt. It is dangerous." The trion would not look at him. "Could that be how you heard the voices?" He stood a little nearer and Venn shrugged. "Touch the ground again, Venn, see if you can tell me how near they are." After his experience with the tree he was strangely reticent to try himself. The trion nodded, crouching and placing a hand in the leaf mulch. He watched as they closed their eyes, fingers digging into the dirt. "Along this path, not far. But I feel . . ."

"What?" said Udinny.

"Anger, I think, hard, black emotion. And . . ."

"We must hurry," Cahan said. And pulled Venn up. "Come, we run."

Running, down the overgrown forest track, ferns whipping past. No voices, no feeling of anyone before them. They burst into a clearing.

"Stop!" Cahan shouted it. Venn and Udinny slid to a stop. Around the clearing were trampled plants and broken branches. "There has been a struggle here."

"How do you know?" said Venn.

"Cahan," said Udinny, "can read the wood the way you or I would read a parchment, Venn. Though perhaps he would struggle to read a pa—"

"I can read, monk," Cahan said. He ignored Udinny's further prattling and moved into the clearing, searching around it, stopping where he found offcuts of vines. Segur sniffed at a patch of ground nearby and Cahan crouched, a smear of red on the grass. "There is blood here, but not much. I think the Forestals took them prisoner." He stood and pointed. "They went that way, south."

"Why," said Udinny. "The Forestal's base is in Wyrdwood, to the north."

"Maybe they have a camp, come, and try to be quiet." They moved on, following the signs of passage through the wood. The fight and capture of Dyon and his party had not happened too long before they came upon it. And it was always slower for a larger party to move, especially one with prisoners, than a smaller one. They found the Forestals quickly enough, or rather they found Dyon and the three with him. Bound and gagged, lying on their sides in another small wooded clearing. The moment Cahan saw them he cursed himself for a fool.

"Dyon!" shouted Udinny and ran towards him, quickly followed by Venn.

"No!" Cahan shouted after them, but too late. He felt the tickle of an arrow behind his ear. Forestals rose from the scrub on either side of the bound men. Segur vanished into the bushes.

"It is a long time," said a voice from behind him, "since I have had some Rai to play with."

"I am not Rai," Cahan said, "if I was you would already be burning."

"Can you rip the life from me and set a fire faster than I can let go of a string, Rai?" That voice, he knew it.

"As I said, I am not Rai. I rip the life from no one."

"You certainly look like Rai."

"But I am not, Ania," he said, the Forestal's name coming back to him. He felt the arrow tip dig in harder behind his ear, hissed in pain.

"How do you know my name?"

"We met before, you lost a bet to me."

Wind blew, branches rattled. Creatures called to one another.

"Well," she said, "the forester returns. You seem to have moved up in the world, and you have some rather nice axes. I bet they would fetch quite the price."

"Let these villagers go, Ania," he said. "They take the message to Harn-Larger that you want delivered. Of treefall."

"Tell your friends to sit with them," she hissed. He nodded at Venn and Udinny and they joined the bound villagers. "Gerint," she said, "take the gag off the leader." One of the Forestals put down their bow and pulled Dyon up, taking the gag from his mouth. "Is this true? About treefall?" asked Ania, her arrow still digging painfully into Cahan's skin. Dyon nodded, terrified beyond speaking. "Why did he not say?"

"They are frightened of you." Cahan heard her click to herself, a satisfied sound, as if that was the way things should be.

"Let them go." Her people cut the villagers loose and they stood, rubbing their wrists and looking confused. "Well," she said, "get on, the sooner you deliver the message the sooner I will have someone decent to rob. Go!" She shouted the last word and Dyon and the villagers turned and ran into the forest.

She did not let Cahan, Udinny or Venn go. The pressure of the arrow tip on his skin never lessened. Cahan marvelled at how strong she must be. "Now they are gone," she said, "you can tell me what is going on up at that village. We saw the soldiers. I wanted the Rai that fled but she escaped me. Now it looks like they prepare Harn for a siege. I am curious."

"You did not rob the soldiers on their way here then?" he said.

"Thought they came for treefall. Tall Sera said to leave them alone. Let them become complacent until they had something worth taking."

"Can we not do this at arrowpoint?"

"I find," she said softly, the arrow digging in a little further, "that people are often more truthful at arrowpoint, Forester."

"I have no intention of lying to you," he said. "I came to find you, I have a favour to ask."

"A favour?" she laughed. "You are a strange one, Forester." The arrow went away, he felt her step back. "Go join your friends over there, then ask your favour. But remember, you and I have history, and there is no Tall Sera to step in and save you today." Stepping slowly and carefully through the leaf mulch, he joined Udinny and Venn, keeping his hands away from his axes, holding his staff light between finger and thumb. Ania stood at the edge of the clearing, her clothing threaded with leaves and vines so that even this close she was hard to make out. Most of her face covered by a hood and only her mouth showed. She held her bow at half draw. He had experienced how quickly she could let loose an arrow, and would take no risks.

"The Rai want the trion," he nodded at Venn. He thought it better not to mention they wanted him as well, it could lead to questions he did not want to answer. "That was why they sent the soldiers, and I gave them a bloody nose for it. They cannot stand for that, we both know it. They will come back to wipe Harn off the map. Dyon thinks he can bargain knowledge of treefall for Harn's survival." The Forestal laughed.

"Soon as try and bargain with the circle wind to stop blowing."

"They are desperate, but they have decided to defend their village no matter what. I will help them."

"If the Rai want the trion," she said. "We should kill them." She lifted her bow. Cahan stepped in front of Venn before the trion even had time to look alarmed. He lifted his hands.

"No."

"I can loose through you, Forester. All you do is save me an arrow."

"It will inconvenience the Rai more if we live. I think they are afraid of Venn." She stared at him. "And Venn is a child." At that she let out a breath, lowered her bow a little.

"How will it inconvenience them?"

"They want the trion alive." She watched, her bow at the ready. "They will have to get close to do that. No sending fire from a distance." Wind blew through the clearing and he hoped it blew away the dislike this woman had for him. As if sensing some change Segur trotted into the clearing to sit by him. Then growled at the Forestal.

"The animal likes you," she said. He nodded.

"And Segur is very choosy." He could not see her face for the hood, but felt she was amused.

"What is your favour?" she said.

"You watch the forest paths, you will know the Rai approach long before we do. If you would tell me of their numbers that would help. How many soldiers, how many Rai come with them."

"You are not asking me to kill them for you?" she said, a crooked smile on her face.

"It is not your fight," he told her. "But knowing their numbers, it will help." She stared at him.

"You are all going to die if they send more than fifty, you know that."

"I am hard to kill." The quiet of the forest settled between them.

"Numbers, and who they bring." She let the rest of the tension fall from the bow. "I can do that. Make sure your villagers know to expect a message from us, I do not want to lose one of mine to a spear."

"They will be safe."

"And we may kill a few Rai for you as they approach. I've got a soft spot for lost causes." With that she whistled, turned and vanished into the forest, followed by the rest of her Forestals. Within moments it was as if they had never been.

"She was not very friendly," said Udinny.

"It's a hard life, being an outlaw," he said. "It breeds hard people." Venn stepped forward; the trion looked worried.

"Why do you think the Rai are frightened of me, Cahan?" they said softly.

"I do not, Venn," he said, "I was only looking for a way to stop her putting an arrow in you." Udinny chuckled to herself, and they began to make their way back to Harn.

47

They took a longer path back through Woodedge. Venn and Udinny followed quietly, they did not ask why he had left the path and he could feel their curiosity with every step. He wondered how long it would be before one of them asked what he was about, and which one of them would speak first. In the end it was Venn, but they did not say what he expected.

"The Forestals are gone," they said.

"Good, I am surprised they bothered following us, they know where we are going."

"No," said Venn, "they did not follow us, they continued south. Now they are gone." He stopped pushing his way through the underbrush.

"What do you mean?"

"I could feel them in the forest. Then I couldn't."

"I have told you," said Cahan, unable to hide his irritation, "not to drift out of this world using your cowl without telling me."

"Ranya's web protects, the forest will not hurt me."

Cahan gave the monk a look, but she was finding a nearby bush very interesting, turning the leaves over to look for anything that might be living there. "The forest does not care about us, Venn. Not in a way we understand."

"I think it does," they said. "And the Forestals are still gone." Venn sounded annoyed, raising their voice.

"You are new to these things, Venn," anger within him smouldering, a struggle not to raise his voice. "Maybe you are not as in control as you imagine." He sank down to one knee, pushed his hand into the dirt and searched for the connection to Ranya's web, part of him angry he called it that so readily. He would speak to the monk when they got some time alone. He blamed her for Venn not listening to him. The web was there, but hard for him to touch. A deep breath. Calmed his mind, damped the fire within. Fear fed it, fear and worry.

Falling.

Upwards.

Life around him. A hundred, thousand, million connections. Each one bright as fire. He felt as though he looked down from the night sky, no, like he was part of it. Travelling through it. The trees, the plants, the life. Them in the centre, bright points. An expanding circle growing around them, like an explosion. The rootlings, startled by Venn's voice. Further out, four points of light, slowly dimming, disturbing the forest as they moved away, not fitting into this place; Dyon and his party, heading towards Harnspire and destined to find nothing good there. No longer his concern. The web spinning around him, dizzying, filling him, taste and sight and sound in silver and black. Something out there, something he did not understand, like an echo, but not of sound. Like a memory.

But no Forestals. No sign of them at all.

He took his hand from the earth, for a moment Ranya's web hung over Woodedge around him. He saw the life as lines running through and around everything that lived. He felt the great net of the fungal mats below his feet and beyond that something wrong, something —

"Did you find them?" said Venn. Shocked out of it. The trion looking pleased with themselves. "You didn't, did you?"

"No," Cahan said. "It must be some Forestal trick. I never felt them before they sprung their trap either."

"Hiding?" they said. "Like, when you hid us from the Hetton?"

"Of course not," he said, rubbing dirt from his hands. "You need a cowl for that." Venn looked a little downcast, and he felt once more as though he had the upper hand before realising something he had never thought about. If he had not known Venn had a cowl, he would not have known. He did not feel it in them the way he did with the Rai. And the Forestals had indeed vanished. That raised possibilities he did not understand, or want to think about. "The Forestals have been in Wyrdwood for generations," he said. "Who knows what tricks they have learned, or how close the great trees hold them." Both Venn and Udinny were staring at him. "Put it from your minds and help me with my task."

"And what is that?"

"I am looking for plants and bushes."

"Cahan, we are surrounded by plants and bushes," said Udinny. Cahan ignored her.

"Do you know what a crownwood is?" From the way they looked at him, they clearly did not. He let out a sigh. "It is a small tree, a bush. A round bole, about as high as my knee, and from it grow long sticks, hundreds of them."

"Oh!" said Udinny, a smile on her face. "Does each end in a pair of wide leaves? And when the wind blows the sticks knock against each other and fill the air with tapping?"

"Yes," he said. "That is it."

"I know it," said Udinny.

"Good," he said, "keep an eye out, I am looking for them, and crosstick bushes, you know them?" Udinny nodded, but Venn looked blank. "It is a bush, Venn, called crosstick because the outer sticks grow across each other to make a cage around the inner leaves. But the inner plant will be hard to see now as it will be in leaf. The outer leaves are bright red."

"That should be easy to find," they said.

"You would think," he looked around. "But I have had no luck so far." They continued on the way back towards Harn until Udinny stopped them with a shout.

"Look!" she said, "is that your crownwood bush?" She pointed through the trees, and now they had stopped he could hear the faint knocking together of its sticks.

"It is, come with me." He ran towards the crownwood bush, Segur bounding around them in excitement. Hundreds of straight sticks grew up from the bole of the crownwood. "We will harvest it, we want sticks that are about the thickness of two of my fingers at the thickest point." He held up his hand, "See, my first two fingers held together, no more than that, and no less." He reached in and took hold of one that looked right. "If you pull on it, low down like this," he began to pull the branch backwards, "it will snap off right where it joins the bole." With a crack the stick came away, startling Segur who leapt into the air and landed with all its fur on end, growling at him. Udinny laughed, and the garaur turned, ran at her and nipped her ankle before vanishing into the undergrowth.

"Iftal's blood," shouted Udinny, hopping on one leg and rubbing her ankle.

"Garaur do not like to be laughed at," Cahan said.

"Ungrateful creature," said Udinny, rubbing her shin, "to think I gave it my last sweetcake."

"So you are the reason my garaur is putting on weight." Udinny looked away. "As punishment, monk, you can go up into the trees and get us floatvine. I was going to send Venn but they can help me harvest the crownwood." Udinny considered complaining, then thought better of it and started wandering about the trees, looking for one that had a good crop of floatvine drifting above it.

"Do we take all the sticks?" said Venn.

"What do you think?"

"No, we don't," they said. "The forest would not like it." Cahan nodded.

"About a quarter of them, that will not hurt the bush, and will do us for now." They set to harvesting the crownwood, while above Udinny cursed in the names of all the gods she knew and a few she may have made up. When she eventually came down, gently descending wrapped in floatvine, they had finished their harvest and bound up the sticks in the floatvine. Cahan gave the tether to Venn. They thought it an honour but the forester had tried to pull bundles of staffs through a wood before and knew how frustrating it would be, it caught on everything. Segur jumped onto the bundle and rode it, looking around the forest like a Skua-Rai in their splendour.

They walked for the rest of the day. Segur quickly bored of its ride and vanished into the forest, rejoining them just before dark. Cahan noticed its mouth was stained with blood, though it had clearly decided not to share its food.

"Still cross with Udinny, I see, Segur?" The garaur whined, and climbed up him to sit around his neck. They camped not long after, though they had still not seen a crosstick bush. They were rarer than crownwoods, considered ill luck and dug up when seen. There were reasons for that, of course, and they had nothing to do with luck.

They found the crosstick bush not long before they sighted Harn. A place Cahan would have expected it to be long gone from. They spent half an hour harvesting it, teasing out the straightest sticks and being careful not to break them. Venn excelled at it, Udinny did not. In the end he sent the monk away to try and repair her relationship with Segur, something she was glad to do as the crosstick sap stung the skin wherever it touched. It was annoying to Venn and Cahan, but Udinny did not have the benefit of a cowl and her skin was covered in painful red streaks. Before the first eight passed they had harvested nearly a hundred sticks from it and the bush itself looked no different.

"We will leave it there, Venn," Cahan said. "Bind these up and add them to the crownwood." Venn looked a little crestfallen as now they knew well enough the annoyance of pulling a long load through a wood. "Do not worry, we are nearly back. You will be done with your burden soon."

"What are all these for anyway?" they asked. The trion sounded miserable.

"Do you remember me saying that with a hundred forest-bows I could stop an army?" They nodded.

"To have a bow, Cahan," they said, "is to be under sentence of death."

"I know, Venn," he replied quietly, "but if I have to make everyone in Harn into an outlaw so that some survive, then that is what I will do." With that he walked away, leaving the trion thinking about what he had said. Realising the danger that was coming, the seriousness of it. They were about to say something, but Udinny came running out of the trees, laughing as she pursued Segur. The garaur yipped and cackled as it ran rings around her. Then she fell into a bush. Coming up covered in leaves and looking as though she was part of the forest herself.

"We are friends again," she said as Segur clambered up to sit around her neck, "I have promised not to bite the garaur, and it has promised not to laugh at me." Then she went cross-eyed and fell back into the ferns, making Venn laugh and whatever they had meant to ask, well, that was forgotten.

48

It was all Kirven could do to walk down to the cells. All she could do to put one foot in front of the other and not collapse, her muscles weakened by grief and worry, her mind blanketed by it.

Rai Sorha had returned from Harn alone. All of her troops were dead.

Kirven did not care about the troops, soldiers died, it was what they were for. But Sorha had not brought back Venn. Her child. Kirven was torn between fury at Sorha for not bringing them back and self-hatred for letting Venn go with her. Why had she allowed it? Why had she let Venn convince her they were ready? Why had she let Sorha shame her into it?

She would find out what Sorha knew and make her pay for this. If her child was hurt, or worse – No, she could not think that. Either way, Rai Sorha was going to suffer a slow and painful death.

Outside the taffistone cells her guards stood silent.

"She is in there?" The guard bowed their head. "Did she struggle?" The guard shook their head. Kirven put her hand on the door. Paused. She would have expected Sorha to fight, Rai never gave in and she must know that her life was forfeit for this. Rai did not forgive failure, and neither did Kirven Ban-Ruhn.

Did Sorha consider her weak? The Rai had already failed once and Kirven had given her a chance. Did she think she would get another? She would not. Kirven would have Sorha's skin. She opened the door, walked in. Sorha sat in the cell behind the taffistone with its faint blue glow – was it brighter? The Rai looked relaxed for a woman who must know her execution was coming.

"High Leoric," she said, a crooked smile on her face. A bow of her head.

"You have failed me." Kirven looked down on her. If she expected fear, or worry, or any form of contrition Sorha did not show it. She scratched her head, stood, her movements languid, uncaring.

"Oh, not only me, High Leoric. People much closer to you than I have failed you," her voice a drawl. She smiled again, walked around the taffistone to the bars. Kirven could not understand what the Rai meant. How could she be so confident when she had failed so completely?

"What do you mean?"

"Your child betrayed you, betrayed me, betrayed all of us, High Leoric." Kirven laughed, but it was a hollow, empty thing. It did not convince her and she doubted it convinced the Rai before her.

"You would say anything to stay alive, Sorha," she said. "You may have lost your cowl, but you are still Rai." Sorha nodded, put her hands on the bars of her cage. "I could have run, High Leoric," she said, "but you and I, we are bound together, I think. You cannot afford me telling them about your traitor child. And I need a patron to survive in our cruel, cruel world." Was Sorha laughing at her?

"You are a fool, Sorha," said the High Leoric, "you should have run. Even if what you said about Venn is true there is a very simple way for me to be sure you never speak of it." Kirven felt the woman's confidence wavering. "And if it isn't true, you are simply a failure." She took a step back. "Either way the outcome is the same, we will not see each other again, Sorha Mac-Hean. You will end your days in a duller's pod, I understand it is a very poor life." If she expected the Rai to crumple the woman did not. She only stared at the High Leoric.

"I lied to you, Kirven Ban-Ruhn, High Leoric of Harn."

"A strange thing to tell me now."

"I did it to protect you." Kirven knew she should go, not listen to what the woman said, but she could not. She was hypnotised by her and, besides, Sorha knew the answer to the only question Kirven had on her mind. The one that burned within her. "You want to know about your child? What they did? If they still live?"

She was trapped and she knew it. To ask was to give the woman a chance, and if given that chance Sorha might somehow get her hooks in. But if she was not here to get the answers she desired, why had she come down to the cells? A death sentence can be signed off anywhere.

"Tell me of Venn. I may make your death quick."

"It is all bound up in the lie I told you." Sorha turned and walked to the back of the cell, sat down. "Do you want to hear my lie?" A knife twisting in Kirven's guts, the Rai trying to assert control even from a cell.

"Speak, or go straight to the duller." Sorha stared at her, her mouth twisted, eyes blank.

"Venn never killed anyone in Harnwood, they never activated their cowl before Cahan Du-Nahere killed Rai Vanhu and Rai Kyik."

"That is not what you said before." Sorha shrugged.

"You had told everyone the child was Rai," that half-smile again. "I went along with it to protect you."

"That is your story?" Kirven made the words into a laugh. Though within she felt as if she were turning to stone. Events had got out of control. Venn's cowl activating had left her feeling almost secure, almost sure she had found safety.

"Why do you think I was so desperate for them to come with me to Harn," Sorha pointed through the wall towards where Kirven presumed the faraway village must be. "I intended to finish what Vanhu had started. For you, Kirven." She managed to look contrite, staring down at the floor. "But I did not know the child was duplicitous, traitorous." Kirven could not breathe, could not speak. Inside she was screaming. Venn was her child, what they did reflected on her. Treachery in Crua meant death.

"Or you lie," said Kirven. "To save your skin."

"I had the false Cowl-Rai. Caged. Ready to bring back to you," she nodded at Kirven. "The whole village were cowed, easy meat. I was going to bring them all back in chains, so you could show what happened to those who betrayed you." Kirven stared, said nothing, would not ask. "Venn let him out."

"No," said Kirven. She could not move. Could only speak that one word. "No."

"Yes," said Sorha, she came to the bars again. An air of desperation as she spoke? Maybe. "Look into my eyes, High Leoric, you will find no lie." She did. Kirven was not sure that you could really see a lie in another's eyes, but she found herself believing the woman despite herself. She wanted to weep, to rend her hair, but not here, not in front of this woman.

"This is excuses. To cover your failure." Sorha shook her head.

"The trion is important, I knew that." The two women were near enough to kiss, staring into each other's eyes, but there was no passion there, no heat, only ice. "Venn sneaked back into the village, to betray us and free the villagers. I had used them to entice Cahan Du-Nahere back. He is powerful, High Leoric, very powerful." She leaned back a little, let go of the bars. "But the dullers did their work. We fought, he and I, one on one."

"And you lost." Sorha shook her head.

"No, I beat him. I am better than him."

"And yet here you are."

"He had followers." Kirven was finding it hard to breathe, the cell room felt small, overly hot. She could not have a real threat to the Cowl-Rai rise, not here, not where she ruled. "Two women stood by him, grey-skinned, fought like demons. Unnatural. I think he is in league with the Osere, using strange creatures come from below. They killed all your soldiers, drove me away. Did not die when they should have." Kirven swallowed. Forced herself to stand straighter.

"You think this story will save your skin? You still failed, you still lost my child."

"You need me," said Sorha.

"Why?"

"Because you have been insulted by Harn and you cannot let that pass or you look weak. And Venn has made you look weak before the Rai, and that cannot pass either. You stand teetering on a pin, Kirven Ban-Ruhn. It is only a matter of time before the Rai make a move on you once they find out you failed again. The only way to show your strength now is to march on Harn, crush it. Bind your child and force them to obey you. Show strength." She leaned forward, her voice soft, a smile on her lips. "But you cannot march on Harn without taking the Rai, they will be insulted if you do. It is when you tell them Harn stood against you, that you will be at your weakest."

"I will take dullers, my own guard and . . ."

Sorha licked her lips. "Galderin, will want to lead, and he will not take dullers with him, not have his power cut off or use anything that suggests he needs help, like your guard." Sorha stared at her. Kirven hated her in that moment, for her confidence, for being Rai, and most of all for being right. "You are trapped, between staying here and being deposed because you look weak, or marching on Harn with overconfident Rai and dying. Galderin may even kill you on the journey." She stepped back again, much calmer. "Cahan Du-Nahere is Cowl-Rai, High Leoric. Without dullers he will take power from some villager and tear your forces apart. But I am a walking duller. I will protect you not only from Du-Nahere, but from your own Rai. Only I will be able to face the Forester of Harn and live." A sudden desperation in her voice. "Kirven, together we can spin a story to the Rai of what happened that does not make you look a fool." The High Leoric stared at Sorha. Counting in her head. Fighting back a dizziness, determined not to show weakness no matter how much panic roiled beneath her skin.

"Or I could never go back to Harn," she said, and as the words came out of her mouth they felt like an option. "This Cahan Du-Nahere, he has never attacked us, he has only ever reacted. If I tell the Rai Venn is dead and this Cahan with them. That you and the trion died for the new Cowl-Rai, if we never go back he might simply never bother me again." Sorha pushed herself against the bars.

"How will the Cowl-Rai react, when they find you have lost their trion?"

"There are other trions," said Kirven. "The Rai are long-lived. Patient."

"This is not the way Rai act," hissed Sorha. "We attack, we face our problems."

"But Sorha," said Kirven. "You forget, I am not Rai." The woman looked shocked, her eyes momentarily widening, and then Kirven turned and walked away. "And neither are you." As she opened the door Sorha began to shout.

"You need me! You will need me!" Kirven ignored her, walking down the corridor. The silent guards said nothing, did nothing as Sorha's shouts followed her. She would have to face Galderin, tell them something. Have to inform the

Cowl-Rai and Tiltspire. Everything was spinning out of control. The High Leoric turned the corner, passed from view of the silent guards and felt as if she were falling. As if a great wind were rushing past her. Fear coming up on her as hard and certain and final as the ground. Her muscles gave way, she made a fist and pushed it against her mouth as she crumpled to the floor. Biting on her knuckles to stifle a scream. Tears flowing as she sobbed, so deeply and so hard that it shook her entire body, and all she could say was one word.

A name.

"Venn," she said, and it was not anger that came close to overwhelming her, but guilt.

49

Harn worked hard.

The first circular pit around the village was almost finished and they had used the spoil from it to make a slope on the far side of the pit, vicious stakes sticking out from it. One of the reborn, the one he had named for his sister, stood on the top of the small spoil ramp before the walls, watching the work. At least that was what he presumed she was doing. She was so still she could have been a statue, placed there at the beginning of the world when Iftal walked and the Osere had not yet fallen. Bridges of split tree trunks had been placed across the pit to allow access to the village, the gates he had destroyed had been replaced and Woodedge around Harn had been cut back by another five paces from where it had been when they left. The air rang with the sound of axes.

As they approached Harn the work stopped, the people stared at him. It made him uncomfortable. Not the stare itself, he was used to them staring. It was that it was not resentful. That he was clanless was forgotten, the armour he wore and instructions he had left had changed him in their eyes. He would almost have preferred that they looked at him with the old resentment, they should resent him. He had destroyed their lives, not on purpose, but had he not been here they would not be forced into making their village a fort. Forced into fighting, and more than likely dying.

He had brought this here.

"Cahan!" Leoric Furin walked through the Tiltgate. Her white make-up once more perfect. "We have been hard at work." As she walked past the reborn the warrior came to life, following the Leoric to meet him, Venn and Udinny halfway between village and forest. "Did you find Dyon, was he safe?" Cahan nodded.

"A little tangle with the Forestals, but I had hoped for that." She cocked her head, puzzled. "They have said they will notify us when the Rai approach, so make sure everyone knows Forestals will be coming, and that they are not a threat." The Leoric nodded.

"We have done well," she gestured towards the village.

"You have," he said. "The pit will be hard for them to get over now." Behind her the bright eyes of the reborn watched him from behind her visor, and he wondered what she thought. She must know how hopeless this was. The walls of Harn were weak, in places they had been removed entirely. Furin saw him staring.

"The wood of the walls was rotten. The warrior," she turned and nodded to Nahac, "said it was better to cut new wood, and that the new wood was harder to burn when the Rai started sending in fireballs." She stepped closer to him. "You must ask them not to talk so plainly in front of the villagers, they fear fire." He nodded. "We will start on the second ring pit shortly."

"You have not asked the reborn to talk less?"

"They are good at giving orders, less so at listening to others."

"Nahac," he said, "you have done nothing but war for generations, you must remember that if you frighten these people they will be of no use."

"They will be of no—" began the reborn but he cut her off.

"We will make them of use. You know as well as I that a battle is lost in the mind before it is lost in the field." She stared at him. "Not everyone's greatest wish is to die." The reborn did not move at first, then gave a slow and stately nod.

"True," she said. "I will keep this in mind." He turned to Venn and Udinny. The monk still had Segur draped around her shoulders. Venn was pulling on the bundle of sticks and muttering under their breath at it.

"What is this gift you bring us," said Furin, pointing at the wood Venn towed behind them. "It does not look sturdy enough to help us rebuild the walls."

"It is not," he said, "it is crownwood staffs and cross-ticks."

"What for?" said Furin.

"Better I tell everyone at once." He did not think the villagers would like what he intended, better to face them all at the same time.

"I will gather them." Furin began to walk back towards the village shouting for her people to meet in the square. The reborn stayed with him.

"Look after her," he said.

"We serve you," she replied. Her voice as dead as she was.

"You serve me, and want something from me," he said. "I want to protect this village, and I need her to do that. They will never trust me the way they trust her." The reborn stared at him from behind the serene face carved onto her visor. "So keep her safe, to help me."

"I had forgotten how complex it is, dealing with the living."

"Get used to it," he said.

"And you will gift us death."

"If it is possible. Yes." The reborn remained still for a

count, then nodded, and turned to follow Furin. He in turn followed her. Cahan slowed to let Udinny pass.

"Not coming, Cahan?" she said.

"A moment, is all, Udinny," he said. "Go with Furin to gather the villagers, bless them if it helps." The monk nodded and as she placed her first foot on the log bridge over the pit Segur leapt from her shoulders and ran for Woodedge. "For such a fierce hunter," said Udinny, "that garaur can be very cowardly."

"It avoids people," said Furin, "maybe it is wise?" Udinny laughed to herself.

"Perhaps," she said, and skipped over the wood bridge. The stakes sticking out of the other side looked new. Cahan glanced down. The villagers had not wasted the old stakes. They had been set in the bottom of the pit. Though he walked slowly, he did not hear Venn's footsteps following across the bridge behind him. The trion was standing on the other side of the pit. They were staring at him, the blue line across their face no longer bright, their shaven head fuzzy with dark hair. As he watched they dropped the tether on the wood, leaving it to bob above the ground.

"What are you doing, Venn?" he said. "Harn needs what you have there."

"But not me," said Venn. "It does not need me."

"It needs everyone, Venn." They shook their head.

"No, I have been thinking about what you said, to the Forestals." They looked away, rubbed their fuzzy head with one hand. "How they came for me, the Rai. They are coming for me. These people," they pointed at Harn, "they need you to fight for them." Venn looked back at Woodedge. "They do not need me. I will not fight, I am just the reason the Rai come here." He felt confusion. Wondered why the trion thought such a thing.

"Venn," he said, and walked over, put a hand on their shoulder. "I am the reason the Rai are coming here. I am the reason they want to wipe out this village. We both know what I am, the new Cowl-Rai cannot allow even the hint of competition."

"But that is not what you said to the Forestals," they looked away, to hide tears he thought. Had he been this worried when he was young, this ready to find fault in himself? He did not remember, but his youth had hardly been normal. Though he did not think Venn's had either from what little he knew.

"The Forestals, Venn, hate the Rai. You know that." They shrugged. "Had I told them what I was, they would have killed us there and then, never even listened to what I had to say." He turned the trion's head back towards him; tears had tracked blue lines down their face. "The Rai are here for us both, true. But I brought them here." He searched for some comfort in his words, but it was a long time since he had offered comfort to any and he found himself wanting. "If you wish to leave, I will not make you stay." He looked back over his shoulder and spoke quietly. "The truth is, it is unlikely anyone walks away from here." The trion stared at Harn. "You know how Rai work, Venn," he said. "You know that everyone in the village will die."

"But not me." They looked haunted. "They will not kill me."

"I would not be so sure, Venn. You have betrayed them." The trion looked away. Looked at the floor. Then let out a long breath.

"They will not hurt me, Cowl-Rai needs me." The words came out in a rush. "The world cannot tilt without me." Cahan blinked. Being the child of the High Leoric meant Venn was important, but what the trion said made them important in a different way. "When the war is won the Rai will gather at Tilt, with sacrifices, lives to take. They feed the power they take into the taffistones before the great stone at Tiltspire." Such misery in their voice. "All those deaths simply because I exist." They looked away. "The power is too much even for the Cowl-Rai. A trion with a cowl must stand between them and the great taff-istone. That is how the world is tilted, how warmth is brought to the north." They looked at him, words coming by rote now, learned and repeated many times. "I am the conduit. I am the pivot and the Cowl-Rai is the lever." A sob escaped them.

"No tilt without you," said Cahan, barely a whisper.

"They will never stop," said Venn, "as long as I am here." Cahan licked his lips, thought for a moment. "They will never stop."

"And you, Venn," he said, "do you survive such power?" They wrapped their arms around themselves.

"No one will tell me." Venn looked into Cahan's face. "I should run, they will follow. I am only one life. I could save the whole village." Cahan stood in the warming air of Least not knowing what to say. Then he put a hand on Venn's shoulder.

"Harn is doomed whether you are here or not, and that is because of me. No matter what you think." His mind racing. Thought after thought. And in among those thoughts, hope, only a little, but that was all that was needed sometimes. "But if you stay, Venn, you may really save this place."

"How?"

"We only need to hold the Rai, Venn, for one day. Then they will pull back and build siege machinery to bombard the village. If they have a couple of really powerful Rai, they will not even need the machinery. But while they prepare, the villagers will realise defending Harn is impossible, and we will escape to the forest with them." Venn looked at him, wondering what this could have to do with them. "But you, Venn, are too valuable for them to drop fire or rocks on us. I spoke truth to the Forestal, though I did not know it. They need you, and they will have to get close to take you alive, they cannot even throw spears at us, never mind fireballs. You give us a chance, Venn.

If any of these people survive, it will be because of you."
The trion stared at him. "So stand straight and bring the
wood. It is more important than ever." He turned back to
Harn. Looking over the wall at them was Ont, the butcher.
Cahan felt sure he was too far away to hear what they had
said, but then again, the woods were strange and sound
could carry.

The butcher turned away.

"Come, Venn," said Cahan. "We have much to do."

With that they walked into Harn, and despite the
holes in the wall and that, maybe on second inspection,
the pit was not quite as deep as he would have liked,
he felt better about defending this place than he had
before.

The people of Harn had gathered before the shrine of
Tarl-an-Gig where Udinny spoke to them. They wore
bright colours, stood together in twos and threes watching
the monk. It was odd, but from a distance Udinny
appeared slightly taller than he remembered, longer of
leg. Some trick of being raised above them on the shrine
no doubt. He also thought they were cleverer than he
gave them credit for. In Udinny's place he would have
torn down the shrine of Tarl-an-Gig, shown that Ranya
had power here now. Udinny had not, she recognised
the people were scared and that they needed familiarity
to cling onto. So she stood before them and told them
one of the old stories, about Iftal, and how much they
loved the people, enough to break themselves apart for
them.

". . . and remember," shouted Udinny, "when the cowls
first came, the people thought them more a curse than a
blessing. They were frightened, because the Osere had
forbidden them. But they had forbidden them because they
feared them." Cahan smiled to himself, thinking on how
she prepared them for what he brought. "Now, I see our

protectors are here," Udinny pointed at him and Venn. "We should hear them, and we should remember not to be afraid."

Cahan was grateful for their words, but knew, no matter how Udinny tried to prepare these people, fear was coming. Fear like they had never known.

50

He pulled the floating bundle of sticks into the centre of the village. The reborn stood at either side of the gates, flanking statues, the villagers were gathered before the shrine. There was a constant chatter in the air. At the Forestgate the gasmaw farmer, Sengui, was using her maws to lift heavy lengths of wood into place. The maws were tethered by a complex-looking net of ropes that used their lift to power a crane. It was a rig he had only ever seen in the military and Cahan wondered if Sengui had served.

Gradually, the chatter died down as the villagers became curious about what he had brought. Cahan undid the bundle of crossticks and put them to one side, then cut the float-vines around the crownwood staffs, letting them fall, clattering into the mud. He watched the floatvines drift up and away into the cold blue sky.

The noise of the staffs falling silenced the villagers entirely. They watched him, some curious, some hostile. The attention made Venn uncomfortable and the trion stepped to the side so they were a little behind him.

"Are you planning a fire, Forester?" shouted Ont, walking

towards him. He held in one hand the large hammer that he had been using to drive in pegs that held the walls together.

"Funny you should say that, Ont," Cahan nodded, "we will need a fire, but not made with these staffs."

"Then why have you brought them, are we going for a walk?"

"We are getting ready," he raised his voice, pulling the attention of the village towards him and away from Ont, "for a show of strength." Cahan looked around. He did not get the feeling that the villagers truly understood what was coming, though there were a few, the guards, Gussen, Aislinn, and Sark who was head of the village's hunters, who he thought might understand. They had fought and they watched him in a different way from the villagers. "We are building strong walls, good defences." Furin walked over to stand by him.

"We hope we will not need them, of course," she said.

"But no god respects a person who is not prepared, yes?" shouted Udinny from where she sat, cross-legged in the mud before the shrine of Tarl-an-Gig. The villagers nodded, the need for sacrifice was understood, simple, what they knew.

"You work hard, and I have seen the pit, the stakes, the slope you have made." He looked around, some smiles. "The new wall comes on apace."

"We intend to build another around it, like what was said." He looked for who was speaking, Sengui.

"Good," Cahan smiled, "that is sensible."

"And strengthen the gates more, too," came another voice.

"I am pleased to hear this," Cahan looked for the speaker, but could not find them, "I am glad you are taking this seriously."

"Once they see they cannot get in," said Manha, the leader of the weavers, "and they know from Dyon they need us to find the treefall, I am sure all will be well."

Cahan nodded, though he knew it was not true. Wooden gates and a wooden wall would not be enough to hold the Rai.

"We can hope so," he shouted, "but as Udinny said, no god respects those of us who do not prepare. So we must prepare." Now he watched them. "You, Manha," he said, "we need armour."

"Like yours?" said a voice, "we would need to work all of our lifetimes twice over to afford even the helmet." Laughter at this.

"Like mine would be good, but as you say, we do not have the time or the riches. Who is the sap puller here?" A couple stepped forward, dressed in the same bright yellows and greens as the rest of the village. They kept their heads down. Did not look at him.

"Us, Rai, I am Gurd, this is my secondhusband, Hadral, our secondwife and firsthusband are in the forest now, tending the taps."

"I am no Rai, Gurd," he said softly. "We need the sap of stingwoods, you know them?" She nodded.

"We keep away from them, stuff burns."

"Yes," Cahan said, "but treated correctly it becomes hard. If Manha and the weavers can make us tunics we can make armour. Like your gate guards wear but newer, better." The sap puller stared at him. Then nodded.

"I have heard from others how it is done, like making sweet sap, then you soak the clothes in it. We will need two vats, at least. It is a lot of work, will take time. Trees cannot be hurried."

"Thank you, Gurd."

"You have not told us about your sticks yet," said Ont, there was something mocking in his words, his voice. "Do you wish us to go out there and beat the Rai with them?"

"No." He turned away from Ont. It was always best to deny people like him the attention they wanted. "Aislinn," he shouted to the one-eyed guard. She did not like him much, but she understood the danger that was coming. She stepped forward but did not speak. "Your spear, did you make it yourself?" She nodded.

"Armwood," she said, "plentiful and the wood is hard. Then I sharpened the end and slow-heated it to harden the wood." She lifted the spear. "It is as good as any I was ever given when I served the Rai, better, I think."

"Can you teach others to make them?" She looked around.

"I can try," she said. It amused him to hear the weariness in her voice, as if the villagers were a lost cause to an ex-soldier such as her. Maybe they were, he knew little of her history. "But them is no good for spears," she said, pointing at the pile of staffs.

"No," he said, "they are not."

"If your sticks are not for spears," shouted Ont, amusement in his voice, "then what are they for?" He could not keep the curiosity from his voice. "We do not all need a staff to walk like you do."

"It is not for walking, Ont," Cahan stared at him.

"What is it for then?" he said.

"War," Cahan told him. Tried to meet the eye of every man and woman there. "Make no mistake, people of Harn, if the Rai are not moved to peace by your walls then we must fight them. They are an army, you are not. They are trained, you are not. We require something to put us on a level with them."

"How will sticks do that?" shouted a voice from the mass of villagers.

"We will make them into bows."

Silence.

Silence for too long. No one spoke. They had been taught to fear and hate bows. To see them as a coward's weapon.

"The Rai will never deal with us if we have bows," said Ont. He turned to the people of Harn. "He wants the Rai to hate us, he wants to fight them."

"You think because we are not soldiers that we are without honour!" shouted another voice.

"You brought the Rai!" shouted another and Cahan realised how brittle the respect he had earned really was. How easily it could be cracked. "Now you bring dishonour! We are not clanless!" The crowd erupted into noise, a clamour, every voice shouting something different. Furin, the Leoric, stepped up, raising her hands and shouting. "Listen! Listen to him!"

But they were not listening, instead they were pushing forward, walking over the staffs, forcing Furin back towards the forester. Fists raised in the crowd, anger on their faces. Fear running through them. From calm to this, crowds were like the geyser rivers of Tilt; calm on top, but with deep and dangerous undercurrents.

"We should take him to them!" shouted a voice.

"They want him!" shouted another. "Let's give him to them."

Violence growing around him. In the distance, he saw the reborn. Murderous statues coming to life, spears held lightly in their hands as they jogged towards him.

Death in the air.

He could taste it on his tongue. Knew if the crowd erupted, if they turned on him, then the reborn would be merciless in their effort to protect him. The death of others was nothing to them. They wanted their own death, and would kill without thought to protect the chance of it. For a count he was helpless, backing away. The mind of the crowd knew it could overwhelm him. Like orits, it cared nothing for individual members, anger and fear controlled it now.

"Get him!"

Backing away, towards the Forestgate, the reborn breaking into a run. Everything spinning out of control.

"Quiet!" this a roar.

Not from Cahan.

A military voice. The sort of voice that was used to command, that was loud enough to be heard over the din of battle. It stunned the crowd, stopped them. They recognised it. One of their own. Sengui. She stood behind the crowd and they turned, their attention stolen by her. "Listen to him." She looked at the crowd. "It hurts you nothing to listen."

"Who are you to tell us this," said Ont, turning to her. The crowd distracted, slowed. "We want to live, not to condemn ourselves by picking up the bow."

"Just because you are big, Ont," said Sengui, "does not make you right."

"We are being led badly," said Ont. "Furin is leading us to our deaths at the hands of that clanless fool because he makes her heart flutter." The crowd were gathering to Ont, his words attractive and Cahan knew why. All the reasons he had avoided people for so long. Ont offered them ease and they were frightened. He offered them a target they understood. A way out through doing what they had been told was right all their lives; turning on someone they believed to be less than them.

"Have you ever fought, Ont?" this from Aislinn, behind her the one-armed guard, Gussen.

"You know I have not," he said, "but that does not mean I do not know when we are making a mistake, when—"

"You have never seen the Rai, Ont," she said. "I have seen them burn a village because the food they gave, the last of their food mind, had mould on it. I have seen them kill a family because a child that could bare speak did not show the correct obeisance."

"This is his fault," said Ont, pointing at Cahan, "his and that trion's."

"Maybe it is their fault," said Sengui. "But we cannot change what is. Now," she looked around, "it may be the Rai come and are ready to deal. And if their price is him," she pointed at the forester, "then I will gladly hand him over if it means our safety." If Ont had said that it would have caused a fury within Cahan, but when the gasmaw farmer spoke he accepted it as sensible. She spoke with a soldier's pragmatism, and she had seen war. He could not blame her for wanting to avoid it. "But, and I tell you this, Ont," she said, "the monk was right. Better to be prepared and not need it, than need it and not be prepared."

"They will kill us all for having bows," said a voice from the crowd. Aislinn laughed.

"How many times have you seen the forester walking into Harn?" She looked at the crowd. "Eh? Many, am I right? And he always has that staff?" Cahan saw confusion pass across the crowd. "Show them, Forester," said Aislinn, "I have suspected it since the first moment I saw you. So show them." Attention back on him.

"Come to the Tiltgate," he said. "Udinny, bring my pack from the Leoric's house." He led them to the open Tiltgate. Stood between the heavy uprights with the crowd behind him, waiting until Udinny dropped the pack at his feet. He took a bowstring from it and hid it in the palm of his hand, turned to the villagers. The crowd hung back, not stepping over the line of the Tiltgate, as if there was some safety to be found in not leaving the place they had always known. But there was no safety for these people, not here.

"I am a man with a staff," he said. "You have known me as that as long as I have been coming to your village." So many eyes, watching, judging. "You have not liked me. I am clanless, no paint on my face, no make-up to wear. Maybe over time some have come to accept me, a few even to welcome me. But all I ever was, or could be to you, is a clanless with a staff. Staffs are common in Crua, right?" Wary looks. He let the string loose, keeping hold of one end so it unspooled. "Watch." He strung the bow, bending the wood into an arc. "Now I am an outlaw," he held the bow up, "someone to be feared and hated." The crowd stared. "Let me show you why." He placed the butt of the bow on the floor. "Most Rai can only project a few arm's lengths from them. You," he pointed at Ont, "pick a tree." He took an arrow from his pack. "Well, Ont?"

The butcher stared.

"Armwood sapling," he pointed, "the one between the two larger burnwoods."

He had chosen a thin tree, thinking to make it harder for Cahan, but the reality was he would help make his point. Hitting the slim tree would only serve to underscore his skill.

Tension the bow.

Sight along the arrow. Taking his time. Take a deep breath.

Loose.

Letting the bow fall to his side. Watching the flight of the arrow, the arc of it through the cold air. It was a beautiful thing, an arrow in flight. Even though its purpose was deadly, the landing an ugly thing of pain and spilled blood.

Breath held in his lungs.

Arrow rising.

Falling.

Hitting the target, shattering the sapling's trunk with a sharp crack, felling the tree. It could not have been more impressive had Cahan picked it himself. There must have been some knot in the sapling for its end to be so spectacular. Gasps from the villagers. A sour look on the butcher's face.

"They cannot hurt you if they cannot get near you," said Cahan. "And if Sengui is right, and you can buy your safety with my life, then you are only villagers with staffs."

"You can teach us to shoot like that?" said Manha, the weaver.

"No." He would not lie to them. "But I can teach you to fill the sky with arrows. Create a storm that none can pass unharmed. That may be enough."

"Come then," said Furin to her people, "I doubt making

a bow is as easy as simply cutting some crownwood. Shall we let the forester show us?" They did not shout, there was no rousing affirmation of what he had done. They were mostly suspicious, but the anger had gone. They headed back to the village until only Ont and Cahan remained.

"I will look forward," said the butcher, "to the moment they hand you over to the Rai." He walked back towards the village square. Leaving Cahan alone.

Deep in the Forest

You are always boy and never Cahan. Sometimes, you do not think that anyone in the monastery actually knows your name. Once, you had thought that Saradis, high priest of Zorir in her finery, cared for you. Had you taken a moment, back on that day at the farm, maybe you would have realised that she never asked your name. Realised that, to her, you were simply a tool.

Of course you do not understand, because you are a child and you think as a child.

Like any tool, you will be useful until you are broken. And then you will be cast away in favour of something stronger.

51

The walls were closing in on her.

It had been happening to Kirven for days. A slow and certain claustrophobia that got worse as time passed. With it came a sense that she was being watched. That every Rai or soldier or servant or monk that passed her knew. They all knew. Only a matter of time.

News would come. People would talk. She would be exposed.

The failure.

Days passed, the light moved across the sky, the Cowl Star danced in the night, and she remained.

But the fear never left.

The walls were closing in on her. There was no escape, the vast weight of Tiltspire was going to crush her and she would crumple beneath the weight of it as if she was hollow. Everything she had cared for gone; only fear remained.

"High Leoric," a knock on her door. Falnist. Was today the day? Was now the time? But surely it would be Galderin, not Falnist, who came, though the trion would enjoy her fall as much as any of them. It would almost be a relief. The knock again. "High Leoric, I have news." How much she wanted to tell them to leave. To go. She looked out of the window. Once more thinking of the possibility of taking her freedom there. Climbing up to the marant landing and throwing herself off, ending her torment falling through the cold, clear air of Harnspire. "High Leoric, there is an embassy to see you." She stood. Walked to the door. Opened it.

"Who?" made the word a challenge.

"They would say very little to me, High Leoric, but they are from Harn," said Falnist, "and they come with a letter of introduction from the Leoric of Harn-Larger."

The walls closing. Tighter and tighter. No room to move. No way to breathe. Harn. And they had already involved Harn-Larger . . .

"High Leoric, are you well?"

"I am well, Falnist," she said, her mouth dry. Now was the moment. Let the walls close? Or throw herself into the air? "Who have these people spoken to?" Falnist looked confused, their face wrinkled up, no doubt some scheme passing through their mind. "Only the guards on the door, they alerted me." They smiled to themselves. "I know you have had dealings with Harn so I thought it might be of interest."

"Did they say why they were here?" Falnist waited a moment, Osere take them they were holding something back. "If you are hiding something from me, Falnist, there will be repercussions." The trion bowed.

"Of course, High Leoric, I was not keeping secrets. It is only that what they said, well," Falnist shrugged and avoided her eyes, "it seemed rather unlikely."

"Tell me." She wondered whether they would deny her. If her power had eroded so far that Falnist dare defy her.

"I think I heard them talk of treefall."

A moment when she found it almost impossible to breathe. Possibilities. Drawbacks. Danger. All came upon her at once. She felt dizzy.

"Put these people from Harn somewhere they will not be disturbed. Let none see them," she said. "They will wait on my pleasure." Falnist stared at her, aware something was happening in the mind of the High Leoric, but not what. "Go!" she said. Falnist bowed and left. She waited. Knew exactly how long it took the trion to walk away from her rooms and go down the stairs. Turn off towards the outside rooms.

She ran.

Down the corridor and through Harnspire, making for the cells. Past the silent guards and into the room that held Sorha.

"I am still waiting for my executioner, High—"

"Quiet!" hissed Kirven. "You said we needed each other, did you mean it?" For once, Sorha did not seem relaxed, uncaring, sure of herself. She was entirely still, as if caught in a trap. Only her eyes moved, watching Kirven. "Well? Did you mean it?" Sorha nodded. A slow nod, not slow to agree, more surprised, as if this thing had come upon her unexpected.

"Yes," said Sorha. So quiet.

"Then we have an opportunity," said Kirven. "One chance."

"What is it?" She licked her lips but her mouth was too dry for her tongue to offer any relief.

"There are people from Harn here."

"We could both be finished then, High Leoric." Kirven shook her head.

"Not if we get our stories straight," said Kirven. "The truth will be lost in the excitement."

"Excitement?"

"They bring news of treefall."

"At Harn?" said Sorha. Kirven nodded.

"How much did they see, Sorha?" The Rai closed her eyes, drifting back to the events in Harn. Feeling once more the visceral terror as the grey warriors cut apart her soldiers.

"Almost nothing, they were shut in their houses, prisoners." She thought, stopped. "Some I had do work, they may have seen the false Cowl-Rai caged. The houses were poor things, full of holes, so it is hard to be sure." Kirven thought for a moment.

"No one knows you are here," said Kirven. "So you have just returned. The people of Harn betrayed you and had Du-Nahere attack you in your sleep."

"The villagers will tell a different story if they are questioned."

"That is why you will be doing any questioning, Rai Sorha," the High Leoric stepped forward and opened the cage, "we are bound together now, for good or ill. We have both failed at Harn and if word of the truth gets out, we will both be seen as weak."

"I will still have failed, High Leoric," said Sorha, "and because of that and what I am, no Rai will stand with me."

"That is why I will put you in charge of my Hetton," said the High Leoric, "as no other wants that job. Now, gather your armour, clean yourself up and we will meet with Harn's emissaries."

Kirven watched the small group from Harn walk down the great room. Past the statues of Tarl-an-Gig, past the flags and the great fires, past the great eight-branched stars of Iftal. They looked small and scared and Kirven Ban-Ruhn thought that good. She wanted them small and scared. She wanted them too frightened to speak lest they say too much. To her left stood Rai Galderin, splendid in his armour, though deeply displeased. To her right stood the reason: Rai Sorha, though she had her visor down. Kirven did not want anyone from Harn recognising Sorha, saying the wrong thing in the wrong place.

She waited until the small group had made its way down the room to stand before her. They knelt. She made them wait. Letting the slow count of time pass and weigh on them. Making these provincial people, far from their home and all they knew, surrounded by a splendour they must find intimidating, wonder if they had somehow insulted her. She did not pity them for what was to come. She could not afford pity. They were a tool, a way of bringing her child back to her with the minimum of embarrassment, a way of keeping her position safe despite all that had happened. It would cost them dear and that was unfortunate.

If unavoidable.

"It is brave," said Kirven Ban-Ruhn, "for people who have betrayed the Cowl-Rai to come and stand before me." She heard a sob from one of them. Fear. It gave her a little strength. Reminded her of who she was. Their leader, a tall, bald man dressed in clothes she would have been ashamed to use as rags, raised his head.

"We," he began, his voice giving way. He cleared his throat. "We deeply regret what happened at Harn. But it was not our fault. The man, Cahan Du-Nahere, was an outcast, unwelcome in our village and . . ."

"And yet," said Ban-Ruhn, her voice as cold and imperious as could be, "you did not tell us we had failed to kill him when my people first came for him. You kept his continued existence secret." She barely moved, stayed utterly still in her throne. Knowing that in her braids and beads and layers of colourful wool she would appear larger than life to them. Something impossibly rich and powerful.

Which, of course, she was.

"We are . . ."

"My soldiers died." She stood, putting a fierceness into her words. "One of my Rai is missing and . . ."

"We will give him to you, and the trion we—"

"Quiet!" she roared it. She could not have them say too much. "Why are you here?"

"To make restitution," the man said, the words quick, high and breathless. He would not look at her, was shaking with fear.

"Your village is not worth even one of my soldiers."

"Treefall!" shouted the man. "There has been treefall. If you can forgive us, we will give you Cahan Du-Nahere and take you into Wyrdwood, we will . . ."

"You will tell us where the treefall is now," said Galderin. He was not slow to realise what really mattered. "We do not deal with people like you, rebels and worshippers of forest gods."

"We are not! We are not!" the man put his forehead to the floor, the ones who had come with him prostrated themselves. "We worship Tarl-an-Gig, we are loyal to the new Cowl-Rai and we hate the forest. We will give you Cahan Du-Nahere, we will give you the apostate monk, we will give you the trion, we will—"

"Tell us where treefall is," said Kirven. "That is a good start."

Silence.

Waiting.

"I cannot," said the man. "I do not know. Only our Leoric knows."

More silence. She let it continue for as long as she could bear. Watching the filthy villagers in their fear before her. She could smell them from the throne.

"You do not know?" Their leader shook his head, looked up from his place on the floor.

"We hope for forgiveness," they said. "And in turn we open our gates to you and give you all you want." Kirven watched the man. Wondering if he was brave or stupid. Deciding that one did not preclude the other. Letting time pass, letting them worry.

"Then we must go to Harn," she said it in a much less severe way, felt the man breathe out, felt his relief. "Go with my Rai here," Kirven waved towards Sorha. "She will find you somewhere to stay. You may stand now." They stood and Sorha walked past her. Kirven touched her arm, pulled her down so she could whisper to her. "Keep the leader alive, find out what the rest know." A nod from Sorha. She watched the emissaries and Sorha leave. When they were gone she turned to Galderin, the stiff wool of her clothes rustling.

"Prepare a force, a large one, two hundred at least. We will wipe Harn off the map. We take dullers to deal with this Cahan Du-Nahere and my personal guard . . ." Galderin almost laughed. Held it back.

"Dullers? For one man?"

"One man trained to be Cowl-Rai."

"But not Cowl-Rai," said Galderin. "We have a Cowl-Rai."

"He killed our soldiers, took my child prisoner. Almost killed Sorha." Did he know they had lied to him? Rai were so hard to read.

"Well," said Galderin, "Sorha is no Rai, not now. And from what she says, he attacked by surprise, at night and with help. I will not blunt my power, High Leoric. What Sorha can do will have to be enough." She nodded, thought him wrong. But could not say why without telling him more than she was willing. Putting herself, putting Venn, in danger.

"How long before we can be at Harn's gates?"

"We will need strong Rai, plenty of soldiers. A show of force will have them open their gates." He stared down the great room. "We cannot loosen our grip on Harnspire either. It will take time to balance our forces. I suggest your guard remain."

"How long," she said.

"The second, or third week of Harsh," said Galderin. Kirven breathed in. Not too long, not really.

But a long time to keep a secret.

52

Uncomfortable days followed and Cahan learned how beaten down the people of Harn were by life in Crua. They did not rail or complain about what he asked of them. Stronger personalities had asserted themselves so they accepted what was as their lot. Cahan was now in charge, he thought, in no small part, due to his armour. There were those, the butcher Ont chief among them, who tried to cause trouble but because he had both their Leoric and Udinny, who was the nearest the village had to a monk, on his side even Ont and his cronies had largely given up.

Each morning the people of Harn woke at first light, they tended their crops or their animals before gathering in the village centre. There the two reborn put them through spear and shield drill. It was boring and repetitious but necessary. Even their Leoric, Furin, joined in. The only villager who was not part of the drill was the woodcarver, Ilda, whose job of making more spears and arrows was too important for her to take time off. She had shown a real skill for weapon making, her arrows were as good as Cahan's and he had no doubt would end up being better.

Venn did not join them.

The trion refused anything they thought would lead to killing. It did not make them popular which in turn made them sullen and withdrawn. While the reborn put the village through their paces Cahan schooled the trion in the use of a staff. He had hoped the villagers would see this as Venn joining in, but suspected it simply looked like they were getting special treatment. Worse, he felt like some of them might think it was a case of the Rai sticking together, being aloof. A void began to grow between Venn and the villagers.

Food was eaten communally after morning weapons practice. Then the villagers went to whatever tasks were required of them. Ilda had a little team of people she thought showed promise that she was teaching how to make arrows. The rest of the village were put to work strengthening the walls of Harn or clearing Woodedge. Children scouted for crownwood and crosssticks to make bows and arrows. Others dried gasmaw gut for strings. Venn helped with these things, but they did it in a half-hearted way that left no doubt they would rather be doing something else.

A brightness for Cahan was that Segur chose to join them. At first it was wary of the villagers but it soon learned who was likely to give it treats. The creature became terribly spoiled.

In the second eight they did bow practice.

At first they had to do it in three groups, due to lack of equipment, but the children of Harn proved excellent at finding crownwood bushes, and soon the whole village lined up outside the walls. Not even Ilda was excused. There had been frustration at first, when people found out how hard the forestbows were to draw. Many of the smaller villagers complained they would never have the strength for it. But he schooled them, it was not only about strength, it was about the right strength, and that strength came with practice. Though whether they had enough time for the practice needed, well, that was unlikely. Once the people of Harn had overcome their distrust of the bows they began to enjoy shooting arrows.

Though even when they laughed and joked, beneath it was tension.

Targets were set and they practised mass launches. At first few arrows had even reached the target, but as time passed and Least warmed, the villagers shot further and further. Even if they loosed a hundred arrows and only a quarter of them hit then that was enough to scare an advancing army, and an army would be a much larger target.

A few showed real promise, and those he made into branch leaders of small groups. He ended up with four branches of around thirty people each. It annoyed him that Ont was one of the best archers, but the man had a natural eye and Cahan was not too proud to use it.

Venn refused to take up the bow. No matter how much he told them that sometimes it was not about using the weapon, but about being part of something, they still refused. In their youth they saw the world as black and white, as simple when it was anything but. His promise that they need never loose their bow in anger fell on deaf ears. To them the bow was for killing, and as such they would have nothing to do with it. So where the forestbows brought the village together, in merriment and in fear, it had the opposite effect with Venn. The trion's stubbornness only made them more of an outsider. Cahan would not have worried if the trion been useful in some other way. But Venn had been raised in such isolation they had no practical skills, and few social ones. They could not plough a straight line, they were frightened of the crownheads and the gasmaws, and any form of physical work involved so many complaints that few people, if any, wanted to work with them.

Whispers began to grow about the trion. Rumour, and resentment. Word reached Cahan that some thought Venn a spy.

In the end, Cahan had to assign Venn to jobs because so few wanted to work with them. People grumbled, but he knew it would be worse if the trion did nothing at all.

Tragedy visited in the last days of Least, as Harsh was returning and Cahan found himself constantly looking to Woodedge, expecting a Forestal bring news of armies moving through the trees. He moved archery practice into the village – if any scout saw the village practising outside the walls then any chance of an arrangement with the Rai was gone. Though of course there would be no arrangement, but he let the villagers believe for now.

He thought he was the only one aware of what was to come but he was wrong.

Pressure kept building until he could no longer pretend otherwise.

More and more often he saw villagers stop what they were doing and stare out at Woodedge. He had convinced himself that these were simple and accepting people, and maybe they did live a little more in the now than he did, maybe their lives gave them no choice. But as each day passed, the knowledge of what was coming began to weigh on them. On Cahan, on everyone. Conversations became clipped and words designed to wound were said. Only Furin, and her uncanny way with people stopped fights breaking out.

It felt like something had to give.

The scream, loud, and full of pain, could not have come at a more inopportune time.

Cahan had sent Venn, along with a man called Darmant, to shore up the ledges they had built along the walls, so that they could see over them and use them for protection. Darmant was a shoemaker and not particularly good at anything, not even making shoes, but he was popular. Always ready with a joke, a smile, or a kind word. Cahan sent Venn with him as he was more patient than the other villagers. When he heard the scream he thought it was

Venn, as it came from where they and Darmant worked. Had they hurt themself? Or finally taxed the patience of the shoemaker so much he had lashed out?

But the scream continued long past that of a short admonition, or small accident. It was the drawn-out wail of agony, of terrible wounds. The villagers froze at the sound, then ran towards it and Cahan followed. Found his view blocked by the crowd. Over the screaming he could hear Venn's voice.

"It was an accident! I didn't mean it! I didn't mean it!" Cahan pushed through the jostling crowd using his elbows, feet slipping on churned up mud. Venn and Darmant had been doing a two-person job. One he thought Venn should be good at it by now. He was wrong. The trion had let go of one of the heavy pieces of wood, the weight of it becoming too much for Darmant who had not been able to hold it. He should have been able to get out of the way but by some quirk of unkind fate, maybe he was tired, maybe because, like Venn, he was not very physical or practical, he had not. The ledge had come down, one of the pegs, used to secure it had caught Darmant, ripping open his stomach.

An agonising wound, and one there was no coming back from. A killing blow. The kindest thing that could be done for Darmant was to end him here and send him on to the Star Path.

A numbing shock passed through the crowd. The jostling stopped. Venn's hands were on Darmant's stomach, blood welling up over them while the man screamed. Venn looked up at the people surrounding them.

"It was an accident," they said. Then they pushed down on the wound, repeating, "Don't die, don't die." There was little hope of that. May as well wish to grow a gasbag and float away.

"You have killed him." Cahan did not know who spoke. But the words spread like fire in dry wood. Growing in strength and menace as they passed through the crowd. The pressure threatening to erupt.

"Darmant!"

"They have killed him!"

"Don't die. Don't die."

"Darmant, the trion has killed Darmant!"

"Don't die, I didn't mean it."

"They are Rai!"

"Don't die!"

"They came with Gart's murderer!"

An ugliness, a swift and growing hate. An outlet for all the fear they had been feeling more deeply with every passing day.

"We need them!" shouted Cahan and the crowd turned on him.

"You brought them here!"

Pointing fingers. Grimaces. Spittle and accusation.

"He brought them here."

You need me.

The fire within him rising, reacting to their anger. The raised voices would be drawing the reborn.

"Don't die!"

Fighting for control. Strong emotions, washing over him.

You are the fire.

"You'll kill us all!"

"They killed Darmant!"

"We should hand them over!"

"Bind them!"

"Burn the bows!"

You are the fire.

And in a moment of inattention. The fragile thing they had been building in Harn was lost. The village may have come together but he was still an outsider. Venn was still an outsider. They would hand them over to the Rai the minute they appeared, no time for thought or question. Cahan had been fooling himself it might be otherwise.

Power, washing over and around him.

You are the fire.

He could burn it to the ground.

"What's happening?"

Burn it all to the ground.

"Is he dead?"

The crowd quieting.

Aggression flowing away.

The power hanging in the air.

The only voice Venn's.

"Don't die, don't die, don't die." Repeated so quickly it was almost one word, not stopping to take a breath. Within Cahan the cowl squirming, the embers glowing more fiercely. He had thought it the approach of violence, but that was not the case.

A cowl always reacted to another user.

Venn was drawing power. Cahan wanted to scream out, "No!" How could the trion do it? After all they had said. In front of the crowd they were taking the Darmant's life?

But they were not.

Venn's power came from the ground, feeding it through themselves, giving it and of themselves to Darmant. The blood around their fingers drying, the terrible tear in Darmant's stomach knitting together.

Cahan did not know what this was.

He did not know this was even possible.

Venn was healing the man, Cahan knew it would be too much for the trion. What flowed in from the ground was not nearly as much as what flowed out. The trion's skin drying, withering, their flesh shrinking and tightening to the bone.

Then they looked at him.

"Venn . . ." said Cahan.

"I didn't want him to die," they said. Then collapsed into the bloody mud.

The crowd silent.

Anger gone.

Darmant looked like he was sleeping, Venn looked like they were a thousand years old. Cahan was unable to speak. The cowl was for killing, for war. That it could heal any other but the user, that had never occurred to him. Was it some property of what Venn was? The conduit, they had said.

No wonder the Rai wanted them back.

"What happened?" said one of the villagers.

"I do not know," said Cahan, and the crowd parted before him as he picked up the body of the trion, light as float-vine, and walked towards the Leoric's longhouse.

Deep in the Forest

The question you had asked the gardener so many times before, falling from your mouth.

"Why, Nasim? Why?" So many whys. Why did they take you away, why do they beat you for the least mistake. Why does your sister hate you so now? Why must you learn to war and hurt? Why, why why? Always the same answer comes back.

"I do not know, Cahan. But all things are linked, Ranya tells us so. Maybe she moulds you for some great purpose."

What great purpose? you thought. To kill and kill and kill to feed a god? To send your enemies, people you did not even know, and the whole world to burn? What is great in that? All had been lies and liars. Only this man, Nasim, was gentle and true. His books fascinating, telling tales of an older god, with softer ways where people came together.

Sometimes you wondered if Nasim wrote those books, if he made them up, because you saw no evidence of gentleness in the world you lived in. Ever.

53

There was a strange atmosphere in the village in the days after Venn saved Darmant. The air was quiet, heavy with shame the way air can become heavy with purpose in the hours before snowfall. Venn slept the sleep of the dead, and whether they would wake from it Cahan did not know. Furin tried to have them put in a bed, and was ready to argue when Cahan said they must be laid on the floor. Udinny quietened her and led her away, leaving him with the trion lying like a bundle of sticks, their breath barely registering. The monk prayed constantly to Ranya for Venn until Cahan sent her away. He did not want others in there with him. So Udinny prayed outside the longhouse and though Cahan heard the drone of it he put it from his mind.

The reborn guarded the longhouse door.

Cahan watched Venn, teetering on the edge of life.

He wondered whether he had looked this bad after the fight in the forest. He did not think he had. Maybe it took more energy to save a life than take one. The gardener, Nasim, might have told him that once, but he had not really understood. Though maybe he should have. Nasim had paid a high price for saving his life, as high as could be paid.

Segur chose to spend its time curled around Venn's neck. At first Cahan worried the trion's cowl might take from the garaur, but it did not. Not that he could have convinced Segur to leave, it was ever a stubborn creature.

So the villagers loosed their arrows, they built their walls, they trained with their spears and Cahan knew all this. They were a buzz in the back of his mind. Sounds that faded into the background the same way the sounds of the forest vanished as you got used to them. They only changed when something was wrong.

He wanted the sound to change.

For something to be wrong.

Some would say be careful what you wish for.

On the second day after Venn saved Darmant, did Venn's breathing become a little deeper? He was not sure. Despite that they were sullen, annoying, often recalcitrant and their ideas about not killing foolish in a land such as Crua, he wanted them to live. He wanted it more than anything.

"Will they live?" Segur hissed at the voice. Cahan turned. Darmant stood in the doorway, letting in cold air. "The grey warriors let me in," he said. "Will the trion live?" He wore the same bright blue tunic he had been wounded in, the front sewn up now. The wool had been cleaned but the bloodstains would never leave, they would always be a reminder of how close he had come to walking the Star Path.

"I do not know." Darmant nodded, face hidden beneath the wide brim of a conical woollen hat.

"It was my fault," he took off his hat, holding it with both hands and twisting it. Not looking at Cahan. "The accident, it was my fault and the village would have killed the trion for it." He stepped forward. "I was impatient to finish, I wanted them to take all the weight of the wood when I knew they could not. I lost my temper and let go, thinking to teach them a lesson by having them bear all the weight." He would not look at him.

"Do the rest of the village know that it was not Venn's fault?"

"I have told them," he looked only at the floor. "They would have killed them," he said again. Cahan nodded. "Whatever I can do for the trion, Rai, tell me and I will do it."

"Do not call me Rai," it was automatic. Though often the villagers ignored his wishes.

"I am sorry." The silence that followed uncomfortable, Cahan did not know what the man wanted him to say so said nothing. Eventually, Darmant replaced his hat and shuffled out of the longhouse.

Cahan continued his vigil, only leaving Venn's side to light the saplamps when darkness fell. He watched Venn and people moved around him, became ghosts. He cared nothing for them. Let the villagers practise, let them die. Darmant was right. They would have killed Venn. And despite how hard they might work at their arms they would give both Cahan and the trion over to the Rai. He had been a fool to think otherwise, and his foolishness had almost killed Venn. The words of the reborn echoed in his ears. "*I can sense death, Cahan Du-Nahere, and it is coming to you.*"

"Water."

He woke with a start. His fingers hurt. The saplamps had gone out. He could hear the soft sounds of sleep from the other side of the curtain.

"Water," A rasp, a croak. Venn. They spoke. The pain in his hands was Segur, gently chewing on them to wake him. He went to the trion, letting a dribble of water from the gourd run into their mouth. At first, no more than to wet their lips. A dry tongue touched the moisture. "More."

"Not too much, you will be sick." The slightest, most imperceptible nod. Cahan stayed, and dripped water into

Venn's mouth throughout the night. Small amounts, almost constantly. In the morning the Leoric came through with Udinny and Issofur, they greeted him but he did not reply. In the days since Venn had been reduced to a husk he had seldom had a word for anyone, and they did not notice that the trion was awake. They went about their business and Cahan ignored them. When the longhouse was empty he leaned in close to Venn.

"When you have the strength, Venn, we are leaving. These people will give in the moment the Rai turn up. We should never have stayed. I was a fool to think anything else." A movement, so small it was barely worth the word. A shaking of their head. "We will talk more when you can, rest for now."

Once the trion had started to improve the process was quick. By lunchtime he was giving them solid food, by the end of the day they were sitting up, one hand buried in Segur's fur. Outside the longhouse villagers trained. Outside the day went on and all those noises that he had become used to continued while he watched Venn. Hours passed, Venn's arms fleshed out, their skin became smoother, eyes brighter. He insisted on them eating, even when they refused. As he struggled to feed them he felt something, a shudder ran through him. A sense that not all was right.

The sounds outside had changed.

Quietened.

Arms practice had stopped.

A predator was in the forest: the instinct of the hunted to not be heard or seen.

Furin pushed her way through the door, spared a momentary glance for Venn but she did not have time for even a word. Her face drawn, the white clay cracked.

"Forestals, Cahan," she said. "There are Forestals at the gate."

Did he care? No, no longer. He would leave these people

who did nothing but let him down. But he had asked the Forestals to come, so he owed them his time at least.

Outside the longhouse it was bright and he had to shield his eyes as he walked, the reborn falling in to flank him. The whole of the village waited, the outlying farmers, too. They held spears and shields loosely in their hands, wore their armour of cloth dipped in sap. The weavers had found some way of adding colour to it and the village was a rainbow of colour quite at odds with the grey atmosphere. Udinny stood among them, she did not have a spear or shield, but she had a bow, and had proved to have some talent with it. She could not loose over any great distance but was unerringly accurate within her range. He had heard some say, "they speak to the wood" for those who can easily pick up a skill, and it fitted Udinny and her newfound ability. He hoped she would leave with him.

"This means they are coming, does it not, Cahan?" said the monk. He did not answer, only turned to Furin.

"Have them open the gates."

"Let Forestals in?" shouted Ont, but he did not continue. Cahan had no patience for his bluster and silenced him with a look. The forester wore the countenance of a warrior that day, and had done since the shoemaker's accident.

"Open the gate!" shouted Furin. Villagers ran to do her bidding, lifting the heavy crossbeam that kept it shut and they imagined would stand the attentions of a ram, or an angry Rai. He had not told them otherwise, and now it no longer mattered as he was not staying. They pulled the gates open and the Forestals walked in. The villagers did not move towards them, or raise a weapon. Only stared as ten, clad in green cloth woven with thin branches and leaves, sauntered past. It looked like Woodedge had come alive and sent its representatives into this place of houses and people. The Forestals looked around suspiciously, coming to a stop before Cahan.

"Three hundred," said the Forestal leader, Ania. "Less about twenty who we killed on the way." Even though he no longer intended to stay, the number took his breath away. It was a lot of troops to send for a simple Woodedge village. "At least one of your people is with them." Ania looked around at the villagers then turned back to Cahan. "When we started killing them, they came after us." She spat. "Better than their usual rabble as well, I lost two so we pulled right back and watched, otherwise there'd be far more than twenty dead."

"Still twenty who won't be here," said Cahan.

"They burned your farm," she told him, "and killed your animals." He nodded again. It saddened but did not surprise him.

"I expected as much."

"We will avenge your animals," said the reborn from behind him. Ania stared at her appreciatively.

"You have some new friends," said Ania. "Who are they?"

"Nothing to do with you," said Cahan, "tell me of the Rai."

"Well, rootlings have put 'em in a foul mood, cos of them I think that I only lost two."

"Rootlings?" Ania nodded at him.

"Aye, never seen them act that way before, constantly nicking stuff from them, throwing things at 'em. They killed a lot of 'em, but there's always more rootlings." She looked around. "Seems you have the forest on your side." Around her villagers looked to one another, unsure what to make of that.

"Thank you for coming, Ania," he said. "And sorry for your losses."

She turned, slowly taking in the village. "Seems you have an army, and a fort for 'em to play in." He said nothing. The Forestal turned to Furin. "We have barely eaten for the last few days, too busy running from them that hunted us."

"We will feed you," she said. "Come to the village fire." She led them over to the fire by the shrine. As Cahan followed he heard a villager mutter. "Forest bandits, why do we need them here?" Cahan turned, it was one of the weavers who had spoken.

"They frighten you?" he said. The weaver shrugged. "Well, they frighten the Rai too." He returned to the longhouse, the reborn went back to guard the door. Venn was sitting inside, eating a bowl of broth by themselves rather than having to be coaxed. Segur sat by them, its focus on the bowl of food and it let out the occasional whine.

"You are gathering strength." The trion nodded.

"It is strange, Cahan, I have drifted as if in a dream, and now it seems my strength flows back from the land." They spooned more food into their mouth and once they had swallowed put the spoon into the bowl and put the bowl down for Segur. The garaur gulped down what was left as if the thing had never eaten before in its life. "The Rai have come?"

"Not yet, but they will be here by tomorrow at the latest. We leave tonight." Venn stared at him. "What is it, child?"

"After all you have done and said, you will leave them to the Rai?"

"They showed what they were, Venn. They would have killed you because they thought you hurt that shoemaker." The trion put a hand on Segur.

"You have been telling me, all along how I must try to become part of them."

"I was wrong." They shook their head. "We will never be part of them. They do not want us. We should not be here."

"No, you are wrong." Cahan did not reply, confused. The trion looked at him. "Can you heal people, Cahan?"

"I cannot, you know that."

"And I did not know I could." They looked down at Segur, who was looking up in hope of more food. "Udinny said all things are linked, through Ranya's web."

"Udinny is a monk, they say a lot of things."

"The forest healed me while I lay here, Cahan, I felt it through the web. I felt Udinny's prayers outside the door. I felt the trees listening and their life pulsing into me. I felt Segur give its warmth. I felt the land. This dead ground," they thumped twice on the hard mud floor of the longhouse, "but it is not dead at all. It fights a war against the bluevein sickness, just like we fight the Rai."

"One illness, Venn, does not make you some sort of sage. You are still weak and healing. You probably half heard these things and constructed—"

"I have never met a Rai who can heal. Neither have you," said Venn softly. "And yet, here I am, about to be in the midst of a difficult battle. If Udinny is right, and all things are connected then surely this is where I am meant to be." The trion looked at him, all innocence.

"Venn," he hissed their name, moved closely so he could whisper. "Three hundred troops and Rai are coming. They will ask for us, and the village will give us up. They are simple people, with a simple understanding of the world. I saw that when they turned against you, I have been fooling myself thinking anything else. They are scared and right to be."

"Maybe you are scared." He turned to find Udinny in the doorway.

"You are not needed here, monk." The words came out as a growl.

"Maybe you are scared, Cahan, that they will not do what you think and give you up. And then you will have to stop running and find a way to save these people."

"There is an army coming, Udinny," he said. "Hundreds . . ."

"Give me a hundred, trained well in the use of the forestbow, and I would break any army the Rai of Crua can throw at me," he turned. Venn looking at him.

"I thought you knew better than to throw my own words

at me, Venn. And, besides, the villagers are not trained well. They are barely trained at all."

"I will not go," said Venn. "I am where I am meant to be. I know that now."

"And I will not stop you going if you wish to, Cahan," said Udinny. The forester stood.

"You are both fools, who are too ready to die," he walked out. The reborn made to follow him and he stopped them.

"Guard Venn," he said, "I need to be alone."

He found himself a quiet corner of the village where he could seethe. Let them all die, what did he care? He was not of them. He was a fool to ever think he may have been.

"Your Leoric has told me your plan." He turned to find Ania, the Forestal, behind him. "Hold the Rai for a day, then lead these fools into the forest once they realise their village is lost." He did not reply. "The forest will probably kill them, you know that?" She picked something from her teeth and looked at it.

"I am not staying for the battle. What they do no longer concerns me." She laughed to herself.

"All commanders get the fear the night before a big fight."

"These people are not worth my life."

"What people are?" she said. "They're all venal, selfish, and only worried about themselves."

"The Leoric is not like that," he snapped it.

"She the only good one?" He did not answer. Not straightaway.

"No."

"And yet, you leave them to die at the hands of the Rai with the rest." She stopped picking at her teeth to stare at him. "It will be hard for any they take alive, the Rai hate those who tweak their noses." She laughed humourlessly. "You strike me as man who carries a weight on your shoulders, I have seen the same in Tall Sera."

"What has your leader got to do with me?"

"If you leave here, the lives lost will be more weight on you and you know that." She stepped closer.

"The Rai will ask for Venn and me, and these people will hand us over. I have been lying to myself about it."

"Maybe they will," said the Forestal, "maybe they won't."

"You are fine one, Forestal, to try and talk me into staying when you intend to be gone before night falls." She stared at him. Blinked. Then reached over and took a handful of arrows from her quiver and held them out to him.

"Ten arrows," she said, "I'll give you that if you stay. Me and mine will hold for ten arrows. Take these as my promise." He took hold of them, though she did not let go. They were very fine arrows, straighter and better fletched than any he had ever owned.

"Why?" he said as they stood, linked by the arrows. "This is not your fight." She kept his gaze.

"I grew up in a village much like this. The Rai came, wanting their soldiers. Our Leoric said we did not have enough people for the farms to give them our young. The Rai took offence and few survived it." She let go of the arrows. "When the ten run out, we are gone. Until then, we will stay here and kill Rai for you."

"There will be no fight, Ania, the villagers will hand the trion and me over. They do not understand."

"Well, if they do that, we shall vanish. We are good at it." She scratched her head. "But maybe they won't."

"I thought you said people were venal, selfish and only worried about themselves."

"But you think there are good people here," said the Forestal, and with that she turned and walked away, glancing back over her shoulder. "Let us hope, for your sake, you are right."

54

A hand on his shoulder, a gentle shake that brought him to the surface of reality, rising from the depths where dots of light impaled the darkness, and the only sound was the screaming of a man he had loved like his own parents.

"They are here." The dream gone, sleep sloughed away like water falling from the leaves of a tree. The face of the Leoric above him. "We cannot tell how many, but Sark reports torches in among the trees." She leaned in close to him, an urgent whisper. "Maybe you should leave, Cahan. Now, in the night. Take the trion, your garaur and run. Take Udinny, too," then she took a deep breath. "And Issofur. Please."

"You want me to go?" Of them all, he had thought, maybe hoped, the Leoric would be the last to want him gone.

"Ont has been whispering in the ears of the villagers, he is a fool but he has enough of them believing they can buy their lives with yours that I will struggle to contain them if they turn against you." Her words were soft, it was easy to believe in the darkness that no one but he and the Leoric existed. For a moment he wished it was so. "It is not me being kind, Cahan. If you stay our village is likely to end up fighting itself and the Rai will simply walk in."

He had heard others say, it is always darkest in the deep of the night and in that moment he understood it. He knew the Leoric felt it too. A sense of hopelessness washed over him. Udinny's, and now Venn's, talk of Ranya's web, of everything being guided, that this moment was meant to be. The idea that the trion, the monk, the village and he were all destined to be in this place. That there was a reason for it. Seemed laughable.

But Venn's ability to heal, something unheard of, it would be invaluable in a battle. They could save lives that would otherwise be lost. And Ania's warning, of the guilt he would carry, he knew she was right about that. "You should go," said Furin again. "Save yourselves, save my boy."

"Will you come with us?" he said, "you know the truth, Furin. You know what will happen here if the Rai are allowed in." She made a noise, a brief expulsion of breath, almost a laugh, but it was one shorn of all amusement.

"This is my village, Cahan, what comes for them comes for me. I cannot leave." She sat back, there were still smears of the white clay she wore during the day on her skin, it made her face look strange, oddly shaped. "Besides, I am hoping the Rai will execute Ont first, so I can see the look on his face when he realises what he has brought on himself."

"I am not leaving." He turned at the voice. Venn. The trion sat up in their bed, rubbing their shorn hair with one hand while the other lay gently on a sleeping Segur.

"You heard the Leoric," Cahan said. "They will hand us over."

"Go, Cahan, you have done enough." There was a calmness in Venn's voice he had not heard before. "But I will not leave Harn."

"Just because the monk says all things are linked, Venn," he hissed, "does not mean it is true."

"Thank you for your vote of confidence," Udinny stepped out from behind the curtain that divided up the longhouse. Then she grinned. "But Cahan is right, Venn, much as I know Our Lady always has a plan. It will be difficult for you to carry it out if the villagers bind you and hand you over to the Rai." Udinny stepped forward, yawning. "I am not saying you must abandon this place, but maybe from the forest you can—"

"We are meant to be here," said Venn, and the trion sounded so sure. So much older in that moment. "You know that, Udinny. Listen and you will know it. Ranya wants us here."

"It is hard for me to hear Our Lady," said the monk. She sounded sad, unsure of herself; a rare thing. "I worry I have fallen from her favour. I share my mind with other voices now and they are loud." Venn looked up.

"Then listen to those other voices. The forest knows." A shiver ran down Cahan, he knew that these two must have spoken, and of things he did not understand. Things he did not like the sound of. Venn turned back to him.

"When I was lost, Cahan, near death, I saw much I did not understand. Spires, greater than of any spire city, glittering in a darkness like no other, speared with light. I heard the Osere begging for release, and I heard the voices of the gods, but not Ranya. Different voices, and they were many." Venn took a shaking breath. "They dream in the darkness." It felt, to Cahan, as though the temperature in the longhouse was falling.

"What do they dream of?" His words were breathless, half spoken. The atmosphere in the longhouse, cold yet feverish, strange in the way it had been before the taffistone when the boughry had taken allegiance from Udinny.

"They dream of fire."

A sharp inward breath.

"Udinny hears these voices?"

"No," said the monk. "I think I only hear the boughry

now, the forest, it drowns out all else." When he looked at her, her eyes shone like a rootlings.

"I did not understand it, Cahan," said Venn. "But I think I heard the forest, too. And it wants us here because the dreams of fire frighten it. And if I must be here so the Rai can take me back, then," their words tailed off, they looked away and they were a child again, fighting back sobs. "If that is what must be it is what must be."

"And you, Udinny?" he said. "Would you leave? Does Ranya, or the boughry, allow that?" The monk's almost ever-present smile was gone. They looked small and lost.

"The forest wants me here, Cahan," she said. "That is all I know."

Cahan heard no gods, no forest, speaking to him. He had been brought up to burn the world. He had experienced the fire. And though all good sense told him to leave, and his own anger said these people did not deserve him, surely it could not be coincidence, the three of them? The fire?

"What of your grey warriors," said Furin. "What do they say?" He turned and as if they could sense when they were talked of Nahac had appeared in the door.

"Stay or go," she said. "Death will follow you, Cahan Du-Nahere."

"I wish I had not asked," said Furin. The reborn shrugged.

Cahan let out a laugh, short and humourless. Furin smiled at him. *It will be hard for any they take alive.* Ania's stark truth. One he could not run from. One he did not want for this woman. Or those villagers he had enjoyed the company of. He had always thought his fate was to die alone but maybe, if he was to die, it was best to do it among those few people he had found he liked.

"I do not know of gods, fire, speaking forests, or death that follows people," said Furin, looking round. "Truthfully, it all frightens me and I wish I had not heard talk of it." She wrapped her arms around herself and Cahan wondered if she also felt the unnatural cold. "But if you stay, when the Rai ask for you, Cahan, I will do everything I can to stop us giving you up."

"I will stay." It did not feel like he chose to speak the words, but once he had spoken them he knew they were right.

Furin nodded, stood, looked around. "The Forestals say they will warn us if the enemy look likely to come at the walls." She glanced down at Segur. "Maybe you should try and sleep, tomorrow will be a hard day." With that she left them alone in the longhouse.

He did not sleep, and neither did anyone else. They did not speak either, only lay with their own thoughts. It was a poor way to spend what he expected to be his last night alive in Crua. In the darkness he felt Segur creep up to sit by his head.

"Old friend," he told it. "You must leave this place. There is no reason for you to die here."

The garaur did nothing but nestle into his neck. It was ever a stubborn and foolish creature.

55

Kirven hated the journey north.

She could have ridden on one of the many rafts, pulled by either crownheads or soldiers, but she did not. It would have made her look weak and she could not afford to look weak before the Rai or their soldiers. So she wore her armour, and she walked with the soldiers and she bit her lip when her muscles ached and the pain of her blisters became almost unbearable. She kept quiet when sleep would not come because she had become too used to comfortable beds in Harnspire. She ate the food, if it could be called that, and she did not complain.

With every step, she felt the slow erosion of her power more keenly.

She had made a mistake in coming, her power was civil not military. Galderin was not slow to point that out either. He could not outright deny her but the group of Rai he had brought with him side-lined her and their troops would not take her orders.

She should have stayed in Harnspire, it became more apparent with every step. She should have known this was coming when she could not bring her guard. Galderin had tried to stop her coming so she had fought him, but looking back he had not fought hard enough to stop her. He had drawn her in. He knew this would weaken her. An easy acquiescence would have been too obvious.

It was still an option to backtrack, to stay in Harnspire, right up to the moment they left. But she had not, because there was Venn. Her child. She could not trust Galderin to bring them back alive. If Venn died in the assault on Harn she was done, and she knew Galderin would exploit it, could even hear what he would say. *"Non-Rai rulers are fine, but not in the north, not where old gods still rise and threaten Tarl-an-Gig."*

She had to be here, to protect Venn from the ambitions of Galderin. But by coming she had played into his hands.

But if she brought Venn back and if she could convince them to come into their power she would be strong once more. The Cowl-Rai needed the conduit. Venn was her only chance.

She had never felt so alone.

Even in the long night when she had waited in the darkness for Madrine, when she had bathed the bruises and sewed up her cuts, there were others with her to understand. The secondwife, the firsthusband. But not now, not here. There was only her.

The troops would not speak to her, she was too important, too high up for them to speak with comfortably anyway. Galderin would speak to her, but he could not keep the condescension out of his voice and if she heard the phrase "a military matter" once more she would scream. At Harn-Larger she had made a final attempt to convince Galderin to bring dullers. That it was the easiest way. Move in dullers, take them up close and neutralise any power Cahan Du-Nahere had, but Galderin had laughed. Not openly mocking her, but mocking her nonetheless. In the way he spoke, the looks he shared with the other Rai.

"But High Leoric," he had said, "we have the abomination for that." Then the conversation was finished.

Sorha, possibly the only one who she could speak with, was at the back of the column. The Rai would not have her anywhere near them, and the troops did not like the Hetton. Now even the possibility of speaking to Sorha was gone, the woman had taken the Hetton and vanished into the forest. Chasing Forestals who peppered the convoy with arrows, and the filthy rootlings that constantly stole from them.

Kirven walked alone on a path she had chosen, stripped the skin from her feet until every single step became agony. Even sleep was no escape, constant nightmares of her first-wife, Madrine, of the night she had punished Kirven for becoming pregnant. Of the terror in the wood, the strange death waiting in the darkness of Wyrdwood.

When they arrived at Harn it looked like nothing special. Ditches dug around its low walls, wooden spikes driven into the ground. It was much like a hundred other little Woodedge villages, she was sure. Much like the place she had grown up in, hated. This one may hold treasure but she would not be sorry to see it burn, as soon as they had Venn back and the information they needed.

She watched Galderin while the troops around him made camp in Woodedge. Darkness was coming, the light above waning as the second eight came to a close. She approached and he made her wait before he turned to her. Pretending he was contemplating the village's defences.

"You cannot make a direct assault," she said. He did not speak to her, not immediately, another small slight.

"I was unaware you were trained in tactics, High Leoric," he said.

"You know I fought," she said, too quick, too defensive.

"There is a difference between holding a spear, Kirven," his eyes lifeless, skin hidden behind thick make-up, "and being the one who tells people where to point it."

"If they hold Venn prisoner," she said, "they are likely to kill them if we attack." Again, Galderin took his time, turned back to Harn. Stared at the walls.

"They have prepared for us, a poor job. The first ring ditch is not even deep enough to stop us walking over it. We should go in now, in the dark. While they are frightened. Finish this."

"You will talk to them first." He stared at her.

"Why?" said Galderin, "they are all going to die, it does not matter when it happens. I have brought strong Rai with me, we could bombard the place with fire now. This would be over before night is fully in."

"You would kill the trion. If Venn is brought out unharmed the Cowl-Rai will look well upon us both." The Rai did not look at her, only at Harn. "Otherwise we are finished."

"You would be finished, High Leoric," he said, turning to her. "Rai survive." Before she could say any more he raised a hand to stop her. "Nevertheless, I will do what I can. I will talk to them, but if they do not know their place." He looked back at Harn. "Well, then they must be taught it."

56

The morning dawned bright and cold. Cahan's stomach hurt, it felt like the small amount he had eaten might come back up.

The villagers stood in two groups before the Tiltgate, one larger than the other. In among the larger group Cahan saw Ont, his great size making him hard to miss. Furin led the other. They both held spears and shields and wore their brightly coloured, boiled sap armour. The bows were nowhere to be seen. The two reborn women stood between them, so still that they appeared to not really be a part of this world, and they would remain that way until that moment they were called upon. The whole scene was wreathed in early morning mist, the light above piercing it in shafts that made him squint and cover his eyes.

Sometimes it took the harshest of lights for someone to see clearly.

That light had shone upon him. He had come through the darkness of the night and seen the truth of himself.

He had run all his life from what he was, what he could be.

And sometimes you must stop running. Realise it was not what you were, but who you could be.

"Stay there, Clanless, do not climb the wall," that from Ont, staring out over the crowd of villagers around him. "We do not want the first face the Rai see to be yours, and for them to think we did all this for you." He gestured towards the walls with a huge hand.

"You did do it for him," Udinny from behind him, walking up with Venn to join Cahan. The look Ont gave her was not the one of a man with good intentions.

"A Rai is approaching!"

A pause in the day. A stillness born of fear.

"Leoric! Come speak with me, Leoric of Harn!" The double wall stopped anyone seeing inside the village, but blocked Cahan's view. He moved so he could see out through a gap between the Tiltgates. The speaker's armour was decorated with the signs and awards of many battles, the carving on it ornate. They had their visor down, the face on it of a grimacing, bearded man. It made him think of Saradis, the Skua-Rai who had taken him from here so many years before. When they lifted the visor he could not tell if the Rai was man, woman or trion, but he knew they were old. Far older than was natural, which meant they were a Rai of some power.

They did not speak again, not at first. Only stared at the wall while they waited for Furin to appear. Behind them, at the skirts of Woodedge, waited their army. Soldiers putting up tents, starting cooking fires from which pillars of smoke were climbing into the air. Poles were being raised to string garlands of small flags in the blue of Tarl-an-Gig and the primary colours of the soldiers' homes. Cahan saw yellows and reds but no green, which meant they had brought no soldiers from Harn county. He wondered if Sorha was out there, or if she had paid the ultimate price for her failure.

He knew what he thought most likely.

"Iftal's blessings to you, Rai," shouted Furin as she stood on the ledge, looking over wall, "welcome to our village." The Rai stared at her. Let their hearts begin to beat faster with worry before he spoke.

"I am Rai Galderin Mat-Brumar," the Rai shouted back, "and I am saddened that you do not open your gates for us, Leoric. We come in the name of the Cowl-Rai and Tarlan-Gig." The Rai's brow furrowed. "We do not understand why you have fortified your village against us, when you also sent me your envoys. It is an odd thing to do." They were trying to sound jovial, but their voice was like the scratching of one tree branch against another. A grating that gradually wore away the bark to create a scar. A wound upon the air.

"My apologies, Rai Galderin," said Furin, and her voice did not waver or show any fear. "But our last experience of the Rai was a poor one, and it frightened my people. Then with the news of the treefall in the forest we have become worried about Forestals as well. Why, only yesterday they were at our gates." Cahan heard a hollow laugh, and looked over to see Ania and her archers, crouched before one of the roundhouses, sharing some dried meat.

"Sensible, then," said the Rai, "to fortify your village." The Rai paused, looking back at their soldiers. "We bring troops to protect you, we bring food, we bring engineers who will build for you. Rai Sorha, who came before, she had been through an ordeal at the hands of the man you know as Cahan Du-Nahere. He is a criminal and a dangerous one. But she overstepped her bounds, hurt your people." These sweet words, like sap oozing from the Rai's mouth, were meant to entice Furin and the villagers, to pull them in the way sap pulled in tiny flyers. But like the sweet tree sap, once they were pulled in they would be trapped and they would be consumed. From the way the villagers were gathering round Ont, and from the way he was smiling Cahan knew they did not understand the danger, they heard only the sweet drip of his words. "I am not here to hurt you or your people, Leoric. I am here to help you. To bring what you need to administer the treefall, together we will bring plenty to Harn. I also wish to apologise for Rai Sorha, who acted badly towards you." Then the false bonhomie fell away, the thorn below the sap revealed. "Now open your gates, and hand over Cahan Du-Nahere and the trion called Venn."

"What if we do not have those people?" shouted Furin, her voice sounded small and thin when compared to that of the Rai, who amplified theirs with the help of their cowl. The Rai did not answer straightaway. Ont said something to those about him and Cahan watched them spread into formation, as he had trained them to when readying for a fight. They did not lower their spears, but they held them ready.

The two reborn now no longer still as statues, they felt the threat in the air. Their spears slid down and they held them across their bodies. A small action but an obvious threat.

"If you do not have them?" said the Rai. "If you have let them go? Then I doubt anyone here will be the sort the Cowl-Rai needs to oversee treefall. In fact, the Cowl-Rai will be very disappointed, and I have little use for those who disappoint the Cowl-Rai." The spears of those gathered around Ont came down. They pointed them at Cahan, Venn and Udinny. Ont smiled at the forester. The voice of the Rai was cold now, cold as deepest Harsh. "You, Leoric Furin, I am afraid will no longer rule here no matter what happens. Accept that with grace."

"Why?" said Furin, and Cahan knew then that she was as strong as any cloudtree, her voice did not waver.

"You have made poor decisions. What sort of Leoric sends away their village's monk of Tarl-an-Gig? Fortunately for Harn, we found him. He told us you cast him aside in favour of some strange wanderer who follows a weak and useless god. You doom your people to an afterlife with the Osere! Deny them the Star Path!" He let the ring of his words in the clearing die out before speaking again. "I have heard the name Ont, from your monk. Let me speak to him. He will be Leoric now." Ont smiled at Cahan. The forester wanted to wipe the grin from his face with his axes.

"He is here, Rai! The man you want," shouted Ont. "We will send him to you!"

The reborn moved like wind. One moment they were by the gate, the next before Cahan. Spears lowered, visors down. Ont's smile fell away, for though he might not have seen them fight he had heard of their prowess. "You promised, Clanless," Ont pointed at him, "that if the village wanted it you would give yourself up." He looked around; not all the villagers had joined him but there were enough, they were shuffling to flank him, spears out. They were scared, and for good reason. If they continued to advance on the reborn it would be a bloodbath. "So is your word good or not?" said Ont.

Anger within Cahan.

The fire growing. The burning within.

The reborn, and him, together? These villagers could not hold them. He would walk over them as if they were not there.

By the roundhouse the Forestals stood, forestbows strung, arrows in their hands. Cahan wondered if they would help him or the villagers, or simply stand and watch. He felt a hand on his shoulder.

"This is where we are meant to be," said Venn. The fire cooled a little and in that space, between the fire and the cooling of it, Cahan found himself lost. There were no good choices here.

"Where is Dyon?" that from Udinny. Shouted at the villagers. "Why make Ont Leoric if he has Dyon? Why not simply bring Dyon forward and have him tell us it is safe and he is to rule?" A pause. Ont's group of villagers stopped shuffling forward. Then one of them called out, Cahan was sure it was Aislinn, the one-eyed gate guard.

"Aye, where is Dyon," she said it loudly and clearly from the front row of the wall of spears and shields. As she spoke she lowered her weapon. "And where are the rest of them that went with him?" The villagers of the shield wall looked to one another, questions were exchanged. Ont's smile fell away.

"Dyon will return with the Rai," he said.

"My firstwife, Grilas, went with them," said a woman among Ont's people. "I want to see her afore we trust the Rai."

"Well?" shouted the Rai from outside the village, "where is Cahan Du-Nahere? Do you have him or not?" Furin looked down on them, on her people, and Cahan wondered what she made of this, of how changeable they were, of how little she could rely on them. Then he saw her nod, and the smallest nod came back to her from Aislinn. It was a grim thing, no joy in it, but he knew then she understood her people far better than he had given her credit for. She knew their fears, their hopes, and how the Rai could manipulate them. She had planned for it as best she could. He turned to Udinny.

"Furin told you to ask of Dyon?"

"She is very wise," said Udinny.

"Rai!" shouted Furin from her place on the wall. "We will gladly hand over who you seek. But there are those here whose loved ones journeyed far to see you. Farther than most in Harn have ever been, and they are worried about them. They would like to see Dyon and his party."

"They will come in with me," said Rai Galderin. "And what you want no longer matters."

"But you know what simple people are like, Rai," said Furin, "suspicious, frightened. It costs you nothing to send Dyon and our envoys back. To calm the people of Harn and ease your way."

"It is poor of them, not to trust me, Leoric," shouted Galderin into the stillness. "I am sent by their Cowl-Rai."

"Cahan," whispered Venn, "why does he not send Dyon and the others back?"

"Could be he does not want to lose face," said Udinny.

"It could be," Cahan lowered his voice so the villagers around him could not hear, "but it is more likely that they tortured and killed them all to find out what they knew. They do not bring Dyon because they cannot bring Dyon." The Rai was staring up at Furin, they slipped their visor back down.

"Very well," said the Rai, "you want this Dyon? I will bring Dyon." He turned and waved a hand, some pre-arranged signal with his troops. Soldiers came forward, walking Dyon with them, his head bowed and his hands bound. The Rai took him from the soldiers, marched him to the edge of the deepest pit that surrounded the village.

"Where are the rest?" said Furin.

"Dead," said the Rai. "It was a dangerous journey." No inflection or life in their voice. "This man, this Dyon. He will teach you a lesson that clearly needs to be learned." He angled his carved visor up at Furin. "That people like you should know their place." The Rai put a hand on Dyon's shoulder, and only now Cahan saw they had gagged him with a filthy strip of material. "There is a punishment for those who do not know their place, my friend Vanhu taught it to me," the Rai was shouting now, making sure the entire village could hear. "It is a trick of the cowl, he called it 'The Ember', because it burns slowly. Starts at the feet and fingers and moves inwards. It only burns the skin." For the first time, there was real joy in the Rai's voice. "Those inflicted die eventually, but it takes days." Dyon was shaking his head, struggling to escape, but he was no match for the Rai holding him. "This Dyon of yours, I will send him back to you with The Ember upon him. You can watch him dying, decide if that is how you also want to die."

Cahan felt a heat, the drawing of power, and his cowl squirmed beneath his skin. Venn's mouth fell open and the trion looked like they were about to vomit. An agonised noise filled the air. Dyon, trying to scream through his gag as he writhed in the Rai's grasp.

"There is a price for defiance," said the Rai, and he let go of Dyon. The man dropped to writhe in the mud before Harn. "Your village will pay that price. Many of you are going to die now, Leoric, because of your choice here. The people must know their place. So you must decide," the Rai looked down at Dyon, "how steep the price your people pay will be." They kicked Dyon. "I will let you come and get this man, you can consider him until the light is at its highest. Think about whether you wish to die like him. I have heard Tarl-an-Gig welcomes no traveller on the path to his star if they come to him screaming."

He turned and walked away, leaving Dyon behind. Cahan felt a weight, all eyes on him.

"Reborn," he said. "Bring the man in." Ont stared at him. He had expected hate from him, but what he saw was shock. Fear.

"Can we really fight them, Clanless?" he said.

"We have no choice," that from the wall. Furin watching as the reborn brought in her second, her friend, in the first agonising throes of a long death.

57

They took Dyon into the longhouse and his screams filled the village with noise and fear. The villagers were stricken. Only now were they realising the truth of what was coming.

If he expected an apology from Ont it was not forthcoming. He communicated only in sneers and found other things to do than look at Cahan. As the light approached its zenith, Furin left the longhouse and came to find him.

"I need to speak to the village, can your . . ." she looked over at the two reborn, once again statues before the gate.

"Reborn."

"Can the reborn watch the walls?"

"I am sure they can, I do not think they even need to sleep." He turned, "Nahac!" At the mention of her name both the reborn came alive, approached.

"What do you wish?" said Nahac. Her silent, unnamed sister watched.

"Watch the wall," he said. "Tell us if the Rai come."

"We will watch," she said and they turned, walking over to take their place on the wall while Furin called her people to her before the shrine of Tarl-an-Gig.

"My people," said Furin. "You have seen what the Rai did to Dyon." She looked around, her voice faltered. "You can hear what they have done." Dyon was no longer screaming, now there was only a low, constant whimper. "Through his pain, brave Dyon has shared what happened to him at Harnspire. All who went were tortured for information then killed, only he survived. I am sorry." She looked over her audience, and Cahan noticed that those whose loved ones had gone on the journey with Dyon were not here. Furin must have told them privately and left them to their grief. "Not only killed, friends. But executed as traitors by the Rai, burned before the great taffistone to entertain the crowd. They have no intention of letting any of us live. We can no longer doubt what Cahan said, they will kill us all if we do not fight."

"This is his fault!" Ont pointed at the forester, his face bent into fury. "He brought this upon us!"

"It does not matter." Furin said it so softly, so matter-of-factly, it stopped any rant that Ont was building up to. "It is where we are, we must accept it if we want to live."

"We cannot fight the Rai," said another voice.

"You are right," said Furin. "But we need only hold them until the light falls," she looked around, let the weight of what she said fall upon them. "We can hold them with our bows, and the help of the Forestals, and the reborn," she waved towards the wall. "Then at night we run for the forest, we will make a new life there."

"What sort of life will that be?" this voice bereft. Already grieving all they had known.

"Better than no life at all," said Furin. "Better than dying by fingerbreadths as fire crawls across your skin the way Dyon does." She raised her voice. "Make no mistake, that is what they will do! They will drag us back to their spire-towns and largers and have us dying as sacrifice or in cages, so all know what happens to those who stand against the Rai." She looked around. "Better, I say, the quick death of blade or spear."

"What of our children?" from the back of the crowd.

"We will protect them as best we can," her face grave, voice low. "But I will open my Issofur's throat before I give him to the Rai." A silence. A pause.

"We have done nothing wrong." Another voice. Plaintive. Confused. Lost.

"True," said Furin. Udinny stared at her in the most intent way Cahan had ever seen. Furin met her gaze. Licked her lips and worry washed across her face, the shudder of leaves caught by the indecision of the wind. She took a breath, gathered herself. "Udinny talks of an older god than Tarl-an-Gig, or Chyi, one as old as Iftal themselves." He saw the villagers look to one another, more confusion. He thought Furin mad to have brought their gods up at such a time. What the people needed was certainty, not a new theology. But she carried on. "Udinny names her Ranya, a god of all things, who touches upon everything." She was losing the villagers, they had been through so much with her and now she was pushing them too far. Cahan wanted to tell her to stop. "I see you, my friends," she shouted, "and I know you do not care for what I say. Do not want talk of gods. Especially new gods." Silence. "When Udinny spoke to me of Ranya, I laughed. What use was this soft god to me, I thought. A god who, Udinny says, nudges and pushes and gentles along those who serve them." Muttering from the crowd now. Furin breathed, looked about her. "But consider where we are."

"About to die!" shouted Diyra, the tanner.

"That was always coming!" shouted Furin. "From the moment the cloudtree fell, it was coming." Silence once more, broken only by the whimpering of Dyon as he burned. "But consider this. Think of what has been sent to us. Forestals, adept with bows who have only ever preyed on this village, now here to fight with us." She pointed at the wall. "Warriors who cannot die, come to us from an ancient battlefield." Then to Venn. "A trion who can heal terrible wounds." She looked up, light in her eyes. "These are signs! And we have the only monk of a forgotten god, to show us how to read these signs. And lastly," she swallowed, "we have Cahan Du-Nahere, who knows how to fight, who has taught us how to fight. Who was trained by monks, to be Cowl-Rai." A coldness within him. Betrayal, that she would spill his secret. He looked at Udinny, she was the only one who had known of his past. She did not look at him. The Forestals, however, they locked eyes onto him as if he were north and they a walknut.

"He is no Cowl-Rai," shouted Ont.

"No," said Furin, "he is not. He denied the power, so as not to be like those we face now. But he has knowledge, and that is a power." She looked around. "It would be hopeless for a village like us to fight the Rai, I have heard many of you say as much. But do not lose hope," she said. "More than you know, more than any of us know, is in play here. Issofur was called to Wyrdwood by the boughry, and sent back unharmed! I believe they did this so Cahan and Udinny could meet the Forestals. And rootlings attacked the Rai in Woodedge. The forest itself sides with us!" She let her words sink in. "We have come to the attention of a god, I think, and they will not abandon us. So Iftal bless us! Iftal bless us and great luck be upon us, for we fight." Silence again, villagers looking to each other. Frightened, unsure. Sengui, the gasmaw farmer, stepped out from the crowd.

"You know me," she said. "You know Aislinn. Know we have fought in many places before we settled here." Aislinn gave her a nod from the crowd. "We did not want to ever fight again. Only a fool does." She licked her lips. "I do not know of gods, I only know of me. Them out there," she pointed past the walls with her spear, "they killed ours, they hurt ours and they will hurt us too. For that I think they should pay, and if Udinny's god, her Ranya, has sent the means for that, in the forester and those with him, then it seems like a fine enough god to me. So let us stand against our enemies in Ranya's name."

And if Furin had lost the crowd, and whether Sengui had won them back, it all ceased to matter.

"Rai forming up!" Shouted by the reborn on the wall.

The battle was coming. Furin was ready for this moment. She turned to the shrine of Tarl-an-Gig behind her, the balancing man made of woven sticks, and grabbed it with both hands.

"I'll not fight under the watch of a god who wants me dead," she shouted. Then she pulled the statue over, standing back and watching it fall into the mud. Her people open-mouthed. Too shocked to act. "Get your bows," she shouted. A count where nothing happened and Cahan wondered if she had lost them, if they would turn on her. "Take up your arms! We go to war!"

"For Ranya!" shouted Aislinn, holding her spear aloft.

"For Harn!" shouted Sengui.

Then all was movement. "Cahan," shouted Furin, "Forestals and branch leaders, come to me. We must be ready."

He joined Furin, with Ania, the Forestal, Aislinn, Sark, Sengui and Ont, the leaders of the four branch units. The village was suddenly full of people running, shouting, finding their places and the friends they were to fight with. The Forestal, Ania, leaned on the staff of her bow, drawing her hood up over her head.

"Cahan," said Furin, "I bow to your expertise in tactics. Tell us what to do." He took a deep breath, held it. The world became dark, the responsibility as it shifted to him unbearably heavy. For a moment he wished he had run. Wished he was deep in Wyrdwood, wished he did not have all these lives laid at his feet. "Cahan?" said Furin again. He closed his eyes.

You are running but you are not running fast enough.

You are running.

Running.

He felt a touch on his arm. Udinny looking up at him.

"No more running," she said.

Let out the breath.

No more running.

"We keep the bows hidden at first," he said. "As few people as possible on the walls. Aislinn and Ont, I want your archers before the Tiltgate ready to loose on my command. Keep your spears and shields near in case they break through."

"Why only half of us?" said Ont. He crossed his huge arms. "And why be somewhere we cannot see the enemy?" He looked to the other branch leaders. "We should meet them with everything." He looked about, confident in his ignorance. The Forestal, Ania, punctured his confidence with a low, hacking laugh.

"You might be big but you're no soldier, are you?" she said. "The Rai will come at the front, thinking us ignorant villagers, be right in some cases." She smiled at him, a mocking thing. Ont did not answer; like most in the village the Forestals scared him. "But, while you're all looking at the Tiltgate, thinking you face your enemy, they send half their people round the back to come at you that way." Ont stared.

"I think we would know if they did not send all their forces, many of us here can count," but his words were bluff, said to try and win back some face.

"You would not," said Aislinn, she spoke more softly, more gently. "Battle is chaos. It is frightening, and it is a place where decisions are no longer made sensibly. They are made on instinct and in the moment. That is why we need people like our forester, who know how to lead in battle, understand tactics. One clear head is worth a hundred soldiers."

"She is right," said Ania, "so let us hope our forester keeps his head clear."

"At least let us see what we loose our arrows at," said Ont, he no longer sounded like a man full of his own importance. Cahan could hear the confusion and fear behind his bluster. He pushed away his distrust, his anger at the butcher for the way he had acted in the past, because Ont must carry his words to those who would fight with them. As must the other branch leaders and now was not the time for resentment.

"I hide you for two reasons, Ont," he said, and a brief moment of surprise on the butcher's face, that Cahan spoke to him like an equal, not an opposite. "First, I want to surprise the Rai. I do not want them bringing shields to protect them from arrows." Ont stared at him, narrowed his eyes. Cahan stepped a little closer, as if to share a thing only with him – though he wanted all around them to hear it. "Second, our strength lies in our numbers not accuracy, loosing arrows as quickly as you can to make a storm that rains down death. I will not risk losing you to spears on the wall. I know your range and I will aim for you." Ont stared at him, he could see a war within the man. He knew what Cahan said was right, but did not want to be seen to be backing down.

"We need to aim," said Ania, "it is a bad decision to put my Forestals behind walls. We have ten arrows for you, don't waste them."

"Aye," said Ont, "she is right. Be foolish to waste their arrows." He nodded, but there was little aggression in him. The Forestal had given him the way out he needed.

"We will put the Forestals on the walls then," he said, "they came here to kill Rai, and that is what they will do."

"A good day for it," she said, and walked towards the wall.

"Can you not burn them all where they stand?" Ont asked him, not mocking, not gruff. "Furin said you were Cowl-Rai."

"I am not," he said. "Though I do have a cowl, Ont."

Did the way the butcher looked at him change? He was not sure.

"You will use it to defend us?"

"It requires feeding," he said, looking at the gathered villagers. "It feeds on life and pain and I will not do that. But I will use my own life if I have to." He looked towards the Tiltgate, imagined the Rai's soldiers massing. "Yes, if it comes to it, I will do that." He turned. "Sengui," Cahan shouted, "did you see to the bridge before the Tiltgate?" She nodded.

"Aye, soon as we knew the Rai were here we cut through the supports, it won't hold many now. And we flooded the pit with filth from the tanners' pits, but you can probably smell that."

"Good, it will be an unpleasant shock for them."

He saw Ont flush at his words, saw fear in his eyes at talk of an assault. Then it ceased to matter. The call came.

"They advance!"

58

They did not advance far.

At first.

The Rai's line was made up of two trunks, one hundred and sixty troops in armour of rough bark. Trunk leaders, in smoother bark armour, stood before them, holding fluttering streamers of small triangular flags that showed their allegiance to the blue and their home county. Behind each trunk commander stood two branch leaders, all flew the blue flags of the new Cowl-Rai, two the yellow of Mantus, one the purple of Stor and the fourth branch showed the blue star on red of Jinneng. For a moment Cahan was shocked to see Jinneng's flag, thinking that the most powerful of the southern counties must have fallen. Until he realised he was meant to be shocked. It was a ruse. If Jinnereng had fallen they would have heard, even as far north as Harn as the war would be over and the whole of Crua would be preparing for the tilt and the great celebrations to follow.

Behind each branch company stood two Rai. Cahan was surprised so many had come, felt sure there would be others he did not see, readying to attack the Forestgate.

It was strange to stand atop a fortified wall, even a make-shift one, and look out at an army set against him. It was frightening, worrying, the weight of responsibility heavy. But at the same time it was exhilarating. As if he were meant to do this.

The platform felt sturdy beneath his feet, the wall provided cover up to his hips. He touched the rough wood, running his gauntleted hand along it. The whorls and grain of wood were familiar things to him. He had known wood almost all his life, worked with wood, lived among it. Half the length of his arm away was the second wall, slightly taller, a gap between the two. Wind whistled around him and in the distance the flags of the Rai army cracked in the breeze. He heard the gentle tinkling of porcelain charms on the flagstreamers. A trunk commander shouted and the Rai soldiers brought their spears up. Behind them the trees, bare in the cold of Harsh, lines of darkness against the sky, skeletal shapes framing the army.

Directly in front of the walls was the circle pit, flooded with filth and filled with spikes. In front of the Tiltgate a bridge. Further out the second pit, with a poor show at spikes before it, barely worth mention and no doubt the invaders would think it proof of the shoddy work of the villagers.

But it was not there to stop them, only as a marker.

Cahan had let his armour grow more elaborate, points at elbow and shoulder, a set of small horns, a face on the visor. All of this felt strangely familiar, as if the world was unfocused, two lives overlapping. One he was and the one that he could have been meeting here. He gripped the wall more tightly and wondered if Udinny was right. Was he led here by Ranya?

"Why have they stopped?" Furin was staring out at them, and the Forestal Ania joined them.

"Posturing," said the Forestal, and spat between the walls. The wind fell, and the smell of the tanners' pits from below made Cahan want to retch.

"They want us to see them," he said.

"Weapons!" the shout of a trunk commander echoed around the forest clearing, bounced off the walls of Harn. Followed by the clap of a hundred spears coming down in unison.

"Lunge!" the soldiers did. With a massed shout of "Anha!" that hit Harn in a wave of sound. Furin flinched, the Forestal only stared with a half-smile on her face.

"Rest!" A shout of "Uhl!" and the soldiers stood straight, spears once more pointing into the sky so they became a forest, one as leafless as Woodedge.

"What are they doing now?" said Furin.

"Showing us how professional they are," he said. "They want us to think about how they are an army and we are not."

"That is what I am thinking about," said Furin.

"They still die," said Ania, and she slipped off her quiver of arrows, standing it against the wooden wall. "They will come to try and talk again." Furin looked confused.

"No one ever wants to fight, Leoric," said Cahan. "Even the Rai, they enjoy cruelty, but war is dangerous and unpredictable."

"More so for them," Ania tapped her bowstaff against the wall. "They want us to give up so they can play with us on their own terms without any danger. But that is not a game I wish to join in with; the Rai like to break their toys." She looked away when she said that, some shadow on her face she hid within her hood.

"Look," Furin pointed. One of the Rai coming forward. As they moved through the troops five broke away to follow them, one bearing a standard showing a gasmaw, tentacles spread to each side of the flag, holding a spear out to each side. They walked slowly, purposefully, stopped fifty paces from the wall. The light above gleamed from their armour, highlighting the sigils painted in glowing fungal juices, a history of violence scrawled across gleaming, shining wood.

Their visor was carved into a smiling face with a sharp nose.

"I am Rai Condorin of Tasspire," they shouted.

"Where is Rai Galderin?" Cahan shouted back.

"Rai Galderin is planning our attack. He does not have time for you." They looked back at their troops before turning back to Harn. "But I was raised in a small village in Mantus, much like yours. The High Leoric has asked me to help you."

"He said we had until the light is fully above," Cahan shouted back.

"And that has passed," shouted Rai Condorin, though it hardly had. "Do your people know how the Rai work?" they raised their visor. They had that strange, stretched look the Rai got as they aged, like they were no longer quite people. Rai Condorin's eyes were very pale.

"They know enough," Cahan shouted back.

"The war in the south needs Rai," shouted Condorin, "the Rai need lives. One life, it can be kept guttering like a candle for almost half a season." Condorin stared up at them, pushing their voice so it carried into the village. "It is not a good way to die, it hurts as much as your friend hurts, the one who is burning, maybe even more."

"You give us a good reason to fight," Cahan shouted back.

"No, if you open the gates, we will only punish you, Cahan Du-Nahere, and the Leoric, and no one else." He wondered why the Rai did not simply lie and tell the Leoric she was free also. "Now, will you open your gates? Save the rest of your people?"

Ania moved so quickly he could not stop her. She grabbed an arrow, nocked it. Pulled the bow to tension and aimed. The arrow cut through the air with a hiss. It hit the Rai in the forehead. Knocking them backwards into the icy mud. They were dead instantly. For a moment the soldiers did not realise what had happened. Then they turned and ran back to their army.

"Does that answer your question?" shouted Ania as the soldiers ran.

"I wanted to keep my archers secret," the forester said.

"And I told you," said Ania, crouching down by her quiver and taking out another arrow, "I came here to kill Rai." Below them, the body of the Rai Condorin lay with their arms outstretched in the mud. Furin was unable to take her eyes from it.

"I have never seen one dead," she said. "I did not think they could die."

"You'll see more dead before the day is through," said Ania, and she stood, then whistled to bring her four archers up onto the wall.

"No way back now," said Furin.

"There never was," said Cahan.

A horn blew, cracking the quiet of a day shocked by death. Then a shout, a harsh, dark, angry voice.

"Ready!" A drummer started to beat their drum. Spears were lowered, soldiers lowered weapons and marched on the spot, filling the air with the percussion of their steps. Cahan felt ice within him. This was it. From now on this village and every life in it would depend on his decisions.

"*Overconfidence.*" The voice of the Trainer of War, as clear as if the monk stood beside him, his lash tapping against his hand in readiness to punish mistakes. "*Overconfidence is a flaw, Cahan, but your lack of confidence is worse.*"

The Rai are so sure of themselves. The thought jumped into his mind and he turned.

"Furin," he said, an urgency in his voice though he tried not to show it in his body. "Bring all our archers to before the gate. And the Forestals from the other wall."

"But you said they would attack from the other side while we were distracted." There was no alarm on Furin's face, only confusion. Behind her Ania watched him, that mocking smile on her face.

"And they will," he said. "They will. But not this time.

Not in the first attack. The Rai are confident, too confident. We are just a forest village to them, they will think they can walk over us. They will expect their first attack to beat us and see no need for fancy tactics." He stared out at the troops. "So we defend this wall with all we have, and we bloody their nose."

"And if you're wrong? If they attack the Forestgate wall?" said Furin.

"They will not." Spoken with a confidence he did not have, but he had committed now and knew a commander who was indecisive was worse than none. "But we shall leave one lookout on the Forestgate wall, someone with a loud voice." He was unduly gruff, and knew it from the look of hurt in Furin's face, but it was too late to undo it. She nodded and climbed down, running over to the other side of the village.

"Advance!" A voice ringing across the clearing.

Now was the time. Now he must hold, must stand here strong and proud while the enemy advanced. Pretend he did not feel any fear or doubt or worry.

The beat of their drum loud in his ears.

The percussion of their steps disturbed his breathing, making it ragged with apprehension. The fear he would fail Harn almost overwhelming. Their slow advance piling on pressure meant to crush him. Crush them all.

"That was well done," said Ania, pulling his gaze away from the troops. "First time you have sounded like you should be wearing that armour." She turned and looked out at the soldiers as they came forward, moving in time to the drum. "Let's hope you were right, though, or it's a short fight." His mouth too dry to reply. Villagers streaming over to the Tiltgate wall. The soldiers coming on. "The cowards are staying out of range," Ania spat over the wall.

The Forestal was right, the Rai remained behind their lines, each with four soldiers standing in front of them. No sign of Sorha either, fools not to use her. She knew the land and the layout of the village. Another sign of over-confidence. Behind him the villagers were milling about. Nervous energy manifesting as chatter.

"How long before you think they are in range," he whispered to the Forestal. He had his markers set but he needed distraction. It was hard just to stand and watch.

"My range? Not long." She looked down at the villagers. "Their range? A while yet, but you know that."

A scream. Dyon, slowly burning alive. The villagers flinched every time the man was overwhelmed by pain. Cahan worried it would break their morale before they even loosed an arrow. He needed to act.

"I will return quickly," he jumped from the wall.

"Quiet!" he shouted, moving among the villagers. "Form lines like we learned." They stared at him. Their faces drawn and worried. "This will be our chance," he said from among them. "They do not think we have any strength. They think you are weak." He lifted his bow "With these. Today. You will show them we are strong."

"They're going to kill us," it was said so quietly he could not tell who had spoken.

"No," he said, "they are not. We are going to kill them. We kill enough, they will withdraw, and in the night we escape to the forest."

But there was no denying the fear in the air.

As real as the beat of the drum.

The percussion of their steps.

The slow advance.

The screaming of a man slowly burning alive.

Nearly three hundred professional soldiers. Eight or more Rai, with all the power that brought. All outside the walls. Here to end these people.

"Organise yourselves as I have shown you." He pushed through them, heading towards the longhouse where the screaming came from. Furin behind him. "I will be back in moments." Inside he found Udinny and Venn, holding

Dyon down while they tried to get a mash of herbs into his mouth.

"What are you doing?" said Furin and she rushed over to them. Dyon let out another scream.

"The fire climbs his body," said Udinny, "we are trying to get some Sleepwragg into him, to control the pain, but he grits his teeth so tightly we cannot."

"His screams," said Cahan, "they are frightening the villagers. Sucking the spirit from them," and him, he knew it but could not say it.

"You would scream if you were burning alive, Cahan," said Furin. He knelt by the man, Udinny and Venn were still fighting Dyon, his body twisted by agony, muscles spasming.

"Sometimes," he said, and reached for the knife on his belt, "it is kinder to stop the pain, especially when pain is all Dyon has left." He drew the knife. Aware of the way all eyes had focused on him. "It is one life, but it may save many. Morale is—"

"No," said Venn. "We cannot."

"You would let him burn by fingerbreadths?" hissed Cahan.

"Venn," said Udinny, "what you did for Darmant, what you said you could do for those who will be hurt, can you help ease Dyon's pain?" The trion stared at the monk.

"I do not know . . ."

"You must try, or you must let Cahan free him," said Udinny.

"It nearly killed Venn last time," said Cahan.

"We only need to get the Sleepwragg into him," said Udinny. "That will quieten him. Help us settle the village." Venn looked about the room. Cahan took a breath.

"Very well. Like a tree, Venn," he said. "Touch the bark and see what you can feel beneath." Cahan knelt, taking the trion's place holding down Dyon's arm as he struggled, gasped and whimpered. Venn nodded, closed their eyes and put their hands on Dyon's torso. As soon as they made contact Venn pulled their hand away and let out a shriek of pain.

"It burns." They stared at Dyon, then looked at Cahan. "Surely you can do this?"

"Cause it? Yes, I can probably do that. Stop it, no. Not within my power." The trion licked their lips. Nodded. Took a breath and placed their hands once more on Dyon. Flinched. And despite that the longhouse was barely warm their brow broke out in sweat. They clenched their teeth. Made a sound unlike anything Cahan had heard before, part pain, part fear. Every muscle in the trion tensed. Eyes opened wide. Staring up into the rafters of the house. Mouth a thin, determined line. For a moment he thought they might have some sort of fit. Then both Venn and Dyon let out a sigh. Dyon's mouth fell open and Udinny spooned in the Sleepwragg. More than Cahan had seen any person given. The monk looked at him.

"He is in a lot of pain," she said.

"That much may kill him."

"A moment ago you were going to cut his throat, so you are a fine one to give medical advice, Cahan." He looked away, felt Dyon's muscles relaxing beneath his grip.

"The Rai are coming," Cahan said, "I have to get back."

"Go then," said Venn, "I will stay with him. Do what I can."

Out into the cold air once more. The frigid atmosphere of a people slowly sinking into a terror that could freeze even seasoned soldiers.

The beat of the drum.

The percussion of their steps.

The slow advance.

On the walls Ania had been joined by her Forestals. They watched the advance. Confusion among the villagers. They had still not formed into their lines properly. They were lost. He opened his mouth but did not know what words would help.

"Branch leaders!" shouted Furin, "proud trunks of Harn! Are you beaten before you start? Your children hide in our roundhouses, if the Rai overrun us what do you think will happen? You think poor Dyon will be the only one that burns?" She sounded angry. What she had seen in the longhouse had filled her with a righteous fury and she grabbed the nearest villager. "Form a line," she said, pushing them into line. "String your bow. And if you cannot string a bow take up a spear, for that is what I will do."

"Ranya brought us here," shouted Udinny, following Furin and taking up a bow of her own. "She has given us all we need to survive. We have Venn, who will heal us. We have Cahan, who will lead us. We have these," she brandished the bow, "which we have been trained to use!"

"If you would live. Then you must fight!" Furin sounded fierce, spear in hand she appeared to him as some feral woman of war. "Follow Cahan Du-Nahere. Obey his words and we will prevail. Do this for your children, as I do it, for Issofur." The crowd, as Udinny and Furin spoke, began to form their lines. Ragged and unkempt, not like the lines of the Rai's soldiers which were perfect and disciplined.

"Thank you," he said to Furin as they climbed onto the wall.

"You just have to know what they need to hear," she said. He nodded and looked back at the villagers. He saw something in their raggedness, in their many colours. He saw the joy of their past, oh gone now, no joy there, only fear. But those bright colours had been done in celebration of life, and created by them coming together. The energy of the village given form. So unlike the uniform lines that marched towards Harn, the men and women who fought, at least in part, for fear of the Rai who ruled them.

"Ready your bows, people of Harn," he said from his place on the walls. Every one of them heard his voice for he pushed it out among them. "And I will get you through this." He held his head straight. "I once told Venn, that given a hundred with forestbows I could break any army sent against me." He lifted his bow. Took a breath. "So, raise your bows, and let us break this one."

It was not true, of course, they were not trained, they were not experts and many of them would die before this was over. But as Furin had said, it was what they needed to hear. He turned. Somehow more at ease.

The beat of the drum. Matched the beat of his heart.

The percussion of their steps. Matched the measured breaths he took as he watched.

The slow advance. That he would turn.

"Nearly time," said the Forestal. She looked out at the advancing line and took an arrow from her quiver. Licked the fletching of dried leaves.

"This will be a long day," said Cahan.

"For you," said the Forestal, "for us it is ten arrows."

59

He saw the battlefield as an archer; imaginary lines on the scrubby, frost-tinged grass marking different ranges. The furthest line he saw was where the villagers of Harn had cut back Woodedge. Out of range of every bow in Harn and where some of the Rai stood, watching their troops advance. The next line was the old Woodedge, the extreme edge of his skill with a bow, and probably the Forestals' too. The approaching army was well inside it.

The next line was where a good archer could confidently pick off single targets. As the army reached that point Ania raised her bow but Cahan put his hand out, a signal to wait. The look she gave him could have broken porcelain.

"I came here to kill Rai," she said, "and their troops if I can't get at the Rai."

"And you will," he said, "but let's not scare them off too early. We need to kill as many as we can. We only get one first chance." She did not look pleased, but lowered the bow. It was strangely quiet then, apart from the steps of the soldiers and the solemn beat of their drummer. It felt like it stabbed right through him every time it echoed across the clearing.

The army of Rai crossed into where a group of practised archers could drop arrows easily for hours without becoming tired. Every step the army made twisting something up inside him. He wondered what it was like for the villagers, if it was easier for them because they could not see the soldiers coming, or if it was harder because all they had was the ominous sound of the drum to warn of the Rai's approach.

He had worried that when Ania had loosed her arrow it might have altered the Rai's strategy. It had not. Their soldiers did not carry shields, only the spears they would use for the assault. Behind the spear carriers came scaling ladders and bridges to get over the pit before the gates. In the centre of their formation they had a battering ram. Behind the first ranks came eight Rai and their standard-bearers, screened by soldiers with shields.

"Had you not killed that Rai," Cahan said quietly, "you would have easier targets now."

"A few flags and shields will not save them," said Ania.

They were not far from where he wanted them. The first row passing the shallow pit, spears dipping as they crossed. It marked the farthest edge of the villagers' range. Nearer Harn than he liked. If the arrows did not stop them it was not far to the wall.

The muscles of his shoulders felt like they had been tied in knots.

The second line of troops entered the killing zone. He balled his fists. He wanted to tell the villagers of Harn to loose, but that was the adrenaline running through him not the warrior thinking. It would be a poor decision. If they retreated after the first volley his best opportunity would be wasted.

Let the Rai get closer.

He needed as many as possible in the killing zone, and if that risked the walls being assaulted then it was a risk he must take.

The beat of the drum.

The slow advance.

The percussion of their steps.

Closer and closer.

"You should loose," said Ania.

"Not yet."

The beat of the drum.

"They are too near."

"Not yet."

The slow advance.

He could see the first line. Look into their faces. Grim and set, weapons down. Some smiled. Maybe they enjoyed the idea of taking the village. Hurting those within. Others looked resigned, as if this was simply another day. Some looked scared. Some were much younger than he thought a soldier should be. Some much older.

"I did not bring my people here for hand-to-hand fighting," hissed the Forestal.

"You brought them here to kill Rai."

"At a distance."

The percussion of their steps.

"Well, get ready, Ania." He lifted his hand, the signal for the villagers to nock their arrows. The reborn were down there among them but he had instructed them to stay hidden unless it was desperate.

The villagers readied their bows, a sound like snow falling from laden branches. He did not look back at them, did not want them to think that he needed to check they were doing it right, though he dearly wanted to.

Closer.

"Ready!" he shouted it, the approach of the soldiers did not falter. They did not know what was coming. "Draw!"

And closer.

The first rank were about to pass out of the killing zone. He could not allow that. The villagers were not skilled enough to shoot short, they had one zone of killing and he must use it.

Now.

"Loose!"

Over a hundred bows loosing at once, a noise like nothing he had ever heard before, one that he had no reference for. The hiss of arrows passing overhead. Some did not make it over the wall, bouncing off the wood around him, some dug in. But most soared. Lines of black drawn across the sky, rising and rising.

Falling.

Screaming. Soldiers staggering, falling. Arrows in arms, and legs. One soldier pierced through the top of the head and killed immediately. Many wounds. Not enough. The soldiers still coming. Beaten on by the shouting of the Rai behind them.

Behind him, the shiver of bows redrawing. He looked to the Forestals, stood with bows in hand. Ania's eyes, like a predator's, waiting for the Rai at the back to come close enough that she knew she could not miss a killing shot. Or maybe for some signal he did not yet understand.

"Will you not loose?"

"Not yet," said Ania.

"You were keen before."

Another shower of arrows.

"I have never seen a mass loosing like this before," her eyes shone. "I am enjoying it."

"It's not stopping them," He watched soldiers struggling through the storm of arrows. "They will be through the killing zone soon." She nodded.

"Then we will loose," she said.

Another rain of arrows. Coming more raggedly now, each villager loosing at their own speed. The soldiers staggered on. Bodies on the ground, but not enough. Soon it would be their turn.

"Ready," said Ania. Her Forestals nodded. "Maytan and Borof with me on the Rai leading them. The rest of you," she smiled to herself and nocked an arrow, drew the bow to tension, "thin their ranks." She let fly. Her arrow powerful and strong. It cut down the standard-bearer of the centre Rai. As the soldier fell Ania was already loosing her second arrow. The air around the Rai exploded into fire. A shield that would burn her arrow to ash before it got near. She changed her aim, one of the other standard-bearers had fallen. Ania loosed past him, the arrow taking a Rai in the neck. Cahan's hands itched for his bow, but for this first assault he would not use it. Once he had served under a trunk commander who stood during a battle, she did not move or attack or defend herself unless she was attacked. He had asked her why, and she had told him it showed belief in her troops, that her branches fought harder because they knew she trusted them.

So he trusted the villagers.

He would be the stalwart tree in the centre of the storm.

The Rai's forces closed, he counted every shortfall, every arrow that hit dirt not a soldier. Gradually, the villagers' arrows began to do their work, they instilled fear in those attacking.

The Forestals did the work better.

Not shooting often. Carefully picking their targets. A death with every arrow. Except Ania's. She only loosed at the Rai, one had fallen, the others were protecting themselves with fire and she wasted her arrows on it. Soldiers were dying, groaning and screaming. A spear was thrown by the attackers, digging into the wood before him then, with a roar, the first rank of soldiers got near enough to attack.

"Ram!" he shouted to the Forestals, "concentrate on the ram!" The Forestals changed their aim. "Woolside spears!" he shouted. "To the wall!" Those villagers with military experience dropped their bows, took up spears and climbed onto the wall. The Forestals killed every soldier on the ram, their ten arrows dwindling.

It was not going to be enough.

More soldiers came on, driven to the ram through the hail of arrows by their trunks and their Rai. Soldiers with ladders ran across the drawbridge, pushed them up against the wall. The first to the top was killed with a spear thrust to the neck by Sark, only to be replaced by another. A face appeared before Cahan and he smashed it in the crown of the head with his bowstaff. Soldiers rushing to give their strength to the ram. Shouting and screaming. The smell of blood mixing with the stink of the tanning pits. Arrows falling. The Rai had moved out of range of the villagers' arrows and all now had burning shields before them. The Forestals were down to one or two arrows each, and as each loosed their last arrow, killing soldiers holding the ram, they withdrew from the wall. Leaving only villagers with spears and Cahan and a stream of soldiers running towards Harn, eager for blood.

The ram was picked up once more.

"Last one," said Ania, and she nocked the arrow, aimed and put down the soldier holding the front right of the ram. It fell, the carved crownhead end digging into the mud before the bridge. "I am done now," she turned to jump from the wall. He grabbed her arm.

"You have more arrows in your quiver." She stared into his eyes. "We have more arrows. Your skill could save a lot of lives here."

"Ten arrows," she said. "It was all I promised."

"We haven't stopped them yet." For a moment she softened, the hard face the outlaw had always shown falling away.

"You cannot stop them," she said quietly, though he heard her quite clearly, even above the roar of battle. "We both know that." Then she pulled his hand from her arm and jumped from the wall.

A scream of rage behind him. He turned, knocked a soldier from a ladder with his bowstaff. Five ladders against the wall now. Soldiers coming up, villagers being forced back along the platform. The air thick with shouting, screaming, crying. He dropped his bow and took up his axes. Below another soldier took their place at the ram and the ram crew ran for the bridge before the Tiltgate. A trunk leader lifted his sword.

"Bring the gates down!" they shouted.

It seemed like every Rai soldier on the field roared. The ram mounted the bridge. He had told Sengui to cut through the supports. The ram came forward.

The bridge held.

A crash as the ram hit the gate.

The bridge held.

The ram backed up. A roar. The ram came forward and smashed into the gates with a huge crash. The entire wall shuddered. Some of the defenders losing their footing. The ram backed up again and the carved end came forward for the third time.

With a groan the bridge gave way under its weight. A whip crack retort of splintering timber. Soldiers pitched into the pit, the ram dragging those who held it down with it. Shocked faces as they fell. The lucky ones died immediately, impaled on spikes, the unlucky skewered through leg or gut or arm, held like creatures trapped in sap.

It is odd how such a thing can turn a battle.

Had they kept coming, even only using ladders, Cahan knew they would have overwhelmed the defenders. They had the numbers for it, the strength. The loss of the ram smashed their morale. One moment they were cheering, then they were screaming. Backing away. First slowly, then quickly, streaming back past their trunks, who screamed at them to continue. But there was nothing to be done, once morale was broken it was almost impossible to rebuild it. The Rai's soldiers ran. Leaving a few troops trapped on the walls and with no choice but to fight, they were lost and they knew it. Some tried to jump over the pit, falling among the spikes. Others continued to climb the ladders to be cut down by the defenders. All along the wall the villagers were jumping onto the platform to shout and jeer at the retreating soldiers. He watched a villager draw a bow.

"Don't waste the arrow," said Cahan, "save it for when they come again."

He found Furin, standing by him.

"A victory," she said, but she did not smile or join in with the whooping and jeering that filled the air around them. "You promised us that." He nodded. "Will they come again today?" He did not answer, he was counting the bodies before the wall.

There were many.

There were not enough.

He looked up at the light as it journeyed across the sky. A small tremor shook the walls.

"They will probably wait until it is dark." Around him the celebrations continued and it made his head hurt. It was too joyous. "How many of ours died, Furin?"

"None," she put a hand on his arm. "You do not look happy about that. Is it not another victory? Proof Ranya stands with us?" A villager picked a helmet off a corpse and threw it over the wall, laughing as they did.

"I wanted a victory, Furin, but I wanted it to cost. We will have a hard time getting them out of the village and to the forest now." Villagers on the wall were stripping the corpses of enemy soldiers of anything valuable. "I wanted them to fight, Furin, but I did not want them to think they could win."

The land rumbled, shaking the walls and no one but Cahan seemed to notice.

"Let them have this moment," said Furin, "we will make them see sense later." He nodded. Though he knew they were likely to pay for this victory, and the price would be high.

60

There was jubilation among the villagers. A festival spirit ruled in Harn. People gathered, talking excitedly of how they had "saved their village" from the Rai. How it was now "only a matter of time" before the Rai offered terms. Those who would once have scorned him clapped him on the back as he passed, congratulating him as if he had done more than simply stand and give commands while the attack had come.

The villagers celebrated.

The reborn stood still as statues.

The Forestals had gone.

No joy within him. He had no wish to celebrate. Without the Forestals terrifying accuracy he did not think they would survive another attack.

"We need people on the walls," he shouted.

"They are, look," one of the villagers, Manha, pointed at the wall where the first attack had come, three or four villagers were up there. Darmant, the shoemaker that Venn had saved, was dancing in a circle, moving their hands through tree shapes in time to some music only they could hear.

"All the walls," he did not mean to growl at them, but it was how the words came out and he felt the spirit of festivity dampen around him. Good, he thought.

"We beat them," said Ont. "They fell like burst gasmaws."

"They will come again," said Cahan. "And this time they will know what to expect from us." He was going to say more, to explain how the Forestals' arrows had helped win the battle, but held back. They did not need to hear that now, it would not help them.

A scream from the longhouse froze the celebrations. The whole village paused, as if struck by the reality of their situation. "Dyon," said the butcher. His voice quiet.

"We need to be ready," Cahan raised his voice. "Branch leaders, join me!" They came running, as did Furin.

"A good victory," said Aislinn.

"They all are, but we must not become complacent. The ram that fell in the pit. Get sap on it, soak it, set it burning so it cannot be used again." Aislinn nodded. "And only open our gate a little. Have people ready to close the gate if the Rai come. And pick up any spare arrows you can." Again, Aislinn nodded and turned. In the middle of the village Sengui was staring at the few gasmaws she had saved from her farm. She stared at them with a spear in her hand.

"They are dying," said Aislinn to him. "Sengui said they would if she moved them from the farm, they are recently shorn of their stings and need rest. She worked hard to make that farm pay."

"Someone is coming!" shouted from the wall.

"Gather spears and shields, be ready," shouted Cahan. "Assemble the bow company."

"Surely they are coming to discuss terms?" said Ont.

"It is Tussnig!"

"Huh," said Furin, "I wondered when we would see him again." Another scream from the longhouse and Udinny appeared at the entrance, coming over to stand by Cahan.

"The Sleepwragg has worn off, Venn is doing what they can for Dyon," said the monk.

"Can you give him more."

"Not yet, it will definitely kill him if we give him more before dark." Furin looked up, the light was almost touching the tops of the trees. She opened her mouth and then shut it as another scream came. "Will Venn be well? We saw what helping Darmant did to them." Udinny nodded.

"The trion says Ranya feeds them, through the ground and the web. I followed Ranya for many years and do not understand it, but I thank her for it." The monk grinned. "Venn does not seem to be flagging."

"Tussnig wants to speak to Furin!" shouted from the walls. Cahan turned to Aislinn.

"While we talk to the monk," he said, "use this time to collect arrows and soak the ram. It should be safe." They nodded and turned for the Tiltgate. "Wait!" They stopped. "Put sap pots all around the ram, and sap over it, but do not fire it, not yet." They nodded, and ran towards the gate where villagers were lifting the log that held it shut. Furin, Udinny and Cahan climbed on to the wall. The monk of Tarl-an-Gig stood before the broken bridge. He still wore the headdress of his god, but it was no longer as makeshift as it had been. His clothes were neater, newer, though he still had the look of some small scurrying creature that should be in a hole rather than parading before the walls.

"Tarl-an-Gig watches this village and he is not pleased," shouted Tussnig. His fury barely contained, all he could do not to scream.

"They were never pleased," shouted back Furin. Below villagers were busy soaking the ram in oil and children ran about collecting arrows fallen near the wall.

"They are a hard god, it is true, Furin. But this is a hard land."

"And yet it seems, Tussnig, some god was smiling on us today." Tussnig stared up at them. It was not the look of a man who was pleased with what he had heard, but neither was it the look of man who had the wit to gainsay Furin.

"Tarl-an-Gig will be avenged!" shouted the monk, and without an answer he fell back on anger. Dancing on the spot and tearing at his robes. "You are cursed, eight and eight! Cursed with your outlaw weapons! The Osere will feast on your eyes!" Cahan, Furin and Udinny stood watching, impassive. Eventually, his fury abated as he realised it was not working. When he spoke again his words were sap-sweet. "I do not want my people hurt, Furin," he said. I care for you, for the people of Harn. It was my home for so long." He stared up at Furin. "Rai Galderin is powerful, Leoric, he will rain down fire on your village if you do not open the gates. Fire!" The monk had nothing but bluster, though Cahan could feel the wind of his words passing across the village. They had listened to the words of Tussnig for so long that to hear him condemn them was powerful.

"Ranya protects this village," said Udinny

"Your forest god is weak," shouted Tussnig, his fury returning.

"But you admit they are a god," Udinny beamed at the other monk. "Before you said she was all my imagination." She gave him a small nod. "I welcome the progress you are making, Tussnig."

"I hope you survive the fire," Tussnig screamed the words, "the Rai take their power through pain, and I will skin you alive and feed your pain to them." Udinny laughed, which only increased Tussnig's ire. Before he could shout more, and his words could blow more ill wind into the village, Cahan interrupted.

"There will be no fire, Tussnig, we both know that."

"Oh, there will be, you will bring an inferno upon yourselves!" He pointed at Cahan. "This is your doing, you doom the people! The people of my village! You send them all to the Osere!"

"These people threw you out," shouted Udinny. "You are not wanted here, Tussnig."

"They were misled!" he screeched his words. Then took a moment, smoothing down his robe and calming himself. "I come now to offer them life! Give us the trion and the forester, Leoric, and we will let everyone else live."

"That is not true," said Furin. "The Rai have already told us that the best we can expect is a quick death."

"But I," shouted Tussnig, "I have negotiated for you! I will save the lives of everyone!"

"You lie," Cahan shouted back. "The trion is too precious for them to throw fire at this village." Tussnig stared up, a grin spread across his face.

"No one is more precious to the Rai, than the Rai, Forester," he shouted. Cahan's heart sank a little at that, it was the first true thing the monk had said. "They will come again, and they will break this village. But, if by some miracle, they do not," he pointed at them, "do you really think the life of one trion, no matter how important, would be more important than making themselves clear on the matter of rebellion?" Tussnig knew his words had landed. gone was the raving and the dancing on the spot. Gone was the look of an animal before it attacked. "And even if they do not bring fire, how long can you survive a siege, Forester?" he shouted up. "Do you have enough food set away to live through all of Harsh?"

"Enough," Cahan shouted, and in the quiet his words echoed out until they were lost in Woodedge. "Our answer is no. Tell your Rai to leave."

"It is sad that you wish for death, Forester," shouted Tussnig, "sadder that you would take this village along with you." As he finished Cahan picked up his bow and nocked an arrow. That was enough to send Tussnig scampering off, cursing him for a coward all the way back to the treeline. Cahan aimed then lowered his bow, Tussnig was not worth the arrow.

"We cannot survive a siege," said Furin quietly.

"No," he replied, watching the monk of Tarl-an-Gig as he ran back, robes flapping. "That is why we must leave tonight."

"Look," said Udinny, and she pointed out to Woodedge. Soldiers with large wooden shields, not a large number, only a few, moving slowly across the scrub towards them. "Are they attacking?"

"Skirmishers," said Cahan, "they will come within reach of our bows and try and get us to waste arrows. If they get near enough to throw spears they may." He looked along the walls, at the villagers standing with their bows. Had an idea. "Udinny, have our best archers, you included, thread leaves and branches through their clothes the way the Forestals did." He jumped down from the wall, followed by Furin and Udinny. "And have someone find one of those cloaks for me. The Forestals have left, but the Rai do not know that." The monk nodded, jumped off the wall and ran into the village.

"I want to look in on Dyon," said Furin to him, as if an answer a shriek came from the longhouse.

"And I would check with Venn." They walked towards the door but were stopped by a group of villagers led by Manha, the weaver. The little group could have been ready for a festival in their brightly coloured armour and made-up faces, the lines and swirls of their clans smudged by sweat.

"Is it true, Furin, that you want us to run to the forest, even after we beat them?"

"They will come back, Manha," said the Leoric.

"And we will beat them again." Furin stepped a little closer, spoke quietly to the woman.

"Without the Forestals, Manha, we would have been overrun. And look about you." The weaver did.

"They have gone?" she said.

"Ten arrows, that was their gift to us, and I think an apology because they brought treefall to the notice of this village. They had a hand in bringing the Rai here." He saw emotions cross the weaver's face. Confusion, anger, then acceptance.

"I will miss this place," she said. "When do we leave?"

"Once the light is gone we will—" He was interrupted by a scream, and one of the villagers fell backwards off the wall, a spear through their chest. The other lookouts ducked below the wall.

"Darmant!" said Manha, her face stricken.

Fear. Sudden and overwhelming. He had thought they would not come before dark. Cahan ran for the wall. On the way passed a villager holding a cloak, ready to make it look like one of the Forestals and grabbed it, throwing it over himself and climbing up onto the ledge. Crouching on the ledge next to a villager named Tyui, their eyes wide, body shaking.

"They killed Darmant," said Tyui. Cahan looked down at the corpse. Venn may have given Darmant his life back, but fate would not be denied.

"How many are there?" he hissed.

"They killed Darmant," said Tyui again. Cahan grabbed them by their shoulders. "How many! Are they coming?" Cahan saw only fear in Tyui's eyes. "Darmant is dead." He let go, turned, cursed the double wall of wood that stopped him seeing through it to the Osere-cursed army outside, and then raised his head above the wall.

No army.

Only the skirmishers. He caught a movement. A spear. He ducked, the spear soared over the wall and fell in the village. He heard a shout, but of surprise not pain. Then scrabbled along the ledge, looking for his bow. Found it. Arrow quiver resting against the wall by it. Took string from his pocket and strung the bow, grunting with effort. He put two arrows between his teeth. Held the bow in one hand, the other held a third arrow.

One deep breath.

This would be a test of reaction times.

One skirmisher he could beat and knew it. But at least five had been coming forward.

Two deep breaths.

Tyui staring at him, the villager lost in their own fear.

A third deep breath.

"It will be all right, Tyui," he said. "I will avenge your friend."

Stood.

Pulling on the string. Sliding the arrow along his forward hand until he had full tension. Feeling the bow vibrate in his hand. The world slowing. His cowl writhed. A skirmisher drew back their arm to throw a spear.

Loose.

The arrow flew. Past the shield. Pierced the soldier in the chest and they fell back with a cry. He turned, taking another arrow from between his teeth. Saw a second soldier about to loose their spear.

Draw.

Aim.

Loose.

The arrow took them in the throat. Third arrow. Draw.

Too late.

The spear coming. The thrower already turning to run towards their lines. Cahan dodged left. The spear hit his shoulder, spinning him, the point scraping along his armour, knocking him off balance. Not enough room on the ledge to regain his balance. A moment of panic as he fell. The arrow loosed, soaring straight up.

Impact. Crashing into the dirt. The breath knocked from him. Villagers all around. Trying to help. Trying to pull him up. Cahan trying to find his voice. The arrow he had shot landed, point down in the mud by his head.

"Cahan!" Furin, kneeling in the dirt by him. "Are you hurt?" He shook his head. Pulled the arrow from the mud.

"The wall," he said it softly, then swallowed. Took a

breath. "Get back on the wall. Those dressed as Forestals."
Fighting to breathe. "The wall. Scare the skirmishers, stop
them coming back . . ." Furin helped him up and villagers
scrambled back onto the wall. Someone, very gently, helped
Tyui down. Others took Darmant's body away. Cahan
climbed the wall, still bent double and struggling for breath.
"If you see a skirmisher," he said to the nearest archer, not
realising it was Ont until they looked at him. "Just draw
the bow, it should be enough to back them off."

"I do not think that matters now, Forester," said Ont.
Cahan leaned against the wall and looked over.

The army was massing. The drums were beating.

The Rai were coming back.

61

He stood on the wall with Furin.

The Rai came quickly this time, the drum beat in time with his fluttering heart. They held shields to protect themselves from arrows.

"You said they would wait until night," said Furin.

"I had hoped they would." The soldiers advanced, not as many coming this time, which he was sure meant they would be assaulting both the Forestgate and the Tiltgate. "We need people on both gates, Furin." She nodded.

"It is going to be harder, isn't it?" He watched the Rai's forces, grim expressions on their faces. The Rai army had not expected resistance on the first attack, now they knew what to expect and would be ready. They would want to avenge their fallen, and they would want to avenge the insult of being beaten by villagers and outlaws. Shouts bounced back and forth among them, though he was unable to make out the words. Soldiers banged their spears against their shields in time with the drum. The noise filled the wooded clearing around Harn. Only when they were nearer could he make out what was shouted. Not words. Names. They shouted the names of their dead.

For a moment, he was tempted to bring the reborn onto the wall, but he wanted them hidden. A surprise for when, not if, the Rai breached the gate. Another chance to break the morale of the attackers, when they found two elite warriors from legend waiting for them.

He took a deep breath. Behind him the archers were in good spirits, sure of themselves after their first victory. He wondered how long that would last. He had half of the best archers dressed as Forestals on this wall. The rest on the other wall and Sengui led the forces there. Cahan held his bow, and would use it this time.

In the field the Rai no longer stood behind small groups of troops, but had warriors walking in front of them with large wooden shields. He picked an arrow and nocked it. Aimed at the leader of the Rai, Galderin, and let fly. He watched the arrow, saw it hit the shield before the Rai but not puncture it. He let the bow fall to his side.

"Yes," he said, "it is going to be harder." The first troops crossed into the killing zone. He raised his hand, readying the archers. Let the attackers come a little further, get as many as possible in range. A flame went up from the rear of their lines. Answered with a roar from the other side of the village.

"The Forestgate!" said Furin and she turned. Cahan grabbed her arm.

"We must trust that Sengui can follow instructions and leave them to it." He looked to her. "This is our wall, Furin. It will need all of our attention." He let his hand fall. "Loose!" The arrow storm began. The attacking soldiers lifted shields above their heads. He heard the drumming of arrows falling, watched the oncoming army for soldiers falling. None did. Cahan started to loose arrows into the front rank, aiming for the throats of those holding the shields. Picking out the trunk or branch leaders when he could. A death for every arrow, his chosen archers copied him, their aim not as precise but they did good work until the front rank lowered their shields, deciding the arrows from the front were more dangerous than the arrows from above. Their shields were not as strong as those used to protect the Rai, they protected them from Cahan's pretend Forestals, but not from his arrows which punched straight through.

It did not matter.

He could not loose quickly enough to do the sort of damage the Forestals had. The soldiers were pushing through the killing zone quickly. The Rai hanging back, not entering the place where a stray arrow could hit them.

With a roar, the forces of the Rai charged. Throwing aside their shields, choosing speed over protection.

"Spears!" he shouted, "spears to the walls!" He felt the platform shaking as villagers ran up the ladders, joining him on the ledge. His chosen archers continued to loose, Cahan along with them. The Rai's forces reached the edge of the pit. Bridge runners came forward, throwing lengths of wood over the pit. Spears were thrown. A villager fell, and another.

"Shields!" shouted from further along the wall. Villagers ducked, hiding behind shields or the wall. For a moment, it felt like he was young, back when he was an itinerant warrior. The air loud with the shouting of the Rai's forces. Screams from the wounded on both sides. The soldiers threw their spears further and better than the villagers could. The thud of a body hitting the floor. More bridge runners, throwing lengths of wood across the pit and against the spiked hillocks on either side. Cahan ignored them. Their bridges were small, no more than one soldier at a time could pass over them. What bothered him was a group who were putting a larger bridge across the pit in front of the gate. In the fury of the attack they had not noticed the sap that the ram had been soaked through with. The pit was bridged.

Soldiers streaming over the pit.

Ladders against the wall.

"Rocks!" shouted Cahan. "Throw rocks at them, do not waste spears!"

The villagers on the wall were holding the enemy. Throwing rocks, using spears on the ladder climbers. Shouts from below. The drums beating faster. The spears coming at them. Screams and shouts and noise. More soldiers rushing across the bridge, carrying more ladders and screaming their fury.

"Fire!" shouted Cahan. Furin held up a torch and he lit the end of an arrow dipped in sap. Waited a moment until the fire had caught. Stood. Drew. Loosed.

The arrow flashed by the soldiers. The warriors had shields up, sweat on faces. Anger, fury, hate. Barely seeing the arrow. The names of their dead hanging in the air like hateful promises.

Nothing happened.

The riot of bodies below continued. Pushing forward as his arrow vanished into the pit. Another ladder being raised. Crashing against the wall. Hooked tops biting. A woman, drawing back an arm to throw a spear, eyes wide, bright with joy as she aimed at him.

The weight telling. Cahan could feel it. The momentum of the battle was with the attackers.

A light.

A small fire beneath the bridge.

Growing.

Billowing outwards, flames following the pit around, igniting the chemicals from the tanners' pits. The crack of sap jars bursting in the heat. The force of the exploding bottles throwing the makeshift bridge into the air, spilling soldiers into the fire below to be impaled as they burned. Screams of fury replaced by screams of pain. Cahan raised his arm in front of his face. Fire hot on his skin. The Rai army backing away from the furious heat.

An exultation within him. Cowl writhing beneath his skin. He wanted to open the gates. Call out an attack. Push forward.

Fought it down.

They could not pass the fire any more than the attackers could. Villagers were jeering from the walls, calling soldiers cowards as they ran. Cahan turned, shouting, "Chosen spears and archers to the Forestgate!" and jumped from the wall. Followed by the villagers he had picked as the best warriors. The rest stayed on the wall. Lost in victory.

Over the forest the light was setting, framing the trees as black teeth against the pinking sky.

Cahan ran towards the Forestgate. Felt something in his gut. The squirm of his cowl beneath his skin. It was reacting to another cowl user, somewhere near.

"Down!" he roared out the words. Saw the reborn, standing with a group of villagers armed with spears, react, throwing themselves at the floor.

A great flash lit the village. A second set of shadows cast. Another light. Framing the wall as a shadow, the villagers on it caught in odd positions, bodies askew, arms and legs in places they should not be as the gate below exploded. The shockwave knocking those villagers to the floor who had not heard his shout. Soldiers, led by one of the Rai, streaming into the village.

"To me! Spears and archers!" screamed at the top of Cahan's voice as he pulled himself up.

"Woolside archers to me! Woolside spears to me!" this from Sengui, sprinting towards him with her spear and shield.

The two reborn by his side, now he needed them. This was their time. Their element.

Villagers running to join him as he pulled the axes from the thighs of his armour. Something nightmarish of this, seen through the flickering fire of the exploded gate. People running. Some with purpose, some in panic. Had the Rai that came through the Forestgate not expended their energy destroying it they would have been finished. But the attack on the gate had taken all they had and, rather than joining their troops, they hung back, letting their troops enter first. The soldiers were loath to act without the orders of their Rai, and set up a shield wall just inside the village. Behind them their Rai leaned on a soldier. The Rai straightened, the soldier slumped as sacrifice was taken from them.

Cahan knew they did not have long.

"Form shields!" he shouted. "Woolside! Form shields! Tanside! To me!" The messy shield wall before him tightened, though he did not think it would stop a concerted charge. "My chosen! Draw!"

Behind him the chosen archers, dressed as Forestals, nocked arrows and brought tension to their bows. The villagers did not have the skill to shoot accurately over the line of their own shields in front of them; they needed direct line of sight, more risk than he liked, but there was little other choice. "Shields down!" The shieldbearers with their spears knelt. The bows loosed. Arrows the length of his forearm streaking through the air. At this range, even loosed by amateurs, they were devastating. It should have been over with the second volley. Had they been better trained, quicker to loose and draw, quicker to get the shields back up then Cahan's prophecy of a hundred archers breaking an army would have been proven true, and by less than twenty bows.

But they were not.

The Rai's forces knew what to expect. They were ready. Heavy shields blocked the second volley of arrows, and though some got through it was not enough. Worse, they had their spears ready. He heard the order. Saw spear arms draw back. Shouted out, "Shields!" But their shields were weak things and the spears cut into their ranks. The woman behind him fell without a sound. One of the reborn added her shield to his own. He heard screaming. He heard the wet thud of sharp wood cutting into flesh. He heard bodies hit the ground. He heard panicked voices. All the familiar sounds of war, all the things he had spent so long wishing never to hear again.

You were running but you were not running fast enough.

All for naught, death came to him. No matter what lies he told himself he could not escape that. He could blame Venn. He could blame the Forestals. He could blame the treefall. But the truth was he had put all of this into motion by coming back to his childhood farm all those years ago.

You need me.

He felt the line wavering. He felt panic beginning in the heat of the bodies around him. The quick breaths, the sobs of fear.

They would break if he did not do something.

The Rai joined their troops. Moving into the second rank, they felt victory was near but still sought the protection of their soldiers' shields and bodies. Fire danced along their ornate armour.

Cahan knew he must act. Another volley of spears would break the villagers.

"Into them!" He screamed it. Charged the shield wall.

As he ran the reborn ran with him. Resplendent in their ancient armour, they looked at home here, among the sobbing and the screaming. A roar from behind as the villagers joined the charge. Another rain of spears. It was a simple act for him to weave among them. The weapons moved as if through heavy sap. He moved like a creature of the water. Silver and fast.

The reborn were even faster. They did not bother to dodge the spears. They relied on speed, running straight for the enemy, a spear in each hand, shields left behind. As they ran one screamed, a monstrous sound that would have been more at home on some creature of Wyrdwood, something with hook-tipped tentacles and a poison-tipped beak that struck from the shadows to drag off its prey. But there was nothing of striking from the shadows about the reborn. They cut through the twilight, through flames, leaping over burning wood. Two slender, armour-clad figures carrying death. The Rai pointed, shouting orders. The soldiers concentrated their next volley on the reborn. The one in the lead, the one he called Nahac, could not escape. The first spear hit her armour, bouncing off. She missed a step but did not stop. Immortal, unable to die, they cared little for tactics.

She ran on.

The next spear hit her helmet, knocking her head back. She ran on.

Two more hit, these punctured her armour, cracking the wood, piercing her body and she screamed. But not in pain, it was a sound of frustration as her body weakened. Another spear pierced her and she fell.

The second reborn ran on.

She had been using the first as a shield and when her sister dropped to her knees she used the body to vault into the air, throwing herself at the enemy shield wall with a spear in each hand. Crashing into them, knocking soldiers back, filling the air with the sound of hardwood against hardwood. A spear through the head of a soldier. Her impact opened a gap in their wall. She did not stop. The gap in the wall left the Rai exposed and she threw herself at them, forcing her spear through their armour. The Rai screaming out in pain.

But it took more than a spear to kill Rai.

This one was old, as Cahan ran towards them he could feel it. Rather than fall, rather than die like they should, the Rai reached out with both hands. Clasped them around the armoured head of the reborn. Cahan felt the pulse of power through his cowl. Felt the fire coming. Heard the reborn scream as the Rai let fire flood from their hands and into her helmet, destroying her flesh, cracking bone in the sudden and intense heat. The Rai let go of her. She fell. The Rai shouted out in victory, but only once.

For then Cahan was among them.

I need you.

So aware of the world around him.

I am here.

His power was small, had he fed it with a life it would have been larger but he had sworn not to. What power he had was taken from the slow seep of the ground and the bright light of his spirit. He could not burn Rai, or throw fire. If he tried to steal life from the Rai their soldiers would cut him down.

But even so, he was quick and he was lethal.

The Rai let go of the smoking corpse of the reborn. His axe took their head from their shoulders.

No stopping him. Axes flashing. None could stand against him. Screaming, shouting, cursing in the name of the Osere. Men and women died under his axes. Blood covered him. He was unstoppable. A fury. A monster. Cutting out a clearing around him. Turning the tide.

The villager's shield wall hit. He felt the impact. Heard the impact. The shouting. They were winning. He was winning.

And then.

Without warning.

They were not.

He became an old man. His armour heavy. His muscles tired. The world a blur.

Before him stood Sorha. It felt as if they were the only two in the village.

"Cahan Du-Nahere," she said, and drew her blade. "I have a most strange effect on the Rai."

62

He could not describe the sudden feeling of loss, of being hollowed out. So long he had denied the cowl then, when he embraced it, it was taken away. He looked for a duller, but there was not one. Only her.

It was her.

To be near Sorha was to be diminished, to become so much less than he was.

Strength fled, he fell to his knees. The villagers began to fall back. As if they had been sapped of their strength just as he had.

"Disconcerting, isn't it?" she said. The Rai's troops, so near to breaking before, reforming around her.

Sorha held a shield on one arm, a sword in her free hand. "You made me this," she said, leaving the shield wall. She spun the sword. "A walking duller." Swung her sword in a lazy arc. He batted it away with an axe, felt the jarring power of her strength through his arm. He stood, it was an effort. His legs barely worked. She began to circle, visor up. Smiling at him. "No reborn to save you this time, Forester," she said, lunged. He jumped backwards. She laughed. "You know, I did not realise how lazy we become as Rai," she brought her sword down in an overhead swing. He caught it on crossed axes.

All he could do to keep hold of them.

She was not even trying. Not yet.

"The cowl, see, Cahan Du-Nahere, it does all the work for us. We are like an old tree, hollowed out by rot, kept up by vines. But when you remove those vines?" She dummied a lunge, he fell for it and she twisted, shouldering him, using her shield to protect herself and sending him sprawling to the floor. "We collapse, Forester, that is what happens." Sorha stood over him. Stepped closer, brought her sword to his throat, touching the weak point between armour and helmet where only sap-hardened wool protected him. "They cannot bear to be around me any more, those who were once my compatriots. They make me lead Hetton now." He felt the pressure building on the sword tip. "Last time we spoke, here in this village, you said that by destroying my cowl you had freed me." The pressure growing. "I did not believe you then, but I understand now. The Rai?" She glanced over her shoulder, the Rai were gone. No doubt withdrawn far from her influence. "They seem strong, but they are weak within. Rotten."

"And you are not?" he said.

"No. I am not." She had the air of one who has seen a vision, had a great truth revealed to them. All the surety of a fanatic on her face. "They will regret the way they have treated me." The point of the sword, sharp and hard against his throat.

"And yet you fight for them."

"For now," she said.

"Join us." She smiled at him, not a real smile, a thing as cold and lost as a flower in the middle of Harsh, destined to quickly die among the frosted grass blades.

"That would require forgiveness, Cahan Du-Nahere," the pressure growing, her muscles tensing. "And I am not the forgiving type."

"Woolside! Tanside! Forward for Harn!" Ont's voice. Sorha looked up. A roar came from the soldiers behind her and they brought spears down. Sorha's sword left his throat, she backed away, still with that smile on her face.

"We are not finished yet, Cahan du-Nahere!" she shouted, "you can't win this. I will be back, and I'll take my time with you." Then he was surrounded by the villagers of Harn, hands helping him up, strength returning as Sorha moved away and the influence of whatever she was abated. He stood. Strong again. In among a shield wall of villagers, scrappy, frightened, sweaty, but there.

"Spears up!" Shouted from the enemy wall in front of him. A hail of spears, coming in. "Shields!" he shouted, but the villagers were not soldiers, not yet. Not quick to obey. Some raised shields, some did not. The spears hit. People screamed, people died. A spear hit him in the chest, bounced off his armour. He wished he could have given the villagers better armour, their hardened wool did little more than offer the illusion of protection. More spears ripped holes in the shield wall. Panic ripping through the people of Harn. The line close to breaking. Their joy at rescuing him ripped away by sharp points, flushed away by flowing blood. The Rai's soldiers pushing forward. He stood in the centre of the line. His voice hoarse.

"Shields! Hold fast! We can stop them!" And maybe if heart and bravery could have held the enemy soldiers then they would have. The Rai's forces smashed into them with a roar, pushing the line back. Practised spears found weaknesses, forced points through, seeking flesh. Shouts of pain, of anger and fury. His axes rising and falling, killing those in front of him. But the soldiers knew Rai. They were ready for him. They knew how to neutralise him and he was quickly faced off by stout shields. His axes, his strength, splintered them but more came. The villagers pushed back. But they were not strong enough. Not numerous enough.

He could feel the moment coming. The moment of loss. They were not soldiers. Fear overwhelming them.

"Hold!" He shouted it more from desperation than anything else. The villagers could not hold, he knew it. Panic taking them. Fear overriding the knowledge there was nowhere to run to. They did not have the discipline of soldiers, or the battlefield knowledge that to run was to die. "Hold!" A scream from their line. Another enemy spear finding its mark.

"Break!"

He did not know where the order came from, but it was what the villagers wanted to hear. They were not trained against such tricks. Not expecting them and the voice said what they wanted to hear. Maybe they would have held for longer without it. But it did not matter.

They broke.

The line melted away around him, the meagre protection of their shields vanished. The Rai soldiers saw their opportunity and ran after the retreating villagers, screaming and whooping.

"Kill them all!" shouted a voice.

"No! They want prisoners!" That from a soldier bigger than the rest, in better armour. A trunk commander. In fury, and desperation Cahan threw an axe, taking him in the head but denying himself a weapon. He did not care. It was useless to care. The only thought going through his mind was that he would die fighting. He would not let Sorha, or the Rai, take him. He did not want to die by fingerbreadths like Dyon.

A soldier came at him, battle-mad, looking for glory in taking down the enemy with the best armour. He lunged with a spear. Cahan pushed it away and cut the soldier's arm from their body. But he was only a vanguard, behind him more were coming. Less foolish, better organised. A shield wall built just for him.

"Come then!" he shouted. "Who would be the one to

say they took down Cahan Du-Nahere! The Forester of Harn?" His bravado bounced off their shields.

Soldiers everywhere.

Harn had fallen.

Cahan tightened his grip on his axe. Stared at the shields before him. Readied himself.

A gap appeared in the shield wall.

Then another.

Another.

A sound, familiar and unexpected.

Arrows.

Expertly shot arrows. Cutting down the Rai's soldiers as they ran into the village. Opening up the shield wall. A cloaked figure on top of a longhouse. Stood, loosed an arrow. A soldier fell. The figure knelt again to pull an arrow from a quiver, nock it. Standing again to loose. Barely even aiming. With each shot a soldier died.

Astounding skill.

Skill he had only seen once. The Forestal, Ania.

More of her people appeared on the roofs of other round-houses and longhouses. Soldiers falling to arrows, suffering the same shocking reversal that the villagers had suffered when the spears were thrown. Arrows flying, Rai troops falling back. Some singly, others in groups using shields. It did them no good. The archers had height and were positioned all around the village, giving them the angle. Those that ran had a better chance, the groups with shields were slower and easier to hit. Cahan retrieved his axe from the head of the trunk commander.

A moment in the darkness. A breath taken.

He stood.

"They are running! Into them!" He screamed it, using the cowl to amplify his voice. "Into them!" Villagers appeared from between houses, cutting down running soldiers. Some threw spears, most missed, but others found their mark. Some used makeshift weapons: a pitchfork as a spear, a spade used as a club, everywhere he looked the routed soldiers were being cut down, trapped between houses. Arrows singing through the air.

Then they were gone.

Harn stood once more.

Though for how long?

63

Thirty had died among the villagers. Young, old, the army of the Rai did not care who fell before it. He saw children among the dead, though he did not understand how they had come to be out during the fight.

In the middle of the village he found the reborn, Nahac, pierced by spears as she charged the line of the Rai. She had fallen to her knees, then backwards, but the spears had kept her body upright. The body of her sister lay prone further down among the corpses of the Rai, smoke drifting from her helmet. Udinny joined him as he examined the bodies.

"Venn is treating the wounded," said the monk.

"And Dyon?" The monk looked away, shook her head. "All we can do is dose him with Sleepwragg, despite the danger, but we are running out of it." Udinny looked at the ground, not at him, and he had the strangest feeling she was only partly here. "Venn helps those who cannot be saved take the Star Path peacefully, without pain. Those that can be saved Venn treats and says will heal by themselves, given time." Udinny smiled, snapping back to themselves. "If we had time." Drumming, and discordant singing drifted over from outside the walls.

"Tell Venn not to do too much, do not let them hurt themselves."

"This way they have," said the monk, "it barely takes any power from them. They work with what is in the body to connect it to Ranya's web." She shrugged. "I do not understand it, but I feel it."

"You feel it?" The monk looked away, shrugged again.

"Ever since I gave myself to the boughry, Cahan, my awareness of the forest has been growing." She looked up at him. "I am changing, do not say you have not noticed?" He nodded, her ragged robe no longer touched the ground because she was taller than she had been, and thinner. Up close he could see a very fine but thick covering of hair across her skin. Not enough for most to notice. He had not noticed until recently, these changes had been slow and subtle.

"I am not sure how much time we have," he said, but Udinny was not listening to him. She was looking at the reborn.

"I thought they could not die," said the monk. She reached out as if to touch the reborn. Then stopped, as if she dare not.

"So did I," he said, stepping nearer as Udinny crouched by the corpse. "I suppose they have got their wish."

"Cahan," Udinny cocked her head, "can you hear that?"

"All I hear is the Rai, outside the walls, making their noise."

"Come closer," she said. He did. Something there. Something little more than a whisper on the breeze, the barest scratch of a tiny creature moving along a leaf.

"Is it the reborn?" said Udinny. "I sense the web but they are not in it." Cahan leaned in closer, put his head near the reborn's mouth. Heard her more clearly. She still lived, in her way. And from her mouth words, drifting slowly to his ear.

"Out . . ." So quiet, so slow it was barely a word. "Out . . ." the whisper on the wind. "Take . . . them . . . out."

"Udinny!" he said. "Help me pull the spears from her." He dragged the reborn over onto her side. Udinny grabbed a spear and pulled. If the reborn felt anything she gave no sign. Her limp body slid in the mud as the monk fought against the suck of flesh against spear, the grind of it against her armour. "You hold her, monk, I will remove the spears." Udinny nodded and they swapped places. Udinny sitting on the reborn's body to hold her still while he used his greater strength to draw out the spears that had pierced her. She did not make a sound, not a groan, not a hiss of pain. When the spears were out the reborn only lay there, limp.

"We should take her to Venn," said Udinny. Cahan nodded, picking up the body. She was curiously light even though she wore full armour. He ran towards the longhouse, passing villagers on their way to the village square where Sengui and Aislinn were calling them. They looked damaged, broken, different from the men and women they had been before the second attack. Ont walked past him, his stare focused somewhere far outside the village, the pretend Forestal cloak still about his shoulders.

"Ont!" The butcher blinked, as if waking when Cahan said his name. "Have the people strip the soldier's bodies of armour, give the best to those who will stand in the front line."

"They will come back?" he said, all his bravado stripped, his bluster bleached thin by battle. Cahan nodded, it would have been easy to score points then, to castigate the man for his short-sightedness and selfishness. But he did not, it would serve nothing but his own sense of importance.

"They will keep coming, Ont," he said, the body of the reborn slack in his arms. "We must ready ourselves to escape into the forest", Ont stared at him, "and we must keep busy, if people dwell on danger they can lose their wits." The butcher blinked again, then nodded.

"I will tell Sengui and Aislinn," he said. "We will keep them working until we can leave." All the fight gone from him, he looked smaller. Cahan nodded.

"Thank you, branch leader," he said, then took the reborn into the longhouse.

The floor full of bodies. The air full of pain. Venn moving from person to person, bent over, pausing by a woman. They put their hands on them. As they did Cahan felt the air shimmer, no one else reacted, no one else commented. The cowl beneath his skin fluttered. The woman before Venn stopped moving, stopped making a noise and then the trion stood, moved on to the next one followed by Furin. The Leoric had a smear of bright red blood on the white make-up of her face. He laid the reborn down and Venn came over, wiping their hands with a rag.

"Can you help her?" he said. Venn knelt and put their hands on her, the trion's face twisted.

"They are dead," said Venn.

"But she spoke to me," said Cahan. The trion looked up at him.

"The others," they said, looking back at the villagers arrayed across the floor. "I can feel the life running through them. I am a bridge, I work with the web to connect them." They looked back at the reborn. "But her? Something animates her, but it is not life. I cannot help her." They stood, about to say more when a scream cut the air, a sound containing more pain than anyone should have to bear.

"Dyon," said Furin. "The Sleepwragg has worn off already." She sounded tired, miserable.

"He cannot be helped?" said Cahan. Venn shook their head.

"I told him, Cahan, what you offered, to let him slip from this life and start his journey on the Star Path. But he will not go." Cahan looked away, amazed at how hard people would cling onto life, no matter the circumstance.

"We cannot stand another attack, can we?" said Furin. He thought on that, licked his lips.

"Maybe one more," he looked around the longhouse, at the dying. "The Forestals have returned, and they are fierce. But it would be better if we escaped now. I have told Ont to get people ready." Furin nodded. Then looked back at the wounded villagers.

"Not all can be moved."

"We cannot leave them," said Udinny. "The Rai will not take our escape well. They will avenge themselves on any left behind."

"Sleepwragg is a kind death," said Furin, "if it is what must be, then that will be the last gift I will give those who cannot be moved. We may have enough." Venn opened their mouth to say something, about to argue, but Furin turned to them. "You know," she hissed, "what the Rai will do. We make hard choices now, Venn," she spoke softly, "we must arrange the wounded into those who will die quickly, those who may linger we have to dose, and those we can move. Will you help me?" The trion looked shocked, their eyes widening. "You ease the path for those with no choice but to take it, but sometimes," Furin touched their shoulder, "it is simply about how many can be saved." She led Venn away, looking to Cahan, and mouthing, "leave this with me". He nodded and left, followed by Udinny.

In the darkness villagers were stripping the bodies of the dead. Others were building travois and packing them with belongings. He saw some villagers standing over the body of the second reborn getting ready to strip her armour.

"Wait!" he said. The villagers stopped. "Strap her to a travois, leave her armour."

"She is dead, Forester," said one of the villagers, softly.

"She is reborn," he replied. "They say they cannot die. So we take her with us. She is likely to walk again before we find a place to stay in the forest." He did not know if that was true, or how long it took the reborn to come back to life, but it was enough for the villagers. They dragged the body away to one of the houses where the travois were being made.

"Planning on leaving?" He turned to find the Forestal, Ania. Her face hidden by her hood, a stick in her mouth that she chewed on.

"From the start I have wanted these people to run for the forest, now they finally understand why and will do as I ask." The Forestal let out a small laugh, a crackle of winter leaves beneath the feet.

"Too late, Forester," she said, and as ever she made the word forester sound mocking. "They have left it too late."

"What do you mean?" She took the stick from her mouth.

"Ten of us left here, Forester, seven came back."

"The Rai are in Woodedge?" She shook her head.

"Not Rai, were it Rai they would be food for trees and sprouting arrow branches from their backs." She dropped her stick in the mud. "It was the same foul things got us before." She spat. "We are of the forest, it accepts us, makes us part of it. But whatever hunted us could hide in it, until they were close and then it was . . ."

"Like you had eaten something rotten?" She nodded.

"Aye, and they did not fall to an arrow to the heart, they kept coming." Cahan was silent.

"Blank eyes, like a cooked fish head?" She nodded.

"Hetton." A blanket of fear settled on him, like snow in the darkness, muffling the sound around him. "How many?"

"I do not know, more than five, less than ten. They surrounded us, circling like hungry animals. Gildan died first. Chaf and Giddick gave their lives so the rest of us could escape."

"Why come back here," he asked, "why not escape further into the forest?" She looked up, bright eyes under the hood.

"I have fought, many times. Hit-and-run attacks, I know how it works. Relies on being faster than your enemy. They were faster than us, would have picked us off one by one as we made for . . ." her voice drifted off. Came back louder, surer. "If I'm going to die, Forester, I'll do it killing Rai. Not running." He thought about what she said, about trying to get through the forest and find somewhere safe with an army of Rai behind them. With the lurking horror of the Hetton picking them off as they went and he knew that he could not do it. He could not lead the villagers into the forest with the Hetton waiting.

But at the same time, to stay here was certain death.

"You're almost out of arrows," said the Forestal.

"Udinny," Cahan turned to the monk, "go and get Furin, we must speak to the village." The monk nodded, her face drawn as she walked away. "How many arrows do you have?" he asked Ania.

"Not enough," she said.

"I will give you what we have left." She looked away, towards the still intact tiltgate.

"You should send people out to gather fallen arrows."

"In the dark? They would stumble about not finding anything until the Rai came and finished them." The Forestal shrugged.

"Without arrows they die anyway." He stared at her, she was a cold one but she was right. There was a delicate balance to be kept here, between the risks he must take for what Harn needed, and the risks that were too much for them all, and would cost him what morale there was left.

"I think I can get us more arrows," said Udinny as she returned.

"That would be good," said Cahan.

"Cahan." He turned, Furin was there with Venn and behind them the villagers were gathering. They looked to him for answers, for hope.

But he had very little to give.

Deep in the Forest

You remember a room, close and claustrophobic with heat. Voices, some high, some low, calling and singing across each other in a twisting intermeshing cacophony as you are brought in. The atmosphere is both celebratory and funereal. You are elated and you are frightened.

Colour and light, dark and flickering. Four great fires lit in the name of Zorir, the god's name spoken by a hundred mouths and each speaker dressed in robes and cloaks of shimmering fungal colour. Before them all, on top of the three stone steps standing and before her throne is Saradis, the Skua-Rai, in her bearded mask, and she sings in a high discordant voice that hurts your ears. You should be enjoying this, this should be a momentous moment for you, a waystick on your path to greatness. But all you feel is fear.

All you feel is fear.

They have put all they are into you, and all you feel is fear.

The singing and drumming and cymbal crashing reaches a crescendo, the monks holding your arms grip you tight because no matter how brave you say you are they know the truth, the weakness and the fear that runs through you. They know you may run at any moment. That here, before Zorir-Who-Walks-in-Fire, before a god whose voice you have heard echo round the throne room, you are all too aware of your betrayal. Surely, here and now is when you are revealed in your utter and complete unsuitability, that your doubt and your lies, will doom you in the eyes of a creature that burns those who disappoint it to ash while they scream and beg.

"Zorir!"

With that shouted name the Skua-Rai cuts her hand across the singing, stopping it dead. In that moment of silence you have never felt so alone. You want your sister, but she is gone. Never worthy of the mysteries. Dead upon a sandy path.

You know that was where your doubt started, she was better than you in all things. Better scholar, better fighter, better tactician and no matter how many times you hear "but she is older", that is all. You know it for the lie it must be. She did not weep into the arms of a gardener. Then weep again for his loss.

But if that was the case. If your sister was more. Then that would mean the Skua-Rai was wrong, and she is infallible, the vessel of Zorir, she is the container of the furnace. She is the one who will be the architect of the future of Crua, and for her you will burn the world, and it will be reborn in glory.

You should not be afraid.

You should be sure, and you should be confident and you should be righteous.

All you feel is fear.

64

Kirven was feeling better than she had for weeks. The attack on Harn was not working out as Galderin had expected. His confidence, so strong before, was wavering. Kirven had not felt welcome at his fire on the journey. The other Rai would move away, sneer at her. Now she found attitudes changing. The Rai, once three of their own had died, became less sure of their position around Galderin, began to look upon him as weak, began to think that maybe she was a better bet for them. A better way to power. To survive.

She had watched the Rai and their troops return, heads bowed with the shame of defeat, and smiled to herself. "Beaten again, Galderin," she thought. "Where is your strength now? Where are your promises to your followers that they would easily roll over these weak villagers?"

Gone, was where.

His army had been held at bay: by one man, a handful of outlaws and the same "weak" villagers he was laughing at only days ago. Now Galderin was the weak one. Now was her opportunity to strike and she would take it. Galderin might be strong in his cowl but he needed the support of the other Rai, and they were quick to change allegiance when it looked like they might be in danger. For all that they revelled in cruelty Kirven thought them cowards at heart, always in the second line of attack and never in the first.

Now they had asked her to a strategy meeting.

She left her tent, walked through Woodedge. She hated the forest, it reminded her of being a child. Of being forced to go into the trees in search of wood, or to check the traps or to gather sap or any of the other tasks the adults, too frightened of the dark between the trees, gave to children. She knew the forest hated the people. Her Rai wife had known her fears. That was why Madrine had once left her tied to a tree in the Wyrdwood for a day and a night, punishment for her pregnancy.

While she struggled Kitath, the secondhusband who fathered the child, had died in front of her. Covered in some sweet liquid that called to orits and their rasping mouthparts had slowly flayed the skin off him while he screamed. His fate was something that Madrine had enjoyed taunting her with, promising it would be hers next time she displeased the Rai. Sometimes, when she closed her eyes, she felt the trees about her, closing in, intruding on her flesh in some unfathomable way.

Kirven fought down a shudder. She had always thought she would die amid the trees, had felt it coming the nearer they marched to Harn. Yet, here was opportunity among them. Life in Crua was like the forest in a way, the fall of one great trunk allowed another to flourish. She would flourish, Galderin would fall.

He had lost.

Twice.

She heard voices as she approached the large tent Galderin had set up among the trees. The remaining Rai were in conference, discussing tactics, and she felt anger run through her. She should have been part of this all along.

She should have been planning with them. Well, that was about to change. Galderin had failed too often.

It was her chance now.

She passed the guards without acknowledging them, walked into the tent to find the Rai standing around a table, Galderin bent over it. On the table bark had been rolled out, and a crude drawing of Harn and the clearing it sat in drawn on it. The two nearest Rai, Vedara and Handlin, turned to her, then turned away. No nod, no acknowledgement of her even though they had invited her. She almost stumbled.

That was wrong.

Not the right reaction.

"High Leoric," said Galderin, standing back from the table. "We were making plans for the final assault." He was calm. He should not be so calm in the face of his failure.

"Another one?" she said. Did she see smiles from the Rai around the table? She hoped so. "I seem to remember the first assault was the only one we needed, and the second was the final one." Galderin stared at her, if looks could kill, she thought.

"Well, Kirven," he said, "we were given poor information, but I suppose that should be expected when it was provided by someone such as yourself, who is not a natural military leader."

"I have fought," she said and immediately wished she could take it back. It had made her sound defensive when she should have sounded sure. "And the information on this place was provided by one of your own." The atmosphere became colder in the tent.

"It does not do," said Galderin, coming round the table, one hand on the blade at his hip, "to compare the Rai with an abomination such as Sorha."

"I told you to bring dullers," she said.

"And that is the problem" said Galderin. "You think like them," he pointed out of the tent and toward Harn, "not like Rai. And we have listened to you beg for the life of your child. We have fought like them because of it. We have not been true to ourselves." A shudder passed through her. He had turned this about. He had made her responsible. "Because of you we have played to their strengths. Not ours."

"We must take the village intact," she said.

"Because of your child." Galderin looked at the Rai around the table. This was wrong. How he was acting was wrong. She stood as tall as she could, made her voice as cold and hard as possible.

"Venn must be brought back to Harnspire alive, for the Cowl-Rai." They were all staring at her now, eyes too pale, skin stretched across the bones of their faces. Inhuman.

"If the trion is alive we are to save them," said Galderin. Then he smiled, and it was the dead smile of the Hetton. "And we have seen no sign of them. At all."

"They probably hide them," said Kirven, panic rising. She fought it back. "If they know they are valuable, they will hide them." Galderin did not say anything, only watched her, his face cold as Harsh now. No pretence at emotion.

At being human.

"We intend to fight like Rai, High Leoric," he made her title into a mocking crown. "No more walking into arrows or traps. We will combine our power, and we will drop fire on those fools in that village. Burn them. Then we walk in and suck the life from anyone left and offer our strength up to Tarl-an-Gig." Despair, ripping into her. He offered his Rai what they wanted most. Life, strength and power.

"No!" Her legs threatening to give way. "If Venn dies then—" He moved so quickly she had no time to escape. She was in his grasp. His hands either side of her face. Her legs almost gave way and he was the only thing holding her up. Her body held against the cold wood of his armour.

"If they die," said Galderin, "there will be other trion,

Rai are long-lived." She had never noticed before just how very pale his eyes were, how empty. "That is something you people simply fail to understand. Your lives are short, we need only be patient and wait for you to make mistakes. You always do." A deeply unpleasant smile. "You have."

"Let me go," she said. Each word a triumph of self-control. "I was put in place by the Cowl-Rai themselves. I am the High Leoric of Harnspire." Did she feel the pressure of his hands on her face lessen? Yes, but only for a second. "I am in charge." The pressure increased.

"No, Kirven, you are not, you are just fuel."

"You cannot," desperate, aware how thin her words were, "how will you explain this to Tiltspire."

"I am sure they know, Kirven Ban-Ruhn," he said, leaning in closer to her, pressing harder, "how dangerous a battlefield is."

"No." Her words the merest breath of wind among the cold trees.

"You were a fool to come here," said Galderin. "I will tell the Cowl-Rai you died running from villagers. None will mourn your loss." She felt the cowl's touch as a caress at first, as if it were the touch of the lovers she had denied herself for so long. Then he rubbed the clanpaint from her face with his thumb. Heat following. Galderin smiled and Kirven began to burn. Opened her mouth to scream. She could not. She tried to struggle. She could not. "You should be glad," he said, "that your sacrifice here will aid the Cowl-Rai. Your life will help us burn that village full of traitors."

"Venn," she thought, "all I have done is let you down."

The pain was excruciating.

65

The villagers gathered in the night, ready to leave.

Outside the walls of Harn the drums sounded once more. The seven remaining Forestals stood on the walls. Every one of the villagers looked worn and worried. All in need of rest. The different colours and stripes they wore on their faces flaking off to reveal the skin below. The agonised screams of Dyon ran counterpoint to the furious rhythm of the Rai's drums. Belongings were tied to travois which floated in the air suspended by dying gasmaws. Discarded possessions littered the ground.

Furin came to stand by him and leaned in close.

"We are down to less than a hundred arrows, Cahan," she said, "I have given them to the Forestals." He nodded, and tried to hide the dismay on his face. Without the reborn he was not sure they could stand. Without arrows he knew they could not. He turned to the villagers.

"We have a hard choice to make," he shouted.

"What choice?" came from the crowd, "it is made. We are running for the forest." Cahan nodded.

"That was our plan, aye." He looked about, the villagers were tired and scared. In the past they had been foolish.

They had made bad decisions. They had treated him like he was less than them.

But in the moment when Sorha's blade was about to fall, when he needed them, they had come.

And not one of them deserved what the Rai would do with them.

"People of Harn." He met their gazes. "You see the Forestals are back." Nods, even smiles. "That is because the Rai left something guarding the forest." No noise, no explosion of shock or horror. They were spent, and only watched him. "Getting past the Rai would always be hard once they were here," he shouted. "But now it is harder. To escape we must leave everything behind, all we own, our wounded, anything that will slow us down." All eyes on him, not looking away, not talking to each other, only watching. "And even then, many of us will die. They will follow, pick us off as we go."

"Is that our only choice?" this was Ont. He sounded like he had nothing left.

"We stay here, and we die. Those that don't will wish they had." There was no kinder way of saying it. There was no point in lying to them.

"Movement!" a shout from the Tiltgate.

"Furin," Cahan said, "I must see what is happening, you need to prepare them for how hard breaking out is going to be." She nodded, and turned on the podium before the fallen shrine to speak to her people. Cahan ran towards the Tiltgate wall, climbing to stand on the ledge next to Ania. She pointed out into the darkness. Drumming filled the air. A line of torches far out in the clearing. It was hard to make out quite how far away they were. For a moment he was tempted to use his cowl, dip into Ranya's web and feel out where the enemy were. A small voice told him this was tactically sensible, while another told him it did not matter they were coming, he should save his energy.

"The Rai are coming," he said.

"Not yet," said the Forestal.

"Why call me?" he asked Ania.

"Figures," she said, "out there. Within arrowshot." She pointed.

"Skirmishers?" She shook her head.

"I would have killed them if it was." Her tone was matter-of-fact, no fear. He stared into the darkness and as his eyes adjusted he began to see what Ania saw. Figures on the battlefield; but not one or a couple, hundreds. Like people but smaller, scurrying across the bloodied clearing before the village. "Rootlings, I reckon," said Ania. "What are they doing?"

"I do not know," he continued to watch. Most of the rootlings were scurrying about the field. Some stood still and the rest ran back and forth to them. Then one of the still rootlings scurried forward, stopping before the gate. He thought, though he could not be sure, that it was the same limping rootling he had freed from the Harn-Larger. In its thin arms it had a bundle of twigs.

No. Not twigs, arrows. The rootling hopped forward, hesitantly, looking up at them. It chittered something and dropped the arrows before the gate.

"They are helping?" said Ania. Then she let out a short laugh. "I had always thought of them as pests." The rootling vanished into the darkness and another appeared, dropping more arrows.

"Send someone to pick them up," he said, "share them out." He stared out into the night before climbing down and returning to Furin's side. The villagers were quiet.

"Are they ready?" he said. She nodded but did not reply.

"We are not leaving," said Aislinn, her one eye glittering.

"You will die," said Cahan, because there was no way to sweeten it. It was the truth. "We will all die." So many faces looking at him. Eyes glittering in the darkness.

"This is our home," said Sengui softly. "We are not forest people like you. And we may not be warriors but we know the truth behind your words. We die here, or we die running through the forest pursued by Rai." She looked about herself. "Given a choice, we would rather die defending our homes than running from them." The other villagers were nodding, watching him.

"We thank you for what you have done, Forester," said Ont. "We do not expect you to stay and die with us. Use the attack to escape, take the Forestals and the trion." He looked around. It was odd, but it looked like the villagers stood taller, were less frightened than they had been. As if by accepting the inevitability of what was coming they had put aside their fear.

"There is no changing your minds?" he said.

"There is not," said Aislinn. Cahan took a deep breath, wrapped his arms around himself.

"Then I will stand with you."

"As will we," he turned to find Ania, standing with two of her Forestals, their arms full of arrows. "We came here to kill Rai. If we're going to die then it's how we want to go."

"What do we do now?" said Furin.

"The travois," Cahan said, "we don't need them. Tip them, cut loose the floatvine and form them into a wall around your longhouse. We must make a line of defence we can fall back to."

"They are not much defence," said Ont.

"No," he said, "but it is better than nothing, and all we have time for." Ont nodded. Behind him some of the villagers had already started removing their belongings.

"What about the reborn?" said Sark.

"Put her in the longhouse and . . ." A feeling, a sudden headache. A weakness in his knees as if he was about to fall. For a moment he thought that it was Sorha, the Rai and her strange ability to sever him from his cowl, but the connection was still there. The hiss of the cowl still in his mind.

A pressure in his ears, like he was going up a steep hill. The trees on the Tiltgate side of the village filled with light, their leaves and trunks suffused with orange. What he felt was power, a gathering of it and the release of it. The light intensified and with a hiss and a roar a giant fireball climbed into the sky.

"You said they would not . . ." began Furin, watching as the fireball soared into the night.

"I did not think they would."

Shock flooded through Cahan. He had been so sure they would not simply fire the village from afar. If they could fight the Rai there was hope. Slim but still hope. But the fire? They could not fight that. It could not be killed, or deflected with a weapon. It could not be reasoned with, and you could not run faster than it.

The great fireball reached the top of its trajectory, beautiful in its own way, and began to fall. He traced its path in his mind. As did every villager standing around him, staring up into the darkness. It would land here, right among them. He did not move. In the back of his mind, he thought, "at least it will be quick".

"We tried," said Furin, staring up like every other. From behind him he heard Ania, the Forestal. She shouted a word Cahan had never heard before. Some command to hers, no doubt she ordered them to run.

"Foci!" screamed into the darkness.

He caught movement from the corner of his eye. The Forestals on the wall jumping down, running towards him. It made no sense. Why run towards where the fire would land? Did they want a quick end to this?

Ania pushed past him, running to the centre of the village square.

The fireball falling, roaring. Bathing them in light.

Ania shouted the word again at the top of her voice.

"Foci!" Forestals, running at full tilt, sliding towards her, managing to land so that each of them either had their hand on her back, or on each other. A strange and ungainly mess of branch- and leaf-clad people.

Cahan felt another surge of power.

This one different, not as harsh, not as hard or as disconcerting. A cowl but not as he knew it.

The fireball filling his view and then, in the final moment, as he raised his face, felt its heat upon his skin, Ania thrust her hands up. Shouted something loud and wordless that stunned the air.

A blink-and-you-miss-it shimmering above them.

Something he did not understand coming into existence. His cowl shuddered beneath his skin and he heard a sound as if a thousand horns played somewhere very far away. The fireball hit. But not them. Not him. Not the villagers. It hit an invisible barrier above them. Created a roof of liquid fire over them and the body of the fireball bounced away, crashing into the edge of the village and immolating a roundhouse. Around him shocked and surprised faces. The Forestals stood back from Ania.

"We need lookouts back on the walls," she said.

"What was that," said Cahan. "You have a cowl? But it is . . ."

"Like mine," that from Venn, standing in the door of the longhouse, how long they had been there he did not know. "I felt what you did," they looked at Ania, "how did you . . ."

"Not the time," said the Forestal, and she pointed at the trees. He felt that terrible power growing again. The Forestals moved around Ania, standing more comfortably now they had a little time, arraying themselves so they were all touching each other. They stood in a triangle with Ania at the head. Another fireball roared into the night sky.

"How long can you do this for?" said Furin.

"Long enough to annoy them," said Ania as she watched the fireball rising.

"How, though?" said Venn again.

"Power is shared among the Forestals and never taken. It is given freely," said Ania. "Now let us work." Cahan nodded.

"Archers and lookouts on the walls!" shouted Cahan. "Make that wall of travois! When they think the fire has done the work they will come." He felt the strange twist of the Forestals in the air again. Like nothing he had ever felt before. The fireball fell roaring. Villagers screamed, ducked, and the shield flickered into being. The fire splashing across it then bouncing away, crashing into the village wall and setting it alight.

"The travois!" shouted Cahan. "Ignore the fire, the Forestals protect us!" Another light grew into being at the treeline. "They will come soon, thinking their fire has done the work! We must be ready!" In the heat and flickering light the villagers looked barely like people, almost feral. "Go!" he shouted, and they did. Pulling over travois and anything else they could find to make a barrier in front of the long-house. Another fireball launched into the sky, hissing and spitting.

"Foci!" shouted Ania.

"What does that mean?" he said.

"It is the word," she replied, but she was not looking at him, she was following the passage of the fireball.

"This must be near to the last," he said. "It requires huge amounts of strength to launch fire like that." The fireball reached the apex of its arc and began to fall.

"To us!" shouted Ania. "Gather around us!" Villagers ran with all they had to get under the shield and again, the frisson on the air, the roar of the fireball, the frightened faces and the moment when the shield flickered into exist-ence. The fire splashing across the surface like liquid, before the mass of it bounced away, crashing into a Tanside round-house. Flame roaring through the village. Some had splashed onto the roof of Furin's longhouse.

"Put that out before it catches!" shouted Cahan. Villagers were already moving, they knew the danger of fire and that it must be stopped before it caught. He ran to help but was stopped short by a shout from the walls.

"Forester! They are coming! The Rai are coming!"

This was it. The final attack.

The last stand of Harn.

66

He had fought many times.

When Cahan was young and full of anger, martial skills were all he had to sell. He thought the heat of battle would hide his pain, he believed his anger a thing that could be spent, that he could use it up. He did not realise that battle was a fire and he was only stoking his anger, every sweep of his axe adding more fuel. A frightened boy became a frightening man. He fed the fire well and teetered over the edge of the conflagration he had been raised to become.

And one day he looked deep into the fire, he felt the heat and knew it would burn everyone, including him. So he turned from it.

It took a long time to put the fire out.

His past meant that it was not alien for him to stand on the walls of a town or a village, watching the enemy advance. Nor was it alien for him to be one of those advancing. He knew the fear of both sides, he knew the excitement of it, too. He knew that the Rai, though they held back, their energy spent on creating the fireballs, would be eager for the fight as much as they feared it. Their cowls burning within them like acid, demanding to be fed. They would be balancing the desire for the pain of hunger to stop, with the knowledge they were vulnerable. The wish to attack, against the wish to stay safe.

He knew all these things.

But he had never stood upon a wall, or advanced upon an enemy sure in the knowledge he would lose. And seeing the troops arrayed against them he knew he would. His hands shook and he placed them on the wood before him, grasped it tightly. As the soldiers advanced his mind showed him images, old and forgotten images, the faces of men and women as they gave up their lives under his hand. The way they screamed, the pain. The flood of power and the things he could do with it.

You are the fire.

He had sworn not to feed his cowl. *Never again.* And already broken that promise once in the forest clearing. He knew it was death by fingerbreadths, the slow hardening of everything that made him one of the people. He could steal life from those advancing, grab one and pull them away to a dark place and take what he needed. It might be enough for him to save the village.

It is not.

The voice was right.

One soldier's life was not enough to face the Rai and the Hetton.

But it was a step towards becoming something worse. Something that frightened him enough to know he must not do it. He must fight with what he had.

And die.

Die with everyone else here.

But die as one of the people.

He looked around. Fire, always hungry, had collapsed part of one wall. The villagers were banding together with their bows. Ania and five of the Forestals stood on the wall with him. Venn and Udinny were in the longhouse seeing to the wounded.

There were worse people to die with. Worse places to die and alone on his farm may have been one of them.

The soldiers of the Rai advanced on the wreckage of the forestgate. The villagers had tried to block it, but it would not hold for long. They would fight them in the village, and withdraw to the longhouse, do their best to protect the wounded and the dying until they joined them. Became more bodies laid out on the floor like the leaves of Harsh in the wood.

"Ready, archers!" he shouted. He had not taken up his bow. Though he knew he would be a better shot than nearly every other. Instead he stood with his axes, and would join those who had only pitchforks and sharpened sticks to fight with when the time came. He wanted the villagers to feel that he trusted them, was one of them, the few he would kill with arrows would make little difference here. Ania looked over at him. Ont had his bow, and stood next to Furin with a bow of her own. She was a poor shot, but that no longer mattered. A few stray arrows would make no difference. Udinny had asked to come, but in the end had stayed in the longhouse to help Venn.

The Rai's soldiers marched into the killing zone, his attention was for them now. "Loose!" he shouted it at the top of his voice. In answer he heard the whistle of arrows passing over him. He watched them land, saw shields raised. A few arrows found targets but no one fell. Ania glanced over at him and grinned. He heard her shout to her people.

"Kill them," she said. The Forestals started loosing arrows, slowly and methodically choosing their targets. A death for every arrow. He saw Ania licking the flights of the arrows that had been made in Harn, straightening them to her liking before she loosed. When the Rai were halfway across the killing floor their branch leaders let out a roar.

"Forward!" A mass of soldiers running at the gate. A shout of "They're coming!" from the other side of the village.

"Put down the leaders!" shouted Ania. Loosing even more deliberately. "Iftal curse the Rai," she spat, "staying back with the second wave, the cowards."

"Furin," he shouted, hands itching for his bow, "come with me, we meet them at the gate." He jumped from the wall, Furin dropped her bow and grabbed a spear. Below villagers ran to join him. Children gathered up the remaining arrows and ran with them to the Forestals who were loosing faster, putting all they had into killing as many soldiers as they could before they breached the ruined gate.

"Form up!" shouted Cahan, "form up!" Around him villagers were crowding together, some with makeshift shields, others with shields stolen from corpses. The shield wall was the best they had made so far. "Good!" he shouted, "good! Get ready to meet them! Stand fast! For Harn!"

From around him raised voices, "For Harn!"

Soldiers, pushing easily through their attempt to block the ruined gate, and among them, shunned even by their own, came four of the Hetton. Broken skin, fishbelly-white eyes, the scent of rot filling the village and making even the stink of Tanside feel clean. Unlike the soldiers they did not run, they advanced slowly, deliberate and sinister. Cahan reached down and grabbed a fallen spear, hefted it and launched it at the nearest Hetton. Rather than dodge the creature caught it. Hissed, and threw it back. Cahan smashed it away with an axe and the Hetton pointed at him, as if in challenge.

"Ania!" he shouted, "the white eyes! They are what killed your people, concentrate your shot!" Ania twisted on the ledge and brought her bow up, two arrows, swift as a stream sent into the back of the Hetton. It stumbled but did not fall. Her Forestals added their arrows. Still it did not fall. More arrows, he lost count of how many before the thing went down. While they brought down the first Hetton the Rai's soldiers formed their shield wall.

Stopped.

A pair of Hetton pushed through it. Terror walking, no

longer people. Creatures that, even to those without a cowl, radiated a powerful sense of wrongness. Cahan felt the strength of the villagers waver around him. Fear running through the line. He could not blame them, he felt it himself.

Behind the line of soldiers a third Hetton jumped onto the wall, not needing ladders. Its body moving loosely, as if a collection of parts barely joined, its armour flaking, cracked and dry. It landed between two of the Forestals, stretched skin face scanning backwards and forwards, a pointed tongue flickered out of a lipless mouth. It hissed again. The nearest Forestal dropped their bow and reached for a spear. The Hetton moved, so quickly it seemed to flicker, flowing around the spear thrust and then the Forestal was dead. A quick stab, barely seen, and the outlaw fell from the wall, clutching at their neck and trying to stem the flow of blood. The Forestal on the other side did not go for their spear, they used their bow. Loosing arrows one, two, three, into the Hetton. The impact of each staggering it but not stopping the creature as it ran towards them. Three, four, upsetting, strangely arrhythmic steps.

The second Forestal fell, run through by the Hetton's spear.

Then the Hetton advanced on Ania. She was concentrating on loosing arrows into the mass of soldiers. Cahan shouted but she was battle-aware, and had already seen the creature. She spun, loosed an arrow at it that punched through the creature's helmet. It paused, shook its head as if trying to shake off a night's drinking, and advanced with the arrow still through its skull. The Forestal loosed another arrow. Turned, looked into the village and found Cahan. She grinned and gave him a quick salute before jumping from the wall. The Hetton followed, loping after her as she vanished between burning roundhouses.

The remaining two advanced on the villagers.

"What are they?" Furin, beside him, holding a shield, eyes wide with fear.

"Hetton, creatures of terror."

She did not reply, only stared at them as they came forward.

Cahan could feel the resolve of the villagers cracking like new ice underfoot. The shouts of battle quieting on both sides. Hetton radiating hate and fear and the sour stink of rot. Hissing to each other as they advanced. The Rai's soldiers held back, as much because they were wary of the Hetton as because they were giving them space to fight. They, too, became quiet. Still.

The Hetton were fear, and they were to be feared.

"Hold the line," he shouted. His voice rang into the night. "Furin, take my place." Cahan stepped out of the line, leaving the warmth of gathered bodies and moving into cold air. The two Hetton, lit by roaring fires. Wreathed in woodsmoke. Fishbelly-white eyes locked on to him. Speaking to each other in their not-quite-understandable language. One went left of him, the other right. Cahan's hands sweating in his gauntlets. His hair wet with the clammy, uncomfortable sweat of fear.

We are ready.

He was ready.

Now was the time, what did it matter if he was a husk by the end of it? They all died here anyway. He let his armour change, spikes growing at elbow and knee. With a thought, and a ripple of pleasure passing through him he changed the smooth spikes on the knuckles of gauntlets to longer, serrated ones for ripping and tearing.

He had seen how many arrows it took to bring down a Hetton.

He knew it would not be easy.

We are ready.

He took up his axes. The world became quieter, like the moment of dawn in the forest before the creatures realised the light had risen. Cahan took a breath. Everything felt very close, very detailed. The ruts in the mud. The flickering fire. The curling smoke. The flaking white make-up on the faces of the villagers. The flaking broken skin on the faces of the Hetton. The thud of his blood through his body.

He took a breath.

Each breath could be his last. The air, thick with woodsmoke and the scent of tanning pits, felt as cold and clean and sweet as if he were sitting by a forest stream.

"Well," he tightened his hands on the axes. Felt his gauntlets extrude cilia to hold them more tightly. The sweat drying up within them as he absorbed it. "You have come for me, Hetton, let us see if you can take me."

67

The Hetton let out a hiss. The one on his right held a sword. The one on his left a spear. Briefly, he wondered about Ania, wondered if she had survived one-on-one with a Hetton. Unlikely.

Then he was no longer thinking.

He was fighting in the flickering light of fire.

Ranya's web, but they were quick. The sword Hetton swung as it came forward. He dodged back and the spear Hetton used its greater reach and the momentary distraction to thrust the spear at him. The strike was good, trying to smash the spear through the gap between chest plate and back plate. He twisted at the last second and the spear scraped along his breastplate. He felt it as a memory of pain, a ghost of what it would have been ripping through skin. He lashed out with an axe and the spear Hetton jumped backwards. The sword Hetton tried to rush him. Then he was fending off sword strikes so hard and strong that each one felt as if a hammer blow. He retreated, trying to watch his step and the spear Hetton at the same time. It was limping, two arrows in its right thigh. Weakness there.

You need strength.

True.

His best chance was to get close to the wounded spear Hetton. Use it as a shield for the moments he would need to suck the life from it and feed his cowl. It was not a life he would take, not really. He would not be killing a person, only removing something terrible from the world.

Was that true? Or was he lying to himself in desperation?

The sword Hetton came in, a dagger in its left hand. Tried to dummy him with the sword. Its skill fearsome. Its focus total. Its speed frightening. Cahan let himself relax into the cowl, let the cowl defend him. Its greatest drive was to live, to continue to be. It had been a long time since he had done this. Strange, to relinquish his body. To see from outside as the sword Hetton came in, weapons striking, and he defended without any conscious thought. The cowl protecting him and itself. It cost him, it hurt, it promised weakness unless it was fed.

While the cowl defended him, he considered the spear Hetton. Saw it coming in, favouring its wounded leg. Saw it draw the spear back for a thrust towards the same place in his armour it had targeted before. It pushed the spear forward. He took control back.

Leap.

Pushing upwards and back, towards the spear Hetton. His body twisting in the air. Over its weapon like smoke curling round a branch. World diminishing. He felt as if he watched from the slow sentience of the forest. He had ample time to plan his next move. The sword Hetton, mid-sweep, the blade coming round and finding only air. The spear Hetton trying to twist as he landed. As he rolled. Coming up behind it. He dropped his right axe. Moved in close, arm around the Hetton's head. So near to it. He wanted to retch, to expel the air they shared. His body reacting violently to the thing's presence. He bit down, pushed revulsion away. Thrust his right fist up and under the jaw

of the Hetton, the spike on the gauntlet going into its brain.
The thing still writhed and fought against him. He let the
cowl flood out, ready to steal the life from the thing and

Corruption.

Couldn't.

His blood rotting in his veins. His organs becoming
sludge. His memories polluted. There was nothing he could
use. It was the bluevein of the fields but magnified by a
hundred, a thousand.

Corruption.

He looked into it. Past the Hetton. Into something, and
something looked back into him.

Then heat. Flowing from him and into the Hetton. He
did not ask for it. Did not want it. Something automatic,
his control overridden. The Hetton stiffened as fire flooded
its brain burning it to ash. It became limp. He let the body
drop. Staggering backwards as the smouldering corpse fell
to the floor.

The sword Hetton on him. Weapons blurringly fast. He
had only one axe. His body shaking, weak from the fire.
Strike. A step back. Strike. Two steps back. Pushing him
towards his lines. Strike. Step back. Strike, a scratch upon
his armour. Strike, a hit on the side of his head. He could
not let it into his lines. The carnage would be terrible. Like
a spearmaw loose among crownheads.

He forced himself to relax, let the cowl defend him. Let
its desire continue to take over. Even weakened he was as
fast as the Hetton. Whatever it was, the cowl was its match.
Though his cowl was passive, only defensive. They held their
own. Defended from its strikes. When Cahan saw gaps, he
took over. Hit back. The axe cutting away the Hetton's armour
which, despite the look of rot, was as strong as his own.

But he was winning. Step by step pushing it back. Taking
the fight to it.

Behind him, the villagers of Harn were shouting.
Screaming encouragement. Chanting his name.

For all it cost him.
He thought it might be worth his life.
To give them.
This.
Win.

Then he was nothing.

Sorha, the corrupted Rai, stepping out of the line of soldiers. Cahan's strength gone. His knees gave way beneath him. The link between cowl and man vanished and she smiled. The Hetton raised its sword, gave a hideous cry of triumph.

Something long and furred and vicious hit it in the face. Chittering and scratching and biting at the white eyes. Segur. A ball of fury and hate. The Hetton hissed. Grabbed the creature and pulled it away, despite all the scratches and bites the Hetton did not bleed. Its opened flesh white and filmy, almost see-through. It looked at the garaur for a heartbeat, then lifted its sword to cut it in two.

"Segur!" Cahan reaching out with his empty hand and then cursed himself for letting the Hetton know the garaur meant something to him. The animal growled and spat and struggled in the Hetton's grasp. The Hetton looked at him, then at Segur and an awful parody of a smile passed across its face. It drew the sword back further.

The song of an arrow cutting through the air.

He expected it to punch the Hetton from its feet but it did not. He heard a scream from the Rai's lines. Then the Hetton made the most awful sound he had heard them make yet. A vile, grating sound, like an arrow tip being pushed along ceramic, setting all his teeth on edge. The thing was laughing. A word slipped from its lipless mouth.

"Miisssssed." The awful laughing sound continued. The sword came sweeping round towards the struggling garaur.

Stopped.

The Hetton let out a sound, an "ack". Cahan glanced

back. Udinny in the doorway of the longhouse with a bow in her hand. By her was Venn, their hands stretched out, grimacing and sweating as they concentrated. Between Segur and the sword was the sparkling form of a shield, a smaller version of the one the Forestals had made.

Shouting from the Rai's lines, he turned.

"No! no!" Past the longhouse he could see Sorha, an arrow sprouting from her shoulder and her soldiers were dragging her away from the front line. Obeying the standing order of "keep the Rai safe". Not understanding why she wanted to stay. They were programmed to protect the Rai no matter what.

Cahan's strength returned.

He punched forward with his spiked gauntlet, hitting the Hetton in the stomach. It let out a sound like someone retching after a night's hard drinking.

"Burn!" he said, and it became fire. Dropping the garaur, taking the last of his strength from him as it fell.

Hands grabbing him, pulling him.

"To the longhouse! To the longhouse! The gate has fallen! To the last line!"

68

He remembered very little between killing the Hetton and entering the longhouse. He did not know which villagers took a man they had once despised and ensured that he lived, even while in fear of their own lives. He vaguely remembered speaking, of saying the same words, "I must fight" again and again and again. At some point, he thought someone, Udinny, or Furin maybe, told him he had fought enough, that he was done now. He could rest.

In the darkness of the longhouse, among the dead and the dying and lost in his own pain, the cowl clung onto life for him.

A brightness.

At first a hazy glow, like the light above through the forest canopy. Then brighter, and brighter, until he stood within a clearing of his mind, the pain ebbing the way the snow melts into the ground. He felt calm and warm and at peace.

"Cahan, wake up, Cahan."

He did not want to.

"Cahan, wake up."

The forest edge shivering and the voice, all crackling leaves and cold breezes, was one he could not disobey.

Eyes opening.

Venn, their face above him, deep lines marring their youth.

"Are you alive, Cahan?"

"Venn," he said it loudly in his head, but it was barely a whisper.

"You have worn yourself away again," said the trion. "I have lent you a little of my strength." Now they said it he knew they had, and he felt how much the healing of those hurt had taken out of them. Their skin looked dry, as if it would flake away at a touch. Their cheekbones stark against their flesh.

"I must get to the fight . . ." Even saying it he knew it as foolish. He had barely the energy to speak.

"They are not attacking, Cahan," said Udinny, appearing behind Venn.

"We do not know why," this from Furin. "But the Forestal, Ania, she is readying the people for the next attack."

"But I am . . ."

"We must move you," said Venn. "I am sorry and I know it will hurt. But we must." Before he could reply he was grabbed, hard hands taking the tops of his arms, dragging him across the floor of the longhouse. The smell of roasting flesh filled his nostrils, the sudden awareness of another's pain flooding into his mind. He did not have the strength to block it. A body across from him. Dyon, Furin's second. Curls of smoke drifting around his face as the ember of the Rai continued to eat away his flesh.

A voice from outside the longhouse. "You are finished, beaten!"

"Cahan," said Dyon, his words heavy with his own pain. "Venn, says," he took in a breath, pulling an agonising hiss through his teeth, "you take strength," another hiss of pain, "from life." His eyes, deep and brown, were bright with pain.

The voice from outside. Rai Galderin. "Give me the trion. Give me Cahan Du-Nahere. And I promise quick deaths for your village."

"I will not . . ." his own words as hard to get out as Dyon's plainly were. Dyon's hand grasped Cahan's arm. He was shocked the man could even move. His blackened skin cracked when he moved, a slow trickle of blood ran across the char until the heat of his body stilled it. The thrill of life coursed between them.

"Gift me the Star Path," said Dyon softly. "Take my life for Harn."

"Cannot," said Cahan. "Promised not to take . . ." The hand, a lump of pain and misery tightened. The heat of Dyon burning his skin, connecting them. Making them strange kin in that moment.

"A gift," he said, and his eyes begged Cahan to take from him, "not to you. To my people. I made a terrible mistake."

Rai Galderin from outside: "I have over two hundred troops left. Give me what I want or I will burn the longhouse you hide in."

"I do not want this—"

"I do not care," vehemence, behind Dyon's pain, "you and I brought this here. Do not deny me."

Galderin from outside: "I will flay alive anyone who escapes."

"Save my people," said Dyon.

"I cannot steal the life from another. It . . ."

"Cannot . . . steal . . . a . . . gift, Cahan Du-Nahere. Take it."

Galderin: "I will make your deaths last for whole seasons of pain!"

"Take it!" hissed Dyon. "Spare them my agony." For a moment, through the link he felt Dyon's pain. His desperation.

"It will hurt," said Cahan.

"It cannot . . . be worse," said Dyon, "end this." Behind him Venn, intent, their stare boring into him. Behind them stood Udinny and Furin. He did not know what they expected. The life of one man would not be enough. It may get him on his feet, allow him to fight a little longer. Maybe he owed them that.

"Please," said Dyon, raising a charred hand, "put out . . . the fire."

We need this.

What could he do?

"Close your eyes. I will put you on the Star Path, Dyon," His eyes closed. Cahan took a breath, and then took the gift he offered.

Behind Dyon a trick.

A trap.

A gift that, though unwanted, was generous beyond price. A well so deep he could do nothing but fall, even as he tried so desperately not to.

Another life, waiting, linked to Dyon by touch. Behind that another and another. Cahan tried to pull away. He could not. There was a powerful force of will behind Dyon. Every man and woman in the village whose wound had put them on the road to the Star Path had made a decision. They had chosen to give their lives for those who still lived, and the weight of that commitment was something that could not be refused.

He tried, but his was not the only will at work, the cowl also had a will of its own and the cowl wanted to survive, to carry on, and for that it needed him. For him to live, it needed power, and when that power was offered, it took.

He stood in a whirlwind of life, flowing around him and pouring into him. More power than he had ever known, there were ten, twelve, sixteen, eighteen, twenty, thirty, lives giving all they had to him. And something of their gift, of their willingness, magnified what was given. As they stepped out of this life and out of his reach, he felt no pain from them, no hate or anger or fear.

This was not the way it had been before.

The world blurred.

Cahan found himself.

Deep in the Forest.

"Your sister is dead, Cahan Du-Nahere." The Skua-Rai's expression is impenetrable, as she looks down on you from her raised throne. "She was murdered by an outlaw. Killed for the bread she held in her hand. Bread she brought for you." The pain within like nothing you have ever known. Like you are on fire. Like you are being eaten from the outside in. "You are angry, and righteously so." She does not look at you, only looks over him while her acolytes, hidden behind masks and cloaks, swing burners full of herbs that make your head swim. It is so hot. Your joints burn and yet you shiver as if freezing. Behind the Skua-Rai is her firsthusband, secondwife and trion. They watch you.

Your anger rises. All the pain, all the unfairness and loss of your life is concentrated here.

A man is brought before you.

"This is her murderer, Cahan."

The murderer is unable to speak as they have cut his tongue out. You feel a pure and white-hot hatred for him, for taking Nahac, your sister. And for so much more that you barely even know. You do not understand that you have been manoeuvred, forced and engineered to exactly this point. Of course you do not understand, because you are a child and you think as a child. You stare into eyes that beg you not to do what you are about to do.

I beg you, not to do what you are about to do.

Do not do this thing.

But you are young, and hurting and angry. And my voice was quieter then.

Do you remember now, Cahan, how I whispered into your ear? Begged you not to?

Do not do this thing. Do not choose to destroy. To corrupt.

You did not listen.

You became the fire then.

You are the fire, Cahan.

You always were.

He wept.

He screamed.

He cried.

He burned.

He grew.

Fire flowed into him, but not the fire he knew. Maybe because they went willingly, he did not know. He felt himself becoming more, not some huge and powerful thing, but an avatar of these people, their lives. He was the mechanism through which they would be avenged, the whole village avenged, all the unfairness of it. Avenged.

He had little time, very little control. There was too much.

Outside Galderin was finishing his speech.

"Bring me those I want! Or die slowly."

Rai and their troops massing. Moving around them. Ania's voice?

"We've beaten you twice. We'll beat you again."

The drums beating as powerfully as his racing heart. The villagers standing together in a tight group, ready to fight and die. The last of the Forestals readying their bows and gathering together their final few arrows. The soldiers of the Rai excited, sure in the coming victory. The Hetton feeling nothing but a terrible hunger. The other Rai, eager to be there at the end and to claim the victory for themselves. Sorha lived, but she was moving away from the village, a small pool of nothing within Ranya's web. A horde of rootlings, hidden in the forest.

He had knowledge: Udinny shot the arrow that wounded Sorha, he felt a quiet pride that her aim was true. Venn had suggested the chain of people that filled him with power. Furin had been the one to convince her people to do it. They had been glad when he fell in battle, because Venn knew they would never have convinced him to take the gift otherwise. That desperation was the trigger.

He should have been angry. Maybe he would be.

But in that moment he cared nothing for morals and why and wherefores. He knew only that there was a fight and they had been losing it.

They would lose it no longer.

We are more than fire.

And the cowl. It was not something separate to him. It was him, and he was it. The destruction, the coldness, the harshness was not in the taking of power, it was in how it was taken. In what was done with it.

So long he had damped down the fire inside, and now it burned hot and pure and fierce and *different*. Not a fire of destruction. Not something to consume. A fire of life. All around him life was burning. He felt it. He saw it. Everything overlaid with the white on black lines of Ranya's web. A hundred dots of life showed him villagers and soldiers and they burned alike, with a white-yellow flame. He felt the Hetton as a distortion of the web, a wrongness within it. The Rai as something similar but not as overt in their corruption, though they were corrupted. He felt all this, and he knew that even with the power flowing through him it would not be enough. He had the fire, the power, but it was a furious thing. Like being given a hammer and expected to make delicate jewellery.

He stood.

He walked.

He moved.

He burned.

The journey from inside the longhouse to the outside was the longest he had ever taken. With every step he held in the fire.

You have had years of practice.

He saw the villagers but he did not. He saw Rai Galderin and their troops but he did not. He existed in and out of this world. The Rai were coming, and now was the time for him to end this. But despite this power being different, all he knew was fire. He would be an explosion. A vast inescapable burning wave.

Fire through the alleyways, through the doors and windows, over the roofs. Nothing escapes. An expending conflagration that sweeps and scours the village until, when it ends, all that is left is you. Standing in a smoking black circle where once those you had known and passed the time of day with had been.

Not again. It could not happen again.

The last push. They were coming, they were coming, but the defenders were not doing anything. They were looking to him. He saw himself as they saw him. A shimmering figure of white, almost too bright to look at, his eyes twin fires from which rose a haze of heat.

It was time. It was time. It was time.

He is the fire.

And there was no other choice but to be the fire.

No.

"Cahan," a voice.

Udinny, a strange smile on her face. Venn by her. They were holding hands. "The boughry asked for my service, and here is where I give it," said the monk. Something in her voice, wistful and sad. "Take my hand."

"I am fire." The words hung in the air, they reverberated around them. "I am fire and destruction. I will burn you."

"Fire is part of nature, it is part of the path," said the monk. "It is death and it is rebirth." Words made of crackling leaves and waving branches. Venn held out their hand, but unlike Udinny their expression was blank, catatonic, almost. Through the awareness of Ranya's web he saw the two were tied together. Vines and leaves reached out from the monk to Venn. As the vines reached the trion they changed into rope and knots of stone and earth. Venn's hand held out to him. He did not want to take it.

He was fire. He was burning. He was death.

Venn took his hand. The ropes around them wrapped around him and as they did became lines of glowing energy. The three of them tied together.

Leaf, to rope, to fire.

The web opened. He saw so much more. No longer only lines of black on white. Venn linked him to Udinny. He saw through Udinny's eyes. He saw through Venn's eyes. They saw through his. They felt what was around them. Life everywhere. The land that gave it. The plants that grew on it. The fire that burned and returned the life to the land.

They saw the village clearing. They saw the trees around it. They saw the burning village. They saw the forces of the Rai. They felt the bluevein in the ground, the slow corruption that poisoned crops. They saw the forest that had been, is and was yet to be. The life of the land, hidden in the ground. The pulsing energy of Crua, the place that kept them alive and fed into each and every one of them. In the trees, in the animals and the plants, the same energy that filled him, given in gift by dying villagers. All linked flowing back and forth in an endless exchange.

And he saw them, from outside. And stood behind each of them one of the boughry, but huge, tall as cloudtrees, arms outstretched. Behind the boughry massed ranks of rootlings, and behind them, legion after legion of swarden. Behind the swarden the Forestmen, those huge wooden statues found at the boles of trees. Ranya's web lay over them all.

Upon Cahan fell a terrible weight, the gaze of the boughry

upon him, upon them all. As if something was expected of him. As if the time was now. He heard the voices of those gathered creatures, a song bright and loud: but incomplete. Cahan wanted to weep. They all wanted to weep.

The focus changed.

Through Venn, he saw what Udinny saw. The life which lay dormant all around. A million seeds and plants all ready to grow. The sleepers in the bones of the land. The bluevein, stretching out putrid tendrils as if searching for them.

We need not be fire.

The voice within him.

We can be life.

His voice. Udinny's voice. Venn's voice. The boughry, too. hearfeelsee

Udinny speaks. Her face before him. Her gentleness, her truth. What she gave was a way. A different path. Between them Venn. A trion, the one between, the balance and the conduit. Energy flowing. Venn taking it up until they became the glowing figure, the avatar of the power Cahan held. Through Venn Udinny provided the focus he lacked. He was the arm that pulled the bow. Venn the string that held the energy ready. Udinny the eye that aimed him.

"It was all worth it," said Udinny, or did not, maybe she thought it. Her mind full of wonder and joy. "It was all worth it for this."

The power flowed from Venn to Udinny, changed by the trion into something new, something life-giving. He heard the scratching sigh of the boughry. And together Venn, Udinny and Cahan touched every seed and every bulb that hid in the ground. The bluevein, scoured away in a wave of pure energy. He felt the reborn, alive and yet not, and his power knitted together damaged flesh, smoothed out burns. The walking wounded in the longhouse found themselves healed.

For the beat of a heart, the quick intake of a breath, the song was complete. The sound of a million small parts suddenly joined in union. A sound that had been once, and should be again.

Then they were back. In the clearing. Before the long-house.

In every handful of dirt and earth. In every place around them, seeds sprang to life. Trees sprang into being. Everything grew. Udinny showed him where the life was and he gave it energy. He directed the flow and direction.

Saplings grew as spears.

Galderin drew his sword. Called fire to his hand. Before he could act, speak, scream in pain, he was lifted from his feet. Shot up into the air on the impaling spike of a new tree. More trees erupted, ripping soldiers and Hetton and Rai apart in their eagerness to grow. The dead sprang from the earth wrapped in plants, marching like swarden to fall upon their attackers. The enemy had no time to scream or run or even to feel fear.

The victory was absolute and total and sudden.

Together, Cahan, Venn and Udinny awoke the ancient anger of a sleeping forest. They awoke what had been subdued by the hands of the people who had lived here for so long. Gave it a target. One moment they were about to die. The next they stood in the midst of a new forest, and around them hung the gruesome corpses of its first fruiting. The dead of an attacking army, pierced by tree and branch.

Cahan heard a sound, as if a great sigh, as if something ancient, old and angry had been appeased.

And it was done.

The power gone. He was a man once more. A man standing in a wood. Venn before him, blinking, confused. Udinny, too. She turned to him, smiled. Reached out a hand.

"It was worth it," she said again, "and now, Cahan, the forest calls for me."

He was going to ask what she meant, but he did not need to. In her eyes, her look, he knew.

"Udinny," he said, reaching out a hand for her. "No . . ."

"It's all right," she said softly, "did you feel it? Did you hear it? I am of the forest now, Cahan Du-Nahere. Nothing of the forest ever truly dies. It is a cycle." And as he tried to touch her a breeze blew up, and Udinny became dust, lost upon it, taken by a zephyr and whirled up among the trees. Pain shot through him, as shocking and hard as if a spear had been thrust through his gut. The monk had done this knowing what would happen, that contact with such power as he held was more than she could ever hope to live through.

She had paid the price the boughry asked of her.

"Ranya's path," he said, "she walked it to the end." He felt Venn by him.

"Cahan," said the trion, and there was something new and stronger in their voice than he had heard before. "Ranya's web is complex, and her path stranger, and longer than we can understand." He looked to the trion, and was surprised not to see grief there, as if they were privy to some secret he was not. Before he could ask any more the trion stepped away.

Behind them the people of Harn, staring up in wonder at the new forest.

"We did not go into the forest, so the forest came to us," said Furin. Villagers turning to stare at Cahan. Then Ont spoke. Going down on one knee before him.

"Cowl-Rai," he said. Each villager followed his action, and the small clearing in the bloody forest rang out with the name he had been raised for, run from, and never wanted to hear again.

"Cowl-Rai."

He wanted to speak. But he could not.

He had run but never fast enough.

Been running all his life, when there was never anywhere to run to.

This place. These people. They were home.

Epilogue

Saradis sat before the taffistone of Zorir-Who-Walks-in-Fire and lit a candle. To all but her this was a sacred relic of Tarl-an-Gig. Only she, the Cowl-Rai, and her second, Laha, knew what this stone really was. Understood that the subtle glow, the seeping blue, was the manifestation of the fire. If anyone found out then, well, she would claim them a liar and she would be believed.

They would not survive long afterwards.

There were definite benefits to being Skua-Rai of Crua, second only to the Cowl-Rai in power.

She watched the candle burn, focused on it and closed her eyes. She visualised the stone in the afterimage of the flame. Grey and as tall as she was, scarred across its face by a great crack. The great "V" where the small fragment from the monastery had been reunited with the great stone. In her meditation she hoped to hear the voice that had been with her all her life, or at least ever since she had first touched the fragment of the blue-tinged taffistone she had found as a child.

Saradis put her hand out, touched the stone and listened. Often, instead of a voice, it was a feeling, something that slid into her mind and gently pushed her in the right direction. Usually she would be unclothed, but today she had much to do, and did not have time for her normal rituals.

"We get closer," she said. "There have been setbacks but the world will still be wiped clean, the fire will come. We will begin all again as you desire." She wondered if Zorir could feel her worry, though she did not think the god cared for such human weaknesses as worry. If there were problems it was for her to sort them. Still, she wanted the comfort of her god's touch, to know her failure could be forgiven.

Nothing.

Saradis bowed her head and sighed.

What was done was done, and nothing was insurmountable. She was the hand of a god, a true god, not some tool of monks used to gain power, and not the lackey of one of their freakishly powerful Rai. Crua had lived under lies and without gods for too long. That was changing now.

She wore the raiment of the pretender, Tarl-an-Gig, but it did bother her. Saradis believed in her cause. She believed totally and utterly and it was that which made her the most dangerous person in the whole of Crua. She would do what was necessary, without guilt and without feeling. She had a higher purpose.

Saradis opened her eyes.

"I give all I am to you," she said before the shrine. "My life is yours, your purpose is mine. Give me strength to make it through this day." She felt some joy then. Had a fragment of her god touched her? Yes. It shuddered through her in waves of pure pleasure that made her gasp. She waited a few breaths until she was sure she could stand.

Now there was work to do.

She passed through the grand hall at the centre of Tiltspire. Along the hall were the banners of Tarl-an-Gig, the balancing figure in black on a background of blue.

Behind them, and larger than them, as all believed was right, was the star of Iftal on a background of many colours, for all of Crua. At the end of the hall, before the window, a huge sculpture of the star, woven from the smallest, though still huge, branches of the great cloudtrees of Wyrdwood. Before it a statue of the balancing figure, one leg bent, knee and arms out. At the right time of day the light above would shine directly through the star and it would appear Iftal spread light all the way down the hall. In the centre of the light, the long shadow of Tarl-an-Gig.

Fitting, thought Saradis. As Tarl-an-Gig was only a shadow, one cast by Zorir, a far greater god.

Rai stood guard along the hall, in armour of wood so hard and shining that it looked black, carved with grimacing faces and painted with glowing icons that marked their journey through the Cowl-Rai's army. The signposts of the path of conquest across Crua. If she stopped, looked them over, she would see herself reflected in their breastplates; a strange and distorted figure passing across the chests of her soldiers. A good metaphor for her. Appear as you must appear, but twist and turn and be whatever was needed for the greater purpose.

She wore all the finery of the Skua-Rai, the high priest of Tarl-an-Gig. Long robes, twigs that had been heated and bent into a cage that held her body upright, forcing her to walk tall whether she felt like she could or not. The mask of the god, blank but for a smile, covered her face; all of this marked her as the second most important person in the land of Crua.

She was not the Cowl-Rai but she was their voice, and the Rai looked to her for guidance because of it.

Or that was what they were told.

The resentment they felt towards her would become murderous if more than the trusted few knew the truth.

She wondered how the Cowl-Rai was today, calm and useful? Or ranting, smashing things, furious for no real reason. Wondered if she would be able to talk tactics, to pick that wonderful mind clean of knowledge to guide the war in the south. Not by doing what they suggested, not usually. They could not win the war, she could not afford that. Not yet. She was not ready. The news she had been given was bad, but not too bad. It may even help her convince the Cowl-Rai to slow their advances.

Though they would not like it. Not at all.

Beyond the hall was the private throne room. None but Saradis and her second, Laha, were allowed in there. The door was guarded by ten Hetton. She did not find them distasteful the way others did, they were servants of Zorir, good ones. Savage and unthinking. Answering only to her.

In the throne room waited the great secret.

The Cowl-Rai of Tarl-an-Gig, saviour of the north. Conqueror of Crua.

Kept in a cage.

She had her back to Saradis, looking out past the bars and through the window. The light behind the Cowl-Rai was beautiful this evening. The windows of Tiltspire somehow made light more real, infusing it with a warmth like ripening seed heads. It lent a certain beauty to everything it touched, from the wooden chair of twisted branches, to the polished stone of the floor. Usually she would go to her knee before the Cowl-Rai, but today she fully prostrated herself, lying with her arms out to her sides, nose touching the polished stone. The cage of twigs around her body dug painfully into her flesh while she waited, unmoving.

The Cowl-Rai wore cheap armour, the same sort most of the fodder, those destined to be chewed up by the fighting, wore. This had made the common troops love them at the start. A clever trick, but they were clever. They did not rise to be who they were without being clever. Fool so many into believing they had power when they had almost none. Saradis was clever, too; together they had ascended to this place and they had congratulated themselves on what they had wrought. They had found a way to give her power.

Maybe they had been too clever.

Too successful. Too quickly.

Now it all balanced on the edge of a blade.

"Saradis. You bring me news?"

The Cowl-Rai spoke like a leader, despite standing in a cage of wood made from trees twisted by bluevein. It had been hard to find those trees. Bluevein killed most things it touched, but it was all that would hold her. Her prison was comfortable. She had a chair, a bed, a table covered in maps and bark she had written her plans on. She had a beautiful view, they were three floors above the city here, she could look right out over Tiltspire.

But a cage was still a cage.

"That you lie down, Saradis, that does not bode well. Given how proud you are." The Cowl-Rai's voice was as warm as the light, as gentle sounding as the soft touch of a lover. "Stand up, Skua-Rai." The Cowl-Rai turned to Saradis. Face hidden by a visor carved into the likeness of a beautiful girl. She removed her helm, put it on the table. "Tell me what news you bring."

Saradis stood. She was taller than the Cowl-Rai though she never felt like she was looking down on her. The Cowl-Rai was beautiful. Or had been. Now her hair was lank as she rarely got to wash it, or herself. Saradis could smell her stale sweat mixing with the scent of the cage full of histi in the corner of the room. Despite this she was, somehow, more beautiful than she had been when she was younger, her bone structure accented by lines of blue, and small shimmering stones embedded in the skin above her eyes.

"It is not all poor news, Cowl-Rai. We found the woman, Tamis Du-Carack, brought into being for Hast-Who-Walks, and they are dead. As is Virag Par-Behian, brought into being for Loun-the-Wet-Blade." The Cowl-Rai said nothing. They both knew this was not what really interested them. Not what they really wanted to know. Saradis waited for an answer and the Cowl-Rai let time pass, the light falling upon them took on a weight of its own.

"Saradis, tell me of Harn far in the north. Does it still stand? Have we retrieved what matters to me. The trion? Can I tilt the world?"

She would never tilt the world, but Saradis knew she did not want to hear that.

"No, Cowl-Rai," said Saradis. The Cowl-Rai did not move, only stood within her cage like a strange statue. The beautiful face, the clothes of a commoner.

"My army and my High Leoric, Kirven Ban-Ruhn, and Galderin Mat-Brumar. Will they return to me?"

"No," said Saradis, and if she could have fled at that moment she would have, despite the cage which should keep her safe. Saradis could feel the rage brewing. Smell the sickly sweet scent of power gathering. "They are gone, Cowl-Rai. Dead. All except the woman named Sorha who escaped. She brought us the news of what happened there." The Cowl-Rai did not explode, she did not reach for her beautiful, willwood blade. She only cocked her head.

"And this because of the forester, Cahan Du-Nahere? He beat an army of mine. He beat my Rai and my Hetton?"

"And still lives." A long gap, how to tell the Cowl-Rai what had happened? How to explain it? There was no good way, better to rip the bandage straight off the wound. "He grew a forest, and ripped apart your army. Killed them all."

Another gap, even longer this time.

"You said he was weak, Saradis."

"He was. Every time I saw him in his youth I was confronted with the fact that I chose badly and I—"

The explosion came with a scream, her power like liquid, dark and noisome. It flooded out of her body. No control, it was wild and furious, smashing into the bars. But they held, the power could not pass. It splashed back over the cage and its contents. Saradis knew, from experience, if it touched any flesh but the Cowl-Rai's it burned, and she knew in her fury the Cowl-Rai cared little for who was in her way. All Saradis could do now was wait until she tired herself out.

It did not take long. Saradis kept her weak.

The fury and screaming abated and when the liquid darkness was gone, the power spent, the Cowl-Rai remained. Collapsed in the cage, kneeling, head bowed, body drained, barely breathing. Saradis went to the cage of histi in the corner, took out one of the struggling animals and threw it into the cage. A thin whip of power from the Cowl-Rai encircled it as soon as it was through the bars. The histi screamed as it was caught, the sound cut off as the life was taken from it. The Cowl-Rai raised her head, the blue lines of her power more apparent against the gauntness of her flesh after the show of temper. She blinked. Breathed heavily. Moved hair from her face. Now more lucid than ever.

"Why am I in a cage?"

"Your power is great but difficult to control. You commanded to be kept this way until it could be controlled." A lie, but one that had served Saradis well.

"Cahan. Where is he?"

"Gone. Fled into the forest with all those that survived the fight."

"The trion?"

"Went with them. But there is good news. There has been treefall in the Northern Wyrdwood."

Silence. For a long time all that Saradis heard was the laboured breathing of the Cowl-Rai. When she spoke again she sounded sure, focused.

"We should take a skyraft off one of the families. It will be useful. The Hosteine family are the weakest of the air nobles. Take theirs from them, Saradis, take it in my name."

"Cowl-Rai," said the monk, "it is not done, the skyraft families are—"

"Word of Harn will escape," said the Cowl-Rai. Her tone hard, calculating. Clever. The woman who had won Crua talking, not the woman Saradis had been forced to cage. "We cannot look weak, especially to our own Rai. Taking a skyraft is audacious, it will address any talk of weakness." She cocked her head to one side. "We will have to slow our advance without the trion. The people will expect the world tilted once the war is won so we cannot win, not yet." It was hard for Saradis not to smile on hearing exactly what she wanted to. "In the meantime, take as many people as you need from the prisons and those villages that provide us little sacrifice or soldiers. Have them executed in the spiretowns, tell everyone they are from Harn. It will distract the people from the war. They love an execution."

"I will have this done, Cowl-Rai."

"Sorha," said the Cowl-Rai, more to herself than the priest. "She is the anomaly? The walking duller?" Saradis nodded.

"She has failed us, I will add her to the execution list."

"No," the Cowl-Rai levered herself up, sat on the chair. Even that small exertion cost her much. "Use her. Send her to find Cahan. Have him brought back here, alive." Then she smiled, and Saradis saw a glimmer of the madness that the stone had brought upon her returning. "I want my brother to know it was I, Nahac Du-Nahere, who should have been chosen. I want him to beg for his life, and then beg to serve me." She looked up, stone-blue eyes focused on Saradis, the madness a turmoil beneath them. "I want him to beg, Saradis, just like you did."

"Of course, Cowl-Rai," said Saradis.

Am I dead?
I definitely remember dying.
This is not at all what I had expected.
It's very dark, for a start.

The story continues in . . .

Book TWO of
The Forsaken Trilogy

Acknowledgements

Book seven of nine.* It seems miraculous to still be sat on my sofa doing this and, as ever, I wouldn't be doing it without my agent, Ed Wilson at Johnson and Alcock and my editor, the wonderful Jenni Hill, and the rest of the team at Orbit.

I hope you've enjoyed your time with Cahan (though whether you would want to be around Cahan, well, I'm not as sure). I suppose, at its heart, *Gods of the Wyrdwood* is about running away. We all run away at times, and even if we don't there are times we definitely want to. From simple running away, sitting at the keyboard and not wanting to start writing to more serious attempts – going abroad, leaving everything you know behind – we tend to find the same thing. Whatever we run away from is still there when we come back. Or, like Cahan, what we are running from is not what we think, it is ourselves, and you can never outrun yourself.

Of course, in a book you get to be a bit more literal about it. Cahan is repeatedly drawn back to where he starts, unable to escape what he is and forced to face up to it. Only with that can he ever find a little peace. Although, clearly peace is not something Cahan is likely to get in the land of Crua,

* Well, there's a fortuitous SF reference to start this afterword off with.

his past is tied up in the future and he can no more run from that than he could escape his farm, the village of Harn, or the strange and unknowable Gods of Wyrdwood.

One of the great things about writing a trilogy of books is you get to take your time and lay the groundwork. The events of *Gods of the Wyrdwood* seem relatively simple, but just like the seeds below Harn, this is a start, and from it something far stranger and more complex will grow. Very little in Crua is how it seems, or what the people who live there think it is and it's been huge fun writing this thing while knowing the places it will go to. I can see the shoots; I am afraid you will have to guess what is going to grow.

And grow it will, as both growth and change are the essentials of being alive and the way people can change fascinates me.

RJ Barker. Leeds
November 2022

meet the author

RJ BARKER lives in Leeds with his wife, son and "a collection of questionable taxidermy." He grew up reading whatever he could get his hands on, and having played in a rock band before deciding he was a rubbish musician, RJ returned to his first love, fiction, to find he is rather better at that. As well as his debut epic fantasy series, the Wounded Kingdom trilogy (*Age of Assassins*, *Blood of Assassins* and *King of Assassins*), RJ has written short stories and historical scripts which have been performed across the country. He has the sort of flowing locks any cavalier would be proud of. RJ's novel *The Bone Ships* was the winner of the British Fantasy Society's Best Fantasy Novel, aka the Robert Holdstock Award.

Find out more about RJ Barker and other Orbit authors by registering for the free monthly newsletter at orbitbooks.net.

orbit

Follow us:

/orbitbooksUS

/orbitbooks

/orbitbooks

Join our mailing list
to receive alerts on our
latest releases and deals.

orbitbooks.net

Enter our monthly
giveaway for the chance
to win some epic prizes.

orbitloot.com